"WHAT IS IT SHAYNA? WHAT HAVEN'T YOU TOLD ME?"

His voice was low and deep and close to her ear. She could feel his breath against her cheek and the rock-hard strength of him.

"I want you to trust me," he said when she remained silent. "Haven't I shown that I trust you?"

She nodded automatically. She *did* trust him—but she still could not tell him.

He held her slightly away from him and stared down at her. "I don't know if you've actually lied to me—but I know that you haven't told me all the truth."

He took her hand that had paused in mid-air, inches from his chest. Raising it to his lips, he kissed it softly. Then he lifted his head slightly, still holding her hand, and his gaze traveled slowly over her face, stopping at her parted lips.

Shayna had never seen such gentleness, and it was all the more amazing because it came from this hard man of war. She knew that making love with him was wrong: wrong because it would be the beginning of something that could never be finished. But she wanted him as she'd never wanted any man.

Other *Leisure* and *Love Spell* books by
Saranne Dawson:
CRYSTAL ENCHANTMENT
STAR-CROSSED
ON WINGS OF LOVE
AWAKENINGS
HEART OF THE WOLF
THE ENCHANTED LAND
FROM THE MIST
GREENFIRE

Saranne Dawson

Spell Bound

Book Margins, Inc.

A BMI Edition

Published by special arrangement with Dorchester Publishing Co., Inc.

Printed in the United States of America.

Digest format printed and distributed exclusively for Book Margins, Inc., Ivyland, PA.

Spell Bound

Chapter One

"Shayna, there's an emergency! We need you at the Institute right away."

"Wh-what happened?"

"I'll explain when you get here. I have to call the others."

Shayna fumbled to punch the button that switched off the vidcom, then fell back against the pillows. Emergency? What sort of . . . ?

A chill shot through her, propelling her from her bed. Surely not! She'd mentioned her fears to Teres only a week ago, even as she tried to downplay them lest she be thought to be engaging in academic politics.

Teres had heard her out in his usual grave way, and had even admitted that the possibility had occurred to him. But the project wasn't yet at a point where the risk seemed great.

She dressed hastily, pulling on a blue jumpsuit, sliding her feet into her favorite soft boots, and then, as an afterthought, running her fingers through her long auburn hair as she left her apartment and headed for the elevator. Surely she was wrong! But what if she was right?

Don't wish trouble where it doesn't exist, she told herself. *Teres is jumpy right now because we're at a crucial stage. He was probably working one of his round-the-clock shifts and discovered some glitch.*

But if that was what it was, he certainly wouldn't have awakened her. The science was far beyond her ability to understand. She was a historian, not a physicist.

Twenty minutes later, still with no idea why she'd been summoned, Shayna brought her aircar to a smooth landing in the lot at the Institute. Her quick journey over the sleeping city had produced no further explanations, but she was still loath to accept the first one that had occurred to her.

She ran across the lot and past the gardens and fountain to the entrance, where she pressed her palm against the white square, then gave her name when it vibrated slightly. The door slid open and she ran through the darkened corridors to the rear, where she knew they would be awaiting her. Everyone else on the team lived in the Institute's own housing. She could have too, but since she was only a consultant and still had teaching duties at the university, she had chosen to remain where she was—on the far side of the city, near the campus.

As she'd expected, they were all there, and she saw that they were clustered around the big plex window that opened to the clean room. Her heart leaped into her throat, but she continued to deny the possibility.

Teres was the first to spot her; then he directed the others to seats at the big round table where they regularly held their conferences. The others moved away from the window, but Shayna approached it, her fears growing with every step.

And yet, when she reached the window and saw her worst fears confirmed, she still could not accept it. Instead she stared dumbly at the one remaining craft, willing its mate to reappear. For a brief moment it did, shimmering at the very edge of reality. She was so stunned at the apparition that a few seconds passed before she realized that she'd unconsciously used her powers to summon its likeness.

Behind her she heard Teres draw in a sharp breath. The image vanished and she turned to him, mortified at her unwitting transgression. "Sorry. I didn't mean to do that. I just . . . wanted it to be there."

Teres nodded and waved a hand in dismissal of her unintended sorcery. Unlike many people, he was totally at ease with her and the powers she had, but never used.

"You were right when you warned me, Shayna," he said sadly. "I just didn't think they'd try anything yet."

A chill slithered along her spine at this further confirmation of her worst fears. "Then it *was* Haddar."

"I think so. At least he's the most likely candidate. Let's join the others."

They took their seats at the table, where eight other men and women sat in stunned silence, most of them still staring at the window.

"Here's what we know so far," Teres said without preamble. "Someone—almost certainly more than one person—got into the building about two hours ago. Kenan is still checking out the system, so all he's sure of right now is that someone gained entrance at that time."

"But surely we know when they left," someone asked sharply.

"Unfortunately, we don't—though I hope we will soon. Whoever it was has virtually destroyed the program—and the backup. But Mazla and Gar are trying to put it together again."

"Are you saying that we don't even know where they went with it?" one of the physicists asked incredulously.

"That's exactly what I'm saying. They covered their tracks very well." Teres shot her a glance. "However, I think we have a suspect. Shayna and I discussed this possibility only a week ago."

All eyes turned to Shayna, who was normally not a major participant in these discussions. She spoke carefully.

"I told Teres that I feared an attempt on the part of Haddar Trikian and some of his allies to hijack the craft. But I had no basis for believing that except for his increasing obsession with the project and his . . . political views."

"Several months ago," Teres said, "I sat in on a seminar where Shayna debated Haddar on the subject of Unification. Most of you know his beliefs, so there's no need to get into them in detail. But he believes that the worst mistake this world ever made was to tear down the old tribal barriers and unify."

He paused and shifted in his seat with a heavy sigh. "Now I think he's going to try to change that by going back to the time when it happened."

The sharply indrawn breaths and bursts of sound from the others showed that only now had they begun to grasp what she and Teres had already guessed: Haddar intended to do the unthinkable.

Questions and comments began to fly back and forth. The project members who were trying to gain information from the computers appeared to report their lack of progress, then vanished again, carrying suggestions from the team.

The talk was mostly technical now, so Shayna paid it little attention. Instead her thoughts were on Haddar, her faculty colleague and nemesis. He'd been livid when she was chosen as the historical consultant to the project. She had been shocked, herself, since she was junior to him on the faculty. But Teres had told her that they'd ruled out Haddar because of his radical views and his reputation for being brilliant but unstable.

Now she knew that she would have to put herself in Haddar's place. Where would he go—and what would be his plan for destroying the Unification? If the computer trail could be reconstructed, the first of those two questions would be answered. At least they'd know where in time he'd gone, and perhaps she could guess what he might be planning to do.

Shayna had joined the project with a mixture of eagerness and uneasiness. Naturally, as a historian, she was thrilled at the possibility that they could journey back in time. But when the most learned minds were unable to answer the question of whether or not the past could be changed by their venture, she was left with a growing sense of dread as well.

Her role in this project was to design the rules under which they would make that journey, then help to select the period and see to it that the people who went would be prepared well enough to pass unnoticed in a world long gone.

The Period of Unification was her particular specialty, and although no decision had yet been made about where they would travel, it was accepted by most of them that that turbulent and all-important period should be their focus.

Until Unification, the world had been composed of many different tribes, with constantly shifting alliances and incessant wars. All resources had been focused on winning those wars, with precious little left over to provide for people's needs, let alone scientific progress.

The initial impetus to change that sorry state of affairs had come from one man, an Amaden warrior who'd convinced his tribal council that it was time to create a lasting peace. The Amadens were both the largest and most powerful of the world's tribes.

Once the decision had been made to seek peace, it had taken most of two decades to bring it about and to create the World Council that continued to rule to this day. All armies had been disbanded and people turned their attentions to science and the arts.

"Shayna?"

She roused herself from her musings as Teres offered her some tea. He looked at her gravely. "If we can't figure out where they went, we'll have to rely on you to make a guess."

She sipped the tea as her stomach began to churn. "And then what?"

"Then we'll have to go after them."

At that instant, Shayna finally realized what she should have guessed before: *she* would have to go after them. There was no one else on the team who had her knowledge of that period, no one who would be able to make the kind of decisions necessary once they arrived.

The prospect both thrilled and terrified her—as the project itself had done. What historian wouldn't leap at the chance to see history come alive? But even with her limited technical knowledge, she knew the dangers too.

Then, abruptly, she realized that she'd forgotten something very important. There was no need for them to hurry. They could take the time to build another backup craft and provide the necessary training. It didn't matter if it took years, because they could still go back to the time that Haddar had chosen.

The adrenaline rush that had accompanied her first thought began to fade, but it left behind a faint residue of disappointment. A part of her had always wanted to go, even though she'd known from the beginning that if they chose the Period of Unification, that wasn't likely. As a woman trying to move about in that male-dominated world, she would have been under too many restrictions.

The hours passed with no further information. Night gave way to dawn. Someone went to the cafeteria and brought back food. Teres spent an hour on the vidcom with the science minister from the World Council, briefing her on the situation. Since it was a weekend, only a few of the Institute's support staff appeared and were told of the situation. A media blackout had been decreed, so at least the news noses weren't pestering them.

Shayna paced the room restlessly for a time, then went down to the gym. Because the project team had been working long hours, a gym had been set up for them, together with showers and barracks-style sleeping quarters. She exercised in a halfhearted manner, then showered and returned to the conference room. One look at Teres's long, narrow face told her that the news was not good.

"They've given up," he said, running a hand through his thinning brown hair. "There's no way the computer is going to tell us where they went, but . . ." He paused, peering at her intently.

"But what?" she prompted when he seemed strangely unwilling to go on.

"There might be another way," he said carefully.

"What do you mean?"

"If we were to leave soon—within the next two hours, according to Gar—we might be able to follow them."

"I don't understand."

"You won't if I explain it, either. I'm not sure *I* fully understand what Gar is saying. But what it comes down to is that their passage through time leaves a sort of trail—a disturbance. Gar figured that it wouldn't last more than twelve hours, real time, and maybe not even that long. But he can program the onboard computer to follow them." He stopped again, once more staring at her.

"I'll go," she said, the words out even before she could think them. "I have to go."

Teres nodded. "You're the only one with enough knowledge to pass—but you won't be alone. We're sorting out now who the others will be."

He took her arm. "Shayna, you can refuse, and we'd understand if you did. We think the craft is ready, but we were planning to test it for another few months before we made a trial run—and then only a few years back.

"It's dangerous too, because now there's no backup craft, but that isn't quite the problem it may seem. It would take us at least another two years to build a replacement and test it, but we would still be able to follow you and retrieve you immediately—your time.

"Nevertheless," he said with a grave look, "you would lose two years of your life here."

Shayna nodded her understanding, although in truth, the complexities of time-travel gave her a headache. In any event, at this moment she was thinking of only one thing: she and Haddar had simply carried their academic disagreements to a new and dangerous arena. She was sure that he was determined to change history—and she was equally determined not to let that happen.

A little over an hour later, Shayna and the two other crew members were assembled in the conference room. The two men were self-conscious in their hastily assembled attire. Shayna was somewhat more comfortable in her long dress because she wore it sometimes to deliver lectures on the Period of Unification. Haddar had on one occasion accused her of being theatrical, and perhaps she was, but her students enjoyed it.

By now they were certain that it was Haddar and two of his allies who had stolen the time-craft. When he couldn't be found, security agents had rounded up several of his like-minded colleagues and had wasted no time in getting the truth from them through the use of drugs. The matter was considered to be grave enough to warrant such extreme measures.

Shayna had already told Teres that she was certain Haddar would have gone back to the Period of Unification. Now, as they waited for Gar to finish programming the remaining craft to follow the "pathway" of the one stolen by Haddar, he asked what she thought Haddar's plan might be.

She'd thought of little else as she'd made her hasty preparations for the journey. "I should have a better idea when we find out where they've gone, but if I had to guess now, I'd say that it's his intention to assassinate Mikal Har-Amaden."

Teres nodded. "That's exactly what I thought—and the council thinks as well. There is no other single action they could take that could change history."

Shayna's mind conjured up an image of the rugged, silver-haired warrior who had fought for peace as brilliantly as he'd once fought wars. No person in world history was more revered than Mikal Har-Amaden. His portrait and statues were everywhere—even three hundred years after his death. His birthday was still celebrated as a holiday the world over.

Haddar had said many times that he regarded Mikal

Har-Amaden as the greatest villain in history. Haddar was himself descended from Amaden nobility. They were and always had been an excessively proud and arrogant people. The fact that Mikal Har-Amaden—a member of the tribal ruling family—had chosen peace, and then persuaded the tribal council to agree, was nothing short of astounding, given the Amaden history of wars of conquest.

Haddar was of the opinion that the Amaden had been destined to rule the world, and that Mikal Har-Amaden had betrayed his own people.

"Well, he shouldn't be hard to find," Larus, the other crew member, remarked. "But it seems to me that he's likely to be well guarded."

"We know from past history that anyone who is willing to sacrifice his life can carry out an assassination," Shayna reminded him. "And Haddar might be willing to do just that." She turned to Teres. "Do we know if they took any weaponry with them—other than stunners, of course?" The small cylindrical stunners were available to anyone, but other weapons were very difficult to come by.

"We know only that they were trying to get their hands on some explosive devices of the type used for mining. But we have no evidence yet that they succeeded."

Teres reached out to place his hands on Shayna's shoulders. "I was asked by the council to tell you that you are free to use any weapon at your disposal—either to bring them back or to kill them."

An uneasy silence followed that statement, during which time Shayna saw the nervous glances that were cast her way by the others in the room. Shayna wished fervently that Teres hadn't spoken—or at least that he'd spoken only to her. But she understood why he had felt it necessary to tell the others.

Shayna was a descendant of a tribe called the Astasi. They were a small sect whose power far exceeded their numbers because they were believed to be the "children of the gods." The Astasi possessed supernatural talents, but had forsworn the use of those talents during the Period of Unification—a vow that had never been broken in three hundred years. And now Teres was telling her that the World Council had given her permission to break that vow, should it become necessary.

"I understand," she said quietly in response to Teres's statement.

The uneasy silence that followed was broken by the appearance of Gar, who announced that he had done his best to program the computer aboard the time-craft. It was time to leave.

There were no lengthy good-byes. Everyone wished them success in the fervent, solemn tones people use when they know that the chances of such an outcome are slim. Even Gar, always so confident of his extraordinary skills with computers, was subdued.

They entered the antechamber to the clean room, where the remaining time-craft awaited them. The door closed behind them and a bright red light came on, informing them that the decontamination process had begun. This was necessary so that time-travelers would not accidentally carry with them any germs or viruses that might prove to be fatal to inhabitants of a different time.

The process took only a few minutes, but it felt like an eternity to Shayna. Now that it was too late, she began to question the anger with Haddar that had propelled her on this uncertain journey. Of course, she had good reason to be angry with him: the man was a menace. But was that reason enough to risk her own life? She personally could not bring herself to believe that the past could be changed even if he succeeded in his nefarious scheme. But better minds than hers on this subject thought it possible.

If they were right, then the world to which she would return might well be a very different—and far worse—one. If she returned at all, that is. A chill slid through her as her mind snagged on that last thought. She glanced at her companions and saw in their faces the same thoughts. They were all betting their lives on the skills of the team, and in a technology that had yet to be proven.

Except, of course, that it *had* been proven, at least to some extent. Haddar and his allies had succeeded in going *somewhere.*

The red light winked out and a green light took its place. The door to the clean room slid open, and Shayna followed the two men into the time-chamber.

The craft was small; there was no need for much space. The journey would be brief in real time, however long it might be in history. And time-travelers took little with them. Each of them carried a supply of the money of the time and the small cylindrical stunners for personal protection that were to be used only in the most dire of circumstances. If there had been enough time, they would have been outfitted with extra clothing and other items common to the time period, but this was a journey made in haste.

Shayna wondered if Haddar and the others had money and weapons. The investigation was continuing, but by the time it produced any results, it would be too late to be of benefit.

Larus, her companion who would be piloting the craft—to the extent that was needed—opened the door. "Off we go, then," he said in an attempt at cheerfulness that wasn't exactly successful.

Conti, the third member of the crew, climbed in first. He was descended from the Amaden tribe and had minored in history at the university. Shayna knew from conversations with him that he'd studied his ancestral tribe. Even three hundred years after Unification the Amadens remained a distinct group, as did the Astasi, her own tribe. Other tribes, however, had intermarried for many generations. The world was now a blend of races where people wore their heritages in the color of their skin, the shape of their eyes, or their heights and builds.

But many of the Amaden and all of the Astasi married only within their tribes. In the case of the Amaden, it was pride; for her own people it was shame, though it was frequently disguised as pride. In a world where science now ruled, the supernatural powers of the Astasi were seen as relics of a shameful past, even though their powers had never been used for evil purposes.

Shayna's accidental conjuring of the vanished time-craft would have met with undisguised horror and disgust on the part of most people, though Teres, being the man he was, had accepted her apology without condemnation.

She climbed into the time-craft after Conti and settled into the front seat on the far side. Larus climbed into the other front seat and closed the door. The clicks of the locking mechanism sounded a note of finality that sent another shiver through her.

The disembodied voice of Teres filled the craft as he and Larus went through the preflight check. Lights flashed and numbers and words appeared on the curved console in front of her. Shayna thought about all the times when she'd dreamed of making such a journey, even though it seemed unlikely that she would ever be chosen.

"We all go with you in spirit," Teres's voice said in farewell.

Larus glanced at each of them in turn. "The journey will last no more than a minute. We don't know if you'll feel anything other than some vibrations from the craft, but it's likely that you won't."

"What would we see if there were windows?" Shayna asked curiously, already feeling claustrophobic.

"Nothing, in all likelihood." His hand curved around the knob on the stick that protruded from the floor between their seats.

The lever shifted almost soundlessly. Some lights dimmed and others grew brighter. Shayna felt the vibrations that Larus had mentioned. On the console, displays changed with dizzying speed. She had never been in the clean room and so was unfamiliar with the craft.

She was about to ask Larus how they would know when they'd arrived and if the display would tell them where they were, when she saw him frowning at one particular display. He had just reached out to punch a button on the console when the craft suddenly began to shake, nearly flinging her from her seat. Her frightened cry was joined by those of the two men just as the lights on the dashboard began to flash wildly. A strange odor filled the craft—something she thought she recognized but couldn't quite place. Sparks shot from the array of instruments—and then there was a final, terrible jolt that sent her head crashing into the console.

Shayna was confused by the sharp, insistent sound that aroused her from her stupor. She tried to focus on Larus, who lay slumped in his seat, bleeding from a terrible gash in his forehead. She reached out to touch his arm and called his name. There was no response.

Fighting panic now, she turned carefully in her seat to find Conti. He lay sprawled over the empty storage compartment next to his seat. In her confusion and fear, it took several seconds for her to realize that his neck lay at an impossible angle. Acting purely on instinct now, she reached back to check for a pulse, and found none. The annoying sound of the alarm continued.

"Larus!" She turned her attention back to him and began to shake him. Getting no response, she felt with shaking fingers for his pulse. It was there, but very faint. And then, even as she pressed her fingers to his warm flesh, it fluttered and stopped.

The alarm filled her mind, its pulsing sound beating in her head, demanding her attention. She tried to focus on the console, but her vision was blurred. And then, suddenly, with a horror greater than anything she'd felt before, Shayna knew what the alarm meant.

It flashed through her mind in less than a second as she was already beginning to scramble with uncoordinated fingers for the door lock. The self-destruct mechanism! She could hear Teres explaining it in his quiet, deep voice.

"It's the ultimate safeguard—and one I fought for. If the craft should crash, it will self-destruct. That way, no one from another time can get their hands on it. We're not worried that they could make use of it, but we *are* concerned about the impact such a discovery could have—particularly on primitive people. It's simply an extension of our determination to leave nothing of our journey behind."

Her fingers finally found the proper buttons and the door swung open. Acting wholly on instinct and totally without thought, Shayna flung herself out of the craft into cold darkness. She fell, and her hands encountered bone-chilling cold. Snow! She blinked and tried to see her surroundings as she pulled herself to her feet. Inside the craft, the alarm continued.

She ran, although to any observer it would seem more of a drunken lurch. The world around her was spinning crazily. Her head throbbed unbearably, and even through the wet cold of the snow, she could feel her ankle throbbing as well.

Then, suddenly, the alarm stopped, and a second later an invisible force struck her, propelling her through the air. After that, she neither felt nor saw anything more.

The storm woke him as it vented its fury on the mountainside and the valley beyond. He lay in his bed listening and smiling, enjoying the vagaries of the weather here. He'd come only two days ago from the south, where the climate never changed, except to vary from hot to unbearably hot. Even the daily period of rain was hot—and the very rain itself.

Lightning flashed beyond the cabin's windows, and thunder tried to shake the sturdy log walls. The day of his arrival here—two days ago—nearly a foot of snow had fallen. Now spring was making another run at the hills and valleys. He always thought of it as a battle, because that metaphor came easily to him.

He got out of bed and peered through the uncurtained window that faced the valley. Gusts of wind-driven rain struck the panes with a faint hissing sound. In the flashes of lightning, he saw it pelting the snow.

If the weather changed—as he knew it would—the snow would all be gone in a day or two, and green shoots would spring from the mud. He was glad to be home, though it was somewhat inaccurate to call this cabin his home. In truth, it seemed that he had no real home anymore, except for the battlefield. But this was his family's land, so he called it home anyway.

He was about to turn away from the window and go back to bed when a bright flash caught his eye, leaving a strange afterimage in his mind. He frowned, holding the image there as he examined it: a great fork of lightning that had seemed to have something in its center that lit up briefly.

After a moment he shrugged and went back to bed. No doubt the storm was playing tricks on his tired brain.

When he awoke the next morning, the storm had long since passed and the air was fresh and cold, though somewhat warmer than it had been the day before. As he stepped outside, he heard the sounds of the snow melting everywhere and breathed in the faint hint of spring in the air. And when his gaze traveled down across the slope to the valley, he recalled that strange image from the night before.

He let it linger in his mind as he fixed his breakfast, then chewed it over as he chewed his food. There was nothing he had to do this day—a great luxury for him—so he decided to ride down into the valley.

His surefooted stallion picked its way down over the rocky slope that was in places slick with melting ice. He didn't really expect to find anything, but the valley was as good a place to ride as any. Before long it would be filled with grazing cattle from his family's ranch, but for now they were pastured closer to the barns.

When they reached the valley floor, his horse began to strain at the bit, wanting to run. He held it in, knowing there could be dangerous chuckholes that would snare a leg and break it. He would let the stallion run when they reached the road at the far side of the valley.

Then maybe he'd go on to the house, where he could count on his brother's cook to provide him with a good meal while he caught up some more on family business.

This casual, unplanned day was a luxury to be savored—especially here in his beloved homelands. There were times when he envied his brother and thought about the path not taken. At such times he sensed the two sides of himself very strongly: the man of peace and the man of war. But the world saw only the latter, and praised him for that.

He turned in the saddle and glanced back at his cabin to get his bearings as he rode across the valley. It was impossible to be certain, but he thought that flash had occurred over the very center of the small valley. And then, when he turned back again, he saw something that made him rein in his stallion.

Off to his right, perhaps a quarter-mile or less away, was a bare spot. The valley was still at least six or eight inches deep in slushy snow, but that one spot, oval in shape, was completely bare, its edges sharply defined. Curious, he pointed the horse in that direction.

A few moments later he was frowning at the spot, trying to guess what had caused it. The grass that had begun to grow beneath the snow in other places was absent here. There was nothing but half-frozen mud in a distinctive oval shape, as though something had rested there.

He began to scan the area around the strange spot, and a few seconds later he saw something else that didn't belong, something that from where he was looked like a pile of clothing: women's clothing, to judge from the pattern and colors.

He let out a sound of surprise as he approached it. It wasn't just a pile of clothing, after all: it was a body. He reined in his horse and leaped from the saddle, then ran toward the rocky outcropping.

She lay facedown on the rocks, the dress clinging wetly to her curves. But it wasn't her body that held his attention; instead, it was that long auburn hair. An Astasi witch? That was impossible. They never ventured beyond their valley, more than a hundred miles to the northeast.

Red hair did exist among his own people, but it was very rare—rare enough to make him approach her cautiously, his hand resting lightly on his holstered sidearm, even though she hadn't moved at all and might well be dead.

He crouched down beside her, staring at the one pale hand that was the only exposed flesh he could see. Definitely Astasi; his own people had much darker, bronzed skin. And now he could see that she wasn't dead, after all. Her back rose and fell slightly with her slow breathing.

He scanned the area, looking for her companions or her horse. But there was no sign of either. None of this made any sense. Why would an Astasi witch be so far from home—and alone? He suspected witchcraft, but couldn't understand the reason for it.

He continued to squat there, frowning. His people weren't at war with the Astasi, but they weren't exactly fond of them, either. No one was. Children of all tribes grew up hearing dark tales of their witchcraft.

Finally he reached out to sweep away the thick curtain of hair that hid her face. She still didn't stir, so he grasped her shoulders gently and turned her over carefully.

She was beautiful—but then they all were. If he'd harbored any remaining doubts as to her identity, they vanished now. She had the delicate features and high cheekbones of the Astasi, and he knew that beneath that thick fringe of dark lashes would be their distinctive green eyes, a strange, pale green the shade of new spring shoots.

He pressed two fingers into the hollow at the base of her throat, feeling for the pulse. It was slow but steady. Her skin was cool, as smooth as marble. He began to check her for broken bones, trying to remain impersonal in his touch but unable to completely prevent a tightening in his groin.

When his hands trailed down over her hips, he felt

something hard and realized it was something contained in the pocket of her dress. He ignored it until he had satisfied himself that no bones were broken, and then he slid his hand into the pocket and withdrew the object.

His dark brows knitted in puzzlement as he stared at it. It was a small, cylindrical object, about the length and thickness of his middle finger, and made of some sort of metal that he couldn't identify. The only adornment on the object was a circular part near the one end that was curved, almost as though intended to fit a thumb or finger.

Ignoring the unconscious woman for a moment, he tried holding it in various ways until he became certain that the circular part must be intended to be depressed by a thumb, though one much smaller than his own. Holding it away from himself and from her, he pressed against the thumb-pad, not knowing what to expect. But nothing happened. He felt relieved, having had the strange thought that it might be a weapon of some sort, though why an Astasi should need a weapon, he couldn't begin to guess. Besides, even if they had weapons, they couldn't have something unknown to him.

He slipped it into his pocket and returned his attention to the unconscious woman, sliding his fingers beneath her head this time. There it was: a knobby lump. Her head must have struck the rock when she fell.

He stood up and whistled for his stallion, then carefully picked up the unconscious witch and laid her across the saddle. His cabin was much closer than the house, so he turned in that direction, even though he knew that he'd find help at the house.

Later he would realize that he'd made a momentous decision by taking her back to his cabin. But at the moment he was operating on pure instinct. Something made him decide that she should remain his secret—for now, at least.

Chapter Two

Shayna awoke to confusion, drifting in and out of consciousness and then hovering somewhere in between. She had only the vaguest of memories: an alarm, the cold, something unseen pushing her. Before that, she could recall nothing, even though she had the sense that the memories were there.

She felt herself being bumped along somehow, being moved in some fashion that her bruised mind couldn't quite comprehend. At one point she heard her own voice crying out in protest—and then a deep voice answering, saying something that didn't quite penetrate the thick fog in her brain.

She was cold and wet, and then she was dry and warm, and she had no way of knowing if either state was real or imagined as she struggled for those elusive memories that would connect all this confusion.

That same voice was talking to her, asking her questions she couldn't answer—except for her name. She gave that several times: her first name and then her full name, putting the words together so that the harsh voice would go away.

But it wouldn't go away. Several times she was shaken—not roughly, but it still made the pain in her head worse. She protested, and the shaking stopped.

When at last she opened her eyes, her surroundings wouldn't come into focus. Shapes she couldn't quite identify doubled themselves before slowly resolving into furniture of a style and composition she recognized from old photographs: pictures of a time when furniture was still made of wood.

The walls confused her even more. They weren't smooth, although it took a lot of staring before she was sure of that. They appeared to be made of many curving pieces of polished wood. After a time, she gave up trying to figure them out.

The room was lit by a soft glow, and she turned her head—very slowly and carefully to minimize the pain—toward the source of the light. Her nose twitched as she caught an unfamiliar odor, and then she drew in a sharp breath when she saw that the light was a flame. But it was a flame trapped inside a column of glass: an oil lamp. She'd seen pictures of them too, and assumed that accounted for the acrid odor.

Suddenly her confusion had an edge of panic to it, and icy fear began to crawl along her spine. Desperately she attempted to place herself by summoning up memories. But all that came were the alarm, the cold, and that shove from an unseen force that had sent her flying through the air.

Go back, she ordered herself. What was the alarm? Where were you when you first heard it? An image flashed through her mind and was gone quickly: a man with a deep gash in his head that was spurting blood. Did she know him? She couldn't remember. She tried to resurrect the image, to examine it more fully, but it refused to come again.

Her restless gaze fell on a dress spread over a chair. Was it hers? It looked vaguely familiar, but it felt wrong, as though she knew it—had perhaps even worn it—but as a sort of costume. She stared at it, trying to place it in history. It looked like the type of dress worn by women hundreds of years ago: long, high necked, showing the dull colors of natural dyes.

Shayna's frustration grew inside her like a gnawing, writhing thing. How was it that such facts came so easily to her, while she couldn't recall what was important? She knew her name, but she didn't know where she was or how she'd gotten here.

Then she remembered that voice, demanding to know her name. She began to listen carefully for sounds beyond the small bedroom, but heard nothing. Was she alone now? Was the voice that of the man with the bleeding head?

Way down deep inside her, in a primitive place where the darkest fears reside, was the truly terrible thought that she was in a worse situation than she could possibly imagine.

Her stomach growled, reminding her that she had no idea when she'd last eaten. She was just thinking about trying to get out of bed when she heard footsteps approaching.

The lamplight barely reached to the doorway, so the figure that appeared and then paused there was in shadow. She knew that it was male, and that it was not the man with the wound. Even in the dim light she could see that he was too big and too dark.

"So you're awake now, witch. I hope you're ready to give me some answers."

The deep voice, which she immediately recognized as the one that had demanded to know her name, echoed through her dazed brain as she struggled to focus her blurry vision.

Witch? It was a term that echoed down the long, long halls of history—one she'd never heard spoken. His accent was strange, too, even though she had no problem understanding him.

He advanced slowly into the room and she saw that he carried something: a coil of rope. At least she thought that was what it was. He stopped a few feet from the bed and she stared at him as her vision temporarily cleared.

It was a harsh face, but not an unattractive one. A faint feeling of familiarity slithered through her. She was certain that she'd seen him before. He has to be Amaden, she thought, with that dark hair and bronzed skin and great size.

He raised the hand with the rope. "I came in here to tie your hands, witch, so that you can't cast any spells. But I've saved your life, and if you give me your word that you won't try anything, I won't tie you."

She stared at him in shock. Spells? The very thought of that forbidden activity disgusted her, and her expression must have shown that.

"Are you going to deny that you're Astasi?" he demanded, his dark eyes boring into her.

She tried to shake her head, but stopped quickly as a wave of dizziness overcame her. "No. I'm Astasi—but it's forbidden to cast spells."

He frowned. "Forbidden? You mean because I saved your life?"

Shayna hesitated. Once again that sense that her situation was far worse than she knew came over her. "Yes," she said, deciding that that was the answer he wanted.

He tossed the coil of rope onto a nearby table. "Then perhaps you'll explain what you're doing here."

Shayna felt tears of frustration stinging her eyes. She had hoped he could answer that. "I don't know. I don't know where I am."

A part of her hated making the admission, allowing this man to know how vulnerable and frightened she was. But the words had come out anyway.

He sat down on a chair and stared at her. "Amnesia," he said. "It's not uncommon after a blow to the head—or a shock of some sort."

Amnesia, she thought. Of course that was it. She knew that he'd spoken the truth because she'd heard of such cases. "Then it will come back—my memory, I mean," she said with relief, talking to herself as much as to him.

He nodded. "Probably in a few days. You have a concussion and you've injured your ankle, though I don't think any bones are broken."

Until he spoke she'd been unaware of the pain in her right ankle. Now she moved it experimentally and winced. She also realized for the first time that she was naked beneath the covers. The thought of how she might have gotten that way made her very uncomfortable.

"Do you remember anything?" he asked.

She told him about the alarm, the man with the wound in his forehead, and about the strange push that had sent her flying through the air. And even as she spoke, a different but no less compelling alarm seemed to be going off inside her, as though warning her that she shouldn't be speaking of these things to him. And when his frown deepened, she became even more certain that she should have kept her silence.

"That's all I can remember," she said finally.

"Describe this man," he ordered.

She did so reluctantly, then said that she couldn't picture him clearly.

"Is he the one who pushed you?"

She shook her head and was punished by a fresh wave of dizziness. When she had recovered, she tried to find the proper words even as she wished she hadn't told him about it.

"No, I don't think so. It felt more like a strong wind, I think."

He was silent for a moment, his dark brows still knitted in a frown. "You were alone when I found you. What I want to know is how you got there. I didn't even find a horse."

A horse? Why should he have expected her to have a horse? Her gaze fell again on that old-fashioned dress, and once more she felt uneasy. "I don't know how I got there," she answered honestly.

The dark, deep-set eyes that bored into her were compelling—and familiar. She knew this man—and yet he'd given no indication thus far that there was any prior acquaintance.

"I'll bring you something to eat," he said and left the room.

He watched her eat the food he'd brought her, her good manners barely able to temper her hunger. And he wondered if she were telling him the truth.

No one really knew all that much about the secretive Astasi. They lived in their secluded valley at the edge of the Amaden lands, where they had always lived, keeping to themselves. Few others had ever ventured there, and those who did were stopped at the valley's entrance. Many believed that the "children of the gods" could heal any disease or injury, and they were the ones who came to the Astasi. Sometimes they were indeed healed, but other times they were told that nothing could be done for them.

The Astasi had been a thorn in the side of the Amaden for many centuries. At various times Amaden leaders had made war upon them, but never with any success. The Astasi, though small in numbers, had succeeded in turning back any attempt to take their valley by employing their magic.

During the course of his own studies of his people's history, he had reached the conclusion that something would have to be done about them at some point. They'd never shown any interest in making war, except to defend themselves, but there was always the danger that they might decide to throw their lot in with the Amaden's many enemies.

He decided that he was being provided with an excellent opportunity to learn something about the Astasi—information that could prove to be very useful in the future. It seemed likely to him that she was, in fact, telling him the truth now. Her confusion seemed real enough, and that bump on her head indicated that something had indeed happened to her.

But what could it have been? It seemed unlikely that

anyone could have captured her—unless it was another Astasi. No one knew for certain what their powers were, but accounts he'd read of those long-ago wars indicated that no one could hope to capture any of them.

Could she have been deliberately cast out from their valley for some reason—some transgression he couldn't even begin to imagine, not knowing anything about their society?

He thought this over while she finished her meal, casting glances at him from time to time. Was her sudden appearance on his family's lands the result of some of their magic? He supposed that could account for that strange oval-shaped bare patch on the ground near where he'd found her. And it could even explain the "wind" she'd described that had knocked her into the rocks. But it didn't explain the man she'd described, or the strange cylinder he'd taken from her pocket and hidden away.

The way he saw it, he probably had a few days to learn what he could about her and her people, and then she would recover her memory and undoubtedly begin to lie to him. If she wasn't already, that is.

Shayna awoke to a darkness that was only partially banished by the bright moonlight that poured through the window. Before she could realize their possible importance, the dreams that had plagued her sleep slipped away, leaving no trace behind.

Earlier he'd helped her to the crude bathroom at the back of the cabin after she'd struggled into her clothes. Now she decided to try to visit it on her own. She climbed carefully out of bed, still wearing the long dress, then stood up cautiously, testing her weight on the injured ankle.

She bit back a cry of pain and tried again. Then she saw a piece of a tree limb leaning against the chair. It hadn't been there earlier, and she realized with a rush of gratitude that he must have put it there for her to use. She picked it up and began to hobble to the bathroom.

There was no hot water, but she did her best to wash anyway, shivering as the cold water splashed over her skin. The tiny window in the bathroom admitted little moonlight, but she leaned forward and stared at herself in the mirror over the sink.

The face that stared back at her seemed to be haunted by memories that could not be summoned: memories she desperately needed. The impact of the moonlight was to deaden the usually vibrant red of her hair and the pale green of her eyes. She reached up and felt the lump on her head. It seemed to have receded somewhat, and her vision remained clear.

The bathroom was located off the small kitchen and she stopped there. A fire was still burning in the stove, keeping warm the kettle of water on top. She fumbled around in the semidarkness until she found some tea bags in a canister, then made herself some tea and cut off a chunk from the loaf of bread on the table. She wished that she had some butter, but couldn't begin to guess where it might be.

Her unfamiliarity with such a simple thing as a kitchen, combined with a near certainty that she'd never known such things truly terrified her because they seemed to touch that deep, dark part of her that hid even greater horrors.

I am alive, and I will be well again, she told herself to stave off those fears. And thus far, at least, her benefactor had been very kind to her, though it was certainly a kindness tempered by wariness and distrust.

That's understandable, she thought. *He is surely Amaden and I am Astasi. Even after all this time, no one completely trusts the Astasi.*

That thought made her frown as a quick image flashed through her brain: another man, tall and wearing a startled expression as she apologized for something.

The image was gone quickly, but this time she found that she could recall all the details: a room filled with computers, the man in question wearing a dark green jumpsuit, other voices, several people working on the computers.

Shayna drew in a quick, sharp breath as the knowledge settled over her, heavy and cold. She did not belong here. She wasn't yet certain what *here* meant, but she knew it was the truth, and that it was a tiny piece from that dark place.

She knew it for two reasons. The first was that familiarity clung to that brief image. It was a place she'd been often, and the tall man was someone she both knew and liked. And she knew the image had pried open a corner of that dark place because she was very certain that that familiar place and this place she was now could not coexist.

Her brain stretched to make the connection beyond herself—to find the reason for her presence here, when she clearly belonged *there.* But nothing would come.

Her body made restless by the confusion in her mind, Shayna got up from the chair and, leaning on the branch, made her way out the front door of the cabin into the star-filled night.

She hadn't been outside yet, but now saw that her earlier guess had been correct. Her temporary home was indeed a log cabin. She had surmised that when she'd finally realized that the interior walls were made of logs. And as she stood there staring at it, she knew that she'd never seen one before, except in pictures—and that it came from a time far removed from her real life.

The extent of her knowledge now was frustrating: bits and pieces of varying sizes, but no overall picture. Connections were missing, and no matter how hard she tried to make them, they eluded her.

The cabin was perched on the edge of a steep hill overlooking a narrow valley, with more hills beyond. He had said that he'd found her down there, but she didn't recognize the place.

She turned her thoughts to him instead. He'd told her nothing at all about himself—not even his name. She was greatly troubled by her total dependence upon him—and even more troubled in a vague way by that lingering sense that he was somehow familiar to her. Tired again from all her thinking, she was about to turn and go back into the cabin when she heard footsteps inside.

He stopped in the open doorway when she spun about clumsily, nearly losing her balance with her injured ankle. He wore the same loose trousers he'd worn earlier, but no shirt this time. Dark hair stood out against his bronzed chest, tapering to a thin line before disappearing into his unbelted trousers. Shayna was shocked to feel a powerfully erotic response to him, when she'd felt nothing more than gratitude and curiosity before.

"I'm sorry if I woke you," she said politely, hoping he wouldn't notice the slight huskiness in her voice. "And thank you for this." She indicated the branch she was using as support.

He merely nodded, then asked if she couldn't heal her ankle herself.

At first Shayna wasn't sure what he meant, but then she realized he must be referring to her powers. She recalled that earlier reference, when he'd intended to tie her hands. He seemed to expect her to use those powers. Didn't he know that she couldn't—that she was forbidden to do so?

"No, I can't," she replied, struggling to understand why she couldn't.

"I thought that the Astasi were great healers," he said as she hobbled toward him.

"We were once—but there's no need for that now."

And as soon as the words left her lips, she knew they were a mistake, that she'd leaped over those connections she had yet to make.

"No need?" he echoed. "I don't understand."

"It will heal itself," she said hastily. "It's much better already."

He stepped aside for her to enter the cabin. They exchanged good-nights and she returned to her room. But he continued to stand there in the cabin's doorway.

His earlier thought that she might have been cast out by her own people returned once more. Perhaps they'd forbidden her to use her powers ever again—or maybe they'd somehow taken them away. But what could she have done to merit such punishment? By casting her out of the valley, they were condemning her to death.

He knew he was treading on dangerous ground and had been ever since he'd chosen to bring her back here instead of taking her to the keep. If he weren't who he was, he might have been able to harbor an Astasi, but under the circumstances . . .

He raised his head to stare at the bright night sky, remembering the storm and the strange lightning that had sent him down into the valley where he found her. And, suddenly, a man who rarely knew uncertainty, let alone outright fear, felt cold fingers creeping along his spine.

Shayna had not known how much his presence affected her until he proved it by his absence. He had a name now: Kaz. She had asked him when she awoke and found him standing outside the cabin, staring down into the valley. He'd seemed surprised and even slightly wary at her question, then had quickly apologized for his failure to introduce himself.

Still, Shayna couldn't help feeling that there could be another reason for his surprise at the question. Contrary to what many people had once believed, the Astasi could not read minds. But they did possess a certain talent for spotting falsehoods, even when they were uttered by accomplished liars. And Shayna was certain that he had lied about something.

Nevertheless, she could not fault him for his hospitality or his thoughtfulness. When she came into the kitchen, she discovered that he had heated several large pots of water for her bath, which he then carried into the big tub in the bathroom, apologizing for what he called the "primitive" accommodations here.

She was still enjoying the bath when he tapped on the door and told her that he would be gone for several hours because he had to replenish their food supply. She assured him that she would be fine, and he must have left immediately.

At the time she'd thought it strange that he'd waited until she was bathing and then had departed in such haste, but when she emerged from her bath a short time later and looked out the window to see if his horse was gone from the small lean-to beside the cabin, not only was the horse gone, but he had already reached the valley.

She was about to turn away from the window when a movement far out in the valley caught her attention. A lone rider was coming toward him. She watched as both Kaz and the other rider changed their courses and met in the middle of the valley, where only faint traces now remained of the snow.

Had he seen the rider coming and then hurried down there to prevent the person from coming to the cabin? she wondered as they both paused briefly, then began to ride away from the cabin together. She narrowed her eyes, trying to get a better look at the other rider. It might have been a woman; certainly he or she was smaller than Kaz.

She had washed her clothes the night before, sleeping in a shirt he had offered her. Now she put them on again and fixed herself some breakfast, which she carried outside. The day was surprisingly warm, considering that snow had fallen only a few days ago.

Suddenly the fickleness of the weather seemed to touch a memory. For a moment she heard a woman's voice. "Shayna, you don't come home often enough. Otherwise you'd remember that spring is a great tease here."

Shivers crawled along her spine, despite the warmth of the sun. "Mother!" she whispered as a fleeting image came to her of a lovely gray-haired woman smiling.

Is this the way it will happen? she asked herself. Will I be tormented by bits and pieces until finally the connections are made? Kaz had said that it would probably happen that way, but she'd hoped that she would awaken to a morning where the world suddenly made sense again.

And yet she knew with absolute certainty that the knowledge she sought so desperately would come with a very high price. There was an old saying about ignorance being blissful—and Shayna knew that she was likely to discover soon just how true that was.

She was grateful for the absence of Kaz's watchfulness, but unfortunately it left her alone too much with her thoughts. When she could no longer stand them, she began to roam about the small cabin. In one corner stood a big piece of furniture that she couldn't identify at first, but she finally decided that it must be a desk of some sort, perhaps with the writing surface hidden behind the curved part. She tried to open it, but saw that it was locked.

Then, after checking to be sure he wasn't yet returning from wherever he'd gone, she went into his bedroom. Her curiosity about him had been limited by her confusion about herself and her unremembered past, but now, perversely, it began to grow in his absence.

The room was only slightly larger than her room and furnished much the same, although the bed was bigger. She pulled open the drawers of the small dresser one by one, but they yielded nothing more than a minimal supply of clothing. So she then turned to the wardrobe standing in one corner.

Shayna gasped. She had expected to find nothing more than the nondescript clothing he'd been wearing—but there, hanging amidst shirts and trousers, was a military uniform. She knew that was what it was because she'd seen them many times in pictures that now flashed through her mind.

She separated it from the other clothing and examined it more closely. From somewhere came the recollection that one's position was determined by the trim on a uniform, but she could recall nothing more than that.

The uniform was dark blue in color, with brass buttons on the jacket and a great quantity of gold braid that crossed the shoulders and hung down in loops along the arms. She thought that if sheer quantity of decoration connoted high rank, he must be a very important man, even though she'd already guessed his age at somewhere in his midthirties.

She began to wonder if this might not be his real home. Perhaps it was only a retreat of some sort. That would account for his comment this morning about the primitive accommodations.

She continued to stare at the uniform as that nagging sense of something familiar about him plagued her once again. And then she noticed a slight bulge in the pocket of the jacket. She reached into it and withdrew a small silver cylindrical object.

What is it? she asked herself, expecting her memory to produce the answer, much as it had several other times when she'd not immediately understood what something was. But this time nothing came, so she put it back, then closed the wardrobe.

When he returned to the cabin and found her gone, he knew that what he should be feeling was relief. Shayna Har-Astasi could be nothing but trouble to him. Even if she weren't a witch, he had no time for a woman in his life right now. Not that he ever had. At some point it might be necessary to take a wife, but he hoped not. The responsibilities of marriage and a family would only overburden a man who'd already taken on as much as one man could be expected to handle.

He certainly had no problem in finding amenable women to warm his bed, and he intended to keep it that way. And in any event, a witch suffering from amnesia—no matter how beautiful she was—wasn't a candidate for his bed. So he should have felt relief at the temptation being removed.

But instead he was stricken with a sense of loss out of all proportion to the reality of the situation. He even wondered uneasily if she might have cast a spell on him despite her assurances to the contrary.

He'd told no one at the house about her, and now his

guilt at that omission was assuaged by the fact of her absence. He'd even gone so far as to steal some clothing for her from trunks in the attic: things he hoped wouldn't be missed by his sister-in-law, whose wardrobe filled several closets.

And then he saw her. Glancing out the window in the kitchen as he put away the food supplies he'd brought back, he spotted her lying beneath a tree at the edge of the clearing. He hurried toward her, irrationally happy to see her, while at the same time fearful that she'd become ill in his absence.

"Shayna!"

The voice was harsh, summoning her back from the realm of dreams. She tried to ignore it, wanting to stay where she was, in her lovely apartment atop a graceful building at the edge of the university campus, surrounded by carefully chosen items collected over the years.

But the voice called her name again, and then a hand closed around her shoulder, shaking her gently. She opened her eyes to find herself staring into a pair of concerned dark eyes scant inches from her own.

She was engulfed by a tidal wave that threatened to drown her in too much knowledge: far more than her brain could process. There was the memory of her dreams, the horrifying memory of the accident with the time-craft—and the more recent memory of this place and this man.

"Are you all right?" he demanded, releasing her.

"Yes," she answered automatically, even though there had never been a time in her life when she was less "all right." Now she understood that dark place in her, that certainty that there were things she didn't want to know about her past. She was lost in time—and she was alone!

She wanted him to go away and leave her there so she could try to think about her situation, but instead there he was, crouched on the ground in front of her, watching her every move as he had been since she'd arrived here.

"I've brought you some clothes," he said. "I think they'll fit."

"Thank you." She avoided meeting his eyes, lest he see just how little she cared for this latest example of his thoughtfulness. As much as she wanted desperately to be alone right now, she knew that she was even more dependent on this man's kindness than she'd realized before.

She started to get to her feet, bracing herself against the tree trunk. He put out a hand to assist her, then withdrew it when she didn't accept his offer. Preoccupied as she was, she still noticed his wariness—and now she understood why that was. Wherever she had landed, it was a time when her people had been both feared and reviled.

"My headache has returned," she told him as she hobbled toward the cabin. "I must rest for a while."

She hurried as best she could into the cabin, then went directly to her room and closed the door behind her with a sigh that was half sob. How she wanted to believe that this was all a bad dream and she was really back in her own world.

She sat down on the bed and proceeded to fit all the pieces together, still hoping against hope that it wasn't real. But once the floodgates of her memory had opened, it had all come out: the Time Project, Haddar's treachery, the hasty journey with Larus and Conti, who were now dead, and the programmed destruction of the time-craft that had now left her trapped in a time that might or might not be where Haddar and his allies had gone.

She had no way of knowing what had gone wrong with the craft. If Larus or Conti had survived, they might have been able to guess, but she lacked that technical expertise. And what did it matter in any event? The craft had self-destructed, and her only hope of ever being able to return to her own world lay with Haddar, who might or might not be here and who certainly hated her.

She lay back on the bed and let herself wallow in self-pity for a time. How could such a thing have happened to a woman who'd led a carefully ordered, scholarly life? She wasn't even the adventurous sort, unlike so many of her friends and colleagues, who regularly cast off their academic personae to climb mountains or sail the oceans or trek into the wilderness.

But she also wasn't the type to wallow in self-pity, either. And even if she were so inclined, now was definitely not the time. She was reminded of that by the sound of his footsteps in the little hallway beyond her room as he apparently went into his own room, then came out again a moment later.

She desperately needed information from him—but how could she obtain it? If this place weren't so isolated, she might be able to make a guess as to what time period she was in. But as it was, she had too little information.

It also occurred to her that the deaths of her companions on this time-journey left her uniquely vulnerable. Not only was she a woman almost certainly stranded in a time when women could not move about freely, but she was also easily recognizable as an Astasi: a witch. And until after the Period of Unification, her people had never left their valley. Most had, in fact, remained there until recent times.

Teres had hoped that assertions by Larus and Conti that she was not Astasi would have covered any of those problems. After all, red hair and green eyes did show up occasionally among the Amaden and other tribes. Her identity had seemed to be no more than a minor problem by comparison with the problems presented by Haddar and his allies. Now that problem seemed insurmountable. Kaz had left no doubt that he considered her to be Astasi.

She thought about him now in light of her recovered memory. Whatever she planned to do hinged on his cooperation—or at the very least, his passive acceptance.

Apart from the fact that he must be a military officer, she knew nothing about him, and she thought now that his profession did not bode well for gaining his cooperation.

Down through the centuries, Amaden warriors had periodically made war on her people, despite the fact that the Astasi had never done anything to provoke their wrath. It seemed that the Astasi's very existence, in the midst of the Amaden lands, was enough.

And yet, presented with what must have been a perfect opportunity to kill her, Kaz had saved her life. The question, she thought, was why he'd done that. And it was one question she could ask without revealing her true identity. Furthermore, his response might well aid her in determining just where she had landed.

One step at a time, she thought as she got up, ready to declare that her headache was gone. When I know where I am, I can begin to construct a story he might believe.

She found him seated at the big desk in the corner, writing in what she assumed must be a journal of some sort. His back was to her and he apparently hadn't heard her soft footsteps. As his pen moved from the inkwell to the page, she wondered how she might steal that journal in order to get a look at it. Perhaps he wouldn't be as careful about locking the desk when he was here—or maybe she could find some way of picking the lock.

Then he seemed to have sensed her presence, because he turned around suddenly, then laid down his pen.

"I want to ask you something," she announced, deciding to forestall any questions he might have in mind.

One dark brow shot up and she thought that he looked slightly surprised—perhaps even faintly amused for some reason.

"I would like to know why you saved my life."

He swiveled the desk chair around to face her and took his time before responding. That faint gleam of amusement remained in his dark eyes.

"Would you have preferred that I left you there to die?"

"Of course not—but you haven't answered my question."

"We're not at war with the Astasi," he said mildly. "Perhaps I was merely curious about why a witch would be on my land. I'm still curious about that."

"I still don't know how I got here," she lied. "In fact, I'm not sure exactly where I am. Am I far from the valley?"

"About one hundred miles southwest," he told her, watching her with that odd mixture of fascination and wariness that she'd seen from the beginning.

"And this is your land?"

"My family's land. I keep this cabin as a sort of retreat."

"Who was that I saw you with down in the valley?" she asked.

"My sister-in-law. She and my brother live in the family home, an hour's ride from here."

"You didn't want her to discover me," she said, making it a statement rather than a question.

He nodded. "It seemed wise to keep your presence a secret."

"Why? Would they want to kill me?"

"No, but my own position is such that it would be . . . difficult."

"What do you mean? Are you married?"

"No, I'm not married. I'm a military officer, and while I personally don't regard the Astasi as being an enemy, there are those who do."

"I see," she said, trying to think of more questions because she feared that he was about to start asking some of his own. Unfortunately she wasn't quick enough.

"Have you remembered anything at all?"

"No, nothing."

"Then tell me what you do know about yourself. You obviously haven't lost all your memories."

She fought down her panic. She could lie if necessary. She knew her people's history and how they'd lived. She affected a shrug. "I know only my name, and I remember some things about the valley and my life there—but nothing that would explain how I came to be here."

"Is it possible that you were deliberately cast out by your people for some reason? Would they do such a thing? I've never heard of it."

No, they wouldn't, she thought. But it did provide her with an explanation. "It's possible," she conceded doubtfully.

"Could they have used magic to send you here?"

"Why do you ask?" She sensed strongly that he had some reason beyond mere curiosity for asking that particular question.

"I saw something the night before I found you down there—something I can't explain. There was a thunderstorm." He stopped and frowned for so long that she thought he might not go on. Was that what had happened? Had they entered this time only to be caught in a thunderstorm? She vaguely recalled discussions about the dangers of entering a time when they didn't know the conditions existing at that moment.

"I'm still not sure exactly what I saw," he went on. "But it seemed to be something caught in a bolt of lightning. Then, when I found you, it was because I'd noticed a bare spot on the ground, even though there were still at least six or eight inches of snow elsewhere in the valley."

The same force that had flung her through the air as it destroyed the time-craft had obviously melted the snow beneath it. And now she knew that it had indeed been a storm that had disabled them.

That meant that it was likely she had arrived in the same time period as Haddar—or so she thought. But if that was the case, shouldn't he have been there as well? She'd understood that they were following his trail. Could the storm have interfered and sent her off course? But what about them? They should have encountered the same storm.

He had spoken again, but she was so lost in her thoughts that his words hadn't registered at all. She looked at him questioningly.

"Could what I saw have been some sort of magic?"

"It's possible," she said carefully. "There are secrets known only to the Elders."

A lightning bolt lasts only a fraction of a second, she thought. *If we did follow Haddar here, that might have made all the difference in the world. He could have escaped it. Or the storm itself could have blown us off course after we entered this time.*

Whatever the answer, Shayna now believed it likely that Haddar and his companions were not far away. But what about their craft? One of the problems that yet remained to be solved was that of what to do with the craft while they were exploring another time. The hope had been that a way could be found to program them to return to their pads at the Institute, then come back for retrieval when signaled by the time-travelers.

Since that particular problem hadn't yet been worked out, Haddar's craft must be here, hidden somewhere. Unless, of course, it too had been destroyed.

Her thoughts returned to her treacherous colleague. She knew Haddar well. While she didn't doubt that he might be fanatic enough to sacrifice his own life for his evil mission, she felt certain that he would try to return—hoping, of course, that he'd be returning to a world that would regard him as a hero.

She had to find out if he was anywhere in the vicinity. But at the moment, she had no idea how she could gain that all-important information.

Chapter Three

In her dreams, Shayna returned to the comforting familiarity of her own world, reliving a life that had perhaps lacked excitement much of the time, but was nonetheless more than satisfactory as far as she was concerned.

She dreamed of growing up in the valley of her people, a much-cherished only child in a close-knit extended family. She dreamed of her carefree student years at the world's most prestigious university, cherished now by a system that placed great value on education. She dreamed of the wonderful year spent traveling the world following her graduation and of the challenges of being one of a select handful who were accepted into intense postgraduate work.

And she dreamed of the years since that time, a period of steady career growth as she became, by age thirty-two, a respected scholar and well-liked professor, upon whom was bestowed the great honor of joining the Time Project.

But an outsider peeking into those dreams would

have noticed something missing from her life—something of which Shayna, most times, was only subliminally aware. She had friends aplenty. Long after the Astasi had renounced their strange powers, people were still drawn to them, as though a residue of magic still clung to them. Some, of course, were put off by that dark part of Astasi history they could never understand, but many more were attracted to it without even being aware of the reason.

Nevertheless, Shayna's life had been almost completely devoid of romantic entanglements. Before she found herself lost in time, Shayna had dreamed of one man, but she'd always kept that fantasy a secret, in a place reserved for impossible and therefore embarrassing dreams.

She relinquished her dreams of home and family and work with great reluctance as she awoke to face yet another day of confusion and fear that she would never again return to that reality.

The first thought in her waking mind was the last thought of the previous day. How could she get herself back through the mysterious channels of time? Without Larus and Conti it would be difficult, if not impossible, for her to travel about, searching for Haddar.

She thought sadly about the years that might be passing back home as Teres and his team built another craft, then came looking for her. But at least they would come. They might be here even now.

Preoccupied by her thoughts, Shayna was slow to notice the low murmur of voices somewhere beyond the thick log walls of her room. When she did, she began to listen carefully. But other than the fact that the voices were male, she could tell nothing.

After putting on one of the dresses Kaz had brought for her, which was rather snug through the bodice, she opened the door just a crack to see where they were. The voices were slightly louder, but the words were still indistinguishable, and she decided that they must be outside. Kaz apparently had visitors, but had kept them outside to preserve the secrecy of her presence.

When she stepped into the hallway, she saw that the door to his room was open. Assuming that the visitors must be out front, she went in there and peeked out the window, staying safely in the shadows of the room.

There were two men besides Kaz, all of them standing at the edge of the long slope that led down into the valley. Both men wore uniforms similar to the one she'd seen in Kaz's closet, but without as much braided trim. They were all facing away from her as they talked, and she still could not make out more than an occasional word.

Trying to piece together the tiny fragments of conversation she could hear was frustrating. She thought they were telling Kaz about some intruders and that Kaz was downplaying the importance of the incident. But where had they intruded? Surely not here, since Kaz had said these were his family's lands, and an incident here would not have brought soldiers.

She drew on her knowledge of history and suddenly realized where the soldiers might have come from. She'd visited the place many times herself: the ancient fortress at Lonhola. It still stood in her own time, preserved as a museum of ancient Amaden power.

She felt irrationally excited at having now identified where she was. The fortress could not be far from here, because the two soldiers spoke of the incident having occurred only the night before. And that fact, together with the information Kaz had given her about the location of her ancestral valley, gave her a sense of where she was in this ancient world. Somewhere not far from here would be the great keep that was still home to descendants of Mikal Har-Amaden.

Lonhola had been built many centuries ago. It would be old even in this time, though it continued to serve as headquarters to the Amaden army until after the Period of Unification, when all armies, including that of the powerful Amaden, had been disbanded. Mikal Har-Amaden had been the last commander of the Amaden army, a role he had willingly relinquished only months before his death.

The location of the great fortress was no accident. It stood near the very center of Amaden tribal lands on a high mountain that overlooked the valley of her people, who were completely surrounded by their ancient enemy. Shayna could remember climbing to the very top of the tallest stone tower, where Amaden soldiers had once kept watch on the valley of the Astasi.

Kaz walked with the two soldiers over to a spot beyond her line of vision, where they must have left their horses. Shayna had stopped paying attention to their conversation, since she couldn't hear it anyway.

Her thoughts instead were on Mikal Har-Amaden. It stunned her to realize that he must be close by. She thought that she would give most anything—except for her return to her own world—to meet that extraordinary man who'd almost single-handedly ended centuries of warfare and set the world on the course it had followed ever since.

What a fascinating figure he was—and yet so little was known about him personally. Many biographies had been written, of course, even in his own time. But in the manner of that period, they'd tended to dwell on his exploits and his speeches, not on the man himself.

The great quest among historians—the dream of all of them—was to find his missing private journals. It was known that he'd kept them, but the family had maintained after his death that they could not be found. Since his death had been accidental, and not the result of some lengthy illness during which he might have decided to destroy them himself for some reason, it had always been suspected that the family had destroyed them. The only problem with that theory was that no one could venture a guess as to why they would have done such a thing.

Kaz reappeared outside, walking back to the spot where he'd been talking to the two soldiers, whom she now saw making their way on horseback down the hillside. He stood there staring down into the valley and she turned her thoughts to the snatches of conversation she'd overheard.

The realization struck her with the force of a physical blow. The intruders might well be Haddar and his companions! If she was right and they were here as well, the fortress at Lonhola would be their target: the place where, sooner or later, they would find Mikal Har-Amaden.

In her own time Lonhola was a major city, but in ancient times it had been a trading town, located on the main east-west trading routes from the great port city of Wantesa to the frontier lands in the west, claimed by the Amaden, but also by several other tribes. Wantesa, the old Amaden capital, was her own home, a magnificent city by the sea that gracefully combined old Amaden architecture with the soaring buildings of her own time.

Yes, she thought. If Haddar is here, he would stay near Lonhola, knowing that Mikal Har-Amaden would show up there at some point. And his knowledge of history would have allowed him to time his arrival to coincide with a period when that was most likely.

She left Kaz's bedroom, deciding that she had to find a way to get him to talk—and then, somehow, she had to get to Lonhola. When she walked into the cabin's main room, she saw that the desk was open and his journal lay there. Apparently he'd been writing in it when the soldiers came. She was curious about it, but at the moment she had more important things on her mind.

"Good morning," she said when he turned and saw her as she emerged from the cabin. "I thought I heard voices out here."

His wide mouth twitched with amusement. "You *know* you heard voices out here because you saw them as well. I saw you at my window."

"Oh." She was surprised because she thought she'd kept herself well hidden.

"At least they didn't see you."

"Why were they here?" she asked. "I couldn't hear what they were saying, except for something about an intrusion."

Instead of answering her immediately, he folded his arms across his broad chest and cocked his head slightly, studying her. "You have an . . . unusual manner about you, Shayna Har-Astasi. You're very direct for a woman."

Oh no, she thought. It was easy to affect the appearance of a woman of this time—but it was obviously not so easy to behave like one.

"My people don't regard women as being inferior," she replied with a trace of defiance. It was true, of course, though she didn't know if he knew that.

"So I've heard," he said with a nod. "As it happens, I don't, either. How are you feeling?"

"Much better," she said, although she knew that what he was really asking was whether she'd recovered her memory. It was time to get some story going in that regard, but she hadn't worked it out yet.

"But you still remember nothing?"

She shook her head, avoiding his dark gaze. Strangely, she was finding it more and more difficult to lie to him.

He took a few steps toward her, then suddenly reached out to lift her chin with his cupped hand. "You're lying to me, Shayna. Perhaps you don't yet remember all of it—but you remember something. Your eyes have lost that confused look."

She moved away from him, startled both by his perspicacity and by her reaction to his touch. She wanted to think of him as nothing more than a temporary protector and a source of information. Certainly she couldn't afford to let her emotions become involved.

"I'm not really lying to you, Kaz. I just don't want to talk about it until I've sorted it out myself."

Once again he tilted his head and regarded her quizzically. "It's your speech too," he said after a moment.

"Wh-what do you mean?" she asked, though she'd already guessed. Even though she was no linguist, she'd been trying to avoid words and phrases that might sound alien to his ears.

"It's different—both your accent and the words you use."

She shrugged, hoping he would write it off to the differences between their cultures. It was very fortunate that the Astasi had led such secluded lives.

"Why were those men here?" she asked in an attempt to steer the conversation out of dangerous areas and back to what she needed. "Are they friends of yours?"

"Aides," he corrected. "There was an incident at Lonhola last night. You know where that is, I presume?"

"Of course. Every time we look up at the mountain, we're looking at Amaden cannons."

"But it's been many years since they were used," he reminded her.

"Still, it isn't very pleasant to be surrounded by your enemy," she persisted. She'd often thought about how difficult it must have been for her people.

"Surely not when you have your magic to protect you," he countered. "You may rest assured that we have enemies enough without looking for war with the Astasi."

That was certainly true, she thought. The world of that time was filled with shifting alliances whose sole object was to conquer the Amaden.

"What was the incident? Surely your enemies haven't come to Lonhola?"

"It's possible that a few agents have, though from the descriptions, at least one of them must be Amaden."

A mental image of Haddar flashed through her mind as she waited for him to go on. Unfortunately, the identity of his companions hadn't been established before she left.

"They attempted to get into the fortress," he went on. "In fact, they very nearly succeeded. It seems that the guards at that gate were asleep—or afflicted by some strange illness, which is what they claim."

Stunners, she thought—then remembered her own. Where was it? She'd forgotten all about it. Perhaps she'd lost it in the valley when she was flung through the air.

Then, abruptly, she remembered. Kaz had it! She'd seen it in the pocket of his uniform jacket before her memory returned.

"What sort of illness?" she asked, thinking that she'd have to get it back from him. It wouldn't work for him, but she could not leave anything behind. What did he think it was?

"They complained of stabbing pains all over their bodies and aches in their bones. Why are you so curious?"

Now she knew that it had indeed been Haddar. What Kaz described was the aftermath of a stunner attack. "I'm a curious person," she replied with a shrug. "Is Mikal Har-Amaden at Lonhola?"

The question was rash, but not as dangerous as it might have been before she knew that Haddar was here. Still, the expression on his face worried her.

"No, he isn't. Why do you ask?"

"Perhaps they're assassins," she replied, knowing that there had been several attempts on his life.

"Why would anyone want to kill him?" he asked, seeming to be genuinely puzzled.

A chill slithered through her. She'd got it wrong. Her mind spun, seeking the reason. He continued to stare at her with a frown. Had Haddar come back to an earlier time—a time when Mikal Har-Amaden had not yet achieved greatness?

Yes, she thought. Of course! It would be far easier to kill him before he became so famous. Much as she detested him, she had to admire Haddar's ingenuity.

"He's a war hero, isn't he?" she replied when he seemed about to repeat his question.

"How do you know that?"

She felt as though she'd just climbed out of one pit only to fall into another. "We have ways of gaining information," she said with what she hoped was a mysterious smile.

He found himself in exactly the kind of situation he hated most: surrounded by uncertainty, with no clear path to the truth. He stood at a window, watching her as she emerged from the woods at the side of the cabin, wearing his old jacket. The weather had turned sharply colder and there was a smell of snow in the air. Winter was returning for one last attack before surrendering to spring.

He should have taken her to the house, where his sister-in-law could have tended to her and then sent her on her way, wherever that might be. Acting rashly wasn't normally part of his nature, and he didn't understand why he'd done so in her case.

He felt that familiar stirring in his loins, but thankfully it was tempered by the knowledge of what she was. He smiled for a moment, remembering the schoolboy stories about witches. They were baseless, of course, the fantasies of boys approaching manhood and just discovering that girls were something other than nuisances or the objects of teasing.

But the fantasies of the adult were not so easy to dismiss. There was something about her that challenged him and awakened those old fantasies. At first she'd seemed only pitiable as she wandered about in a daze, with gray clouds of confusion in her green eyes. She still seemed troubled, but now she walked differently and talked differently as well. Even in his sister-in-law's cast-off dress and a jacket many sizes too big, she had a pride and dignity that seemed almost masculine to his eyes. Combined with the curves not even her present clothing could disguise, plus her delicate-featured beauty, it was more than enough to trigger the memory of those fantasies.

But even more than her obvious physical attributes, it was her behavior that intrigued him. He knew that she must be tempering her naturally assertive behavior because of her present dependence on him, and he wondered just what he might see if that were not the case.

What could have happened to her? Was she here because she'd been cast out by her people? He'd never heard of such a thing happening before—and he surely would have heard about it.

What seemed more likely to him was that she'd left the valley on her own, and then something had happened to her. He thought about that story she'd told him when she was too confused to have lied: a man with a wound on his forehead and how she'd been pushed or thrown by some unseen force. He was familiar with the confusion that could come over men in the thick of battle, and suspected that something like that had happened to her.

Roving bands of outlaws weren't unknown, but it seemed highly unlikely to him that they would have strayed so far from the main roads, deep into his family's lands. Besides, if she'd been attacked by them, she would have used her magic to repel them. Alone among women, the witches of the Astasi could travel anywhere with no fear, even though they didn't do so. And outlaws would have known that.

But all of this was mere speculation engaged in to avoid his darker thoughts: thoughts of treachery. She'd been entirely too interested in the details of that incident at Lonhola, and too quick to spin some outlandish tale about its purpose.

Over the centuries, his people had often worried about the possibility that at some point the Astasi would ally themselves with the enemies of the Amaden. In numbers alone, the Astasi could never be a force to be reckoned with, but when one combined their magic with their location, deep inside Amaden lands, there was more than enough cause for concern.

In light of that, he knew he had to consider the possibility that she'd come here deliberately, and had faked the accident and the memory loss. Even her suggestion about the goal of the intruders at Lonhola took on the form of a subtle threat when seen in that light.

But that meant that she had to be a consummate actress—or that she was using her dark powers to affect his judgment.

If only he knew more about those powers. Many attempts had been made over the years to discover just what talents the Astasi possessed. But other than their magic fire and their ability to create illusions on the battlefield, little was known. There were stories about their healing abilities, of course, and other tales about how they could summon the rains necessary for their crops. But were they capable of more subtle methods: of prodding the mind against its better judgment, as some claimed?

He was appalled at the thought of such a thing, but he knew that he could not discount it completely. It occurred to him as he saw her head toward the cabin, with the wind whipping her unbound red hair, that he was sharing his solitary retreat with a wild creature that might strike out at him at any time.

"I'm sorry that I've been dishonest with you, especially since you've been so kind to me," she said as she shrugged out of his jacket without waiting for his assistance.

"You were right, of course: my memory has returned—or most of it, anyway. I left the valley because I was angry, and I allowed my anger to make me foolish—not for the first time." She gave him a rueful smile. "I'm not the first to leave the valley, either. Others have done it, but at least they had the good sense to disguise themselves first."

"Why were you angry?" he asked.

She shrugged. "It's a very long story, Kaz—but perhaps one that you could understand. Life goes on in our valley as it always has. Nothing ever changes there, while outside, the world is always changing. For years now, I've climbed the hills and looked at that world, wondering what was out here. Your guns were always enough of a reminder that we had to remain in the valley, but since there've been no wars for a long time now, we mostly ignore them.

"I had a disagreement with my family—and so I left. That much I remember clearly. I also remember seeking shelter from a storm. I must have fallen asleep.

Then I was attacked by two men. I got away from them, but they stole my horse and my belongings."

He didn't believe a word of her story. "Why didn't you use your powers against them?"

She turned away from him for a moment, then slowly turned back again. "I probably shouldn't be telling you this, but our powers don't work during thunderstorms. Or rather, they do work, but the risk is too great. People have died doing that, as though by calling on their powers, they have drawn the greater power of the storm into themselves."

Now he was beginning to believe her. He thought about the strange thing he'd seen during the storm. "Are you sure that you didn't try to use your powers?"

She frowned at him in confusion for a moment, then shrugged. "I can't be sure. But if I did, I suppose that could account for what you saw." She shivered. "If I did that, then I'm lucky to be alive. Perhaps the lightning did strike me, after all. That could explain my being thrown against the rocks, couldn't it?"

He nodded. Either she was telling the truth or she was very quick-witted, to have adjusted the story to his prompting.

"Where were you going?" he asked, getting back to the most easily spotted problem with her tale.

"I don't know. I was just riding. I realized that I had to stay off the main roads because I'd be recognized."

He couldn't dispute that, so he asked what she intended to do now.

She sighed. "I'll have to go back to the valley. I was hoping that you could help me. If you could just get me some sort of disguise, and a horse, of course . . ." She looked at him hopefully.

He was stunned by how much that thought disturbed him. She was a problem he didn't need right now—and yet the thought of never seeing her again . . .

"It will have to wait," he told her. "There's a storm moving in. When it is over, I'll see what I can do."

"Thank you, Kaz." She paused for a moment. "There's one other thing. I seem to have lost my talisman. It's a small silver cylinder. Would you happen to have it?"

He withdrew from his pocket the object he'd been carrying for the past day, after first having left it in his uniform pocket. The thing still troubled him for some obscure reason.

"That's it!" she cried with pleasure as she reached for it.

He was sure that her pleasure was feigned. He held on to it. "What is it?"

"I told you, it's a talisman. We all carry them." Her tone had changed from one of pleasure to thinly disguised annoyance.

"What is it made of?" he asked, staring at the object.

"I don't know," she replied in the same tone. "They're passed down from one generation to the next."

Ignoring her for a moment, he walked over to the lamp and bent to examine it more closely, as he'd intended to do when he'd put it into his pocket. Now he could see that there was a tiny hole at the rounded end, and when he turned it to peer at the other end, which was flat, he saw a series of numbers and letters etched there.

He glanced up at her suddenly and caught an expression of pure terror on her face. It was gone quickly, replaced by a patently false smile, but he knew then that what he held wasn't just a talisman.

"I'm keeping it until you tell me the truth about it."

"I have told you the truth!"

Acting on an impulse he would never understand, he pressed his thumb against the pad on the object and pointed it at her. And once again, he saw her flinch instinctively for one brief second.

"It's a weapon of some sort," he said, knowing suddenly that he was right, even though he would certainly know if such weapons existed.

"No, it isn't. Why would I need a weapon?"

He slipped the cylinder back into his pocket. "When you first woke up, you told me that you couldn't use your powers."

"I was confused. I was probably thinking about the storm."

"Then maybe this is something you can use during storms."

She threw him a challenging look. "If that were so, then I would have used it against my attackers, wouldn't I?"

He said nothing. She was right—but she was still lying about something. "I'll give it to you before you leave," he said after a moment.

The storm came, just as he'd predicted. At first there were only a few wind-driven flakes. But then they began to fall thicker and faster, whipped into a fury by the howling winds. Shayna paced around the small cabin restlessly while he sat in a chair reading and pretending to ignore her.

He wasn't, though. She could feel his eyes on her, and several times she caught him at it. Then it was she who had looked away quickly, embarrassed by her reaction to him. The air in the cabin seemed to be thick with tension, though they hadn't spoken for several hours. In that tension were echoes of their disagreement, mixed explosively with a powerful eroticism.

Outside, a storm was raging, piling snow against the cabin, marooning them here together. Inside, it seemed that with every passing moment their outer shells were melting, leaving only a raw, primitive longing she had never felt before.

But disconcerting as that was, what was far worse was her growing need to be honest with him. What was it about him that made it so difficult for her to continue lying?

She stared out the window at the blizzard. There was something about Kaz that reached deep into her. It was her sense of him: the things she knew and the things she didn't yet know, but had already guessed.

He was a decent and gentle man, in a time when the measure of manhood didn't generally include those qualities. Men of his time were measured by their power and their fighting skills, not to mention their ruthlessness. She suspected, though, that he could be ruthless when necessary, and she knew that he must be very good at fighting, since he'd apparently attained a high rank at a relatively young age.

She frowned. How was it that his name meant nothing to her? If she was right about his ascension in the military, she should have come across his name. The Amaden of that time hadn't always done a good job of chronicling other parts of their lives, but they had certainly left volumes about their military exploits—housed ever since then at Lonhola.

A chill went through her, leaving in its wake an unbearable sadness. He must have died young, before true greatness could have come to him. Still, there might be mention of him somewhere. When she returned to her own time, she would have to search the records.

If she returned, that is. What if Teres and the team faced the same problem they'd faced with Haddar: not knowing exactly where they'd gone in time? She had to find Haddar, then prevent him from carrying out his scheme—and finally, persuade him to return—assuming that his craft was hidden somewhere around here.

She wondered if perhaps she should try to find the craft instead of looking for Haddar. She could then return and get some help to deal with him.

Her thoughts returned to Kaz. She couldn't do anything unless he helped her. She turned away from the window to find him just getting up from his chair. In the flickering glow of the lamp and the light from the fireplace behind him, she stared at a face that continued to seem vaguely familiar to her.

"I'm going out to check on my horse and bring in some more wood," he said as he picked up the old jacket he'd lent her earlier.

"How bad will this be?" she asked, wishing foolishly for the weather forecasts that were always available on the vidcom.

He stared out the window. "Bad, I think—especially

with the wind driving the snow. But we have enough provisions."

"Tell me about yourself, Kaz."

The look he gave her was slightly wary, belying his casual tone. "What would you like to know?"

"How old you are. Where you live when you're not here. About your family."

He turned away from her to gaze into the fire. A log shifted, breaking the silence in the room. Beyond the thick log walls, the storm sounded like a living thing: a wild animal trying to get at them. The effect wasn't unpleasant, however, even though it created an intimacy she knew was dangerous.

Shayna's questions weren't idle ones. She wanted to learn all she could about him so that she could research him when she got home—*if* she got home. She continued to believe that she would, because the alternative was too terrible to consider. Even the loss of a year or so of her life now seemed a small price to pay.

She was pleased that Kaz seemed to have accepted her story, because that meant it was likely that he would help her, believing he was only aiding her in returning to her people's valley.

"I'm thirty-three," he said, still staring into the fire. "And mostly I live in Wantesa, though I'm often at Lonhola as well—or on a battlefield somewhere. Besides the married brother I mentioned, I have a sister, who is also married and lives in Wantesa. My father died a few years ago and my mother lives with my brother and his family."

"Why aren't you married?"

"There hasn't been time for that."

"Because of the wars, you mean?"

He nodded. It was becoming obvious to her that he intended to say as little about himself as possible.

"What is your rank?" she asked as she searched her memory for the structure of the old Amaden military.

"I'm a brigadier general." He gave her a slight smile. "Are you an expert on the Amaden military?"

She returned his smile. "No, I'm just curious. Isn't that a very high rank for one so young?" If her memory served her correctly, it certainly was.

"If you survive enough battles, it isn't so difficult," he said dryly.

There must be something about him in the histories, she thought. Despite his disclaimer, there surely couldn't be many men who'd attained such a rank at his age.

"Why did you decide to go into the military?"

His look suggested that no one had ever asked him that question before. "I didn't really decide; I just always knew. What will you do when you go back?"

She couldn't suppress the look of surprise that appeared. Go back? For one brief moment, she was sure that he knew the truth about her. And then, with a wave of relief, she realized he meant back to the valley. "What I've always done," she replied with a shrug. "I'm a weaver."

It wasn't exactly a lie, which made it much easier to say. Weaving was her chief hobby. She had a large loom and even hand-dyed her own wool, utilizing methods that had been old even in the time she was in now. The work gave her great pleasure and seemed, somehow, appropriate for a history professor.

"But you weren't happy there," he pointed out.

She wished that this conversation hadn't veered off track, because she feared that he would catch her in a lie, or ask a question she couldn't answer correctly.

"I was happy enough. Sometimes I do rash things. Leaving the valley was one of them."

He smiled. "A fiery temper to go with your hair?"

That was definitely not true, but she nodded and managed to return his smile.

"You're not married?"

She shook her head.

"Isn't that unusual? Surely you're of an age when most women would be married."

"I'm twenty-seven," she told him, shaving five years off her real age. She knew he'd accept that because people tended to age much more rapidly in his time. She had guessed him to be about five years older than he was.

When it seemed that he was waiting for an answer, she said that she simply hadn't found anyone she wanted to marry.

"Your people do marry, then?" he asked, surprising her.

"Yes, of course."

He stretched his long legs toward the fire. "There have always been so many stories about the Astasi. One of them was that Astasi women take several husbands."

"That was true many years ago, but it was because there weren't enough men. It was mostly men who fought the Amaden—and many of them died. But that hasn't happened since the wars stopped."

"Your people must hate the Amaden."

"No, we don't. Or at least most of us don't. We wish only to be allowed to live in peace. But we are constantly reminded of your distrust of us—every time we look up at Lonhola and see the cannons."

And she remembered how Mikal Har-Amaden had won her people's trust by removing those cannons. The Astasi had been the last people to sign the compact that had ended war forever. Even with the removal of the cannons, it had been rather remarkable that they'd decided to place their trust in Mikal Har-Amaden. Strangely enough, Astasi writings of the time hadn't given any reason for that decision to trust him, but it was known that he visited them many times.

Following a lengthy silence, Kaz said in a soft voice, "Perhaps one day there'll be no need for cannon anywhere."

Startled by his words, she stared at him. "But then what would *you* do?"

He chuckled. "So you don't believe that a man of war can become a man of peace? You're wrong, Shayna. There are some who love war, but most of us long for peace more than the average citizen."

"Do you think that's likely to happen?" It gave her a

very strange feeling to be asking a question whose answer had come long ago for her, but was still in the future for him.

"I think it's possible. Everyone grows weary of war. It remains only for someone to tap into that longing."

He was right. As a historian, she knew that all the factions had grown weary of war, but it still would have continued indefinitely if it hadn't been for the boldness and courage and persistence of one man. And every historian she knew agreed that only the most decorated and powerful warrior of the time could have brought it off.

"Do you think such a person exists?" she asked. Obviously he knew Mikal Har-Amaden, and probably knew him well. She was very curious about what he thought of him.

"Perhaps—but no man can act alone. And he can't act at all until his authority is unchallenged."

She waited for him to volunteer a name, and when he didn't, she was greatly tempted to do it herself. But she recalled his earlier surprise when she'd mentioned Mikal's name. So far he seemed to accept her for what she said she was, and she couldn't afford to arouse his suspicions.

"You will help me to get home, won't you, Kaz?" she asked, hoping she was right about his believing her.

He nodded, but his dark eyes seemed to be searching her face for something. She met his gaze, but with great difficulty as a soft heat stole through her. She knew, with both pleasure and fear, that he was as attracted to her as she was to him.

She looked away, suddenly engulfed by a great and deep sadness. She couldn't be falling in love with him; she barely knew him. And yet she already felt something for him far stronger than she'd ever felt before.

Suddenly she had a brief but strikingly clear vision of herself, back in her own time, standing on a hilltop she didn't recognize, filled with a yearning for a man dead for three centuries. The pain that came with the vision was excruciating, beyond anything a person should have to endure, and she unconsciously wrapped her arms around herself as tears sprang to her eyes.

The vision lasted but a fraction of a second—but the pain lingered until it was replaced by a sudden awareness of him as he moved closer to her, then gathered her slowly and carefully into his arms.

"What is it, Shayna? What haven't you told me?"

His voice was low and deep and close to her ear. She could feel his breath against her cheek and the rock-hard strength of him.

"I want you to trust me," he said when she remained silent. "Haven't I shown that I trust you?"

She nodded automatically. She did trust him—but she still could not tell him the truth. The protocol she'd helped to develop for the Time Project stated that at no time could a time-traveler admit the truth about his or her origins. In the rush to get here, none of them had signed the protocol, but she knew she was morally bound by it, nonetheless.

He held her slightly away from him and stared down at her. "I don't know if you've actually lied to me—but I know that you haven't told me all the truth."

He took her hand, which had paused in midair, inches from his chest. Raising it to his lips, he kissed it softly. Then he lifted his head slightly, still holding her hand, and his gaze traveled slowly over her face, stopping at her parted lips.

Shayna had never seen such gentleness, and it was made all the more amazing because it came from this hard man of war. She knew that making love with him was wrong: wrong because it would be the beginning of something that could never be finished. But she wanted him as she'd never wanted any man.

She leaned toward him and he moved to her just as slowly—and their lips met. The kiss was tentative, careful, uncertain—and all the more powerful for that. The full force of his hunger washed over her and settled into her, igniting her own desire. The storm continued unabated outside, rattling the shutters and the door, but it served only to make their small space more intimate.

Despite their mutual hunger, they moved slowly. She threaded her trembling fingers through his thick, dark hair and pressed her lips to the pulse-point at the base of his throat, where she felt the rapid throb of his heart. He kissed her earlobe and with tongue and lips traced a line along the curve of her neck.

Her dress was high necked, with a long row of tiny buttons. Both the dress and the chemise beneath it were stretched tight against her hardened nipples. He licked at them through the thin layers of cloth, sending tremors through her and making the pressure of the fabric unbearable: pain tempered by pleasure.

She began to undo the buttons, her fingers trembling and uncoordinated. He watched her as his own fingers blindly sought the buttons of his shirt. The bodice of the dress pooled around her waist; his shirt was tossed aside. She reached for the straps of the chemise, but his fingers closed over hers, pushing it quickly from her shoulders.

They lay down against the thick rug and he knelt over her, not touching her with his hands as his lips moved slowly over every inch of exposed flesh. Impatient now and wanting to feel him against her, she drew him down until he fell on top of her, then quickly rolled them both over until she lay atop him.

"Be patient, my witch," he whispered into the deep hollow between her breasts. "We have time."

His words pierced the sensuous, heated fog in her brain. She stared at him, her eyes wide with sudden pain. Then her eyelids fluttered down protectively as he kissed each of them.

"We want each other, Shayna. Let that be enough for now."

She nodded. He was right, even in his ignorance. It would be enough—because it had to be.

Time unfolded in slow motion against the incessant drumbeat of passion. They held each other and caressed each other until their remaining clothes became an impediment, a last holding-back. And then they lay naked and entwined, with the firelight casting a ruddy glow and deep shadows over them as they explored each other.

By the time he entered her, she was aching and moist and eager to have him fill her. They stared into each other's eyes and saw what they needed and wanted to see as the primeval rhythms of love caught them up and became everything. She arched against him, and his strong fingers dug into her and lifted her still more and they moved together until the moment shattered and melted and left them both trembling with aftershocks.

Chapter Four

A tentative light crept through the uncurtained window. Shayna's eyes fluttered open, then closed again. A smile curved her lips as memories of the night drifted through her still-dozing brain. She felt the need to stretch, as though to reassert control over her body. But she remained still.

Kaz lay on his side, one arm grazing the sensitive undersides of her breasts and one long, bristly leg thrust between hers: solid and real and not a dream, after all. She smiled again, the smile of a woman who has been well loved.

The bed was rumpled and warm, and the linens carried the scent of lovemaking. They'd fallen asleep, only to awaken at some point—both of them rather startled to find they were not alone. She knew that *she* was accustomed to sleeping alone, but she wondered about him. Surely a man capable of such passion must have a woman—or perhaps women—somewhere. And yet he'd seemed as startled as she was to discover that he was not alone.

He'd lit the lamp on the table beside the bed, saying that he wanted—needed—to see her. And then he'd made love to her: slowly, deliciously, and very thoroughly, with none of the hesitancy that she realized only after the fact had marked their first mating. He was inventive and completely uninhibited, and afterward she'd smiled to herself, thinking that social historians, who'd claimed that this period was marked by stilted, formal relations between men and women, were very wrong.

Or else, she thought, I have found a truly extraordinary man. She liked that thought and felt its truth—a truth that had been stealing into her mind quietly over the past few days. Accustomed as she was to the men of her time, she'd been slow to remember that men of this time would have been very different. Kaz was different, but she realized only now that the gentleness she'd seen in him could not be common to men of his time.

She had found an extraordinary man, all right—but she could not hold him. For one brief, self-indulgent moment, she dared to let herself consider the possibility of telling him the truth and then persuading him to return with her. She knew it was impossible, of course. The protocol warned against forming close relationships for that very reason. Given that they didn't yet know if the past could be changed, the risk was far too great.

And in any event, she knew that her own return might be nothing more than wishful thinking.

Still, the thought lingered in the dream-place of her mind as she shifted carefully, not wanting to disturb him just yet, but wanting to study his face, as though a part of her couldn't yet believe that he was real.

He was indeed a handsome man in that rough-hewn way of the Amaden. The light was growing brighter, and now she saw that he had a few silver hairs scattered amidst deepest black. She wondered again why it was that he seemed somehow familiar to her. Surely if she'd seen his photograph, she would also remember his name.

She frowned. Photography would have been in its infancy in this time. All that remained in her time were some old, sepia-toned photographs that had long since become blurred.

She wondered if she might have seen a picture of him at a later age. She lay back against her pillow again, mulling over this new thought. She'd seen those photos at the museum at Lonhola many times, so it was possible that she had seen him, and had simply not paid attention to the names.

She raised herself up to stare at him once more. This time her movement caused him to stir slightly, though his eyes remained closed. A half-smile curved his lips briefly before he settled down again. He had a wide, utterly masculine mouth and a tiny cleft in his square chin.

The knowledge came to Shayna slowly, stealing into her consciousness like the softest of whispers. She tried to deny it, but the whisper became more insistent. That mouth. That face. The scattered silver in his dark hair.

Suddenly she felt dizzy, confused. Her lips formed the protest. She shook her head and stared at him again. It was impossible—sheer madness! It could not be!

She was trembling badly as she extricated herself from him. He stirred again and frowned slightly—and her horror grew. She stumbled from the bed, but her legs would not support her and she had to brace herself against a table. And all the while, she could not drag her gaze from him.

Finally she forced herself to gulp down some air. Then she began to back slowly away from the bed until she reached the doorway. She clutched it for a moment, then fled, naked, down the short hallway to the main room. The morning air was cool and she shivered, though the chill she felt owed more to the thought tormenting her than it did to the temperature of the air.

The first thing she saw when she entered the main

room was his journal that lay open on the desk, where he'd left it after writing in it the day before. She wrapped her arms around herself and stared at it. When she first came here she'd wanted to read it, but after she'd gotten to know Kaz she'd felt the need to respect his privacy. Perhaps he'd sensed that, because he'd left it out several times.

Shayna was now shivering so badly that her teeth were chattering. She stumbled back to her room and wrapped herself in a blanket, then sank down onto the bed. This had to be some sort of temporary insanity—perhaps a delayed reaction to all that had happened to her, coupled with some unconscious wish to make her old fantasies merge with the beauty of last night.

That must be it, she decided, grasping at the explanation she'd offered herself. And then, to lend the explanation even more credence, she told herself that there was no reason why he should have lied to her about his identity.

Wrapped in the blanket, she padded quietly across the hall to his room. He was still sleeping, but now he lay on his back. She studied his face again. That prickling uneasiness continued to crawl through her. Add twenty-five or thirty years . . .

She fled the bedroom for the second time and walked determinedly out to the main room—and to his desk. The journal lay open. Half of one page was filled with bold handwriting. Pushing down her guilt, she began to read. It was an account of a battle—which one she couldn't guess, since the page made no reference to time or to the identity of the enemy.

She reached out to flip back a page, hoping for something that would sound familiar to her, even though she'd never studied the wars of that time in as great detail as military historians had done. Her own interests lay more in the political and social arenas.

One name immediately leaped out at her from the previous page: Darwana. She drew in a sharp breath. The Battle of Darwana had been important for several reasons—but chief among them was that it was the battle that had established Mikal Har-Amaden's reputation as a master strategist and the greatest military hero of his time. In its aftermath, he'd been made second-in-command of the Amaden army, even though he was still very young.

That dizziness returned and she leaned against the desk for a moment as the words on the page tumbled about in her mind: a recounting of the battle strategy, but without one mention of Mikal Har-Amaden, whose strategy it was supposed to have been.

Could history be wrong? Had a mistake been made that had given him credit where none was due? A part of her already knew that was impossible, but she clung to the thought anyway—until she turned back to the first page of the journal.

That page contained only two lines, written in Kaz's bold handwriting: the name Mikal Har-Amaden, and the date this particular journal had begun, two months before the Battle of Darwana.

Shayna sank into the desk chair, her eyes glued to that name. The man she knew as Kaz was in fact Mikal Har-Amaden! She had seen Kaz writing in this journal and the journal belonged to Mikal Har-Amaden.

A part of her continued to refuse to believe it. How could she not have recognized him? She closed her eyes, then conjured up the image of Mikal Har-Amaden that was known to everyone in the world. There were photographs of him, mostly at the museum at Lonhola, but even they had been of a much older man. And the image in her mind now came from the painting that had been done of him by the greatest portrait artist of the time. The original hung in a place of honor in the World Council headquarters, though there were copies of it everywhere.

He had been painted at the age of fifty-six, less than a year before his death. Assuming that "Kaz" had given his correct age, and she thought he had, the man in the painting was twenty-three years older than the man who lay sleeping only a short distance away. And yet she still could not believe that she hadn't recognized him.

"Twenty-three years," she whispered. Twenty-three years, during which time he'd fought many other battles and then fought just as hard for a lasting peace. Twenty-three years for the lines to be etched into his face and for his black hair to turn to silver.

A wave of unreality engulfed her. As though for the first time, she now understood the true meaning of the journey she'd undertaken. Mikal Har-Amaden slept a few steps away, while she thought about the greatness that was still in his future—and far in the past for her.

An ironic smile sprang to her lips as she recalled her waking thoughts about what an extraordinary man he was. And a flush of embarrassment followed quickly as she thought about her old fantasies. She'd fallen in love with this man years ago in the midst of her studies.

First had come the awe and admiration—something all students of history felt toward him. She recalled one of her early professors—himself an Astasi—saying that while it might or might not be true that the Astasi were the "children of the gods," it was indisputable that Mikal Har-Amaden had been touched by something beyond man's understanding.

And there was, of course, the famous quotation of Maltus Har-Amaden, the preeminent historian of Mikal's own time. It was carved in the marble base of the huge statue of him that stood in the plaza in front of World Council headquarters. "He wore the cloak of greatness lightly—as only the truly great can do."

But Shayna had at some point allowed awe and admiration to be carried further. She'd given him a wholeness that he lacked in the dry histories, investing him with all the best personal qualities that she thought a man should have. And then she'd fallen in love with her own creation.

The thought came to her now, in all its awesome truth, that she had seen some of those very qualities in the man she knew as Kaz. Most of all she'd seen passion. The Mikal Har-Amaden of the history books harbored one passion only: the end of war and the creation of a lasting peace. In her fantasies she'd carried that passion into a far more personal realm—and last night had proved that it was indeed there.

A part of her remained in denial of this astonishing revelation. She couldn't yet reconcile the giant of history with the man who'd made love to her. Her gaze focused again on the journal and she realized that before her lay the object of every historian's dream: one of the missing journals.

The historian in her temporarily took over her mind and she began to read it from the beginning, where he recounted the formation of the alliance that had provoked the war that ended with the Battle of Darwana. But before she had finished the second page, she heard a sound—and turned to find him standing there.

For one brief moment, Shayna saw not one man, but two: her lover, Kaz—and the Mikal Har-Amaden of the portrait. Then the man of the portrait faded as Kaz started toward her.

His thick, dark hair was rumpled and he needed a shave. He wore only a pair of loose-fitting trousers. She felt a fleeting but powerful embarrassment to be seeing him like this, even though he'd just come from the bed where they'd made love, and she already knew his body as well as she knew her own. And in that embarrassment she recognized an acceptance of who he was.

"Why did you tell me your name was Kaz?" she asked in a tone that was more accusatory than she'd intended.

He frowned at her and his gaze went briefly to the open journal on the desk. "I didn't lie."

Relief swept through her, trailed by a thin line of disappointment. She'd been wrong. But just as she began to wonder how she could be wrong, he went on.

"Kaz is a pet name my family uses. It began when I was a child and my grandfather was still alive. I was named after him, and they called me Kaz to distinguish between us. My middle name is Brokaz."

"Mikal Brokaz Har-Amaden," she said. She'd known that, although his full name was rarely used.

"What's wrong, Shayna?" Then, after a brief hesitation, he asked, "Do you regret last night?"

She shook her head, not trusting herself to speak. She didn't regret it—but now it seemed that she couldn't accept it, either.

He closed the remaining space between them, then threaded his fingers through the long auburn curls that spread over the blanket she still clutched around her.

"When I woke up alone, I thought perhaps you were only a dream. Come back to bed with me, Shayna. Make it real again."

She tried to swallow the huge lump in her throat and tried as well to still the pounding of her heart against her ribs. How could she return to that bed now that she knew who he was?

"Shayna," he said, taking her hands and drawing her to her feet, then cupping a hand beneath her chin to force her to meet his gaze. "Even now you don't trust me. You conceal something from me. But last night you gave yourself to me willingly. You wanted me as much as I wanted you. How can knowing my full name make a difference?"

Shayna had to stifle a bubble of hysterical laughter at the question she knew he asked in total innocence. She wanted to flee from him—and from her knowledge. She wanted him back in the pages of history where he belonged, not truly a man but a giant.

"I . . . I've heard of you," she said, forcing down yet another burst of laughter. It must surely be the understatement of all time.

Then she recalled that she had mentioned his name before—and he hadn't admitted to his true identity. But why? Did he distrust her reason for being here?

"You still haven't told me why it matters to you," he said in that deep, calm voice that barely hinted at an order. She remembered the historian, Maltus, referring to his air of quiet authority and his legendary patience.

She thought fast, seeking an answer he could accept. "I thought you were just an ordinary Amaden soldier—but instead you're a great hero. I know that our people aren't at war now, but. . . ." She let her voice trail off, hoping he would accept her admittedly weak explanation. Then, to forestall any further questions, she went on the offensive.

"I even mentioned your name, after your aides were here, and you didn't tell me who you were."

He ran a hand through his already disheveled hair and rubbed his stubbly cheek. A part of her found the gesture endearing, but a greater part was shocked at the ordinariness of it all. Other men could appear this way, but not the greatest man their world had produced.

"I thought it best not to tell you," he admitted. "I couldn't be sure of your purpose here."

"But you found me unconscious," she blurted out. "How could you think I had . . . ulterior motives?"

"For the same reason you're upset at learning who I am. Our people have a long history of suspicions."

She turned away from him and walked over to the window, then drew in a sharp breath when she saw how deep the snow was outside. She had half turned to him when he came up behind her and wrapped his long arms around her.

"Come back to bed with me, Shayna. Forget who we are."

Forget who he was? The laughter welled up in her again, but so too did that aching hunger for him. She trembled with the force of it as his fingers found their way beneath the blanket to caress her intimately.

He took the low moan that poured from her lips as an affirmation, and swept her into his arms. When they reached his bedroom he set her on her feet and pulled the blanket away from her, then sat down on the edge of the bed and drew her close, between his legs.

His beard was pleasantly rough against her skin as his lips and tongue traced slowly along her curves, tasting every square inch of exposed flesh. The sensual assault made her legs tremble until they could no longer support her, and they both fell back onto the bed in a tangle of arms and legs.

"Have you cast a spell on me, little witch?" he asked

with a smile. "I've never wanted any woman as I want you."

She recoiled at his teasing use of that term, but before her lips could form a denial, he had claimed them again and she knew no denial was necessary. He didn't fear the powers she was forbidden to use, even though in this time no such prohibition existed.

Their lovemaking unfolded slowly, layer by layer, as they pleasured each other and themselves. His big, hard body quaked beneath her touch, and she trembled at his intimate caresses. Driven by an increasing urgency, they still clung to each moment, savoring it to the fullest. Shayna let her body feel what her mind could not grasp: that this was a union of more than bodies, a hunger for more than physical release.

He lifted her atop him and each watched the swift tide of passion that inundated the other until they could bear no more and closed their eyes to the final, shuddering moment of ecstasy.

Mikal lifted her carefully, then settled her against himself as the aftershocks quivered through them both. He was still dazed by what had happened between them, but he ignored the dark whisper that reminded him of her magic. She might be a witch—but what was happening here was real.

He'd been attracted to her from the beginning, even though she was Astasi, but he hadn't intended to give in to that attraction, and he still couldn't figure out just when the moment had come that he could no longer control the urge to possess her.

As long as she'd been sick and confused, he'd buried his desire beneath an urge to protect her and a stricture against taking advantage of the situation. But once she'd regained her memory and he saw her strength as well as her beauty, he was lost.

He caressed her as she lay quietly beside him, lost in thoughts he couldn't reach, but wanted very much to know. They had moved too quickly, he thought, but without regret. They knew each other intimately, but not well. He wanted to tell her that he needed to know her thoughts as well as he now knew her body, but he remained silent, still rather dazed by the force of this need.

Women had never played more than a peripheral role in his life. He enjoyed their company—especially those who walked along the very edges of acceptable behavior by speaking their minds. And he had taken pleasure in bed as well, but mostly with women who made their livelihoods by pleasing men. Now, in Shayna, he saw the two come together.

He propped himself up on one elbow and bent to kiss her. "I love you, Shayna." The words were inadequate and were coming far too quickly, but even now he could hear the steady dripping outside as the snow began to melt.

He'd expected—hoped—for a response from her. But instead she only stared at him. He couldn't read her thoughts, but he sensed that his words had brought her pain as well as pleasure. He kissed her again as his thoughts raced. He was a very determined man, and he had no intention of giving her up.

"We'll find a way. You don't have to return to the valley."

She turned her face away from him and he saw a tear trickle down her cheek. He kissed it away, then drew her head around to face him.

"Maybe I've spoken too quickly, but those are words I've never used before."

When she spoke, her voice was thick with pain. "Kaz," she began, then stopped. "Mikal, you can't love me. It just isn't possible."

She tried to turn away again, but he grasped her face between his hands and held it, forcing her to look at him. "Do you love me?"

She nodded. "But it doesn't matter. We can't stay together."

"Yes, we can. I'll have to leave here when the snow melts, but you can stay until I've made some arrangements."

She blinked away her tears and frowned. "What sort of arrangements?" He thought she sounded more frightened than hopeful, but he hurried on to explain.

"I'll find a place for you in Wantesa. I'm there more than I'm at Lonhola, and it would be better because it's bigger."

"Have you forgotten that I'm Astasi?" she asked, her expression suggesting that he'd lost his senses, which he thought wryly just might be the truth.

"I can arrange a disguise for you. There is a woman I know who's in the theater. She can get you a wig and whatever else is needed to disguise you. And she'll help you with everything else as well. It can be done, my love. I know it can.

"You'll like her. Her name is Bettena Halward. She's both an actress and a playwright—a woman of great talent. We can trust her completely.

"I've known her for some years now. She was once the most sought-after actress in the theater, but she's past forty now, and there are no longer many good roles for her. So she turned to playwriting. I supported the production of her first play and will continue to do so until people accept that a woman can have important things to say."

"Does anyone know that you're doing this?" she asked, seemingly both surprised and intrigued by his story.

"Some people know. It wasn't my intention to keep my patronage a secret, but Bett insisted on it. She thinks it could harm my military career."

He smiled and bent to kiss her softly. "Have I convinced you?"

"I must think about it. Will you be there—in Wantesa, I mean?"

He nodded. "I have to tend to a few matters at Lonhola first, but then we'll go to Wantesa. I have a house there, but it's too well known for me to be able to keep you there."

Listening to the echo of his last words, Mikal felt a powerful urge to tell her that it wasn't his choice to hide her away. Most of the men he knew kept mistresses, but he didn't want to think of her that way.

He ran a finger along the gentle curve of her cheek. "If it were possible, I would ask you to marry me."

She stared at him for a moment, then shook her head violently and was out of the bed before he could stop her.

There was no place for her to go. Shayna realized that only when she reached for the latch on the door. She was appalled to realize that not even her nakedness would have prevented her from fleeing the cabin. She choked back a sob and clenched her fists helplessly. What was happening to her? She'd never behaved irrationally in her entire life.

Well, she was entitled to some irrationality now, wasn't she? After all, Mikal Har-Amaden had just declared his love for her and asked her to marry him.

Shivering, she wrapped her arms around herself and walked over to the hearth, then sat down and drew her knees against her chest. Tears were stinging her eyes, but she ignored them as she tried to think. But just as she was beginning to calm down enough to consider her situation, he appeared, carrying a blanket that he placed around her shoulders before going on to the kitchen.

She listened to him clattering about and wondered what he must think of her. It was a safe bet that her reaction wasn't exactly what he'd expected. Was he leaving her alone because he was angry with her—or did he somehow understand her need to be alone now?

Tears ran down her cheeks and she brushed them away with the edge of the blanket. She felt so adrift, so very lost—and yet she could not allow herself to cling to him.

Think, she ordered herself. *What should you do? What* can *you do? Right now, you're a virtual prisoner here, but even when the snow melts, that won't change.*

A bitter smile curved her lips as she realized that from the standpoint of her mission here, she was exactly where she should be: close to the man whose life she'd intended to save. She made a sound that was half sob and half laughter. Oh yes, she was close to him, all right. Her body still bore his imprint. His scent lingered on her skin. His soft words of love still echoed through her brain.

She would go to Wantesa with him because she had no choice, and because it meant that she could protect him from Haddar until she could find a way to persuade Haddar to give up his evil scheme. Then, if Haddar's craft hadn't been destroyed, she would go home.

She tried to conjure up an image of her home, but what came instead was that portrait of Mikal, staring down at her from the wall in the lobby of the history building.

Then, suddenly, the younger version of Mikal Har-Amaden reappeared, bringing with him a breakfast tray. The stern, silver-haired giant of history was transformed into a man with rumpled black hair and a day's growth of beard. He set down the tray and then lowered himself to the floor beside her.

"You think I'm mad, don't you?" he asked.

She stared at him in confusion. If anyone appeared to be mad here, surely he must think it her, not himself.

"I don't know what the customs are among your people, love, but if they're the same as ours, then you must think me mad for declaring my love so quickly." He chuckled. "Perhaps I am mad. But I'm accustomed to making quick decisions. It's necessary when I'm leading men into battle. I know you have secrets, but whatever they are, they can't change what I feel—or what I want. I want you with me, and if you cannot truly be my wife, then you will be the wife of my heart."

"Please stop, Mikal. You don't understand."

"Just tell me this, my love," he said, taking her hand. "Do you truly love me?"

"Yes," she whispered. For longer than you can possibly know, she added silently.

He kissed her—a soft, lingering kiss that promised

what she knew they could never have. "Then we will find a way."

The snow was melting rapidly under the sun's warmth. Mikal told her that he must leave soon: tomorrow or the day after. He would stay at Lonhola no more than two days, and then return to take her to Wantesa.

In the meantime they indulged themselves, spending many hours in bed or sitting before the fire. She encouraged him to talk about himself and his life, while avoiding as much as possible talking about herself.

It was early evening and they were comfortably ensconced before the fire, when Shayna discovered the first real discrepancy between the man of history and the real Mikal Har-Amaden. He had been speculating about the next source of trouble for his people—a question she could have answered for him easily.

"Will it ever end?" she asked, referring to the incessant wars.

"It will end," he stated firmly. "It will end when the others recognize that we are destined to rule."

Very fortunately, he was turned away from her as he spoke. She stared at him in shock, unable to believe her own ears. This man, who had worked most of his life against incredible odds to set up a system of world government in which all shared equally, was telling her that the Amaden were destined to rule that world.

"We are already the most powerful," he went on. "And we have the best government and the largest share of resources."

"But Mikal," she said, choosing her words carefully, "you cannot hope to have lasting peace if you attempt to rule everyone."

He looked at her in surprise. "There is no other way, Shayna. If we don't rule, then we will have to continue to fight."

She searched her mind for a way to dispute that. "But our two peoples have been at peace for several generations now—and the Amaden do not rule the Astasi."

"Not openly," he admitted. "But you yourself have

spoken of the cannon trained on your valley. We are at peace because, despite your magic, you can never hope to defeat us. For the same reason, we must disarm our enemies while keeping ourselves strong."

Badly shaken, she got up, saying that she would make them some tea. She went to the kitchen and put on the kettle, then tried to reconcile the words she'd just heard with what she knew to be his future.

In his biography of Mikal that was widely regarded as being the most authoritative source of information, Maltus had said that Mikal had always dreamed of bringing all tribes together into one great council. And no one had ever disputed that. In fact, part of his greatness lay in the difference between him and other Amaden, who were known to have believed what she'd just heard from Mikal's lips.

Now it appeared that Maltus had been guilty of the worst sort of treachery found in her profession: rewriting history. She shuddered to think that Mikal might have much in common with Haddar, after all—at least at this stage of his life.

What changed him? she wondered as she made the tea. When did he come to realize that peace could only be realized by sharing power equally?

When she returned to him, he began to ask her about her people, and about her life in the valley. She answered easily enough, drawing on her extensive knowledge of Astasi history, though her mind remained on his startling revelation.

"Why did you tell me when you first came here that you couldn't use your powers?" he asked suddenly, after she'd told him about the life that wasn't hers.

She had no recollection of having said that, but assumed she must have, since it was true in her own time. The decision to renounce their magic had been made a condition of joining the World Council: a condition imposed by the man who was now asking her the question.

Shayna felt herself becoming entangled in the tricky web of her own lies. Then she recalled the tale she'd told him about being attacked and how she couldn't fight off the men because her powers were diminished by the storm.

"I must have been thinking about that storm," she said with a shrug.

"Then you *can* use them?"

She nodded warily, hoping that he wouldn't ask for a demonstration. Like most Astasi, she believed that all those powers remained intact, but no one knew for certain because they hadn't been used for centuries, except for rare instances of unconscious conjuring such as she'd done at the Institute. As the Astasi became less and less conscious of their powers, accidents like that could happen, since they'd long since lost the skills necessary to hold them in check.

Shayna knew that her people had continued to use their magic in secret in their valley for some time after they'd agreed to renounce them. But those harmless practices had ceased more than two hundred years ago, as the Astasi became more concerned about being accepted by the world at large.

"I've been worried about leaving you here alone," Mikal said. "But you will have your magic to protect you."

She hid her relief and nodded. "Do you have reason to think that someone could come?" she asked, thinking that unlikely—unless either Haddar or her rescue crew might come.

"No. Only a few people other than my family know about this place. But I'm concerned about those men who tried to get into Lonhola. It's not that far from here, and after they escaped it seems likely they'd be avoiding the roads."

He frowned as he drained his cup of tea. "That incident troubles me because it makes no sense. What could they have hoped to accomplish? There are over a thousand men at Lonhola."

But only one that they were interested in, she thought unhappily. "But three men who are willing to sacrifice their lives might still be able to accomplish something," she said, trying to find a way to get him to accept that he could be in danger.

He threw her a surprised look, and when he spoke, there was a sudden wariness in his voice. "Do you read minds, Shayna?"

"No, of course not." She knew that many people had believed the Astasi could read minds, but it wasn't true. He studied her in silence for a moment, and she couldn't be sure whether or not he believed her.

"That's just what I'd been thinking," he said finally. "But even if it's true, what could they have planned to do?"

He stared at her thoughtfully. "When I told you about them, you suggested that they might have planned to assassinate me. Why did you say that?"

She smiled and shrugged. "I didn't know you were you, then."

"Even so," he persisted.

"It just occurred to me, that's all. I thought it might be some men bent on revenge because you'd recently defeated them."

"No, it couldn't have been that. From the descriptions, I know they weren't Latti or Bandera. One was Amaden, but the other two didn't belong to any identifiable tribe."

That didn't surprise her. Except for the Amaden and her own people, no one belonged to any identifiable tribe in her world. More than two hundred years of intermarriage had taken care of that.

"Well, I intend to get to the bottom of it," he stated firmly. "I'm planning to question those guards myself when I get to Lonhola."

Shayna could only hope that the guards had nothing to say. If they had caught even a glimpse of the stunners that Haddar and the others had used . . .

"I know you can protect yourself—but I will still worry about you, my love."

His dark eyes searched her face almost desperately. "Promise me that you will be here when I return."

She stretched up to kiss him, and the pleasure was tempered by the pain inside her. "I will be here, Mikal."

He mounted his horse and rode away through the woods, disappearing from view very quickly—but not before he turned briefly in the saddle to look back at her.

Her promise echoed in the warm spring air. It was a promise she might not be able to keep. If Haddar showed up, or if the rescue crew arrived, she would be gone.

It would be so much better that way, she told herself. *The longer I stay with him, the more difficult it will be to leave him.* Even now, the pain seemed unbearable.

She pictured herself back on the lovely, sprawling campus, walking into the graceful lobby of the history building, where a copy of his portrait hung in a place of honor. She imagined herself teaching her courses and being forced to use his name frequently.

I cannot escape him, she thought. I will never escape him. But would it have been any different if he'd been just Kaz, and not Mikal? She knew that she wouldn't need portraits and statues and history books to remember him.

Tears rolled down her cheeks as she prayed silently to the old gods she hadn't acknowledged before to bring Haddar or the rescue team here and help her return to her own time.

Chapter Five

Shayna spent the day in an agony of waiting, tormented by her thoughts. What if Haddar and the others encountered him on the way to Lonhola? What if the guards remembered seeing stunners in the hands of the men who'd attacked them?

And those were just her immediate fears. Lurking darkly beneath them was the fear that she would never be able to return to her own time. With Mikal's departure, that fear had returned. It was scarcely a case of "out of sight, out of mind," because she knew she'd never forget him—but she didn't belong here and she couldn't spend the rest of her life living a lie.

It wasn't her nature to wait helplessly for events to unfold. She'd never been in such a situation before, where she had so little control over events. And that was yet another reason why she couldn't stay here. She could never live as women in this time had lived.

When she finally accepted that worrying would accomplish nothing, Shayna turned her thoughts to the man who'd become the center of her very existence. She still felt a sense of awe. There wasn't a historian alive who wouldn't have given everything he or she possessed to meet Mikal Har-Amaden. And she had not only met him but was loved by him.

How had it happened? She thought uneasily about how quickly he'd fallen in love with her. Was it possible that there was magic involved? The subject of possible unconscious spell-casting on the part of the Astasi had been debated by them and by others for years.

Those who, like herself, had chosen to leave the valley were invariably successful in any endeavor they undertook, which had naturally led to suspicions on the part of others that they were using their magic. Three hundred years after Unification, the Astasi still stood at the edges of society: accepted for their accomplishments but still suspected of dark magic.

The sad truth was that she just didn't know if she might have subconsciously influenced Mikal to fall in love with her—and she never would know.

What she did know, however, was that she'd already broken the protocol she herself had helped to write. She'd gotten herself into a position where she could influence the course of future events—and in a way no one could have anticipated. Mikal was destined to become the most important figure in history—and he loved her.

I must get out of here, she thought desperately, *and I must prevent Haddar from carrying out his scheme even if it means using my magic to accomplish that.*

She stared at her hands, remembering how Mikal had threatened to tie them to prevent her from casting a spell. It was a common belief among outsiders that an Astasi could not invoke magic if he or she lacked the use of his or her hands. In the ancient battles between her people and the Amaden, it had been common practice for Amaden soldiers to cut off the hands of wounded Astasi.

The fact was, though, that it wasn't true. Her people had traced the ancient runes more as a matter of tradition than of necessity. The powers that lived within them could be invoked readily enough without that.

She was sitting in the clearing in front of the cabin, where the sun had melted away the last traces of snow. And now she lifted her hands, staring at them as though they were no longer a part of her. Centuries of being told that magic was unnatural and evil had its effect upon her. Mikal's affectionate use of the term *witch* echoed through her mind. It was not a term her people had ever used, but instead was one flung at them by disapproving outsiders.

She began slowly to trace the ancient runes as she invoked the names of the old gods. No one had taught her this; there was no necessity. It was bred into her as deeply as her red hair and green eyes.

At first she felt only disgust with herself, but as the ancient powers began to flow through her, disgust turned to acceptance—and then to pride. Her body tingled pleasantly and she began to feel as light as the warm spring air.

Still, the first faint traces of the ancient fire that glowed along her fingertips startled her and even frightened her. Without thinking, she closed her fists and it vanished. When the fear had subsided, she found herself deeply satisfied. She had proved that she could use her talents if it became necessary.

Then suddenly she heard the snap of twigs in the nearby woods and whirled around, fearing that Mikal had returned. But instead, a doe stood in the shadows, its delicate head turned in her direction. She stared at it, then got up and began to walk toward it.

The animal didn't move as she approached it, though she could see its graceful body trembling. She reached out to stroke its neck softly. Then she stepped back and released it from her spell. Within seconds, it had vanished into the thick woods.

Mikal returned just before sunset the following day. He'd told her to stay close to the cabin, but she had decided to go for a walk in the valley, hoping that she might find the other time-craft hidden there somewhere. There were thick woods and rocky outcroppings where it could have been concealed, but she found nothing.

She was just starting back up the hillside to the cabin when she saw him riding down toward her. He was still wearing his splendid uniform, and she was reminded of the statues of him on horseback that decorated so many public parks and plazas. Once again she was overcome by the knowledge of who he was, and she came to a stop, unable to cope with the emotions that flooded through her.

When he came to a stop and reached down to draw her up into the saddle, she saw that he appeared to have even more gold braid on his broad shoulders. But before she could question this, he had settled her sideways in the saddle and his mouth was covering hers.

"I thought you had gone," he said in a voice thick with emotion.

"I just went for a walk," she replied huskily as she traced the outline of his firm jaw with one trembling finger.

They rode back up to the cabin in silence and she decided that he must not have learned anything more from the guards. Surely if he had, he would be accusing her of complicity with them—an irony she would prefer to forgo.

When they reached the lean-to where the horse was stabled, he swung lightly out of the saddle, then lifted her down and into his arms.

"How is it that I hunger for you so much after less than two days?" he asked, his dark eyes searching her face. "Are you sure that you haven't cast a spell on me?"

She cringed inwardly, but managed to return his scrutiny. "Do you really believe that?"

"No. I think I fell in love with you even before you were well enough to be casting any spells. On the way back here, I was thinking that I've probably been in love with you all my life—with the idea of you, that is."

"What makes you think that?" she asked as he began to unsaddle his horse. It was an eerie echo of her own thoughts about him—but she at least had had a figure from the history books to fall in love with.

He turned to give her a smile. "There must have been some reason why I could never bring myself to fall in love with any of the women my family tried to foist upon me."

He set down the saddle and paused for a moment, his expression suddenly sober. "It seems to me that I was always waiting . . . waiting for someone. Sometimes I thought I could almost see her, as though she were just on the other side of a veil." He laughed self-deprecatingly.

"It's in my journals—not the one here, but an earlier one. I'll show it to you when we get to Wantesa."

Shayna swallowed to get rid of the lump in her throat. She'd read the journal that was here and had been vaguely disappointed because there was so little in it that was personal.

He fed and watered the horse and they started to walk back to the cabin. He draped an arm over her shoulders. "Am I overwhelming you?"

"Why would you think that?" she asked, hiding her amusement at the truth to his words he couldn't possibly know.

He shrugged. "I've always been told that I can be overwhelming at times, by men as well as women. It's not intentional. But when the way seems clear to me, I don't always check to see if others find it to be so clear."

Shayna smiled. He was speaking almost exactly the words she'd read about him in Maltus's biography. It explained his amazing persistence that allowed him to change the world. She slanted a glance at him, something she'd begun to do when she needed to reassure herself that he was a man, and not the great hero.

"Have you been promoted?" she asked. "It seems that your shoulders are gleaming more brightly than when you left."

He glanced down at them. "Yes. I've been made second-in-command of the army."

And in less than a year, you will be the commander in

chief, she said silently. *And after that . . .*

She never had the chance to finish her thought because the moment they stepped through the door into the cabin, he swept her up in his arms and strode off to the bedroom.

His hunger was too great to allow for gentleness, though she could feel him fighting it. The fires within her that had been banked since his departure leaped up again, threatening to consume her.

It was only during these times in bed with him that Shayna could almost forget who he was and how impossible their love was. He was no longer Mikal Har-Amaden, but a man of solid, warm flesh and passion.

Their lips and fingers were greedy, seeking pleasure while giving it—abandoning their separateness in pursuit of that unique wholeness. Their bodies quickly became an erotic landscape to be explored with the eagerness of children who considered nothing to be out of bounds.

But from the beginning, there was a frantic quality to their lovemaking this time, a need to reassert their ownership of each other. Neither of them wanted it to end, but both of them were carried toward that ending, helpless to slow down the relentless pounding of the ancient rhythms of love.

Shayna welcomed him into her, crying out as he filled her with himself, his hands gripping her as though he would send all of him into her and create another being out of both of them. And in that final moment of blind ecstasy, it seemed that he had succeeded.

He collapsed on top of her, bracing himself on trembling arms as she stroked the smooth, sweat-slicked skin of his back and felt the small flutterings of passion burning itself out—too quickly.

The waves of sadness that washed over her caught her by surprise. For these all-too-brief moments, she had let herself forget, and now she paid the price in pain. He rolled off her, then drew her against him, his bristly arm curved possessively around her. She wondered if the pain would be different if he too knew the impossibility of their love.

She hated those thoughts, hated to be reminded of the lies that surrounded their love and could so easily devour it. Love and lies did not belong together. If he were still Kaz, she might have cast aside her ethical obligations and told him the truth. But the man beside her could not know the truth.

Even so, she toyed with the idea. Would it comfort him in the difficult years he faced to know that he would succeed? There surely must have been times when he'd doubted his ability to achieve his goal. Historians all marveled at his single-minded pursuit of what must have seemed to be an impossible dream.

The records of those years had all been written by others, so no one knew what private anguish and doubts he must have suffered. For that reason alone, his journals had been the life's quest of many historians.

I could ease that pain for him, she thought. I could give him that gift.

But if she told him the truth, would he believe it? Or would it ruin this small time they had together, because he would think her mad?

Lost in her own thoughts, she was slow to realize how quiet he was. She lifted her head from his chest to find him staring at her with that faint frown she'd seen so often, as though there were something about her that he had yet to puzzle out.

She kissed the furrows between his dark brows. "Why do you stare at me like that, Mikal?" she asked, knowing she was treading on very dangerous ground, but unable to stop herself.

"I don't understand why you're hiding things from me. Why can't you be honest with me, Shayna? How can I prove to you that you have nothing to fear from me?"

She nearly laughed at his innocent question. He had it wrong. She had nothing at all to fear from him, but he could have quite a lot to fear from her: knowledge that could change his life forever.

She sat up in the bed, having reached her decision quickly. "I know that I have nothing to fear from you, Mikal. I trust you—more than you can ever know. But I must ask for that same trust from you.

"There are things I cannot tell you and will never be able to tell you." She hesitated as a lump formed in her throat, then forged on in her dance with danger.

"But what I can't tell you has no bearing on us, on our love. I would never do anything to harm you, and I won't allow any harm to come to you. But when I tell you that you are in danger, you must believe me."

His frown deepened as he searched her face for the words between the words. "How do you know that I'm in danger?"

"I can't tell you that. You will have to trust me."

"Can you see the future?" he asked after a moment's silence.

Shayna turned her head to prevent him from seeing her shock, covering the movement by shifting her position on the bed. The Astasi had always been widely believed to know the future. It was true that there had once been some few among them who had visions, though they'd always been unpredictable. But if that talent still existed, those who possessed it kept it to themselves.

The irony of his question made her want to cry—or to laugh. She saw the future, all right—more of it than he could possibly imagine. But it didn't require magic; although to him, the Time Project would surely seem like magic.

He was waiting with that great patience of his for an answer, and she chose a careful middle ground.

"I can't see the future—but I can sense certain things. It's hard to explain. But you must be very careful, Mikal."

"Are you thinking about those men who tried to break into Lonhola?" he asked, pulling himself up into a sitting position.

"Yes—at least I think so. Did you get descriptions of them?"

He nodded, then gave them to her. There was no doubt in her mind that Haddar was one of them. And from the description, she guessed that one of the other two was a student of Haddar's who shared his beliefs. Mikal's description of the third man surprised her the most, because it sounded like it might be one of the staff from the Time Project: an engineer whom she'd seen often, but didn't know well.

That could certainly explain the seeming ease with which Haddar had accomplished his scheme. Before she left, Teres and the security people had been considering the possibility that Haddar had gained the cooperation of someone connected to the project.

"Do you know them?" Mikal asked.

"I know who they are—and they are the ones you must fear. They will try again."

He was silent again as he turned to stare out the window. When he returned his attention to her, Shayna saw what she least wanted to see in his eyes: distrust. It felt like a knife through her heart.

"I questioned the guards. One of them thought that he saw something in the hand of the Amaden: something small and silver. He said that the man seemed to aim it at them, and after that he remembers nothing, until they all woke up in pain."

He got out of bed and picked up the trousers to his uniform that he'd hastily discarded. She watched him, knowing what was coming next and wondering how she could respond.

He held up her stunner. "Is this what they saw?"

"It couldn't have been. I told you that it's an Astasi talisman—and you said they weren't Astasi."

"It's not a talisman, Shayna," he said, shaking his head. "It's a weapon of some sort. I knew that after I aimed it at you that time. You couldn't hide your fear.

"And there is something else I don't understand. Before you knew who I am you suggested that those men might have been trying to assassinate me. But if you knew that, then why didn't you know who I really was?"

Tears of frustration stung her eyes. Her secret was threatening to tear them apart. "I told you before, Mikal. There are some things I cannot tell you."

"But there is a connection between you and these men, isn't there?"

"Only in the sense that I know what they intend to do."

He turned the stunner over and over in his hand, staring at it. "How could such a weapon exist? It isn't Amaden, and none of our enemies could have such a thing without my knowledge."

"Your enemies have them. That's why you must be careful." Then, when she saw the look of horror on his face, she tried to explain.

"I don't mean that all of your enemies have them—only those three men."

"Those three men—and you. Where did you get it?"

"Mikal, you must trust me and believe me when I tell you that no one else has them and no one else can get them."

"I want to know how it works."

"There's no way I can show you without causing you to suffer the pain that the guards suffered."

His persistence irritated her, even though she understood it. He was a warrior, and weapons were his business.

"Was it created with Astasi magic?" he demanded.

She hesitated. If she said yes, he might well believe her. But then he would see her people as being a threat. She shook her head.

"You ask too much of me, Shayna. I'm a man who loves you, but I'm also responsible for the safety of my men—of all my people."

She got out of the bed where they'd made love and began to dress. It was over. She had to leave here. She could not live with his distrust, though she certainly understood it.

Still naked, he sat down on the edge of the bed, toying

with the stunner he continued to hold. "What are you doing?"

"I'm leaving here, Mikal. I don't blame you for not trusting me, but I can't stay."

"I won't let you leave."

She sat down in a chair and pulled on her boots. "You can't stop me, Mikal—and don't try."

Then she got up and started toward the bedroom door. But before she could reach the hallway he was behind her, grasping her arms and then holding her hands prisoner. She didn't struggle.

"I know you think I can't cast a spell if I can't use my hands, but that's not true. Let me go!"

Rather to her surprise, he did. Relief flooded through her. A spell wouldn't have done him any harm, but she didn't want to be forced to use her magic—and certainly not on him.

"Where are you going?" he asked, following her as she started out of the cabin.

"Home."

"You can't walk all the way to the valley."

"Yes, I can. Who would dare to harm a . . . *witch?*" She flung the words at him as she opened the door and stepped out into the last light of the day.

Then, suddenly, she stopped as something brushed against her mind. The sensation was so strange that at first she couldn't identify it. And then suddenly she knew. The powers she'd summoned earlier hadn't vanished. Once awakened, they'd remained there, just beneath the level of consciousness. And what she was feeling now was danger!

Abruptly she turned around, then grabbed his arm and drew him back into the cabin.

"What is it?" he asked in confusion, pulling away from her and starting toward the door again. "Did you see—"

"Stop, Mikal!" Even as she spoke, the power behind the order flowed from her. He froze, his hand still outstretched to push the door open again.

She left quickly, not wanting to see him that way. It

sickened her to know that she'd done such a thing to him, even though it was necessary.

The shadows were already deep in the woods that grew close to the cabin on three sides. She scanned them, knowing that it must be Haddar and the others. If it were a rescue team, she wouldn't have felt that powerful sense of danger. She started in that direction.

"Haddar!" she called. "I know you're out there. I want to talk to you."

For a long moment there was only silence. She continued to walk toward the woods, praying that he had nothing more than a stunner. Surely if he had he would have used it at Lonhola. Stunners had a very limited range, since they were intended for personal protection.

Then, just as she reached the edge of the woods, a twig snapped, followed quickly by more. She stopped and peered into the darkness beneath the trees.

"Come out, Haddar!" she ordered, wishing she could see him so she could use her powers. She had no compunction at all about using them on the likes of him.

He emerged slowly from the shadows, followed by the other two. She saw that she had been correct about their identities. All three of them held stunners trained on her.

Without consciously intending to do so, she summoned forth her own protection. When they saw the eerie blue glow around her hands, they halted, but they continued to point the stunners at her.

A standoff, she thought. She might be able to succeed in subduing them before they could use the stunners, but it was doubtful—and far too risky. If she failed, she would be out for long enough that they could get Mikal, especially given that he was now helpless to escape from them, thanks to her spell.

Pure hatred glittered in Haddar's eyes—a hatred he'd never let her see before, though she knew of its existence. The other two glared at her as well, but she sensed a fear in them that was missing from Haddar.

"I knew they'd send you after me," he said with a

sneer. "We should have taken the time to destroy the other craft, instead of—"

He stopped abruptly, as though belatedly realizing that he shouldn't have started.

"Instead of what?" she demanded, ignoring the growing heat in her hands.

"I didn't think it would matter, because they could just build another. So I had Akmad here make some changes in it instead."

"What changes?" She asked as a chill slithered along her spine.

"He programmed it so that they wouldn't know where it went—just as you couldn't have known where we went. How did you get here?"

"The pathway effect," the engineer named Akmad said with disgust.

Haddar shot a glance at him. "What's that?"

"Some of the team thought that the passage of the craft through time left a sort of trail that could be followed for a short time."

"Why didn't you . . . ?" Haddar waved his free hand in dismissal of the topic, returning his attention to Shayna.

"I know he's here. We followed him."

"Yes, he's here," she acknowledged. "But you can't touch him, Haddar. You won't even get near him because I've placed a spell of protection on the cabin."

This was a blatant lie—but she could have done it if she'd had the time. And she'd noticed how they all kept glancing uneasily at the fire surrounding her hands, which by now were aching from the effort required to produce it and control it.

Haddar glanced toward the cabin, scowling. "You're not permitted to use your powers—witch."

She thought how very different that word sounded coming from him, as opposed to Mikal. "Not in our own time, but I can here. And I will. Give up this scheme of yours, Haddar, and come back with me. If you do no harm, the council will deal leniently with you."

"I'm not foolish enough to believe you, witch. If we

can't get him now, we'll get him another time. You can't protect him forever."

They began to back up, melting into the darkness of the woods. Once again she thought about using the fire, but she could still see the gleam of their stunners, and she couldn't risk it. Nor could she cast a spell. The effects weren't always instantaneous, and she doubted she had the skill to entrance all three of them at once. So she stood there, seething with helpless rage. Then Haddar's voice called out from the darkness.

"You've taken the great man as your lover, haven't you, Shayna? That makes you no better than me."

She raised her hand to strike, but forced herself to close her fist and banish the fire. A sound escaped from her that was half sob. He was wrong! The difference between them was that she wanted only to love Mikal and protect him—while Haddar wanted to kill him. But his taunt had struck a chord, nevertheless.

She listened as the sounds of their departure continued and then faded away. The sense of danger went with it. They were gone—for now. But they just might return later. She turned back to the cabin, but instead of entering it, she began to circle it slowly, murmuring ancient words that came to her lips as surely as if she'd spoken them many times in the past.

When she was satisfied that she had protected them, she pushed open the cabin door and nearly collided with Mikal, who stood exactly as she'd left him, frozen as though about to reach for the door latch. His eyes were open but blank, and she felt a sharp pang of guilt and pain at what she'd done to him, even if it had been for his own protection.

She slipped past him, then turned to stare at him. Spells—especially those cast in haste as this one had been—were tricky. She couldn't be sure what he'd remember of the events immediately preceding it.

She thought about their argument over the stunner. He would certainly recall that—unfortunately. After giving it some thought, she decided that the only thing she could do was to carry on where they'd been and hope that he wouldn't notice the passage of time. Under other circumstances, that wouldn't have been a problem because not much time had in fact passed. But it was just growing dark when she'd started to leave—and now it was full dark.

She shuddered, only now realizing how close she'd come to walking away and leaving him here for Haddar to find. If she hadn't felt that sense of danger . . .

Well, she *had* felt it. For better or for worse, she truly was a witch now. Haddar was right.

Thoughts of Haddar brought back that conversation between him and the treacherous engineer. If he had done as he said, there would be no rescue team, because they wouldn't know where in time to search for her. They couldn't follow the pathway because of the time it would take to build another craft. And when they did build one, they would almost certainly search for her at a much later time, making the same mistake she herself had made about Haddar's intentions.

But she couldn't let herself think about that now. Instead she had to release Mikal from his spell. She opened the cabin door again, then waited a moment to be sure there was no danger. If Haddar returned, he wouldn't get inside—but he might be lurking in the woods.

Her senses told her that he was gone, so she turned and released Mikal, then without waiting to see what would happen, she fled into the darkness.

Mikal felt a jolt, as though something had struck him. His head ached and there was a strange pain in his right arm. He blinked a few times, thinking that it seemed to be darker than it had a moment ago. What was he doing? And where was Shayna? The clear memory of their lovemaking came back to him, and in spite of his confusion, he smiled.

Then he remembered the argument—and her flight. He ran through the open door, calling her name, terrified that something had happened to her—or that she would never return.

"I'm here," she called from the darkness.

Then, as he felt relief wash over him, she emerged from the woods and began to walk slowly toward him. He met her in the small clearing and wrapped his arms tightly around her, thinking that he never wanted to let go.

"I'm sorry I ran off like that," she said softly.

Mikal loosened his hold on her and stared hard at her. That soft, apologetic tone sounded false to him. But then everything was feeling strange just now. His arm continued to ache, although his head was no longer throbbing. But all his thoughts seemed to be wrapped in gauze.

She slipped out of the circle of his arms and then took his hand. He let her lead him back into the cabin, then nodded distractedly as she said that she would make some tea. Something had happened to him. He snatched desperately at his memories—and by the time she reappeared, he knew.

"You cast a spell on me!" he said, too shocked at the moment to be angry.

For a moment he thought she would deny it. She ignored him as she handed him a mug of tea, then sank down in a chair.

"Yes," she said, glancing briefly at him. "I did. I'm sorry, Mikal. I was angry and I wanted to get away from you."

His anger began to bubble up now. Mikal was not given to rages, and this one caught even him by surprise. He flung the mug of tea against the hearth, then jammed his hands into his pockets to prevent them from doing any more damage. When he finally looked at her, he saw her staring at the shattered mug as though she too could not believe him to be capable of such a thing.

"Don't ever do that to me again," he said quietly, in a voice his men would have immediately recognized as being dangerous. "Do you hear me, Shayna?" he demanded when she continued to stare at the broken crockery.

She turned to him and nodded. He saw regret in her eyes—but not the fear he would have seen had she been anyone else.

"I was angry, Mikal . . . and hurt. You say you love me, but you don't trust me."

"How can I trust you, when you yourself admitted that there are things you won't tell me?"

"Not 'won't,' but 'can't.' There's a difference."

"Not to me, there isn't."

A long silence followed, during which she stared into the mug of tea she held. He waited, striving to regain his patience but not quite succeeding.

"You have sworn an oath of allegiance to your tribal council, haven't you?"

He nodded impatiently.

"And nothing—not even your love for me—could make you break that oath, could it?"

"No, but—"

"I have sworn an oath too, Mikal, and I cannot break it, either."

"Then you're saying that the Astasi—"

"No, my people have nothing at all to do with this. And you have nothing to fear from those to whom I've sworn an oath. They would never harm you." She smiled a strange sort of smile.

"They wish you well, Mikal, believe me. In fact, they sent me here to—"

She stopped suddenly, then nervously lifted the mug to her lips.

"They *sent* you here? So it wasn't an accident. What . . . ?"

"There *was* an accident," she insisted. "I didn't lie about that."

"But you were sent here—to me."

"Please, Mikal, I can't say any more. But you must be very careful until those men are caught."

She drained the mug and stood up. Her movements seemed to lack her normal grace, as though she was very tired. She started toward the kitchen, then swayed slightly and put out a hand to brace herself against the doorway. He ran to her and caught her up in his arms.

"What's wrong?" he asked, all his anger gone now. "Are you ill?"

She laughed into his chest. "No, I'm just tired. Casting spells is hard work—especially since I'm not used to it."

He chuckled in spite of himself. "See to it that you remember that." Then, as he once more became aware of the ache in his right arm, he asked her about it.

"That was a mistake," she said. "I told you that I'm not used to casting spells. You were reaching for the door handle and I just left you that way."

"For how long?" he demanded, trying not to think about the horror of what she'd done.

"Not long. I just wanted some time to think." She stretched up to kiss him. "I really am sorry, Mikal. It won't happen again."

But had it happened before? The question hammered at him. Could she have cast a spell that made him fall in love with her? Could a spell be that subtle, that insidious?

Who was this woman he loved? For one brief moment, before he surrendered himself to that love and swept her up into his arms, Mikal Har-Amaden could hear that question echoing down through a dark abyss, filled with all the old stories of Astasi sorcery.

They stopped at the crest of the hill. Before them, across a narrow valley, high atop its own hill, stood the keep, its golden stones aglow in the morning sun. The flag of the Amaden clan fluttered in the morning breeze from the highest tower.

The sight was disorienting, and Shayna knew that it was but the first of many such scenes she would encounter. Buildings from his time still stood in Wantesa as well. She couldn't see his face as she rode behind him, but she could sense his quiet pride, and she wanted to tell him that she'd been to this place, that it would still belong to his family three hundred years from now.

The Har-Amaden of her own time were direct descendants of his older brother, and although they had lived for many generations in a palatial home on the outskirts of Wantesa, they maintained the great keep as a country estate. Once a year, during the summer, they opened the keep to select groups, and several years ago Shayna had been included in a group of historians.

The Amaden had always been a tribal society, and Mikal's ancestors had been the most powerful clan in that society. It was one of those ancestors who'd united the far-flung tribes several hundred years before Mikal's time.

He urged his horse forward and they started down the hillside. Shayna tensed as she wondered about the reception she would receive. Mikal had informed her that they would travel to Wantesa by carriage, with a soldier guard composed of men from his own clan, whose discretion could be guaranteed.

She was glad that he seemed to be taking her warnings seriously, but she still worried about his family. They knew she was Astasi because Mikal had already sent them a message from Lonhola, and they surely could not be pleased. As they rode across the open valley, she imagined them peering out the windows and wondering if he had fallen under a witch's spell.

Her arms encircled his trim waist and she pressed her cheek to his broad back, loving him all the more now for his acceptance of her, even as she hated herself for her lies and half-truths. The fear was growing in her that it would all come out at some point because she would become so entangled in the web of her deceptions that she would have no recourse but the truth: a truth he would never be able to accept.

And even though she knew that he loved her, she could feel his doubts growing, and she could hear them in the small silences and see them in certain looks he gave her. Bit by bit, day by day, they would gnaw at him until they had destroyed that love. It would be much better that way—but it was not what she wanted.

They crossed the valley and started up the bare hillside to the keep. In her own time, this hillside was covered by a beautiful rock garden and shaded by tall trees. She could see the ornate carriage that awaited them, and a group of soldiers milling about. Perhaps they could leave without facing his family.

But as they reached the forecourt, three people emerged from the keep, pausing just outside the great carved doors. Shayna tensed and Mikal put a hand over hers and squeezed gently.

"They will accept you."

They may well pretend to do so, she replied silently, *but they will secretly be wishing me back to the valley and out of your life.*

She could feel the eyes of the soldiers on her as Mikal dismounted and then lifted her from the saddle. She was entirely too conscious of the ill-fitting dress that was probably a castoff from the one woman who approached her now.

Mikal introduced her to them, and Shayna felt a rush of warmth for his brother, Derik, who came forward without hesitation and kissed the hand she belatedly extended.

"You are welcome here, Shayna," he said with such sincerity that she had no doubt he truly meant it. There was a strong resemblance between Mikal and his older brother, though Derik's features were less harsh and his dark hair was already thinning on top.

The greetings she received from Derik's wife Hana, and from his mother, were cautiously polite, and she was reminded that in this time, it was the women who were the keepers of family pride and traditions, since they were prevented from taking part in the larger world.

Her hope that they would leave quickly was doomed as Mikal's mother invited them to come in and rest a while before resuming their journey. Still, as she was led into the keep, she was curious to see it. Mikal's descendant, who had played host to her group, had told them that the place had undergone considerable renovations and refurbishing over the years.

And so it had. She was struck by the simplicity, even

the austerity, of the place. No structural changes were evident here; as she recalled, those consisted of changes in the kitchen and the addition of numerous baths.

They crossed the nearly empty foyer, where the great stone staircase led to the upper floors, then passed through open double doors of ornately carved dark wood into a parlor that was completely at odds with the large foyer.

Her gaze was drawn immediately to the huge marble fireplace, and she remembered her host saying that the marble had been quarried on family lands. It had a faint pinkish cast to it that provided a warmth to the entire room.

But here again Shayna felt that disorientation. Hanging over the fireplace was a huge portrait she'd seen during her visit—but not in this location. The portrait that hung there in her own time was another painting of Mikal, done by the same artist who'd painted the one that hung in the council headquarters.

She had liked that portrait, she recalled. He had seemed less stern, more human—as though somehow softened by being surrounded by his family's ancestral home.

She walked over to examine the portrait that hung there now and smiled, remembering how strange it had seemed to see the great man as a child. It was a family portrait, and Mikal, the youngest, was no more than three or four. In it, he wore an impatient look that was at odds with his reputation—as though he'd been interrupted at play and could barely wait to return to his toys.

"The artist captured me perfectly," Mikal said, coming up behind her and startling her out of her reverie. "The day he painted my expression I'd just been given a pony of my own, and needless to say, I had other things in mind than sitting there."

"He's not telling you the best part, Shayna," Derik said as he clapped a hand on his brother's shoulder. "We'd all gotten dressed up in our best for the portrait. I was supposed to be keeping an eye on him, but he managed to slip outside and stomp through a few mud puddles. So he was actually wearing his second-best clothes."

The next hour passed pleasantly enough as they drank tea and ate the excellent food carried in by the maids. She did her best to convince these people that she wasn't the witch they believed her to be, but she thought that she'd succeeded only with Derik.

Then, as they were about to leave, Derik's wife, Hana, put a hand tentatively on Shayna's arm and leaned toward her. "Come with me for a moment. I think I can find something more suitable for you to wear for your journey."

Surprised by the gesture, Shayna followed her up the staircase and along the mezzanine, where portraits of Mikal's ancestors glowered at her from the stone walls.

Hana led her into the master suite, where Shayna recognized only the huge tapestry that covered most of one wall. Hana opened a large wardrobe and began to search through its contents.

"Here," she said, pulling out a soft blue gown. "I think this will fit you better."

Shayna thanked her and stepped behind a folding screen to change. "I'm sure Mikal will arrange for you to be better outfitted when you arrive in Wantesa," Hana said brightly, but in a tone that hinted at disapproval.

The dress did indeed fit better and Shayna thanked her, then decided to try to allay her fears as best she could.

"Hana, I want you to understand that I will never do anything to harm Mikal, or to cause him trouble. It was his idea that I accompany him to Wantesa."

"Yes, I know that," Hana said, avoiding her gaze. "And Derik is probably right that Mikal can get away with such a thing. But why did you agree?"

"Because I love him," Shayna answered simply. "I may not always be with him—but I will always love him."

Rather to her surprise, Hana smiled at her. "Well, Derik also said once that Mikal would never fall in love with an ordinary woman.

"My mother-in-law said that when Mikal was born, the midwife told her that he was destined for greatness. She was a seeress."

Shayna merely nodded, turning away from Hana so that she couldn't see the tears that had sprung to her eyes.

Chapter Six

Shayna awoke with a jolt. She'd been dreaming about home again, and for a moment she was confused by her opulent surroundings. But that ended abruptly as Mikal leaned across and took her hand. The rhythmic clip-clop of the horses' hooves and the gentle swaying of the carriage had obviously overcome her determination to stay awake in case Haddar tried to waylay them.

"We're nearly to Wantesa," Mikal told her. "I thought you might like to see it from the top of this hill. It's a good view."

She smiled and nodded. Before she'd fallen asleep, he'd been trying hard to convince her that she'd like her new life in Wantesa. So she'd seen firsthand his legendary powers of persuasion. It wasn't so much the words he used as it was the air of absolute certainty that he managed to project.

But then, of course, she'd wanted to believe him—or had wanted him to think she did. After her unwise brushes with the truth, she was determined to fit herself completely into the role of an Astasi witch who'd abandoned her life in the valley.

A footman opened the carriage door and Mikal stepped out, then helped her alight from the carriage. They had pulled off the road, where other carriages and riders and horse-drawn carts continued to move along, most of them headed into Wantesa.

She took Mikal's proffered arm rather belatedly, which drew a smile from him as he leaned toward her. "Don't worry. Bettena will help you learn everything you need to know."

Indeed, she thought. Someone had better do so. She might be as well versed as anyone in the history of this time, but understanding history and being forced to live in it were two very different things. Back at the cabin, she hadn't been forced to deal with society's expectations of women, but now she'd not only have to wear their uncomfortable clothes, she'd have to behave like one.

Mikal led her up a sloping hillside, and when they stopped at its crest, her gasp of surprise was wholly involuntary, though not for the reason Mikal must be assuming.

One thing had not changed in three hundred years. Wantesa was then and remained the world's largest and most beautiful city, blessed by its perfect location at the edge of the sea, surrounded by dark hills on three sides and the crescent-shaped harbor on the fourth.

In her own time, Wantesa had swelled to sprawl along those hills and even beyond, into the valleys to the north and east. But the city that lay before her now was confined to the valley, except for the ancient fortress that stood guard on the highest of the hills.

Ignoring the city itself for a moment, Shayna stared instead at the fortress. In Mikal's time it would be filled with soldiers; in her own time it was filled with administrators. The fortress was the administrative building for the university. And on the plateau behind it would one day rise all the other campus buildings.

She turned her attention to the city. She'd seen many

photographs taken not long after this period, and it occurred to her that most of them had probably been taken from this very spot.

"It's very beautiful," she said, knowing that he was waiting for her to say something. And it was true. Wantesa was built entirely of the same golden stone used at his family's keep. Before her own time, when the quarries that provided that stone had been depleted, a great deal of effort and expense had gone into creating a synthetic stone that matched it, so that even in her time Wantesa glowed a mellow golden shade. The size of new buildings was carefully restricted to prevent them from overwhelming the old city before her now.

Tears slid down her cheeks as she began to pick out familiar landmarks: the old marketplace that was in her time a charming combination of small shops and restaurants and miniature parks, the old college that she knew Mikal had attended, which was an art museum, the grand old houses clinging to each other along tree-shaded streets that were still the homes of the wealthy, though no longer the exclusive province of the Amaden.

She shifted her gaze back to the hillside just below the fortress. Where there was now only dark forest, her home would one day stand: a handsome building of synthetic stone built into the hillside and composed of spacious apartments occupied mostly by university faculty.

"My home is down there, on that street that lines the park," Mikal told her, gesturing. "I sent a note to Bettena asking her to find accommodations for you in her neighborhood, if possible. It's only a few blocks away, in an area that's home to many artists and theater people."

Shayna nodded as she blinked away the tears. She knew the area, and it still remained that way: home to artists and musicians and theater people. She visited it often because she had friends there.

She knew Mikal's house as well. Although it had at some point passed out of his family, there was a small plaque on the stone wall that separated it from the street that announced it had once belonged to him.

She thought about the times when she'd walked past it, wanting to see the inside, wanting to walk where he had walked or to sit in the hidden garden where he must have sat. She'd felt the same way toward Lonhola and toward his family's keep, but those had been large buildings that had seemed less personal.

Mikal hooked a finger beneath her chin and drew her around to face him. "I hope those are tears of happiness, my love. You will be happy here; I promise you that."

He took her hand, and when she glanced at him, she saw a grim determination in his face as he stared down at the city. "I wish I could take you home with me now. We will marry, Shayna. When others get to know you, they will accept you."

He truly believes that, she thought, astounded at his capacity for forcing his will on those who would thwart his plans. She could almost believe it herself—except that it hadn't happened.

Mikal would never marry. Everyone assumed that he must have had mistresses, though historians of that time were too discreet to have mentioned them. Although it was unusual for a man of his position not to have a wife, no one thought much about it, assuming that his work had been his life.

Standing here now, with his hand curved warmly about hers, Shayna wondered if her arrival here had prevented him from marrying. Could it be that he would love only her for the rest of his days?

Yes, she thought as a painful lump grew in her throat, *it is possible—because I will always love him, too. Even before this, I loved him.*

A little over an hour later, the carriage passed through the open gate in the stone wall surrounding Mikal's home. He'd been quiet the whole time, but she knew what he was thinking. He was still bent on finding a way for them to marry. But for all the great successes he would know in his life, this would be his great failure.

Then, just as he extended a hand to help her from the carriage, a sudden thought struck her. *I must have found a way to get back to my own time,* she told herself. *If I hadn't, he would have married me at some point.*

But no sooner had that thought come than it slipped away into the murkiness of her situation and the fear that had brought her here. If the past could be changed . . .

"Bettena is here," he told her, pointing to a small carriage that stood nearby. "I know you will like her, my love—and she will like you."

Preoccupied as she'd been with too many other thoughts, Shayna had given little attention to the woman she was about to meet. She'd been very surprised when he'd told her about his patronage of the first great woman playwright—a secret that had survived the centuries—but she hadn't thought much about the woman herself.

She'd studied all of Bettena's plays, of course—including the ones she had yet to write. They were wonderful, and many of them were still performed regularly by the university's classical theater group. She was still thinking about those plays when they entered Mikal's house and the woman herself appeared in the foyer.

Bettena was a striking woman: not beautiful by any standard, but not forgettable, either. She was several inches taller than Shayna, with a longish face and a slightly hooked nose between bright black eyes with thick lashes. Her hair was a mass of black and gray, barely tamed into a knot at the back of her head.

Her bright red lips smiled at Mikal and she rushed to him. They embraced and Mikal kissed her cheek, then held her away and laughed. "I can see that you've been busy in my absence. You have a few more gray hairs."

They both laughed and Shayna knew that this must be an ongoing joke between them. Then, before Mikal could introduce them, Bettena reached out both her hands to Shayna.

"Welcome to Wantesa, Shayna. I can already see that you're very beautiful, but there surely must be more to you than that. Mikal has been surrounded by lovely women for years." She peered closely at Shayna.

"You haven't cast a spell on him, have you? What an interesting thought!"

Shayna smiled, albeit a bit nervously, since, try as she might, she still couldn't quite dismiss that possibility. And when she glanced at Mikal, she saw something flicker briefly in his dark eyes that suggested that if that possibility hadn't occurred to him before, it might be now. She smiled and shook her head, knowing that for now, there was nothing either of them could do about their suspicions.

"You haven't disappointed me, Bett," Mikal said dryly. "I knew that not even an Astasi witch could put you off stride. But I hope you haven't told anyone else about her."

"Of course not! I did, however, mention the possibility that a younger cousin might be coming to stay with me for a time."

Mikal grinned. "An excellent idea! But do you have room?"

"I do now. I used that excuse to suggest that Traya find her own lodgings. It's time to force her out from under my wing."

She turned back to Shayna. "Traya is a young actress who'd been staying with me until she could get herself established. But she's done that—so off she goes! Now all we have to do is to turn you into an Amaden and come up with a suitable story."

"For someone of your talents, that shouldn't be too difficult," Mikal observed.

Bettena laughed. "Your money and my talent, Mikal. In no time at all we'll make her the talk of the city."

Shayna stared at her reflection in disbelief while Bettena laughed delightedly, obviously proud of her work.

"I think we're ready to venture out to some shops," Bettena said as her dark eyes swept over her creation.

"It's time to start putting our story around."

"I can't believe that you could change me so much," Shayna said with dismay, unable to take her eyes off the mirror.

"Well, get used to it, dear. We don't want you fainting from shock every time you pass a mirror. Swooning is fashionable in some circles, but it's very inconvenient. Besides, Mikal isn't the kind of man to be attracted by that."

The transformation was truly astounding. Bettena had gotten her a luxuriant black wig of real hair. Shayna fingered it tentatively, hoping that there wasn't some poor woman out there somewhere with a bald head.

Then she'd set to work with her huge supply of cosmetics, working on Shayna until she felt more like a canvas than a woman. But the results had obviously been worth the effort. Her skin was several shades darker and her face actually looked somewhat fuller, with far less definition to her delicate features.

Only her eyes remained the same, but even there, there was a subtle difference, thanks to cosmetics and the colors Bett had chosen for the small wardrobe she'd assembled for Shayna before her arrival.

"Don't worry about your eyes giving you away," Bettena said as she put away her store of cosmetics. "Instead, you can worry about Nerela scratching them out when she sees you."

"Who's Nerela?" Shayna asked as jealousy slithered through her. Was she Mikal's mistress?

"She's a stroke of good fortune," Bettena said with a grin. "She arrived in Wantesa only six months ago, but she's already parlayed her eyes and her very limited talent into a gold mine. Green eyes are very rare among the Amaden, as you probably know, but she has them. So that will make yours less unusual."

She apparently saw Shayna's relief at this information. "She's not his mistress. As far as I know, Mikal doesn't have a mistress at the moment—though not for lack of effort on the part of a very large number of ladies." She smiled again.

"Of course, there are those who believe *I'm* his mistress, but that's not true. Mikal and I have been good friends for years, but never more than that.

"He's a good man, Shayna—one of very few who are capable of having a friendship with a woman. And very fortunately, he's also a very wealthy man. I'm afraid that I didn't put away much money while I was still on the stage, and if it weren't for Mikal, I'd be forced to teach now, rather than writing plays."

"I think you'd make a very good teacher," Shayna commented, thinking about all the instructions Bettena had given her to help her play the role of a lady in this society.

"I probably would be, but it's not what I want to do. What I want is to write plays for women—about women. Until I started, there wasn't a single play being performed that portrayed women as being anything more than decoration, or as harridans of the worst sort. It was very frustrating to me." She sighed.

"And it still is. My second play drew a much larger audience than my first, but I'm still not really accepted."

But you will be, Shayna thought, wishing she could tell Bett that. Even in her lifetime, her plays would achieve success—and three centuries later, when only theater historians would remember the names of most of her contemporaries, the name of Bettena would still be known to all.

Shayna was delighted to have made the acquaintance of this fascinating woman, but she was aware of the fact that, once more, she was treading close to the line established by the protocol. Her knowledge was a terrible burden—a far greater burden than she'd anticipated when they'd sat around the conference table, drawing up the rules for contact with people from another time.

The two women left Bettena's apartment and set out for a day of shopping. Bettena explained that she had accounts at all the best shops and would put Shayna's purchases on those accounts to help establish that Shayna was her country cousin who'd fled her small-town life after the death of her husband six months ago—that being a sufficiently long interval that she wouldn't be expected to remain in mourning.

"Of course," Bettena had said, "it would be helpful if you could manage a tear or two upon occasion for dear Paulus. And if you can't do that, then at least contrive to look wistful from time to time."

But Shayna forgot about her "widowhood" as they made their way through the shops. Instead she became the historian again, totally entranced by the daily lives of people and the beautiful city.

Bettena, it seemed, was known everywhere: not just by the shopkeepers, but by other customers as well. She explained to Shayna that she'd recently undertaken various forms of charity work.

"If there is to be a revolution, it must begin with the women of the upper classes," she told Shayna. "The others are too busy just trying to hold their lives together."

"A revolution?" Shayna echoed in surprise.

"A woman's revolution. I'm not foolish enough to believe that it will happen in my lifetime—but it *will* happen. I like to think that I'm sowing seeds that will bear fruit years from now."

And so they would, Shayna thought, already eager to carry back this bit of information. Bettena's plays were often credited with helping the status of women, but no one had apparently known of her other efforts.

"There is one young woman for whom I have great hopes," Bettena went on. "She is the only child of a wealthy merchant and she is already chafing at the restrictions placed on women. She confided to me when we were working at a settlement house that she has no intention of ever marrying because she won't let some man get hold of her money."

"What's her name?" Shayna asked, having already guessed who it might be.

"Milia Danfor. Her father owns a fleet of merchant ships."

Shayna hoped that she'd have the chance to meet her. Milia Danfor was credited with starting the suffrage movement and with pushing for laws that benefited women.

"We've had quite a few talks," Bettena said, pausing to peer into the window of a shop. "Her father is a tyrant, but he's very indulgent where she's concerned. I think, though, that if he knew what's in her pretty head, he'd have a fit of apoplexy. I, of course, am encouraging her as much as possible."

Then Bettena turned from the shop window and smiled, her gaze fixed on someone behind Shayna. "Good day, Estella. How nice to see you. Did you know that your brother has returned? I saw him just last night."

Shayna turned to see a tall, dark-haired woman of about her own age. She was striking rather than beautiful, and her clothing marked her very clearly as being a woman of considerable means. Even before the introductions were made, Shayna had guessed that this was Mikal's sister. She bore a strong resemblance to their mother.

It also became apparent as the women talked that there was no love lost between them. Shayna was certain that Bettena had enjoyed informing Estella of her brother's arrival in Wantesa—a fact of which Estella had obviously been unaware.

"Very good," Bettena said with satisfaction after Estella had gone. "That will establish how you met Mikal."

"But his family already knows about me," Shayna told her.

"Yes, but she doesn't—and I'm sure they won't tell her. Estella is a terrible gossip and she could never be trusted to keep a secret. I sometimes have difficulty believing that she even belongs to the family. It's a case of a woman with no mind of her own who simply latched onto her husband's thoughts. And he's a horror, believe me." Bettena laughed. "Well, I suppose that any family that has someone like Mikal must also have his opposite."

They finished their shopping and then had lunch at a ladies' tearoom. Shayna felt as though she'd walked onto a theater stage—with the playwright beside her. One of Bettena's most popular plays had a scene in a tearoom, and she saw that the set decorators had done a very good job of re-creating what lay before her now.

Once again Bettena seemed to know everyone, and Shayna was introduced to at least a dozen women, one of whom bore the last name of a friend and faculty colleague. She was startled to realize that she might well be meeting her friend's ancestor, and that made her think for the first time of her own ancestors. It would be interesting for her to meet them as well, she thought. But it wasn't likely she could get to the valley.

Shayna was so caught up in this new world that Bettena was showing her that she at first didn't recognize the man who tipped his hat to her as she and Bettena were about to climb into the carriage outside the tearoom. Then suddenly she froze.

"Haddar!" she exclaimed. He had done as good a job of transforming himself as Bettena had done for her.

He gave her a smug smile. "Are you enjoying yourself, Shayna? I hope so—because you won't be for much longer. We know he's here, and we know where he lives."

Shayna cast a quick glance at Bettena, who was frowning at Haddar, then stepped beyond earshot of her friend.

"Haddar, this has to stop! You must return. *We* must return. Mikal has a good description of you and your friends, and his men are looking for you." She paused. "And I've warned him that you might attempt to assassinate him."

She saw with some satisfaction that Haddar appeared to be shaken by that piece of news. But he recovered quickly and sneered at her.

"Pillow talk, Shayna? Does he know everything?"

"No! But I'm warning you, Haddar. The council has given me permission to use my powers if necessary—and I will!"

For one brief moment she had the great satisfaction of seeing fear in his eyes. But once again he recovered quickly.

"Why are you here alone? Where are the others?"

"Looking for you," she lied. "And we're all under orders to bring you back any way we can."

He studied her in silence for a moment. "I think you're lying. Something happened, didn't it?"

Out of the corner of her eye, Shayna could see Bettena watching them closely, and she suddenly realized that she was going to have to explain this scene.

"I must go. I assume you've already found out where I'm staying. If you come to your senses, come to see me."

And without waiting for a reply, she turned on her heel and walked back to Bettena and the waiting carriage. For one brief moment she feared that Haddar might pull out his stunner and strike her down. But when she turned toward him again, he was walking rapidly away.

"Who was that?" Bettena asked the moment they were seated in the carriage.

"A man I met right after I left the valley," Shayna lied, then added, "I'm afraid he's become somewhat obsessed with me."

"I'm surprised that he recognized you. Will he talk, do you think?"

"No, I don't think so. If I'm right about his intentions, he won't want to see me have to return to the valley."

But Bettena's question terrified her. Would Haddar do just that? It would certainly be a way to get rid of her, because if it became known that she was Astasi, she would be forced to leave Mikal.

Her pleasure in the day had vanished. Instead she was plunged back into the darkness of her lies and her fears for Mikal's life. And then she had a new fear as well. What if Bettena mentioned the incident to Mikal? If she did, he would almost certainly realize that it was the same man who'd tried to break into Lonhola.

"Please don't mention him to Mikal," she implored

her new friend. "I can handle this myself."

"No, of course I won't," Bettena assured her quickly.

But that did little for Shayna's peace of mind. She felt herself drawing ever closer to a horrible dilemma: either tell Mikal the truth, or weave an ever more elaborate set of lies that would sooner or later ensnare her.

Mikal couldn't seem to stop staring at her. Shayna wondered if he found her more attractive now that she looked Amaden. But it was no more than a passing thought. He'd fallen in love with her knowing she was Astasi—and a witch. Only now, in her disguise, was she beginning to realize just how extraordinary that was. If people of her own time still tended occasionally to regard the Astasi with a certain uneasiness, those of his time—and particularly the Amaden—looked upon her people with outright fear and loathing. She knew from her studies that many Amaden had urged that the Astasi be eliminated completely.

And yet Mikal loved her. That love shone from his dark eyes every time she looked at him. Bettena had already commented on it and had teased him that he should control himself better, since they were already the center of attention.

The three of them were dining at the city's most elegant restaurant, in a spot that had long since been transformed into a lovely park. Although Mikal wore formal evening clothes rather than his splendid uniform, it was immediately apparent to Shayna that everyone there knew who he was. He'd already received numerous congratulations on his recent promotion.

As Shayna watched him accepting the praises and congratulations, she thought about the words the historian, Maltus, would one day write about him: that greatness sat lightly on his shoulders. It was true, she saw now. He didn't disavow his heroism or his brilliance in battle. To have done so would have been disingenuous. Rather, he accepted it, but in a way that suggested he deemed it to be no more praiseworthy than if someone had remarked on the color of his eyes or the faint threads of silver in his hair. It was part of who he was, and nothing more.

She found herself being awed by him all over again: seeing not the gentle and passionate lover but the great man of history. And that had the effect of reminding her of her true situation here, and of the reason she'd come in the first place.

What could she do? She certainly couldn't be with Mikal all the time. Neither could she be certain that he had taken her warning about a possible assassination attempt seriously. From the conversation, she knew that he must spend his days in very public places: mostly at the large building in the center of the city that housed the Amaden tribal council, with its elected representatives. And from what she could gather, when he wasn't there he was at the fortress on the hill overlooking the city, where he apparently maintained an office.

It seemed unlikely to her that Haddar would try to attack him in either place—at least not at this point. Haddar might be willing to give up his life in a suicidal attack, but Shayna doubted that he was desperate enough to do that yet.

If only she knew what Haddar was capable of. Did he have any weapons other than a stunner? Stunners couldn't kill, but this was a time when guns were readily available, and she had to assume that he'd gotten hold of one of the small, crude handguns of the time.

Shayna chafed under the ridiculous restrictions placed upon her because of her sex. She wanted to try to find where Haddar and his henchmen were staying, but as a woman, she couldn't roam about the city easily. Furthermore, it seemed likely that they would be staying at one of the many small inns near the harbor, where sailors of many races and tribes stayed. Haddar was Amaden, but his companions weren't, and they would attract less attention there.

"Shayna?"

She blinked, pulling herself from her thoughts to look up into Mikal's dark eyes.

"You haven't touched your soup," he pointed out gently. "Are you ill?"

She shook her head and picked up the silver spoon. She'd already discovered that the food of this time was quite good—but there was far too much of it, and since she'd come to Wantesa she'd learned that the diet of the wealthy, at least, was one that would have horrified the people of her time: thick, rich sauces and huge quantities of meat. Mikal had ordered for them and it had sounded to her as though he were ordering for an entire army.

She glanced over at Bettena and saw the frown of concern on her handsome face. Bettena hadn't mentioned the encounter with Haddar again and had seemed satisfied with Shayna's story about his obsession with her. Neither, insofar as she could tell, had Bettena mentioned the incident to Mikal—but Shayna knew that could change, regardless of Bettena's promise, if she believed Shayna was worried or frightened.

She felt that sticky web of lies wrapping itself about her again and forced herself to pay attention to the conversation. Bettena was talking about her new play. She was having second thoughts about certain scenes even as the cast began to rehearse. Shayna was very familiar with the play, since it was one of Bettena's most popular. She had, in fact, seen a performance of it only a few months ago—three hundred years later, of course.

"Why don't you just carry through with the dollhouse imagery?" she suggested. It was introduced early in the play as a metaphor for much of her heroine's feelings of entrapment, and the scene Bettena was talking about now was much later in the play.

Shayna was feeling rather proud of herself for having suggested this—especially since she knew that the change would in fact be made. Strictly speaking, she was tampering with history, but it seemed to her to be a minor transgression. After all, Bettena was free to accept or reject her suggestion—though Shayna knew that she would accept it.

But the horror of her mistake washed over her in ice

cold waves as soon as the words left her lips. How was she to explain her knowledge of the play? She was appalled to realize that she could have been caught up by such a stupid blunder.

Bettena remained silent. Her body had gone very still. Mikal glanced from one woman to the other, clearly puzzled. Shayna thought fast. She'd seen a manuscript at Bettena's that must be the play. And Bettena had gone out for a time in the afternoon.

"I read it while you were gone," she said with a smile and a shrug. "I hope you don't mind. It's very good."

"The dollhouse," Bettena echoed softly. Her gaze remained on Shayna for a time, then flicked briefly to Mikal. "Yes, that's an excellent suggestion. Let me think about it and we'll talk later."

Shayna could barely restrain the sigh of relief that wanted to come out. She'd managed to escape a trap of her own making. The young waiter appeared at that moment to take away their soup dishes and bring the next course. This world that she didn't belong to seemed to settle down again.

"Come with me," Mikal said, laying a hand on her arm as the carriage pulled up in front of Bettena's home.

"Is that wise?" Shayna asked, even as tiny curls of heat began to unfold within her. She'd spent only one night away from him and already she wanted him as though they hadn't seen each other for months.

He smiled. "Nothing about this is wise, so we risk nothing by pushing it further."

She nodded, and he left to see Bettena to her door. The two of them stood there talking for a moment, and Shayna's desire for Mikal was quickly drowned out by fear. What if she were telling him now about Haddar? Or had she made another mistake, and Bettena was talking about that? Bettena had been unusually subdued after the discussion about her play, and Shayna could only hope that it was just because she was thinking over the suggestion about the dollhouse.

She held her breath as Mikal climbed back into the

carriage, then released it with a sigh when he leaned over and kissed her with soft passion.

"You make a lovely Amaden, but I prefer you as a red-haired witch."

She laughed. "I'm afraid that there's less red hair now. Bett had to cut it so that it would fit under the wig."

Mikal leaned back in his seat as the carriage pulled out. "You like her, don't you?"

"Very much," Shayna replied honestly. "She's been very kind to me."

"She's quite intrigued by you. In fact, she says that you might well become an inspiration for her next play."

Shayna couldn't quite stop the small cry of surprise that escaped her lips. Since she wasn't a student of theater history, she couldn't be certain which play was Bettena's next, but what had come immediately to mind was her personal favorite: *Shadows*. It was an unusual play—different from her others—and that difference had been the subject of much speculation over the years.

Shayna felt a chill that was half fear and half wonder. *Shadows* was the story of a woman who was invisible, a woman who moved through people's lives, transforming them in many ways but without their ever being aware of her presence.

She looked over to see Mikal watching her intently in the light of the carriage lamp. And she thought, "That's exactly what I am." She was a shadow moving through their lives: unknown and unknowable. As a result of her passage, Mikal would never marry, and Bettena would write a play that would confound her future admirers.

She shivered and Mikal reached over to pick up the shawl that lay on the seat beside her. He draped it across her shoulders.

"Don't worry, love. This isn't as dangerous as you may be thinking. No one will see you come to my house because we'll be inside the walls, and I'll get you home before dawn."

She very nearly laughed at this reminder of the fact that he was, after all, a man of his own time, concerned about a woman's reputation. But she was touched by that concern, nevertheless.

The carriage moved slowly down the street where Mikal lived, a narrow street of walled homes and huge old trees. Then, just as the carriage halted so the driver could open the gate, Shayna felt a sudden sense of danger.

Across the street from Mikal's house stood several thick-trunked trees close together. And just as she peered out into the darkness, she saw a figure slip from behind them and run off. She caught only a quick glimpse, but she was relatively certain that it was Haddar's student accomplice.

"What is it?" Mikal asked sharply. From where he sat, he couldn't have seen the man.

"Someone was behind those trees," she said, though she knew that he must be long gone by now. The street was very dark, except for scattered gas lamps on the stone walls of the houses.

Mikal leaped from the carriage and ran into the middle of the street, and she called after him, "Mikal, he could be armed!"

But no shots rang out, and when Mikal returned to the carriage, she saw that he had a pistol in his hand. She hadn't even known that he was carrying one. Perhaps it had been in the carriage.

He ordered the startled driver to get inside the walls, then rejoined her after he had closed the gate. Shayna took some small satisfaction from the fact of his being armed. It must mean that he believed her about the danger.

He took her hand to help her from the carriage, then drew her into his arms as the driver continued on to the carriage house at the rear of the property. But much as she craved the comfort of his arms, Shayna knew that there was something she could and must do first. She pushed away from him.

"Go into the house, Mikal. I'll join you in a few minutes."

He stared at her as though she were mad, and even in the midst of her fear, she nearly smiled. Mikal Har-Amaden wasn't accustomed to being ordered about—and certainly not by a woman.

"I'm going to cast a spell," she said bluntly. "It will protect your home—and you. I'll stay inside the walls."

"No."

"Don't be foolish, Mikal! You know I can protect myself—and now I want to protect you as well, at least when you're here."

"Then I'll stay with you while you . . . do it."

"No, you won't. You'll distract me. It won't take long."

She knew that he might indeed distract her, but the real reason she wanted him to go inside was that she didn't want him to see her employ her magic. She could just barely accept those powers herself, and she knew it would be just as difficult for him. Knowing about them was one thing; seeing them was quite another.

They stood there in the darkness, facing each other stubbornly. She could almost hear the clash of strong wills in the quiet of the night. And she was not unaware of just who this man was that she was ordering around.

"If you don't go inside now, I'll leave—and then I'll come back later and cast the spell."

He stared hard at her for a long moment, then abruptly turned and walked toward the door. She waited until he had closed it behind him, savoring this small victory perhaps more than she should have. But how could she not take a small measure of satisfaction from having just bested a man who was not so far removed from godhood? It felt as though the delicate balance of their relationship had just shifted in her favor. And she was aware, too, of a need to assert herself in this world that believed women to be inferior to men, even though Mikal, at least, claimed not to share that view.

And he doesn't feel that way, she reminded herself. In his final years he had lent his great prestige to the cause of women's suffrage and to changes in other laws as well.

She walked toward the wall, feeling guilty over having provoked the confrontation. She could have found another way to accomplish this. It was even possible that she could cast the spell from inside the house, where she surely could have slipped away from him for a few moments.

Fear and stress are driving me to dangerous mistakes, she thought, wondering how long it would be before one of those errors became irreparable.

Her powers came with surprising speed and almost no effort on her part—which did little for her peace of mind. But she gathered them within her, then began to push them toward the wall.

The wall completely surrounded the property, including the large gardens at the rear. It was high, but not so high that one man couldn't boost another to the top. Furthermore, there were huge old trees along the street, with large branches that spread over the top of the wall. She figured that sooner or later Haddar and his men would try to climb it, because trying to kill Mikal in his home would be easier than attempting to assassinate him in public.

She made her way slowly around the inside perimeter of the wall, her mind focused on her task. But as she reached the gardens at the rear, she could nonetheless sense that Mikal was inside the house watching her. She imagined what he would see as he peered out into the darkness: a dark shadow surrounded by a faint bluish light, and an equally faint glow along the wall for a few seconds. Was he recoiling in horror? She thought that she would be if the situation were reversed.

When she reached the back corner and turned to make her way along the far side of the property, she paused briefly and glanced toward the house. No lights were visible in the rear, but she knew he was there. She could feel his presence as a sort of deep, powerful hum inside her. She'd never felt that before and assumed it must be because she was using her magic.

She finished her circuit and sent her powers back down deep inside her, imagining them as a molten lump of blue fire smoldering there. The feeling was not unpleasant, though, and she still felt that pleasurable tingling that accompanied their use.

She smiled as she thought what would await Haddar and his men if they tried to scale the wall. Probably it wouldn't kill them, though she couldn't be sure—and quite frankly she didn't much care. In all likelihood, if one of them were killed, it would be the result of being toppled from the wall by the force of the magic.

She thought that she really should warn them about what she'd done, and that brought her back to trying to find out where they were staying. But before she could give any further thought to that, she became aware again of Mikal's presence and turned to see him standing in the open doorway, silhouetted by the large gaslight chandelier in the foyer.

She wanted to flee into the night rather than face his disgust with her, but a hope that he would understand propelled her to him. She couldn't read his thoughts from his shadowed face, but when he stepped back and she entered the house, then turned to face him, it was all there in his eyes. She saw love—but she also saw fear.

It isn't so very different from the way I feel, she thought suddenly, though the cause of that fear was very different. *I love him, but I too fear—fear that I will hurt him or that I will make that one terrible mistake that could alter the future.*

"What will happen if anyone tries to get over the wall?" he asked.

"I'm not really sure. The spell will prevent them from getting onto the property, but beyond that I don't know. I've never done this before." She added that last hoping that he would understand that it was difficult for her.

He closed the gap between them and cupped both hands around her face. "It seems to me that you're very uncomfortable using your magic. Is that part of the problem you were having that made you leave the valley?"

She was shocked that he'd guessed her discomfort. She shook her head. "I wouldn't be uncomfortable using it if I were there. Everyone uses magic in one form or another there."

"Then you're uncomfortable because of my reaction?"

She nodded.

He released her face and drew her into his arms. "I can't pretend that it doesn't bother me, but I knew you were Astasi when I fell in love with you, Shayna. Believe it or not, it's easier for me to accept your magic than it is for me to accept that you must pretend to be Amaden."

She tilted her head back and stared up at him. There was nothing he could have said right now that could have made her love him more than those words had done.

Their lips met, and a moment later he picked her up and carried her up the curved staircase to his bedroom.

"Take off that damnable wig," he ordered in a voice thick with desire. "I may have to tolerate the disguise in public, but I want *you* in my bed."

She smiled and pulled out the pins that held it in place, then tossed it aside and shook out her red hair. He reached out to touch it. "I'm sorry it had to be cut."

"Mikal, please don't blame yourself for this. I don't blame you."

He smiled bitterly. "I don't much like a world where fear and hatred can keep people apart."

She stared at him as his words echoed through her brain. Could this be the reason that he would work so hard all his life to end the hatred and fighting? Had she already affected that future? If so, she had no regrets. She smiled at him.

"Then work to change it. Make a new world where all people can live in peace."

He reached for her. "Right now all I want is to make love to you. The world can wait."

And so it did. Once more they created a separate world for themselves, a place where two people who should never have come together could meet in a hot, fierce passion. If he was less gentle than he'd been before, she understood that. He'd seen that part of her he couldn't capture, and his desire to possess what he could became even greater.

She too needed to feel his love, needed to surrender all of herself to him and to take as well. Her body, so recently possessed by ancient magic, seemed to be melting from his caresses. And when he thrust into her, he drove them both to dizzying heights—and then into mindless oblivion to a place where she would have gladly spent the rest of her life.

And in that one all-too-brief moment when they shuddered together, she looked into his eyes and let herself believe that it could happen.

Chapter Seven

"Shayna, there is something I must ask you."

Shayna felt a thrill of fear run through her as she nodded. She was sure that Bettena was about to bring up that incident with Haddar. They were breakfasting in Bettena's apartment the next morning. Shayna was tired after a night spent in Mikal's arms, followed by a predawn return to Bettena's.

"Can you read minds?"

Shayna hid her relief as she shook her head. But then, even before Bettena spoke again, she suddenly recalled that conversation over dinner, when Bettena had seemed surprised at her mention of the dollhouse in her play. Uneasiness replaced her very short-lived relief, and she wished she hadn't been so quick to deny that she could read minds.

"Then how do you explain the fact that you brought up the use of a dollhouse in my play? You said that you'd read it—but if you had, you would know that it isn't there."

"But you were thinking about it?" Shayna asked, her

mind racing to find some way out of this latest disaster.

Bettena nodded. "Yes. I visited a friend a few days ago, and she had just bought a very elaborate dollhouse for her daughter's birthday. I watched the child playing with it and thought about how little girls are taught to think of the home as being their world. It's been on my mind ever since."

Shayna told herself—with limited success—that she wasn't really responsible, then. Bettena would have changed the play even without her interference. Then she thought about the other play—the one Bettena had yet to write—about an invisible woman who changes the lives of those around her.

"We can't truly read minds, Bett," she said honestly. "But there are times when we pick up certain thoughts or feelings, especially if those thoughts or feelings are very powerful. Since we've been together so much lately, I must have picked up something without trying. I'm sorry if I've upset you."

"You haven't," Bettena said, her dark eyes sparkling. "All you did was to confirm my own thoughts. I'm going to change the play and include the dollhouse."

Bettena continued to talk excitedly about the changes while Shayna breathed a quiet sigh of relief. Another disaster had been avoided. There'd been a few times in her life when she'd regretted being Astasi, but she thought that she would never feel that way again. Without her people's history of magic to cover her mistakes, she would probably have gotten herself into an untenable situation before this.

The two women finished their breakfast and carried their cups of tea with them as they went to enjoy the sunny morning from the small balcony off Bettena's living room that overlooked a large garden.

"Bett, I need your help with something. I won't be angry if you won't or can't help me—but if you agree, Mikal must not know."

"If I can help, I will," Bettena assured her. "And as to Mikal, he's a dear friend, but I don't feel any obligation to run to him with your confidences."

"Thank you. I really appreciate it. I don't like to hide things from Mikal, but this is something I must deal with on my own."

"That man," Bettena said.

"Yes," Shayna acknowledged. She wasn't surprised that Bettena had guessed. The lie she'd given her at the time was a weak one. "I need to find him. He has two friends who aren't Amaden, so I think they're probably staying in one of the inns near the harbor."

"But who is he, Shayna? How did you meet him?"

Shayna threw her friend a look of regret. "I met them right after I left the valley. They're violent, evil men. They tried to kill me just because I'm Astasi. I got away by casting a spell on them, but I should have done more.

"When we ran into him here, I found out that he knows about my cousin. He left the valley a few weeks ago, after a quarrel with his family. I'm sure that he'll return once he calms down, but this man claims that he and his friends know where Mevas is staying. And if they find him before he comes to his senses, they'll surely kill him."

"I'm not surprised," Bettena said, shaking her head angrily. "There are still many people who hate the Astasi because they fear them. But can't your cousin defend himself with his own magic?"

"Mevas is only fifteen," Shayna explained. "His powers are not yet fully developed. I could try to find him, of course, but given the way he feels about our family right now, nothing I could say to him would send him back. In fact, it could only reinforce his determination to stay."

"But if he hates the Astasi so much, you're in danger as well."

"No. After what I did to him and his friends, he won't try to harm me again."

"What do you intend to do to them if we find them?" Bettena asked curiously.

"What I should have done when I first encountered them. I'll cast a spell on them that will take away their memories of us both."

Bettena gaped at her in openmouthed astonishment. "Can you really do that?"

"Yes," Shayna said, though of course she couldn't. "I didn't do it then because they caught me by surprise and such a spell is more difficult than the one I used to get away from them."

"Still, even if he can't actually do you any harm, he could cause problems for both you and Mikal," Bettena said, frowning.

"Exactly. I was wondering if you might know someone who could help me find him. I know it would be impossible for me to track them down myself."

"I know just the man, and he owes me a favor—more than one favor, actually. He's an actor and he spends much of his time drinking in the harbor taverns. I'll get word to him right away, and when he comes here, you can give him descriptions of these men.

"Then, if you have to go down there to meet with them, I know someone else, another actor, who can take you there. I wouldn't trust Hari to be able to protect you, and you'll need good protection in that part of the city."

"Well, you've done a proper job of tarting her up, Bett. I hope you know that my reputation is going to suffer as a result of this favor."

"Ha! Your reputation is quite beyond suffering, Jan. In fact, she's an improvement on your usual companions."

Shayna laughed as she stared at herself in the mirror. Bettena had suggested that it might be a good idea for her to look as though she belonged in the waterfront area—and now she did. She wondered if Haddar would even recognize her. Instead of the black wig, she was now wearing one in a pale blond shade that Bettena had assured her was all the rage among prostitutes. Then she'd applied makeup with a very heavy hand—and now she stood back, admiring her work as Jan lounged in the bedroom doorway, watching.

Janteg Halvis was the friend Bettena had persuaded

to take her to the inn where Haddar and his allies were staying. Hari had found them quickly, as Bettena had said he would.

Bettena hadn't mentioned Jan's name until he showed up, and then it hadn't been necessary. The young man she met was still years away from his fame, but Shayna recognized him immediately. A friend of hers had written a biography of him, and even though the photographs in the book showed a man some ten or fifteen years older, there was no mistaking that craggy face with its brooding dark eyes.

Still, it made her wonder how she'd known him immediately, while she'd failed to recognize Mikal, whose face was so much better known. She thought that she would never again doubt the mind's ability to deceive itself. At the time Mikal had found her, she'd thought she was in a later time, and so had shoved aside the nagging voice that told her he looked familiar.

Bettena had hired a small open carriage for their expedition to the city's seamy underside, explaining to Shayna that her own carriage would be too ostentatious for such a trip.

"Not that the toffs don't go down there, of course," she'd added with a chuckle. "But they don't go in daylight."

Having been told she was new to the city, Jan kept up a running commentary as they drove slowly through crowded streets. He knew nothing of her relationship with Mikal, having been told only that she wished to confront this man who'd been harassing her. Shayna thought that he suspected there was more to it than that, but he had said nothing.

They were seated together on the leather bench as Jan drove the open carriage, and as she turned to him at one point, she remembered the jagged scar that she'd seen in the photographs. It wasn't there now: a thin, ridged line running from the corner of his eye down along his cheekbone. Obviously he'd acquired it at some later date.

Shayna was getting better at handling such things,

but each time it happened, she still felt that eerie disorientation. Furthermore, she was becoming convinced that the whole idea of time-travel was too dangerous. The temptation to insert oneself too deeply into people's lives was just too great.

They were now passing through the very center of the city, moving at a snail's pace in the heavy traffic. There were men on horseback and women in elegant carriages, and large, heavy carts carrying goods. In another hundred years these same streets would be choked with automobile traffic and the noxious fumes they brought. Then, finally, they too would be gone, replaced by the underground transport of her own time, and the streets would be reclaimed by people and trees and gardens.

If it hadn't been for Jan's comment, she would never have seen Mikal, because she was lost in thought over the many changes this wonderful city would see.

"Well, there's the hero and his entourage," Jan remarked dryly. "Have you met him yet? He's a friend of Bett's."

Mikal was just getting out of his carriage as they inched forward. They were now opposite the building that housed the Amaden government. He didn't look her way as he strode toward the entrance, surrounded by a phalanx of uniformed men. But even if he had, she was certain he wouldn't have recognized her. Nevertheless, she was still relieved when the traffic began to move again and they left him behind.

"Yes. I met him the other night," she told Jan, assuming he would learn that sooner or later.

"I met him at a party Bett gave after the opening of her first play. That was before the Battle of Darwana had made his reputation, though he was still well known, of course, because of his family."

"What do you think of him?" Shayna asked curiously as he turned onto the street that led down to the harbor. Ghosts of buildings that wouldn't exist for several hundred years lined the streets in her mind.

"I studied him all evening because he intrigued me. I

don't think I've ever seen a man so totally comfortable with himself—even though he was clearly out of his element at that party. Everyone else there was in the theater.

"Bett said that that's what money and power does, but I think it was more than that. Mikal Har-Amaden has a presence that owes nothing to his wealth and position."

He turned to her with a grin. "I've been trying ever since to mimic that quality, because the best actors have it too—but unlike him, they have to work at it."

"He's very . . . impressive," she agreed, since some sort of comment seemed to be required.

"He's not married, either," Jan said as he guided the carriage off to the side of the street, easing it in among several others whose horses were tied up to hitching posts. "See that house over there—the one with the red shutters?"

Shayna nodded, assuming that must be where Haddar was staying. She pushed aside her thoughts about Mikal and began to concentrate instead on how she was going to handle this meeting.

"I have it on good authority that the general has been known to visit there. Of course, it might just be for the gambling."

"Oh." Shayna belatedly realized that it wasn't an inn.

"The best in the city," Jan said with a grin, then peered at her closely. "You're not shocked, are you? I'd forgotten that Bett said you came here from the country."

She covered her queasiness with a smile. "I may be from the country, but I'm not an innocent, Jan."

"The inn where your man is supposed to be staying is only a few blocks. It's easier to walk."

They got out and walked across the street. Just as they reached the house Jan had indicated, a trio of women emerged and Shayna saw that they all had the same pale blond hair: clearly wigs like her own. Then another woman hurried out to meet them and Shayna drew in a sharp breath. She had long red hair and very pale skin. Surely, she thought, staring unabashedly at the woman, she can't be Astasi.

All four of the women had reached the street by the time she and Jan were passing the house, and Shayna saw immediately that the woman was in fact Amaden, but had apparently lightened her skin with makeup. She was confused for a moment as the women stared at her, then abruptly realized that they probably thought they were seeing the competition.

"They're not bad," Jan said teasingly after they'd passed the women. "But they can't hold a candle to *you.*"

Shayna laughed. "I don't think I'm going to thank you for that compliment."

In truth, the women were lovely, or they would have been without the garish makeup. She was trying hard to quell that twinge of jealously she'd felt when Jan had mentioned Mikal's visiting the place. She knew it was foolish. For all that he seemed so different in some ways, Mikal was still a man of his time.

"Was that one woman pretending to be Astasi?" she asked Jan.

He nodded. "Astasi impersonators are very popular. The customers like to pretend they're with a witch. There are some fortune-tellers who pretend to be Astasi too."

"I thought most people hate the Astasi."

"No. The military hates them because they fear them, but most people are just fascinated by them. I know several people who have gone to their valley on the pretext of needing to be cured of some illness. But they're always turned away."

Shayna found this information very interesting. It reminded her that virtually all that was known of this time had come from the military historians, not from ordinary people. And it explained why her people had been accepted after they'd signed the Unification Pact. Once Mikal had persuaded them to renounce their magic, no one had really feared them.

"I suppose that out in the country where you come from, there are still people who think the Astasi are evil, but no one here believes that anymore."

Shayna had to hide her smile. Jan was obviously trying to impress her with his sophistication. But he was right about one thing: in this time, the differences between city-dwellers and their country cousins were very great. That wouldn't change for another hundred years or so, when technology made the world much smaller.

"Did you grow up in Wantesa?" she asked, knowing that he hadn't.

"No, I grew up in a little village in the north, called Werand. You've probably never heard of it. But I got out of there as soon as I could."

Once again Shayna smiled inwardly. There was no one in her world who had not heard of Werand. It had long since grown into a city, and thanks to its location in the foothills of the Ice Mountains, it had become one of the most popular vacation destinations in the world.

She commented on the fact that the streets here were nearly deserted, and Jan chuckled. "This is a nighttime place," he reminded her. "With luck, we'll find your man sleeping one off."

A block farther on, he pointed out a gray wood-frame building similar to many others on the narrow street. "That's it: The Gamecock. If Hari got it right, you'll find him in room two-oh-three."

They entered the inn. On the outside it had appeared to be marginally better than its neighbors, but when she entered the small lobby, she decided that any attempt to dress it up had stopped at the door. The place was dark and shabby and it smelled of a combination of things Shayna didn't want to think about.

An elderly man was dozing behind the high counter just inside the door. Without disturbing him, Jan leaned over the counter to peer into the dark corner where the boxes were.

"We're in luck," he told her as he took her arm and led her toward the stairs. "The key is missing, so he must be in."

When they reached the top of the staircase, he stopped and turned to her. "Do you want me to wait outside while you talk to him?"

Shayna nodded, grateful for his thoughtfulness, which probably hadn't come easily, since she was sure he was very curious.

"Okay, I'll stay out of sight. Just make sure he keeps the door open. If he closes it, I'll come running."

They walked down the empty hallway, and Jan stopped several doors away, gesturing her to proceed. She strode up to the door of room 203 and knocked loudly. She'd already rehearsed what she intended to say, but she was very conscious of Jan's presence. If Haddar began to shout . . .

She heard a shuffling sound behind the closed door, and then it opened a crack. But the man who stared blearily at her wasn't Haddar, and it wasn't one of his allies, either.

He opened the door wider, and Shayna winced at the odors that swarmed out of the room. He leered at her with broken, yellowed teeth.

"Come in, girlie. Did Shem send you, then?"

Shayna backed up a bit to get as far away as possible from the smell. "I'm sorry. There must be a mistake. How long have you been in this room?"

"Since yestiddy noon. Come in." He reached out to grab her, but Shayna took several steps away—and then Jan hurried to her. When the awful little man saw him, he just slammed the door.

"I take it that's not your man," Jan said as they moved farther down the hall. "Hari might have gotten the room number wrong."

Shayna stared at the line of closed doors, thinking that she certainly didn't want to knock at any more of them. "Can we check with the man at the desk downstairs?"

"Exactly what I had in mind."

When they reached the dark little lobby, Jan went up to the high counter and rapped sharply on it. The old man jumped nervously, then glared at Jan. Jan described Haddar and told him he'd been led to believe he was in room 203. The man stared at him as though he might be deaf. But when Jan produced a gold coin, the man's hearing returned quickly enough.

"Left yestiddy, they did—all three o' them. One o' them—the young fella—couldn't hardly walk. Looked like he hurt hisself somehow."

"It sounds as though you don't need to worry about him anymore," Jan said as soon as they were outside.

Shayna nodded, breathing the salt-scented air gratefully. If only that were true.

As they walked back toward the carriage, Shayna let herself believe for a time that Haddar might have given up and gone back. The man at the inn had said that Haddar's young student was injured, and she had immediately guessed that the injury might be the result of a failed attempt to climb over the wall at Mikal's. Perhaps they'd seen the futility of their evil mission and given up.

She tried to put herself in Haddar's place. When she'd seen Mikal this morning he'd been completely surrounded by armed soldiers, so it was obvious that he was taking precautions. Therefore, attempting to assassinate him in public would be nearly impossible. Furthermore, it now seemed likely that Haddar hadn't managed to get his hands on any weapons other than stunners, which meant that he was limited to the crude weapons that existed in this time.

And now, if she was right about the source of the student's injuries, Haddar knew he couldn't hope to get at Mikal at home, either. So what course of action was left to him?

But long before they reached the carriage, Shayna discarded her hope that he would return home. Haddar certainly knew that he faced severe punishment. She wasn't sure what crimes he would be tried for: certainly the theft of the time-craft, but possibly even attempted murder.

Violent crime was rather rare in her time, but it did exist—and the punishment was harsh. Those convicted were sent to an island patrolled by the security force's boats and hovercraft. Prisoners were left to rule their own prison, and the results were anything but pleasant. Haddar was a proud man, and she could not see him risking such a punishment.

No, she thought with a chill, *he will not return to that. He will return only if he accomplishes his goal, because then he would be returning to a very different world—probably one ruled by his people, the Amaden.* He obviously was convinced that the future could be changed, or he would never have come here.

"They probably found out that someone was asking around about them," Jan said, breaking into her thoughts. "Hari isn't exactly discreet at the best of times, and when he's down here, he is definitely not at his best."

"Yes, I think you're right," Shayna replied. But she considered it just as likely that her warning to Haddar about the soldiers had driven him away.

As they were passing by a tavern, two soldiers suddenly emerged. Shayna saw that one of them was carrying several pieces of paper. The two men reached the sidewalk just as she and Jan were passing, and the soldier who was carrying the papers hailed them.

"We're looking for these three men," he told Jan after his gaze had swept over her appraisingly. "Have you seen them?"

Shayna stared at the three sketches. They were remarkably accurate—especially the one of Haddar. She remained quiet, glancing covertly at Jan as he studied them with a frown. She'd given him their descriptions.

"Try the Gamecock, just down the street. I saw some men who looked like that coming out of there yesterday."

Shayna groaned inwardly. She knew that Jan was just trying to help her by siccing the soldiers on Haddar and his men, but he might be getting himself into trouble as well. When the soldiers talked to the old man, they would find out that the two of them were also looking for their quarry. She at least was in disguise and unlikely to be recognized, but Jan's identity would be much easier to establish—especially since he was an actor and perhaps already fairly well known.

"Well," Jan said, watching the soldiers as they hurried down the street toward the inn, "that's interesting. It appears that you're not the only one they caused trouble for. But I wonder why the military is looking for them, instead of the constabulary."

"I met up with them not far from Lonhola," Shayna said, already trying to adjust her story in case Jan was questioned later. She and Bettena had told him that the men had accosted her en route to the city from her village. "Perhaps they caused some problems there."

"That would explain it," Jan said. "Well, I think it unlikely that they'll be bothering you again, with the soldiers after them."

They passed the bawdy house again. Two women were seated in a swing on the big front porch. One of them was either the same woman Shayna had seen earlier disguised as an Astasi, or else there were two Astasi impersonators in the house.

It really bothered her to think that Mikal had frequented such a place, even though she tried to remind herself that such behavior was common among men of his class and time. But the truth was that she didn't want him to have feet of clay. She was still struggling with the contradictions between the giant of history and the very real man he'd become to her.

She recalled a professor saying once that heroes such as Mikal Har-Amaden had become nonexistent once communications improved. If Mikal had been born a century later, his face would have been plastered across the pages of the tabloids. But in Mikal's time, journalists as well as historians maintained a careful distinction between the public and private lives of heroes.

She smiled sadly, recalling how she'd sat in that class so smugly, convinced that not even the most intrepid journalist could have found anything unsavory about Mikal Har-Amaden. Even at the age of eighteen, she'd already put him on a pedestal. But then, so had others. From their very first history lessons, they were all taught that he was a flawless hero.

She was wondering idly if she would tell others what she'd learned about him when Jan suddenly stopped, then took her arm and began to propel her toward a street vendor who was pushing his cart slowly along.

"Let's have some ices," he said. "Have you had them before?"

She told him that she hadn't, and they went up to the man. He was pushing a wooden cart that she now saw was filled with shaved ice. Nestling amidst the ice were waxed paper cones of very thinly shaved ice in a variety of colors.

"Well, what flavors have we here?" Jan asked eagerly.

When the man told them what he had, they both chose raspberry. Jan paid for them and they stood there nibbling at the ice. It was very good, though sweeter than she was accustomed to. She'd already noted that the people of this time seemed to be addicted to sugar. Recalling her history, she remembered that the Amaden would have just made peace with the land far to the south where sugarcane was grown.

She exclaimed delightedly over the ice, since she knew Jan would be expecting that, and then he asked if she'd had ice cream.

"No," she lied with a frown. "What is it?"

"Ahh, it's wonderful! It's made from frozen, flavored cream and sugar. Only a few places have it. You must try it." He paused for a moment.

"There are so many new things now. Some people are beginning to call this the Age of Discovery. I've heard that someone has invented a horseless carriage. A friend of mine actually saw it. It runs on a gasoline engine." He stopped. "Do you know what gasoline is?"

Only that it was responsible for polluting the air for a couple of centuries, she said silently as she shook her head. Jan went on to explain about oil and gasoline while she thought about his remark. The Age of Discovery hadn't stuck, since it was subsumed into the Period of Unification, but it was true that many important and life-changing discoveries had been made at this time. Jan was enumerating them now as she thought about an old argument among historians over the importance of those discoveries in bringing about peace.

Many historians—herself included—believed that Mikal's grand scheme had been successful at least in part because these discoveries and inventions had filled people's minds with the hope that the world could indeed become a better place.

She was staring at the remains of her ice cone and thinking about how such small things had played their part in history, when Jan suddenly made a nervous sound. She followed his gaze and saw the two soldiers approaching them. Immediately she berated herself for not having insisted that they get out of this place quickly. She had no real fear for herself because she believed that her disguise would hold, but she feared that Jan was in trouble.

"The clerk must have told them that we were looking for their quarry," Jan said as the two soldiers hurried up to them. "I should have thought of that."

The soldiers were polite but insistent. They demanded to know why Jan had inquired about the men they were seeking. Before he could respond, Shayna spoke up.

"I was the one who was looking for them," she told the soldiers. "I asked him to accompany me. I believe that one of them is a man who's been bothering me. I've just arrived here in Wantesa and he accosted me on my way to the city—near Lonhola."

"When was this?" The one soldier asked sharply.

She told him. He looked her up and down. "And what exactly did you mean when you said that he was 'bothering' you?"

His tone, which was half contempt and half amusement, made Shayna realize her mistake. She'd quite forgotten her temporary disguise.

"I choose my companions," she replied coldly, drawing herself up in a semblance of righteous anger. "And I didn't like his looks. He seemed to me to be dangerous."

She was hoping that he believed her, but when he

ordered the two of them to accompany him and his partner to see their captain, she felt the first faint stirrings of real fear. Still, she wanted to protect Jan, who was completely innocent in all this.

"Very well," she said icily. "But I can tell him nothing more than I've already told you. And there's no need for my friend to come along. He was only trying to help me."

"I'll come along," Jan said, taking her arm.

The soldiers got their horses and directed them to what was apparently a small garrison near the tribal headquarters. Then they rode directly behind Jan and Shayna as they made their way back to the center of the city.

"I wish you hadn't felt the need to protect me, Jan," she said as they rode through the increasingly congested streets. "This isn't your affair."

"I couldn't let them take you to the garrison—not in that disguise. They'd be wanting to do more than question you."

"Oh," she said, silently berating herself for having forgotten the position of women in this time, and especially of the kind of woman they assumed her to be.

Shayna had to suppress a shiver as they passed by the guards into the small garrison. She knew she didn't dare invoke Mikal's name to get her out of this, and she wondered how much influence Bettena would have, should it become necessary.

They were led into a small, bare room that contained only a battered table and four chairs. The door locked behind them with an ugly sound.

"Well, if it comes to that, we'll get Bettena down here," Jan said. "She'll back us up."

"But will they pay any attention to her?"

"They will if she uses Mikal Har-Amaden's name."

Shayna sank into a chair, hoping it wouldn't come to that, but already trying to formulate a story for him. Still, if Bettena got in touch with Mikal, she would no doubt tell him the tale Shayna had given her. So whatever lie she told Mikal, it would have to conform to that.

It was another of those moments when she felt that web of lies tightening around her, threatening to smother her.

One of the soldiers returned with a tall, austere-looking man who was apparently the captain. She repeated her story. He asked for more details involving her encounter with Haddar and his allies. She did her best to provide them, but she could see that he was skeptical. Deciding that it was because she looked like the type of woman who wouldn't turn down any man, she edged closer to the truth.

"I know what you must be thinking about me—but I'm not a prostitute. When we set out to search for them, we didn't know where we might have to go, and it seemed best if I looked as though I belonged in that area."

The captain peered hard at her and then nodded. She breathed a silent sigh of relief, certain that he believed her. Her accent and her bearing would surely have convinced him. But she had gotten out of one trap, only to fall into another, more dangerous one.

"Then please explain to me why you were determined to find this man in the first place. From what you just told me, he'd only approached you once since you arrived here in Wantesa—and then he did nothing more than make some unpleasant remarks. It seems to me that a woman in your situation would simply have avoided him."

Angry now, Shayna glared at him. "I didn't want him to be following me around."

"And exactly how did you intend to prevent him from doing that?" the captain asked with a slight sneer.

"I was planning to threaten him myself," Jan said, speaking for the first time.

The captain glanced briefly at him, then returned his attention to Shayna. "When he accosted you near Lonhola, was he carrying a weapon of some sort—a small silver cylinder?"

Shayna wasn't prepared for that question, but she shook her head quickly. "I didn't see anything."

The captain stared hard at her for a moment, then got up and left. The other soldier followed him from the room, and once again the door was locked behind them.

Jan said that perhaps it was time to call upon Bettena for assistance, but Shayna barely heard him. She could hear only the sounds of her carefully constructed world tumbling down around her.

To all outward appearances, Mikal was a man of infinite patience. He had that quality of being able to remain utterly still and attentive, even as his mind ranged far from the discussion, with only a small part of it attentive enough to catch something important.

The tribal elders, most of whom were his relatives, had called him here to listen to his appraisal of the situation among their recently defeated enemies. He'd accomplished that in his usual succinct fashion, and now, for the past two hours, he had been forced to listen to their own assessments and their arguing among themselves.

His mind drifted toward the evening—and Shayna. He wished they were back at the cabin. Being separated from her was more difficult even than he had guessed. He thought about her creamy, smooth skin and how she trembled beneath his touch—as he trembled from hers.

Then he found himself wondering—not for the first time—how many lovers she'd had before him. His jaw clenched briefly before he remembered where he was at the moment and once more adopted an expression of quiet interest.

It was an interesting question, though he'd never get an answer because he wouldn't ask it. In some ways she seemed as skilled and as assertive as any of the women at Veranna's—but in other ways, she seemed almost virginal.

He barely managed to restrain a smile as he thought about the two women there who posed as Astasi witches, and he wondered if Shayna would be offended or amused. It was as difficult to guess as anything was with her.

He was being very patient, certain that at some point she would be willing to be honest with him. But for now she was guarding her secrets closely. It was possible that she'd told Bettena things she hadn't told him, but he knew better than to ask Bett.

The door behind him opened. "Your pardon, General, but there's something I thought you might like to know."

Mikal turned to see the captain who'd been put in charge of the search here in Wantesa for the men who'd attempted to break into Lonhola. "What is it, Captain? Have you found them?"

"No, sir. But we have two people over at the garrison, and I think the woman knows something she isn't telling us."

Mikal got up and excused himself from the meeting, then listened to the captain's story as they started toward the garrison.

Shayna was seated in one of the chairs, her back to the door. Jan was pacing back and forth in the small room, then pausing to look out between the bars in the single, tiny window. He was saying that it was time to insist upon their rights as citizens not to be held against their will without being informed of the charges against them. Shayna was about to say that they should be patient and not anger their interrogators, when the door behind her opened. She saw the stunned look on Jan's face—and only then recalled that they'd seen Mikal earlier, going into the adjacent tribal headquarters.

"General," Jan said. "I'm Janteg Halvis. We've met before, at—"

"I remember," said the familiar deep voice. "You're an actor."

Shayna didn't move, even though she knew that her failure to turn toward him would seem strange. She was paralyzed with fear. Even her mind seemed frozen, unable to begin to find a way out of this. Mikal knew nothing of her supposed encounter with Haddar and his allies, unless Bettena had told him her tale, and she doubted that. How was she going to explain her failure to tell him, when she'd known they were the men he was seeking? Even if he accepted the rest of her story, he'd never accept that omission.

Mikal was now standing before her, on the other side of the table. She kept her head down, staring at his powerful hands that rested on the high back of a chair. Perhaps he wouldn't recognize her, especially if she kept her gaze averted, feigning shyness.

"The general would like to hear your story, miss," the captain announced.

The light in the room was dim, coming only from one small lamp affixed to the wall, plus the small amount of daylight that came through the narrow, heavily barred window. She remained silent, wondering if she could change her voice as Bettena had instructed her. She risked a quick glance at Mikal, then lowered her gaze again. She'd seen no sign of recognition on his face.

After another prompting by the captain, Shayna told her story. Fear thinned her voice, and she did her best to adopt a country accent. Mikal didn't interrupt her, and by the time she finished, she knew that even if he did recognize her, he wasn't going to admit it here.

She glanced up at him once more. *He doesn't recognize me,* she thought incredulously. *He can't be that good at concealment. He sees what he expected to see: a woman pretending to be a prostitute.* She was reminded of her own failure to recognize him at first because she'd expected him to be much older. And yet there was the question of Jan, and the fact that he knew Jan to be a friend of Bettena's.

"It seems to me, miss, that it would have been better for you to have either avoided this man, or to have reported him to the constabulary."

"Perhaps that's so," she replied, emboldened beyond caution now. "But they would have done nothing—and

I wanted to be sure he didn't cause me any more problems."

Nothing changed in Mikal's neutral expression. "Did he have a weapon of any kind?"

She shook her head as she lowered it again. It was too difficult for her to keep looking at him. "No. They already asked me about that. I didn't see any weapon."

"Well, I think you have no need to fear him anymore, because he appears to have left the city. And if not, we'll soon have him."

He turned to the captain. "Let them go. They've told us all they know."

The captain nodded, but Shayna could see that he disagreed with Mikal's assessment. Still, he followed orders. As soon as Mikal had left the room, he escorted them to the gate, where they'd left their carriage.

As soon as they'd driven through the gate and out onto the street, Jan let out a sigh of relief. "I think if the general hadn't come, they'd still be questioning us. That captain didn't believe our story." He paused and glanced at her briefly as he guided the horse through the heavy traffic. "I can't say I blame him. I don't believe it, either."

"What do you mean?" Shayna asked, startled out of her thoughts about whether or not Mikal had recognized her.

"I guessed from the beginning that something else was going on here, but it's probably just as well that I didn't know." He turned again to grin at her. "It's always easier to lie if you're lying honestly."

She laughed, partly at his humor and partly because she might have escaped yet another time.

"He didn't seem to recognize you," Jan said as the carriage came to a temporary halt in heavy traffic. "Didn't you tell me that you'd met him just the other night?"

"Yes, but only briefly—and I didn't look like this."

"Still, I would have thought he'd recognize you, with those Astasi eyes."

Shayna covered her surprise quickly as she realized

that the term must be used to describe any Amaden with green eyes. But the remark made her more certain than ever that Mikal *had* recognized her—and that this episode hadn't yet played itself out.

Chapter Eight

Shayna could not relax, even though she tried very hard not to show her nervousness. She and Bettena were dining once again with Mikal, who had brought along another man, a banker who seemed very interested in Bettena. The man was a distant cousin of Mikal's and had apparently met Bettena before.

I'm safe enough for now, Shayna thought as course after course arrived at their table. He won't say anything with this man here, and perhaps not even in front of Bettena.

She had told Bettena what had happened, and Bettena had confirmed her fear that Mikal must have recognized her. "The wig and the paint couldn't hide you from him," Bettena had said. "The man is clearly in love with you—and he's far from being blind."

So she ate her dinner and contributed to the conversation and tried not to think about what lay ahead. She hadn't yet come up with an excuse for her failure to tell Mikal that she'd encountered Haddar and his men. By the time they left the restaurant, Shayna had adopted an attitude of fatalism. He would question her, she would be unable to give him answers—and that would be that. Mikal loved her, but no love could stand up to lying for very long.

I've done all that I can, she told herself. *He is well protected. Now I must get Bettena to find me some men who can help me track down Haddar. And failing that, I must go back to the valley and search for their time-craft.* She didn't want to think now about what would happen if their craft had also been destroyed or couldn't be found. It had become increasingly clear to her that she could not expect any help to arrive. Teres and the others would certainly have been able to build another craft, but they were undoubtedly seeking her in a later time, years from now, when Mikal was already engaged in his great quest.

Outside the restaurant, she discovered that she was to be left alone with Mikal very soon. Somehow his companion had arranged to see Bettena home in his carriage, leaving her to go with Mikal.

He was quiet as the carriage made its way slowly along the streets, and still silent as they entered his house. She wished suddenly that she'd pleaded a headache or tiredness, but she knew that would only have postponed the inevitable.

He didn't draw her into his arms the moment they were alone in the house, and Shayna knew with cold certainty that he would never do so again. What should never have begun between them was now over.

Of all the emotions she was feeling right now, the most powerful was the terrible pain of knowing that he would go through his life alone, never forgetting how he'd been betrayed by the woman he loved. Perhaps *betrayal* wasn't the right word, but she knew that he would see it that way. Lies between lovers were the worst sort of betrayal.

"It's a pleasant night," he said, breaking the long silence. "Let's sit in the garden."

The garden was lovely, filled with the mingled scents of many flowers carried to them on the soft breeze.

They sat in two cushioned wooden chairs placed at right angles, with a table between them.

"Do you mind if I smoke?" he asked, drawing out a thin cigar.

She shook her head. She'd smelled them several times since she came here and thought the odor was terrible, but perhaps he needed it, just as he might need the brandy he'd poured for himself after she'd declined. *He's in pain too,* she reminded herself. *This is as difficult for him as it is for me.*

"Must I ask for an explanation, Shayna?" he said in a soft voice.

"I . . . I wasn't sure that you'd recognized me."

He stared at her in obvious disbelief as a wreath of smoke curled around his face. "Even if you somehow managed to change the color of your eyes, I would have known it was you. In fact, I knew it was you even before I saw your face, despite that ridiculous wig and the dress."

"I have no reason for not telling you that I'd seen them," she said. "At least no reason I can give you."

"So we're back to that: your secrets. You love me, but you don't trust me."

"I do trust you, Mikal. I told you before that I've taken an . . . an oath. And I can't break it—not even for you."

"I've thought a lot about that oath," he said, his dark eyes hooded as he stared at her through the haze of cigar smoke. "And I'll be damned if I can think of anyone other than your own people to whom you could have sworn this oath. But you already said that this has nothing to do with them."

"It doesn't. And I also told you that the people to whom I've sworn it are not your enemies."

"How can you be sure of that?" he challenged. "We have many enemies—a constantly shifting array of them. You've lived a very sheltered life in your valley, and you can't possibly know that much about the situation."

His patronizing tone drew forth an anger from her that she hadn't expected. But then, it felt as though *all* of her emotions were close to the surface just now.

"I know far more than you can guess, Mikal—more even than you yourself know." She regretted her rash words—but too late.

"That's impossible," he scoffed. "Don't play these games with me, Shayna."

She hated seeing him like this: so arrogant and patronizing. It was yet another reminder of those feet of clay that she wasn't willing to grant him.

"I know it's impossible—but it's also *true*."

For one brief moment, she saw the beginnings of doubt in his eyes, though she wasn't quite sure what it was that he doubted.

"You can't possibly know that these people aren't my enemies—or soon to become my enemies. What hold can they have over you that you're unwilling to tell me the truth?"

When she said nothing, he went on. "I think that your people are involved. I think that they've somehow convinced you that an Astasi alliance with some other tribe could end the wars. But what they really intend is to destroy us."

"No, Mikal, you're wrong. The Astasi will never fight the Amaden again."

"There are some among our tribal council who believe that it's time we destroy the Astasi so that such a thing can't happen."

She was horrified. It hadn't happened, but how could she be certain it wouldn't happen unless she took some action—unless she changed the future?

"Do you agree with them?" she asked.

"No—and at the moment that may be all that is saving your people." He gestured at her with the cigar. "Understand this, Shayna. Your people might have been able to defend themselves in the past, but we're much more powerful now. Men will die, but Astasi magic is no longer a match for our weaponry."

"Will you promise me one thing, Mikal? Will you promise me that if the decision is made to attack the Astasi, you'll talk to me first?"

"I can't make such a promise, Shayna. I can't trust you not to warn them. They'd still lose, but I could lose more men."

"If it comes to that, I will tell you the truth," she said, getting up from her chair. "But that truth will change everything."

He got up too. "Including the way I feel about you? Will it change that as well?"

She didn't look at him as she shook her head. "No, Mikal, but it will cause you great pain even so. Please take me back to Bettena's now."

She started to turn away from him, but he reached out and wrapped a hand around her shoulder, drawing her back again. "You never intended to stay here, did you?"

She met his gaze and heard the pain in his voice and knew what it must cost him to let her see his vulnerability.

"I can't stay, Mikal, but I do love you, more than I can ever say."

When dawn arrived the next morning, Shayna was still awake, sitting on the small balcony of Bettena's apartment. She was barely aware of its arrival, having unconsciously willed herself into a sort of trance that her people had once used regularly.

The Astasi believed in the importance of what they called the "inner life"—the life of the mind in all its depths. Whenever an Astasi had an important decision to make, or sometimes when the lives of those around him became too burdensome, he retreated into himself for a time.

Shayna knew about this, of course, but she'd never before felt the need to practice it—until now. And even now it was wholly unconscious, as though her mind had slowly slipped into that state without any prompting.

The only thing that was certain was that she had to take some sort of action. Until now it seemed to her that she'd merely waited passively for events to shape her actions. It wasn't her nature to be passive, but the shock of finding herself alone in this strange world had inflicted that upon her. Now she knew that she had to break free—to chart a course for herself.

Noises from the kitchen finally roused her from her stupor. Bettena's housekeeper had arrived, though Bettena herself had probably not yet awakened. Shayna came out of her trance feeling a mixture of exhilaration and trepidation. She had reached a decision, but it was one fraught with both difficulties and dangers—and not just to herself.

Mikal's face swam in her mind's eye: that moment when she'd turned at Bettena's door to find that he too had turned. Neither of them had said a word on the brief trip from his house to Bettena's, and the silence continued as he had walked her to the door. But she had seen the naked pain in his dark eyes—and now she feared that that would be the image she would carry with her for the rest of her life.

There was nothing more she could do for Mikal—but too much that her continued presence here could do *to* him. She had protected his home and he was protecting himself in public. With soldiers searching both the city and the countryside for Haddar and his men, it seemed likely that they would lie low, for a time at least.

She had decided to go to her people. She thought it unlikely that Mikal was right about them conspiring with another tribe against the Amaden, but she couldn't be sure. In the history she knew, it hadn't happened, but Shayna was haunted by the possibility that it hadn't happened only because she herself had arrived to change things.

Then, after visiting them and satisfying herself that there was no conspiracy—or preventing it from happening if there was—she would try to find Haddar's time-craft. She would have to assume that it had landed not far from her own ill-fated craft; after all, they had followed its pathway. If she found it, she would then return to her own time and get some help to deal with Haddar.

If she didn't find it, she would then return to Wantesa and begin searching for Haddar again—unless, of course, he'd already been captured by the soldiers.

Beyond that, she could not go—not even in her thoughts. There were only so many plans she could make, only so many eventualities she could consider. She felt like a blind person, feeling her way cautiously through unknown and unknowable terrain.

"Bettena, I must leave . . . and I need your help."

"Leave? Do you mean that you're going to return to your people?"

Shayna nodded. "I must. I've been very selfish. My family will be worried about me."

Bettena looked relieved, but only for a moment. "But you're not certain that you will be coming back to Wantesa, are you?"

"No, I'm not," Shayna replied honestly. She thought about how both Mikal and now Bettena had somehow known that her stay here would be only temporary. Was it possible that at some deep, unconscious level they both knew that she did not belong to this place and this time?

She decided that it was likely that they had guessed only because she was Astasi, because her people were as much aliens as she was in this time and place.

"But what about Mikal? Does he know this? I cannot believe that he would let you go."

"He knows," she said, though that wasn't quite true. She hadn't said *when* she would leave.

"Mikal loves me, but he knows that we can never make a life for ourselves. I know that it troubles him greatly that I can only be his mistress."

"But he has no intention of keeping you as his mistress! He told me that we would be introducing you as my cousin who was recently widowed, and when an appropriate amount of time had passed, you would marry."

Shayna was stunned. It was true that Mikal had spoken of them marrying, but she'd thought it only wishful thinking. She was reminded again of how determined he could be—something she knew better than he did at this point.

"That will not happen," she said softly. But she wondered. Her love for Mikal whispered to her that perhaps it could be. She could rewrite history and be there for him, at his side as he transformed the world.

But if she were here, would he spend the remainder of his life single-mindedly pursuing that goal? Or would his love for her interfere?

Bettena had been quiet, but now she spoke slowly, her dark eyes boring into Shayna. "You know that, don't you? You've seen the future."

"Yes, I have." It was a relief to speak those words, even though Bettena believed them to be the result of her magic. And so she pushed it further.

"Mikal will be a great man, far greater than he or anyone else can know now. He will change the world, Bettena."

Bettena continued to peer at her intently. "I think that those of us who know him well will not be surprised. But why can't you be with him? You've passed well enough for an Amaden."

"Because I can't. Mikal must be free to play the role destiny intends for him. My presence could change that."

Bettena leaned across the breakfast table and took Shayna's hand. "You know more about this role he is to play than you've told me, don't you?"

"Yes." She squeezed Bettena's hand. "I am glad that he has you for a friend, Bett. He will need friends like you."

She drew in a deep breath. "What I need from you is help with yet another disguise—and some money as well. Can you turn me into a man?"

Tears were sparkling in Bettena's eyes, but she brushed them away and laughed. "I can't turn you into a man, but I think I could make you look like one—unless someone looks too closely. Why do you want that?"

"Because I must travel alone."

"But I could take you in my carriage to Lonhola, and from there you could return to the valley safely as a woman—certainly as an Astasi."

Shayna had considered that, but she wanted to travel alone, in case she encountered Haddar on the way.

"No. I appreciate the offer, but I must travel alone."

"All right, then. Do you want to leave today?"

"Yes, if that's possible."

Shayna guided her horse off the road and up the slope to the same spot where Mikal had showed her Wantesa for the first time. She dismounted and stood there, gazing at the beautiful city whose golden stone glowed softly in the midday light. When she saw it again, would it be this city—or the city of the future?

Then she shifted her gaze to the restless sea that lapped at its shore. A wave of unutterable sadness swept over her. Twenty-four years from now, that sea would claim Mikal's life—just at the time when he should have been able to relax and enjoy the fruits of his success. The historian Maltus, writing about Mikal, had said—or would say—that Mikal had lived as long as it was necessary for him to live, and that he had gone to his death knowing that.

She turned the horse back to the road, raising her face to the breeze to dry her tears. She had a long way to travel—and a very uncertain future. The irony struck her that she knew Mikal's future and she knew the futures for Bettena and for Jan as well, but she could not know her own.

As she rode along, passing others on horseback or in carriages and carts, she silently thanked Bettena's skills. No one was paying her any attention at all. Bettena had cut off still more of her hair, then hidden what remained beneath a visored cap of a type commonly worn by workingmen. She'd also acquired the rough, nondescript clothing such men wore, and then she'd carefully applied makeup that subtly hardened Shayna's features. With the visor of the cap pulled as low as possible, and the loose clothing hiding her curves, she would pass.

Her voice was the chief problem. It was low for a woman, but still recognizably female—at least until Bettena had coached her. Shayna had already decided not to stay at an inn and to carry her food with her, but she thought that if it became necessary for her to speak briefly with anyone, she could manage to sound like the youth she appeared to be.

Bettena had been concerned about her sleeping outdoors, but Shayna reminded her that she didn't look prosperous enough to be a candidate for robbery—and besides, if she were truly in danger, she had her magic to protect her.

So she rode until dusk, then found a well-used campsite that was fortunately unoccupied this night, and settled down as comfortably as possible beneath the stars. By this time tomorrow, she would reach the valley.

Shayna already knew that she would be forced to break the protocol when she found her people. The Astasi population was far too small for her to simply blend in. But she also knew that, of all people, the Astasi were most likely to accept that she had come to them from the future. They were a people who lived with magic, and even though she hadn't arrived here through magical means, they would believe that and accept her.

Her willingness to break the protocol in this case made her realize that at least a part of what kept her from breaking it for Mikal was that, unlike her own people, he wouldn't believe her.

She was aware too of the fact that she was willing to change the future if necessary where her people were concerned, while at the same time she was unwilling to take that risk with Mikal. But in the grand scheme of things, in the long history of their world her people were unimportant—no more than an oddity. The same was not true of Mikal Har-Amaden.

It was late the next day when she first saw the great fortress high on its craggy peak. For just a moment

Shayna could believe that she was back in her own time. Lonhola and the land around it were essentially unchanged because the entire area, even including the small village at the base of the mountain, was part of a historical area. People in costumes mimicked the real villagers of this time.

But she shook off her homesickness and turned onto the road that led through the village. She could not afford to let her mind wander now, because this was the dangerous part of her journey.

At the far side of the village, the road forked. A broad thoroughfare began its winding way up the mountain to the fortress, while a narrow road led into the forest toward the pass that was the only way in and out of the valley.

Her timing was good, she thought. The shadows were already lengthening along the narrow trail. She was riding a dark horse and was dressed in dark clothing, which should also help to make her invisible to the guards in the fortress tower. She didn't know if they patrolled this road, but if she encountered any challenge, she was prepared to say that she was seeking the healing powers of the Astasi. Bettena had said that no one was prevented from going to the valley to seek such help. The soldiers were only interested in making sure that no Astasi left. And Shayna thought that they probably also checked to be sure that no one other than Amaden made the journey, lest they be foreign agents trying to enlist the Astasi's help against the Amaden.

So it didn't really surprise her when she heard hoofbeats behind her and turned to see two soldiers approaching. In spite of her dark clothing and the deepening shadows, the guards had spotted her from the tower.

She stopped and waited for them, carefully hiding her fear even as her heart thudded rapidly and seemed about to rush up her throat. She would use her magic on them if necessary, but she didn't want to risk that.

"What's your business here, lad?" the one soldier demanded.

"I'm wantin' their help," Shayna said. "It's said they'll cure people."

"And just what is it you want to be cured of?" the soldier asked as his companion circled around her.

"It's m'heart, sir. It's weak and sickly." She was hoping that her slight build would back up her claim of illness.

"So you're not afraid of the witches?"

"Oh no, sir. M'da knows people they've helped."

"Well, it's likely you'll have to wait till morning. You'll see the camping place. Don't go any farther than that until they come to you—if they come at all, that is."

They clattered off down the road, and Shayna was barely able to prevent herself from riding just as hard in the other direction. She'd made it! In a short time she'd be safe with her people.

She kept her horse to a slow pace as she rode on through the narrow pass. She wasn't at all sure that the guards in the fortress tower could see her now because it was very nearly dusk and she was deep within the forest, but she didn't want to arouse their suspicions again. They couldn't follow her into the valley, but she feared doing anything that might cause trouble for her people.

As she rode along she thought about her ancestors. She came armed with a great deal of knowledge about them, but she wasn't one of them. The Astasi of this time were so isolated, and therefore were inclined to be highly suspicious of the world beyond their valley—with good reason.

She, of course, had nothing to fear from them. The very fact that she would be admitted to the valley eliminated any possibility that she was an impostor. The valley's entrance was guarded by a powerful spell, as it had been from the beginning, and continued to be even in her own time. The reason the spell still existed was that no one knew how to remove it.

Visitors to the valley in her time simply bypassed the spell by arriving in hovercraft or by private aircars. Those few who traveled the road she was taking now were met by Astasi guides. Scientists, including some who were Astasi, had studied the spell for years now, seeking a way to eliminate it. The spell was an annoying, if unimportant, vestige of a time everyone wanted to forget.

Shayna was curious about these people, who included her own ancestors. The Astasi had never kept written records of their lives, their practices, or their beliefs because there was no need for written records. Instead information was simply passed down from one generation to the next, on the assumption that they would all continue to live in their valley forever.

In Shayna's case, that had proved to be true. Several of her family continued to live there. But entire families had left the valley, beginning two centuries ago—a hundred years after Unification. And even before that, a few had gone to find new lives in the outside world.

She thought that most of what she knew of her people would prove to be true, but there was always the possibility that misinformation had crept into the storytelling over the centuries, or that important information had been lost, perhaps deliberately. It would not be far off the mark, she suspected, to say that the Astasi were inclined to paranoia.

Even so, she doubted very much that the Astasi would contemplate an alliance with another tribe against the Amaden, with whom they'd now lived in peace for some years. Mikal was right when he said that Amaden weaponry was far superior to Astasi magic, but she was certain that the people she was about to visit couldn't know that, and therefore believed themselves to be secure in their valley even with Amaden cannons trained on them.

The path she was following climbed a steep rise, then dipped again, and at the bottom she could just barely make out the narrow gap between high rock walls that was the spellbound entrance to the valley. Dusk was rapidly turning to darkness, but she could see those familiar stone sentinels and was immediately engulfed in a wave of nostalgia.

As a child she'd hiked many times to this place to feel all that remained of Astasi magic. All children in the valley did it, and so too did children and even adults returning to the valley for a visit. The Astasi of her time were clearly of two minds where that spell was concerned. They spoke often of wanting to be rid of it, and yet they came here to feel its magic.

She brought her horse to a halt in the clearing near the entrance, where the trampled ground showed the remnants of many campfires built by those who came here in the hope of being cured. They waited here until an Astasi came to meet them. Many were turned away, but some lucky ones were cured.

The ancient healers among the Astasi were very judgmental people. They could look into the hearts and minds of those who sought their assistance, and only those deemed to be good people were cured. But although the people of this time didn't know it, whether or not they were healed also depended on the progress of the disease. The healers never attempted a cure if they knew there was no hope. But if the terminally ill were good people, then they could at least take away the pain and allow them to die in peace.

Bettena had told her that few people actually came here to be cured, however, because the Amaden feared the Astasi too much, and as their own medical science improved, they placed their trust in that.

Shayna urged her horse forward again, already anticipating the feel of the spell, and then remembering only at the last moment that her horse might well feel something too.

She kept a tight rein on the animal as she rode toward the stone sentinels. Its ears went up and it snorted, but it obeyed her commands.

Then the feeling came: a soft warmth and a tingling that touched every fiber of her being. Her hands, which clutched the reins tightly, glowed with the blue fire, and an even paler nimbus of blue totally surrounded her.

The horse snorted with fear and shied, trying to back away from the narrow passage. But she kicked it, urging it forward—and then the feeling died away and they were into the valley.

Shayna sent soothing thoughts to the horse and patted it as she stared at the long, narrow valley spread below her. It was the valley of her birth and of her childhood—and it wasn't. The Astasi who remained in the valley continued to live in stone houses much like the ones she saw now, but in her own time they were much larger, and only a few retained the thatched roofs.

The fields below her were still planted, but at the end nearest the village, there was now a landing area for hovercraft and aircars and a visitors' center staffed by Astasi volunteers. In her teens, Shayna had been one of those volunteers, who served as guides to outsiders visiting the valley. People from all over the world came here, though their numbers were carefully controlled, and they always had many questions.

In the growing darkness, she could just make out the near end of the village, where lamps had already been lit in the tiny houses. The spot where her own childhood home stood lay at the far end of the village, which was hidden from her now in the darkness.

The horse had recovered from its fright and they rode on, down the steep path to the valley floor, and then on through fields that had recently been planted. The valley of the Astasi had some of the richest farmland in the world.

It was full dark by now and the moon hadn't yet risen, so she was nearly upon the riders by the time she saw them. She'd been expecting that. There were those among her people who could sense the disturbance in the spell even in her own time. Her mother was one of them.

She brought her horse to a halt and waited for them, straining to see them in the darkness. There were three of them: two women and a man. They stopped a short distance away, blocking the narrow road. After waiting for them to speak, Shayna raised both her hands in the old formal greeting.

"My name is Shayna. I have come—"

"We know who you are, Shayna," one of the women said, her voice as gentle as her demeanor. "Welcome to your home."

"You knew I was coming?" Shayna asked in surprise. Even though there'd always been far-seers among her people, somehow she'd thought that their talents wouldn't extend to visitors from another time.

"Yes. We have known of your presence ever since you arrived here."

"Do you mean since I arrived at the entrance to the valley?"

The woman smiled. "No. We have known about you ever since you parted the veils of time and arrived in this world."

"Oh." Shayna wondered if they thought she'd used magic to accomplish that, and whether or not she should tell them the truth. She decided to wait.

They introduced themselves, and she learned that Amika, the woman who'd spoken, was a direct ancestor of hers, or so she claimed. Shayna had no real way of knowing. The Astasi hadn't kept family records any more than they'd kept records of their lives.

"The gods have sent you to us at a very troubling time," Amika told her as they rode toward the village. "They must regard you highly to have worked such powerful magic through you."

Well, thought Shayna, that seems to answer my question about how they think I got here. "What are these troubles?" she asked.

"That can wait until tomorrow, after you've eaten and rested," said the man. He had pure white hair and a deeply lined face and was much older than the other two. Shayna guessed that he was one of the Elders, the elected leaders.

She saw, as they entered the village, that the news of her arrival had spread quickly. People stood silently outside their homes, watching as she passed by with her escort. The attention made her nervous. She'd known that they would be curious about her, but she hadn't expected to be thought a messenger from the gods.

They rode on through the village, and then she was alone with Amika as the other two turned into their own homes. Before they'd even reached Amika's little house, Shayna knew that it must stand on the same piece of land where her own family home was now located.

The first thing she saw as Amika led her through the doorway into the cozy cottage was a loom with a partially completed tapestry. Drawn to it, she bent to examine it in the lamplight, then drew in a sharp breath.

Only a small portion of the tapestry was completed, but she knew it was the one that hung on her mother's wall. The colors had faded badly over the centuries, but it was this tapestry that had given her her own interest in weaving.

"This is lovely," she said to Amika. "The colors have faded, but my mother still has it." It felt surpassingly strange to be telling her ancestor this, but Amika merely smiled.

"That is happy news. As I work at it, I often wonder what will happen to it—or even if I will finish it before my eyes and hands grow tired."

She offered Shayna simple but good food, but she asked no questions. Finally, unable to contain herself any longer, Shayna asked her if they understood that she came here from a future world.

"Yes." Amika gave her a lovely smile that reminded Shayna of her grandmother. "Do not think we are not curious, but the Elders have decided that it would be unwise for you to tell us about it. It is enough for us to know that the Astasi still survive."

"We not only survive, but there are still Astasi living in this valley. I myself grew up in a house on this very spot."

Amika smiled again, but put a finger to her lips as an admonition to Shayna to say no more.

She was not averse, however, to answering Shayna's

many questions about life here in the valley. Shayna discovered no discrepancies between her knowledge and Amika's descriptions. The Astasi used their magic in the normal course of their lives: to bring the rains or hold them off, to cure illness or soothe a crying child, and to move heavy objects.

They were far more religious than even the most devout people of her own time, which she'd already guessed. They worshiped all the old gods separately, devoting much of their time to this activity.

Amika was unmarried, though she was well past the age when most Astasi chose mates. This was unusual, but not unheard of. Astasi marriages required the agreement of the Elders, who sometimes decided that couples were not suited to each other. Shayna learned that this had happened to Amika, and that the man in question was now married to someone else. Amika accepted what she called the "will of the gods" and was not bitter.

That, of course, had changed long ago. Couples still sought the approval of the Elders in Shayna's time, but if they didn't get it, they married anyway in a civil ceremony outside the valley. Receiving the blessing of the Elders was to be cherished, but only because it guaranteed a happy life together. Her parents had received such a blessing.

As she lay in the too-soft bed that Amika provided for her, Shayna thought that it was just as well that the Elders had forbidden her to talk of the future. She suspected that these people would be unhappy if they knew that the Astasi had long ago given up their gods and that most had left the valley to live in the outside world.

She fell asleep wondering what troubles these people believed had caused the gods to exercise their great powers and bring her here.

Chapter Nine

Shayna ached. Every muscle in her body was protesting. She couldn't believe that she'd let herself get so out-of-shape in such a short time. But ladies in this world didn't exercise—unless, of course, they were Astasi.

The Astasi were commonly believed—at least in this time—to have been austere and rigid and very serious. They were, in a way, but they engaged regularly in ritualized dancing as part of their worship of the gods. "Dancing," to the rest of the world in this time, meant stately, slow movements, but to the Astasi it meant leaping and spiraling and doing things that no normal human being could do. And Shayna, to all intents and purposes, had long since become a "normal" human being.

The Astasi who remained in the valley in her time still danced, as Shayna herself did as a child, but these dances were a pale imitation of the dancing she was drawn into now, because the proscription against using magic didn't yet exist.

At home, in her own world, Shayna had discovered

some years ago, to her delight, that science had very nearly caught up to Astasi magic. There were places one could go—just beginning to appear when she was in college—called Lo-Gravs where in special chambers of lowered gravity one could leap great distances and do many of the things that the Astasi had once done with their magic. She'd been going there for years now, and was renowned among her friends for being outstanding in this new dance form.

But in the month before her hasty departure for this world, she'd been very busy and had stayed away from the Lo-Gravs—and now she was paying the price. She'd already been stiff from the long ride on horseback and had foolishly hoped that the dancing would improve the situation.

Shayna was just barely able to drag herself off to the warm springs after three hours of dancing. In her own time, men and women shared the baths, wearing minimal skinsuits that would have scandalized her present companions. But in this time the sexes were, of course, separated—and even so, the women wore light shifts into the fragrant, bubbling waters.

She sighed with relief as she slipped into the scented waters, and after a few moments she smiled with her memories. Every teen in the valley sneaked out to these waters as often as possible—and they certainly didn't wear skinsuits, either. It had been going on for generations, though each new generation thought they were the first to do such a daring thing.

But if the waters were relaxing her abused body, they were doing little for her mind. A whole day had passed, and still she knew no more about the troubles Amika had alluded to. Her arrival had occasioned an entire day of singing and chanting and dancing and feasting.

Shayna was very uneasy with the role ascribed to her by her ancestors. It was clear that they all believed her to be a messenger from the gods themselves. She wanted to be honest with them—and perhaps she would be at some point—but discretion seemed to be called for until she knew more about these "troubles."

Yet another feast awaited the dancers—Shayna included—when they emerged from the baths. She'd thought it impossible for anyone to eat more than the Amaden in the sumptuous meals she'd enjoyed in Wantesa, but there was even more food here.

But she soon found herself devouring the delicious dishes with as much gusto as the others. Her body definitely needed the fuel now that it hadn't required in her largely sedentary life in Wantesa.

The dinner was served at long tables set up outdoors, but when it was over, Shayna was quietly invited to join the Elders in the assembly hall. Her overfull stomach lurched unpleasantly as she followed them to the large stone building at the center of the village.

"We are very grateful for your presence among us, Shayna," said Wyk, the Prime Elder. He was the man who'd come to greet her upon her arrival. "The gods must surely hold you in high regard to have sent you to us."

Shayna merely nodded. If the gods held her in high regard, it certainly wasn't because of her devotion to them. She hadn't given them a thought since she'd left the valley at eighteen—and even before that had regularly incurred her parents' wrath for her failure to worship them properly.

"Have they spoken to you of our troubles?" another of the Elders, a rather austere-looking gray-haired woman, asked.

"No, they haven't," Shayna replied. If she'd ever heard their voices in her mind, she would probably have sent herself off to a psychiatric facility without once thinking that it could be the gods.

They told her the story, taking turns speaking, with one of them picking up where the last left off. It seemed that two agents from the Maccavi tribe had somehow managed to get past the Amaden guards at Lonhola—probably in disguise—and had then approached the Astasi with a proposition.

If the Astasi would join with them and the Guntal—the Maccavi's neighbors and frequent allies—together they could crush the Amaden and free the Astasi from the ever-present danger of war. The Maccavi agents swore that the Amaden were about to attempt to annihilate the Astasi, and an Astasi truth-teller had said they were not lying.

The Elders, who were usually of one mind about things, found themselves on both sides of this issue. Some believed that one final war, though regrettable, was necessary so that they could live in peace forevermore. But others believed that since the Amaden had left them in peace this long, they were unlikely to attack now. And a few Elders even suggested that the Amaden could not be defeated, no matter who was aligned against them.

The food she'd eaten congealed into a hard, cold lump inside Shayna as she listened to this. She was inclined to think that those who believed the alliance could not defeat the Amaden were correct, but she also knew from Mikal that his people were in fact considering war against the Astasi.

She was silent for a time after they had finished, as her mind whirled with the possibilities and permutations. It had been many years since either the Maccavi or the Guntal had taken up arms against the Amaden, and if they were planning to do so now, it suggested to her that they had hopes of enticing other tribes to join them.

The Amaden were by far the largest and most powerful of the tribes, but they'd been victorious only because they'd never faced war with more than one or two other tribes at one time.

The fact that she knew that this alliance would never come into being gave Shayna no satisfaction at all. She no longer knew what to think about past, present, or future. It was entirely possible that it hadn't happened because she herself had stopped it.

And just as that thought came to her, she felt a strange tingling sensation throughout her body. It was similar to what she felt when she'd passed through the spellbound entrance to the valley and what she experienced when she called upon her powers—but there was also a difference.

She drew in a breath, half fearing that she was about to hear the voices of the gods. She heard no voices, but a certainty settled into her that the future was hers to mold.

She let her gaze travel over all of them slowly, then got to her feet. "You must not make this alliance. If you do it will mean the end of the Astasi, and the gods have sent me here to show you that that must not happen.

"There are those among the Amaden who would try to annihilate you. But you have one very powerful ally—and he will stop them."

She paused as an image of Mikal filled her mind: the Mikal who had turned back to stare at her that night at Bettena's, his eyes filled with pain. She forced herself to go on.

"This man is Amaden—but he is a good man. He will spend the rest of his life trying to bring peace to all the tribes—and he will succeed. One day he will come to you and ask you to sign a pact that all others will sign as well.

"He will also ask you to renounce your magic—and this too you must do."

She sank to the floor again, with her own words still ringing in her head. She didn't look at them just yet, because she knew the effect of her speech—especially the final part. And now she understood why her people were willing to give up their magic—something that had always confounded historians.

"But if we renounce our magic, we renounce the gods!" one of the Elders said, breaking the long silence.

Shayna looked at her and shook her head. "You need not renounce the gods. Our magic was a gift that can be returned to the gods because it will no longer be needed in the world to come. It was given to us because we were so few in number and feared the Amaden. But because of Mikal Har-Amaden, you will never have to fear the Amaden again."

She met the eyes of each of them once more, then got

up again. "I will leave you now. Tomorrow I must leave the valley."

She bowed her head and steepled her fingers in the formal good-bye, then left the assembly hall. As she made her way back to Amika's, she whispered to the warm night breeze: "Mikal, I have done what I can. If only you could know just how much I do trust you."

"She has gone?"

"Yes. I thought you knew." Bettena averted her gaze. It was too painful to look at him now. The Mikal she knew had always kept a careful check on his emotions, but the man who stood before her now made no attempt to hide his raw, naked pain.

"She left yesterday morning to return to the valley."

"Alone?"

Bettena nodded. "I disguised her as a boy. She declined my offer to take her to Lonhola in my carriage. She said that she had to travel alone."

Mikal paced around the living room for a few moments, then dropped heavily into a chair. Bettena laid a hand on his shoulder, then sat down across from him.

"Did she say why she was leaving?"

It was a question Bettena had hoped he wouldn't ask—but of course she knew he would. "She said that her family would be worried about her."

Something in her tone drew Mikal's attention. "But you don't believe that," he said, making it a statement and not a question.

"I'm . . . not sure what I believe, where Shayna is concerned." She sighed. "Perhaps it is just because she's Astasi."

"That's not it," Mikal said firmly. "She is Astasi, of course—but there's something else."

Slowly, sometimes haltingly and totally without his usual eloquence, Mikal told her everything: the strange light he'd seen in the storm, how he'd found her in the valley the next day, her warning about possible assassins, her knowledge of the men who'd attempted to break into Lonhola, her mysterious "oath" that she couldn't break, and her insistence that her people were not involved.

As he spoke, he withdrew the stunner from his pocket and toyed with it. When he had finished, Bettena asked him what it was, and so he told her about it too, and how it resembled the weapon used by the strangers at Lonhola.

"But what sort of weapon is it, Mikal?" Bettena asked, frowning.

"I don't know. This one doesn't work, or at least it doesn't work for me. But it left the guards unconscious, and when they awoke they were in considerable pain that lasted for several hours."

He stared at it. "I haven't told anyone else about this one."

"But it must be Astasi—something they've created with their magic."

"She says it isn't, but I agree with you. It couldn't have come from anywhere else. We have paid spies in every foreign army and we'd know if something like this existed." He stood up and began pacing again, still clutching the silver cylinder.

"No one else could have such a weapon. Our weaponry is far superior to that of any of our enemies—and to that of our allies as well." He held it up. "This weapon cannot exist, Bett—unless it was made with Astasi magic."

"Then if those men who tried to break into Lonhola had them . . ." Bettena shivered.

"Exactly. If they had them, they must have gotten them from the Astasi. They weren't Astasi themselves."

"Could they have been in disguise?"

Mikal shook his head. "The one who used his weapon was clearly Amaden, and the other two had dark eyes, though their tribes are unknown."

Bettena nodded. "Yes, you're right about the one man being Amaden. I saw him myself, and he wasn't wearing a disguise."

Mikal had been standing at the window, but now he

spun about sharply. "You saw this man? When? Where?"

"I couldn't hear most of their conversation because Shayna drew him away. He asked her in an unpleasant way if she was enjoying herself, then said that she wouldn't be much longer. Then he said something about knowing that 'he's here' and that they knew where 'he lives.' I thought at the time—and still think—he was referring to you."

"I heard the word 'council' and I thought I heard her say something about orders to bring them back—dead or alive."

"But how did Shayna explain this?" Mikal demanded.

"She didn't, exactly—or rather, she gave me two different stories, one at the time and then another one later. I don't think either one was the truth, but I didn't pursue it."

"Dammit, Bett! Why didn't you tell me about this?"

Bettena was startled by his explosion of anger, but she answered calmly. "Shayna specifically asked me not to tell you. She said she would handle it herself—and then she asked for my help to find him."

"What were the stories she gave you?"

Bettena repeated them. "As I said, even though the second story made some sense, I still think she was lying. But I also think I've gotten to know her well enough to know that she wouldn't lie to me without a very good reason, so I didn't challenge her."

She was silent for a moment, then sighed heavily. "Too many things about Shayna seem strange to me. I kept trying to tell myself that it was because she's Astasi, but I think it's more than that.

"Anyway, after she left yesterday, I went to see an old friend. Several years ago she took her father to the Astasi healers because the doctors couldn't find the source of his illness. They cured him. She stayed there, just outside the entrance to their valley, for several days, and the healers came many times.

"I questioned her about them: how they spoke, how they behaved. She was on the stage once herself, and so she's very observant. And of course, she was also very curious about them."

Once again Bettena stopped talking. Mikal was about to prompt her when she went on. "Mikal, from what she told me, they didn't sound or behave at all like Shayna. The healers' accents were very different, and they often had difficulty understanding my friend's speech. They were also very hesitant and quite shy—as you'd expect people to be when they've lived in such isolation."

"What are you saying, Bett: that Shayna isn't Astasi? She is. She cast a spell on me—and then she put a protective spell on my house. I saw it. I saw the . . . witch's fire."

"Is it possible that she has come from someplace else?"

Mikal shook his head. "If there were Astasi anywhere else, we would certainly have known about it long before this."

"Several things continue to haunt me about her, Mikal. First of all, there's her self-assuredness. It's very . . . male. She tried very hard, at least when we were in public, to behave as women here behave. But when we were alone here, she was very different. I saw it in many small things that you perhaps never saw.

"Then there was the matter of the dollhouse." She went on to explain that to Mikal, then said, "She said that she must have unconsciously picked up on my thoughts, that that can happen sometimes if those thoughts are very powerful. She was assuming that I'd been thinking about adding the dollhouse to the play all along—but I hadn't been. In fact, I'd all but forgotten about it until she mentioned it."

"I have seen that self-assuredness in her," Mikal said. "In fact, it's one of the things I love about her. But I just assumed that it was because she's Astasi."

"I don't doubt that she's Astasi. But there is something more."

"I must find her, Bett."

"I'm not sure she'll permit that. She has seen your future, Mikal."

"What do you mean?"

"She told me that you will be a great man, that you'll change the world. And when I asked her why she couldn't stay with you, she said that you must be free to play the role destiny intends for you, and that her presence could change that."

"Nevertheless, I am going to find her, Bett—even if I have to go to the valley of the Astasi myself."

Mikal was more nervous than he wanted to admit even to himself. As he rode along the narrow path, he kept glancing up at the guard tower, knowing that they could see him down here. Those who needed to know had been told that he intended to deliver a warning to the Astasi. He intended to do just that—but he also intended to find out if Shayna was still in the valley.

Armed with Bettena's description of Shayna's disguise, he'd inquired about visitors to the Astasi and had learned that she'd come there. But no one had seen her leave—so either she was still there, or she'd left under cover of darkness, which is what the guards had assumed.

Word had reached him the day before that the Maccavi had sent emissaries to the Astasi, disguised as Amaden seeking to be healed, and that the Maccavi and possibly their allies the Guntal were hoping to form an alliance with the Astasi to make war on his people. As a result, the pressure to annihilate the Astasi was growing stronger.

So far Mikal had prevailed, but he didn't think he could prevail much longer, unless he received the sworn oath of the Astasi Elders that they would not ally themselves with the Maccavi.

Strangely enough, Mikal would have opposed war against the Astasi even if Shayna had never appeared in his life. He regarded the Astasi as a unique race, which of course they were. But while that inspired fear in others, it led him to want to preserve them in much the same way he sought to preserve rare animals that had been hunted to near-extinction.

But he was Amaden and he was now second-in-command of the army, and if he believed the Astasi posed a threat to his people, they would be destroyed.

The path climbed a steep rise, and when he reached the top, he saw before him the spellbound entrance to the valley. He'd been here before out of curiosity, but that was many years ago, when he was in his teens. He'd come with a boyhood friend to catch a glimpse of the Astasi when they appeared to heal several people. The image was still vivid in his mind after all these years. It was then that he'd told himself that the Astasi must be preserved.

He rode on to the campsite just outside the entrance to the valley, then dismounted and tethered his stallion. No one was there. The soldiers told him that fewer people came here now than in past years.

He walked toward the entrance, tensing as he came closer to those stone walls. He hadn't done this before, but he'd heard what happened, and so was prepared for the sudden paralysis that came over him. There was no sensation of anything pressing against him, but he could not take another step forward. Finally he backed up, then returned to the campsite to wait.

While he waited, he thought about Shayna—and about his conversation with Bettena. She had confirmed everything he himself had felt about Shayna, even though he might have wished that she hadn't. It would have been much easier to continue to believe that he was seeing qualities in her that didn't exist, simply because he loved her.

He drew out the cylindrical weapon that he carried with him always and stared at it. He didn't yet believe that it was all he would ever have of her, but he was edging closer to that. The sun reflected off its surface as he turned it over and over. He intended to demand that the Astasi explain it as well.

After a time, when he could no longer bear to think about Shayna, Mikal's thoughts turned to the prediction she'd made about him to Bettena. Just how was he supposed to "change the world"? As far as he could see, the only way that would happen was if he could inflict such devastating losses on his enemies that they had no choice but to accept Amaden rule.

It could happen, he thought. Year by year the enemies of the Amaden grew weaker because they lacked the resources and the numbers to wage constant wars. It seemed likely that one day they would either surrender to the will of the Amaden, or be defeated so decisively that no further battles would be possible.

Mikal had never doubted that his people would prevail one day. The Amaden were clearly meant to rule the world.

He had been alone with his thoughts for about an hour when the Astasi came. When he first saw the woman standing there, he thought for one brief moment that it was Shayna. But then he realized that the only similarity was in their hair and their eyes. This woman was older and smaller.

As she stepped through the spellbound entrance, Mikal got to his feet and started toward her. She said nothing until he came to a stop several yards away.

"You have not come here to be cured." Her gaze swept over his uniform.

"No. My name is Mikal Har-Amaden, and I've come to speak to the Elders about a matter of great importance."

"Mikal Har-Amaden?" the woman echoed. Shock was evident in her face. "You must wait here. I will tell them."

Then she stepped through the entrance and a moment later had disappeared from his view into the forest. Mikal was surprised. He'd expected to have some trouble persuading the healer to bring the Elders. Furthermore, it seemed that she had recognized his name, and that made him uneasy.

Of course, Shayna could have spoken of him—but why would she do that? Once more he was left with the certainty that there were some very important things he didn't know—and needed to know.

The Elders arrived just when Mikal was beginning to think they would refuse to see him. There were seven of them: four men and three women, all of them dressed in the plain gray clothing that all Astasi wore, or were presumed to wear. A white-haired man introduced himself as the Prime Elder. Mikal explained who he was.

"Word has reached me that agents from the Maccavi have already tried—or will try—to persuade you to form an alliance with them against my people."

"Yes, they were here," the Prime Elder acknowledged calmly.

Mikal had expected them to deny it. He looked at each of them in surprise, and they all nodded, except for one woman, whose gaze on him was so intent that it made him very uncomfortable. He was able to tear his eyes away from her only when the Prime Elder spoke again.

"There will be no alliance. We will not make war upon the Amaden. The gods have spoken."

Relief swept through Mikal, though he took care not to let it show. Still, he felt the need to reinforce their decision.

"That's very wise, because you could not hope to defeat us. Our weaponry is much stronger now."

"There is no need to boast, Mikal Har-Amaden," the Prime Elder said in that same quiet voice. "It does not become you. Our messenger from the gods told us that you will be a great man one day, and boastfulness is not necessary for such a man."

Mikal was dumbfounded—and even a bit embarrassed. "You had a messenger from the gods?" He'd always heard that the gods spoke directly to the Astasi.

"Yes. She came to us from the future, to tell us that we must not go to war, and to tell us that you would protect us."

Mikal actually felt his skin begin to crawl. Cold sweat prickled his face. "A messenger from . . . the future?"

"Indeed." The Prime Elder might have actually been smiling, but Mikal was too shocked to be certain. "Do you not believe in the future, Mikal Har-Amaden?"

Mikal ignored the gentle taunt as he swallowed a few times to get rid of the sudden dryness in his mouth. "Wh-who was this messenger?"

"Her name was Shayna."

"Was? Do you mean that she's gone?" Mikal knew at some level that he was making a total fool of himself, that he looked and sounded like anything but the deputy commander of the world's most powerful army. But he was unable to do anything about it.

"Yes. She is gone."

"Where did she go?" he demanded, relieved to find that his voice was almost normal, even if his mind was still reeling.

The old man shrugged. "I assume that she went to the world she came from. Why does it matter?"

"It matters because I love her and I won't let her go!" Mikal nearly shouted the words, unable to stop himself.

"Sometimes love means letting go, Mikal Har-Amaden."

And with those soft words, they all turned and disappeared through the entrance.

Shayna left the valley after dark, but before the moon had risen. By the time its silver light flowed over the land, she was well away from Lonhola and its watchtower. For the first time since her arrival here, she knew the satisfaction of having accomplished her goal—even if it wasn't the objective of her mission.

She had barely slept last night after her meeting with the Elders. Her belief in the old gods, so absent from her life, had come flooding back on a tidal wave of fear. It was, she thought, a strange quirk of human nature to disavow the gods until one either feared their wrath or needed them desperately.

Her fear had been that the gods would speak to the Elders and tell them that she'd lied—that they hadn't sent her at all. She was even half convinced that they would strike her down for her deception in their names. But neither thing had happened.

She was also certain that she'd overplayed her hand by telling the Elders that the Astasi would have to disavow their magic. She should have left that for Mikal to deal with when the time came. The chances were that none of the present Elders would even be alive by then.

As she rode along through the silver-washed land, she still felt a prickling fear when she thought about that speech she'd given—and the certainty she'd felt that she was changing the future. But if she had, she'd changed it into the future she knew, the future being lived by millions of others now.

She had fallen asleep just before dawn, then awakened at noon when Amika tapped on her door. The fears of the night vanished as Amika told her that the Elders had talked through the night and, in the end, had accepted the will of the gods. Amika had been somewhat rattled because she said that never before had the Elders even considered challenging the gods. But there would be no alliance with the Maccavi against the Amaden, and if the time came when Mikal Har-Amaden asked them to give up their magical gifts, they would do so.

As the day wore on and Shayna spoke to others, she discovered that most people were relieved that the alliance had been rejected. The Astasi were not and never had been a warlike people—unlike their neighbors, the Amaden.

But the thought that they might be called upon to give up their magic was a very different matter. What Shayna heard that day was the beginnings of the quiet rebellion that would continue for a century or more. The Astasi would agree to give up their powers, and for the most part they would hold to that agreement. But long after they signed the pact, those who remained in the valley would practice magic secretly among themselves.

Even in Shayna's own time, there were suspicions that a certain amount of magic was being practiced.

Young Astasi known to have talents for healing left the valley and became physicians, then returned again, and almost certainly used their ancient magic in conjunction with the skills they'd learned.

And several years ago, when there'd been a terrible drought in the Amaden lands around the valley, heavy storms had drenched the valley itself at crucial times, guaranteeing an abundant crop. Meteorologists had all sorts of explanations, but many people—including Shayna herself—suspected that someone in the valley had called the storms.

Then, of course, there was the indisputable fact that whatever an Astasi chose to do with his or her life, it was done well. The Astasi were invariably in the front ranks of their professions and among the top university students.

Shayna smiled to herself, wishing that she could have told Amika and the others that Astasi magic would survive. She knew that would have pleased them.

The eastern sky was glowing with pale light by the time she reached the intersection where the road from Lonhola met the wider road that led straight to Wantesa. She reined in her horse and thought about that city she would probably never see again—at least not in Mikal's time.

Mikal was a warmth inside her, surrounded by the cold, hard pain of reality. And reality for her was finding the time-craft. She turned the horse's head away from Wantesa and followed the road east instead, into the rising sun and into Mikal's family's lands: back to that valley where her time here had begun.

The road bisected Mikal's family's lands, passing through many acres of farmland. She noted that while the crops looked good, they were not as lush and healthy as those in the Astasi fields. She wondered if, years from now, when the Har-Amaden saw that difference, they would regret the proscription against magic that Mikal had imposed. Of course, by then, the Har-Amaden fortune would be spread more widely, into shipping and banking and numerous other things. The family was still one of the wealthiest in the world, with farflung interests.

The Har-Amaden family also employed more than their share of Astasi scientists and engineers and business executives. Since the Astasi had never been wealthy in the sense that it was defined by the rest of the world, it was the Har-Amaden who had helped the first Astasi to leave the valley to obtain university educations. They'd built the hospitals and libraries and had, in general, brought the outer world to the valley—all with the agreement of the Elders. During those first years, when the Astasi who left the valley had felt the need to remain together, the Har-Amaden had maintained a handsome residence facility at the edge of the campus for them. It was now a museum devoted to the history and arts and crafts of her people.

Shayna had always taken a secret pleasure at her people's close relationship with the Har-Amaden family because of her nearly lifelong fascination with the man who had started it all. Mikal's will had left all of his considerable fortune to be used to assist the Astasi in joining the world after centuries of isolation.

Historians had credited his interest in them to the fact that he was the first outsider to have contact with them, other than those who'd come to be healed. But Shayna knew now, in that deep, warm part of her, that Mikal had done it for her. Her passage through this time had changed the future in several ways.

As she rode toward the valley, hoping to find Haddar's time-craft, Shayna knew that when she returned to her own time she would strongly recommend that the project be disbanded—after they had dealt with Haddar, of course. Perhaps it would be possible for others to go back in time without changing things or without causing pain to themselves or others, but she doubted it. And the temptation to fix things—to make changes—was simply too great.

The road climbed a hill, and when she reached the top she saw the Har-Amaden keep in the distance, perched on its own hill at the center of the family's lands. Tears came to her eyes as she realized that, without truly thinking about it, she had come to be very certain that she would be returning to her own time. Her time with Mikal was already receding into the realm of dreams, slowly becoming an extension of her earlier fantasies about him.

Traffic on the road was becoming heavier now by midmorning, but no one paid her any attention. She was once again a poor youth, making his way somewhere on a nondescript horse. She could only hope that the disguise held and no one else would be in the rocky valley she had to search.

Less than an hour later, she reined in the horse and pretended to be checking its one foot as she waited for the traffic on the road to clear. She didn't want anyone to see her turn into the valley.

Then, when she was finally alone, she remounted and set off quickly, hoping to be beyond the hill that separated the valley from the road before anyone could see her. As far as she could tell, no one did. When she reached the top of the hill, she could see Mikal's cabin, nearly hidden among the tall pines and hemlocks on the hill that rose from the far side of the valley.

She made an involuntary sound, half cry and half sob, as she stared at it and let her mind fill up with memories: his tenderness, his passion, that moment of surprising anger when he'd tossed the mug against the hearth.

But most of all, she realized now, she was remembering that slight frown she'd see on his face when she caught him staring at her. Perhaps at the time she'd been too busy worrying about her own situation, and then trying to deal with the stunning realization of who he really was. But now it seemed to her that he'd been puzzled by something about her, and she wondered if, in the years ahead, he would ever come close to figuring it out. Surely, in the years to come, when he talked to the Astasi, he would inquire about her. Would they tell him the truth? Was it possible that someday, Mikal would know where she'd come from and why she couldn't stay?

She hoped that would be the case—that instead of feeling betrayed by her, he would one day understand what had happened.

Brushing away her tears, she started down the hillside into the valley. She had been able to search only a small part of it on foot that day, but now she should be able to cover it more easily. It was, she thought, a perfect place to hide the time-craft, because it was filled with a mixture of thick stands of fir and huge rocky outcroppings.

When she reached the bottom of the hill, she paused to let the horse drink from the small stream that meandered through the valley. Then she began her search.

By the time she stopped to let the horse rest and to eat some of the food that Amika had kindly given her, Shayna had covered about a third of the valley and had even discovered two small caves. Neither of them was large enough to have contained the time-craft, but she wondered if there might not be others that were larger. She knew that the time-craft, like hovercraft and personal aircars, was very light and could easily be towed with a long bar that fit through a ring in its nose. And she also knew that Haddar would hide it very well—not just because of the danger of someone from this time finding it, but also because he wouldn't want anyone following him to discover it.

She resumed her search, and by day's end had covered only half the valley. So she camped out, sleeping on the hard ground and trying to ignore the growing doubts that she would find it.

Mikal went through the hours after his meeting with the Astasi in a sort of daze that alarmed his aides, who began to wonder if the Astasi might have cast some sort of spell over him. Somehow he managed to compose a message to his superior, the commander, saying that the Astasi had given their word that they had no intention of making war. Then, after sending one aide back to Wantesa with the message, he dismissed the other one and sought the isolation of his cabin, arriving there just after dark.

Such was his mood that he didn't even bother lighting a lamp. Instead he sat on the cabin's doorstep in the darkness and stared unseeingly down into the valley.

Why was he even considering that the Astasi Elders could have spoken the truth about Shayna? He knew they dwelt in a world of magical beliefs about the powers of the old gods. To them, a visitor from the future, sent by those gods, wouldn't have seemed at all unusual. For all he knew, they received *all* their messages from the gods in that fashion—or believed they did, which was the same thing.

And Shayna knew that the Astasi were in danger; he'd told her that himself. She might very well have concocted a story about coming from the future with a warning about the dangers of an alliance.

No sooner had that thought begun to soothe his dazed brain than he saw his error and realized that he still wasn't thinking straight. She couldn't have posed as a visitor from the future to her own people, who would surely have recognized her.

His thoughts turned to Bettena's comments about her that had been confirmed by his brief contact with her people. Shayna was different, and she lacked their distinctive accent.

He withdrew the little silver cylinder from his pocket and stared at it, only now realizing that he hadn't inquired about it. But he'd never been able to accept that it was an Astasi weapon; their weapons were magical in nature. Yet he remained certain that it was in fact a weapon.

Mikal's own thoughts about the future had never extended beyond assuring his own people's dominance. So, while the Astasi elders had offered an explanation for the mystery that was Shayna, he couldn't accept it. Their magical beliefs might have convinced them, but Mikal was sure there must be another, more logical explanation.

What seemed most likely to him was that there was in fact another Astasi enclave somewhere that had managed to remain hidden all these years. That still didn't explain the weapon, but it was a start, and something he could accept.

He awoke the next morning knowing that he should return to Wantesa and get back to the busy routine of his life that was the only way he could hope to get her out of his mind. He knew that he hadn't yet accepted the fact that she was gone from his life, and it would be better to be busy when that finality struck him.

Briefly, he thought about the houses of pleasure and the women there who knew how to tend to his needs. But he also knew that he wouldn't go to one of them. In fact, as he got up from his lonely bed, Mikal knew, with a sudden certainty, that he would never want any other woman.

After making a breakfast that he didn't really want, he left the cabin and started toward the lean-to, where he'd left his stallion. His gaze swept over the valley without any real interest—until he spotted something down there.

He stopped and frowned, then returned to the cabin to get his spyglass. When he trained it on the distant figure, he still couldn't see it well. He'd assumed that it was one of the family's many farmhands, though he couldn't imagine what he'd be doing down there. But his vision was improved enough by the spyglass that he could dismiss that belief. Not even the lowliest farmhand on Har-Amaden lands would be riding such a poor excuse for a horse. The family bred fine horses, and even farmhands and house servants rode the sleek animals for which the Har-Amaden stables were famous.

The figure disappeared from view and Mikal stood there uncertainly. Then he saddled his horse and rode down into the valley.

Chapter Ten

Those niggling little doubts that had crept in earlier were now beginning to assert themselves more strongly as Shayna explored each rocky outcropping on foot, then returned to her horse and moved on to the next possible hiding place. Only now was she beginning to admit to herself that her chances of finding the time-craft here had been dubious at best. It could have landed miles from this valley. The fierce winds of the storm that had destroyed her own craft could have interfered with the computerized tracking system, or even put it out completely.

Still, she pressed on, hoping against hope and not daring to consider what she would do if she didn't find it.

She drew nearer and nearer to the hill where Mikal's cabin stood. There was only a small portion of the valley remaining to be searched, but it was particularly rugged terrain, which was why she hadn't covered it while Mikal was gone that time.

She knew that the cabin was visible at least part of

the time, but she kept her eyes away from that hill. She wanted no reminders of him now, no stealthy little thoughts that if she didn't find the time-craft, she would be forced to go back to Wantesa. She dared not return to the Astasi, lest that destroy her credibility as a visitor from the future sent by the gods, who would surely have been able to effect her return.

Finally she reached an area where the landscape was as jagged as anything she'd ever seen. Great walls of rock jutted up at odd angles, forming miniature canyons between them. She tethered her horse to a misshapen fir and let her hopes begin to rise again. Of all the spots she'd seen in the valley, this was the place she herself would have chosen to hide the craft. While there might be occasional visitors to this valley, surely no one would ever find a reason to climb over these rocks, risking life and limb where small pebbles could make it difficult to find purchase. Getting the time-craft in here couldn't have been easy, either, but with three men, she was sure they could have managed it.

She slipped through a narrow opening and then began to climb over the rocks, peering down into one crevasse after another. Each time she scaled another dangerous height, she expected to see it—and when she finally did, she blinked in disbelief.

The time-craft sat, apparently undamaged, deep in a crevasse and shadowed by overhanging rocks on all sides. She could see a few scrapes along the side exposed to her view, but she knew that wouldn't have damaged it. The craft was made of an alloy developed especially for this purpose, and she'd listened more than she wanted to to Teres and the engineers extolling its virtues.

Shayna stared at it, momentarily dazed by a combination of exultation and grief. Here then was her way home—and her way out of Mikal's life forever. She would probably have to come back with those sent to find Haddar, but she would stay well away from Mikal and simply assist the others as best she could.

She clambered down the rocks to the craft, but when

she was still some fifty feet away from it, a well-remembered sound struck her ears: the alarm!

She stopped, balanced precariously on a ledge. Her heart pounded in her ears, mingling with the incessant bleat of the alarm. She had not given any thought to this. In the haste of their departure, no one had explained to her how to get inside the craft, let alone how to disable the alarm. No doubt Larus, the dead pilot, had intended to explain all that to her when they arrived.

She tried to remember how long the alarm had sounded before her own craft had self-destructed. It seemed to her now that it had been many minutes. Every fiber of her being was screaming at her to get out of there, but she hurried down the rocky face, slipping and sliding and then finally landing in a tumble next to the craft.

With the alarm shrieking, she made a quick circle of the craft and ascertained that it was undamaged. Then she tried the recessed handle that opened the door, thinking that if only she could get inside, she could find a way to disable the alarm and the self-destruct device. Everything had been clearly labeled, as far as she could recall.

But the door would not open. She scrambled around to the other side and tried that door as well. It also refused to move. Shayna realized that it must have been programmed to admit only the crew. Probably there was a password, since she saw no handprint scanner.

Tears of frustration nearly blinded her as she gave up and started back up the slope, hoping that as she moved beyond the range of the scanners, the alarm would stop and the craft would not self-destruct.

She was about three-quarters of the way to the top of the rock formation when she allowed herself to look up. For one brief instant she thought she saw a figure up there, peering down at her, and for an even briefer moment it seemed to be Mikal. Then the alarm stopped—and she was hurled against the rock wall.

* * *

Mikal reached the valley floor and turned toward the rocky area where the rider had been heading. He couldn't begin to guess why any of the farmhands would be down here, let alone why someone who didn't belong on his family's lands would come to this place.

When he reached the rocks, he discovered the horse, tethered to a scraggly tree. His gaze ran expertly over the animal, and he was more than ever convinced that it couldn't belong to a farmhand. He raised his gaze to the rocks, frowning.

As a child, he'd come out here to climb these rocks. Once, when he was twelve or so, he and his cousin had come here and his cousin had fallen, breaking a leg. After that, Mikal's parents had forbidden him to come here and he'd obeyed them. The damage done to his older cousin's leg had left him with a permanent limp, and Mikal, who had already decided upon a military career, wasn't about to risk his future to climb rocks.

His earlier glimpse of the rider, through the spyglass, had suggested that he was young, though not a child. Still, Mikal was concerned for his safety. He might have no business being here at all, let alone climbing dangerous rocks, but injury or death seemed to be too high a price to pay for such a minor transgression. Besides, the remote possibility remained that it *was* one of the farmhands or house servants, and like the rest of his family, Mikal felt a strong sense of responsibility for them.

So he left his stallion to graze on the coarse grass that grew along the base of the rocks, and began to climb. He quickly discovered that while he wasn't as agile as he'd been all those years ago, he now had the advantage of superior strength. He reached the top of the first rockpile and paused to scan the area. There was no sign of the youth, so he continued down and then up again, now beginning to enjoy the challenge.

He was partway up the steep precipice when he heard the sound. A chill ran through him. His senses immediately identified it as being an alarm of some sort, but he'd never heard its like: a shrill pulsing sound. He was fairly certain that it was coming from the deep crevasse he thought lay just beyond this next peak.

He continued to climb, drawn by that impossible sound. There was another way to the top that would have been easier, but he struggled upward on this more direct route as the sound grew ever louder.

And when he finally reached the top and peered down into the crevasse, a cry of surprise escaped his lips and he actually blinked a few times. What he saw below him was impossible! The source of the shrieking alarm was a vehicle of some sort. It was somewhat larger than his carriage, but without wheels of any kind. It was made of some unknown substance that must be metal, and painted in a dull gray-brown shade, nearly the same color as the rocks surrounding it. The front was tapered nearly to a point, as was the rear, but fins like those on a fish projected from the rear. There were no windows, but he could make out the outline of a door on the side facing him.

All these observations were made in a matter of a second or two as the alarm continued to shriek its unknown warning. Mikal felt a great urge to turn and run, but he remained rooted in place, staring at something that couldn't be.

Then suddenly, out of the corner of his eye, he caught movement, and saw that someone was climbing up the rocks beneath him and slightly to the left. He moved closer to the edge and saw the rider he'd spotted earlier, a slender youth in rough workman's garb. He was about to call out when suddenly the alarm stopped—and then he was knocked backward by some unseen force.

He landed heavily some ten feet back from where he'd been standing. His shoulder collided painfully with a jutting piece of rock, and for a moment he felt dazed. But he shook his head and picked himself up and hurried back to the rim.

The strange vehicle was gone! He stared in disbelief. Not a trace of it remained down there. Still dazed by the invisible force that had struck him and now further confused by the disappearance of something that shouldn't have been there in the first place, Mikal was slow to remember the youth.

Then he saw the figure sprawled unmoving across a narrow ledge. "Shayna." Her name poured from his lips even before his brain had quite processed the fact. The cap she'd been wearing had blown off and he saw that familiar red hair. Forcing himself to be careful, he began to climb down toward her.

She was lying in a dangerous position, the upper half of her body already out over the ledge. Any movement at all on her part could easily send her plunging down into the crevasse, some fifty feet below. His passage loosened some pebbles and several of them struck her.

"Shayna—don't move!" he shouted as he hurried on, terrified that he wouldn't reach her in time.

But she didn't move, and for the last few yards of his difficult descent, his fears turned instead to the possibility that she was dead. But by the time his feet touched the ledge, he could see that she was still breathing. It was an eerie replay of that time he'd found her in another part of this valley, but Mikal had no time now to consider the possible connection.

Shayna opened her eyes, and the first thing she saw was her green cap, lying at the bottom of the crevasse. Then she became aware of her position, and instinct warned her not to attempt to move until she could find a way to do it safely.

Then something struck her back and legs: pebbles, she saw as a few of them rolled past her eyes and down into the crevasse. At the same time she became aware of a strange numbness in her limbs.

I'm paralyzed, she thought with horror—just before she heard the voice.

"Shayna—don't move!"

Mikal. Surely it couldn't be him. But then she was recalling the figure she'd seen above her before the blast. And she could hear him now, climbing down behind her. More pebbles struck her, then skittered off the ledge. Mikal. He must have seen the time-craft.

Terrified as she was about her own condition, Shayna felt a welcome relief. Now there would be no more lies between them. Now she could tell him the truth and he would believe her.

She sensed that he had reached the ledge, though she couldn't move her head. His hand touched her back and she felt its warmth all the way through her paralyzed body.

"Shayna, don't try to move. Are you hurt?"

"I can't move," she said in a hoarse voice. "I can't move anything. The blast."

She felt his fingers begin to probe her spine, carefully but firmly, all the way from the base of her neck to her hips. She thought about how wonderful it was to feel his touch again, even in these circumstances. And then, as his fingers began to probe her hip joints and her legs, she realized that if she could feel them—and she certainly could—then she couldn't be paralyzed. Or could she?

"Nothing seems to be broken," he said when he'd finished. "I'm going to pull you back from the edge now."

She expected pain as he grasped her hips and pulled her gently back onto the ledge, but she felt nothing. Very carefully he turned her over onto her back.

She was startled to see this younger version of Mikal, since the man he would become had been occupying her thoughts ever since her departure from Wantesa. It amazed her that she could have so quickly reverted to that other image.

"You saw it, didn't you?" she asked.

He glanced away from her briefly, looking down into the crevasse. Then he nodded. "Can you move yet?"

She focused on moving her fingers and saw that she could just barely accomplish that. She wiggled her feet experimentally. But she still couldn't move her arms and legs. They felt leaden.

"Nerve damage from the blast," she said. "But I think the feeling will come back." Even as she spoke, she could feel a tingling sensation traveling through her arms and legs.

He stood up and raised his head to the top of the rock cliff. "You'll never be able to climb up there. I'm going back for my horse. I can tie a rope around the saddle and pull you up that way."

She stared at him, knowing that he needed to focus on the task of getting her out of here. It was something he could understand. He knelt beside her again, then reached out to brush away the hair that had fallen across her face. His fingertips lingered on her cheek, but in his eyes she saw confusion—and perhaps fear.

"Don't move. It will take me some time to get back and then bring my horse." Once again his gaze went down into the crevasse. "Will you be safe here?"

The question was asked in a strange, hesitant tone, and she realized he must be thinking that the craft could reappear or that something equally incomprehensible could happen.

"I'll be safe," she assured him.

She lay on the ledge and watched as he made his way back up to the top of the rocks. *Oh, Mikal,* she thought, *what have I done to you? What effect will this have on your life—and your work? Have I changed everything?*

Then she realized that she would never know the answer to that question. Now she was trapped in this time forever. She could no longer let herself hope that Teres and the others would ever find her.

Or perhaps they would find her, one day years from now, in the time they were undoubtedly searching in at this moment. Shayna's head already ached, and the complexities of time were beyond her at the moment, so she turned her attention instead to her battered body.

She discovered that she could now move her arms and legs, although they still didn't respond to her commands very quickly or easily. But she wasn't really concerned. She'd already realized that this must have happened to her the last time—when her own craft had self-destructed—but she'd been unconscious because her head had struck a rock. She didn't know how long she'd been unconscious then, but by the time she came to, she had recovered the use of her limbs.

Furthermore, she was farther away from the timecraft this time, and she'd already been pressed against the rock, which had probably absorbed most of the ultrasonic waves that had destroyed it. She would be all right.

She was surprised when she heard Mikal calling out to her again. It seemed that her thoughts must have been as sluggish as her body was, because she thought he'd been gone only a few minutes. Yet there he was, once more descending the rock face, this time with a strong rope slung over his shoulder.

By the time he reached the narrow ledge, she had managed to pull herself into a sitting position. His eyes met hers, but slid away quickly. She saw him glance again into the crevasse, as though he expected the timecraft to have reappeared, perhaps through Astasi magic.

Was that what he was trying to tell himself? she wondered. From his perspective it probably made the most sense. She was beginning to realize that the truth wouldn't come as easily for Mikal as she'd assumed. Her people's reputation for magic had helped her many times up to now, but she feared it was about to become a problem.

"How are you feeling now?" he asked, still doing his best to avoid her eyes. Or so it seemed to her.

"Better," she replied. "I can move everything, but not very well. I'll be all right, Mikal. This must have happened before."

She waited for him to ask what she meant, but he didn't. Instead he brought the rope around her chest just beneath her breasts and then secured it with a double knot. His touch seemed cool and impersonal and she felt guilty about her own reaction.

After satisfying himself that she was tied securely, he stood up, thrust two fingers into his mouth, and whistled twice. In spite of her fears, Shayna had to smile at his boyish behavior. It was yet another of those moments when the man of history and the man she loved seemed irreconcilable.

A few seconds later the rope around her chest grew taut, and then she was struggling to stay on her feet and away from the sharp rocks as she was hauled slowly up the face of the cliff. Mikal climbed with her to assist her as his unseen stallion drew her upward.

Finally they were at the top and Mikal ordered the horse to stop. It obeyed immediately, then pawed the ground and snorted its disapproval of human foolishness.

Shayna fumbled with the knots, but her uncoordinated fingers couldn't manage to undo them, and Mikal did it for her. Once again his touch seemed impersonal, and she thought that she might as well be a stranger he'd chosen to help.

As he left her to go to his horse, she thought that his behavior was similar to what she'd seen when she first met him: cool, impersonal, and wary. The difference this time was that she knew it didn't reflect his feelings at all, but rather was an attempt to hide his confusion. His mind simply could not comprehend what he'd seen. She felt an impossibly wide gap between them now, and wondered how she could bridge it—or if she could bridge it at all. If he decided that the time-craft was the result of magic, there was no way she would be able to convince him of the truth.

He led the horse to her and lifted her into the saddle, then said he would lead the horse and asked if he should tie her to the saddle.

She gripped the front of the saddle, but weakly. "I think you'd better tie me."

He secured her to the saddle, then set off over the rocks. Shayna thought that she would have given quite a lot to be able to read his mind, as her people were often suspected of doing. But even without that, she knew that his brusque manner was covering a mind in great turmoil.

She realized now that an interest in the future, which some years from now would first express itself in the form of science-fiction novels, was well beyond a man of Mikal's time. Even apart from the Astasi, this was a time not very far removed from a superstitious belief in magic of all kinds.

Besides, Mikal was a warrior. If he gave any thought at all to the future, it would be from that mind-set. A world of peace, where mankind could turn its attention to something like time-travel, would be quite beyond him—even though he himself would create that world.

Never before had Shayna felt the gap between them to be so great. Up to now she had been trying so desperately to fit herself into his world, but now she must try to explain her world to him, though how much of it she didn't yet know.

His silence continued all the way back to her horse, where his only words were to tell her that she should continue to ride his horse and he would ride hers back to his cabin. She said only that she was sure she could now manage without being tied, since she would have the reins to hold on to. He untied her, and they started toward the cabin.

Even though his continued silence was painful to her, Shayna was grateful for the time it gave her to decide how much and what she should tell him—or whether she should let him believe that it was all Astasi magic, which she was sure was what he wanted to believe.

By the time they reached the cabin, Shayna had regained full use of her limbs, and her headache had receded. When Mikal inquired solicitously about her condition, she told him she was fine, even though she was tempted to lie. With the confrontation now staring her in the face, she still wasn't sure how to handle it.

It was ironic, she thought, that she had so often wanted to tell him the truth and had so very much hated lying to him—and now that she could finally tell him the truth and probably make him believe it, she wanted to retreat once again into deception.

And beneath all this, waiting for her attention, was the unresolved question of her own future.

Mikal fed and watered the horses while she stood

there staring down at the valley, where first her own time-craft and now Haddar's had been destroyed, leaving her trapped in a place she didn't want to be with a man she loved but couldn't have.

He unlocked the cabin and as he did, she began to wonder for the first time how he had happened to be here. He'd seemed to be very busy in Wantesa when she left.

They went into the cabin just as the wind began to pick up and thunder rumbled in the distance. She waited for him to ask his questions, but his silence continued and she recalled how he'd done that before: waited for her to explain herself. In his time, the science of psychology was in its infancy, but more than one historian had remarked that Mikal Har-Amaden had possessed an instinctive understanding of human nature. Questions could make a person become defensive, but silence was neutral and, with most people, would lead more quickly to the truth.

"How did you happen to be here?" she asked, partly out of curiosity and partly to stave off the inevitable. Then, realizing that she'd said nothing about his rescuing her, she thanked him for that.

He had settled down into his big, comfortable chair near the hearth while she remained standing—a clear breach of etiquette in his time that almost certainly resulted from his mental confusion.

The look he gave her when she thanked him was one of hurt surprise, and she realized now how very formal she sounded.

"I came here yesterday, after talking to the Elders."

"The Elders? You mean the Astasi Elders?" She was stunned.

He nodded, then went on to explain that he knew about the Maccavi's attempts to form an alliance with the Astasi, and that he'd gone there to warn them against taking such an action.

"What did they say?" she asked. She was surprised that they'd been willing to talk to him—at least until she remembered that she'd told them about him.

Mikal looked away from her. "They said that they'd already decided against such an alliance because the gods had sent a messenger from the future to warn them against it."

"I see," she said, grateful for the fact that they'd left her out of it, though it probably didn't matter. Except, she thought, that it does leave open the option of letting him believe that what he saw was Astasi magic.

"I was about to return to Wantesa when I saw you down in the valley. I didn't know it was you—or maybe, somehow, I did."

He still wasn't looking at her, and, as she stared at him, Shayna saw something she'd never expected—or wanted—to see in this man: vulnerability. Not the touching vulnerability he had displayed in his love for her, but a very different kind. She understood it, because it was similar to what she'd experienced when she'd awakened to the confusion of amnesia in a strange world.

"Bettena said that you were different—and that it wasn't just because you were Astasi. I'd felt that too, but it was part of what I loved about you, so I didn't really question it."

He'd said *loved*—in the past tense. She heard the rest of it, but only that one word stuck in her mind.

He glanced briefly at her. "I understand now why you were lying to me. Are these men from the future too?"

"Yes. That was their craft that self-destructed. Mine was destroyed when I arrived, before you found me. They're programmed to self-destruct if they become disabled or if someone not authorized to enter them approaches them."

She knew she was retreating into the role of teacher, and she was also aware of the fact that she'd dropped her carefully cultivated accent. But there was no need any longer for pretense of any kind.

"How far in the future?" he asked, still staring into the empty hearth.

"A little over three hundred years." Just speaking those words had the effect of making her see him and this tiny cabin as though through a long, dark tunnel. She sank onto the stone hearth.

"Three hundred years," he echoed. Then he reached into his pocket and withdrew the stunner. She'd temporarily forgotten that he still had it, and now realized that he'd probably been carrying it around all along, trying to figure out what it was.

"It's called a stunner," she told him before he could ask. "It's a weapon many people carry for personal defense. It can't kill. It emits rays that act on the nervous system." She thought what a minor, unimportant thing it was, and yet, because he was a warrior, it was something that would, of course, be of interest to him.

"Is this one broken?" he asked.

"No. They're programmed to work only for the person who owns it. It would still work for me."

"Programmed?"

She tried to explain. "Years from now, there will be machines that can think, called computers. And they'll just get smaller and smaller and be able to do more and more. The tiny computer inside the stunner is programmed—or told what to think. When I press my thumb against that pad, the computer reads my thumbprint and knows it's me. Everyone's thumbprint is slightly different."

He set the stunner on the table, then turned to her. He looked dazed, she thought—and no wonder. The gap between them was widening with every word she spoke. She wanted to go to him, to hold him, to tell him that she loved him. But she remained where she was.

"Why did you come here?"

This was the tricky part. Should she tell him the whole truth, or make up some story he'd probably believe in his present condition? He might believe almost anything right now, but she knew that sooner or later he would begin to think more clearly.

If it weren't for Haddar and his actions since he came here she could have gotten away with a lie. But Haddar had tried to break into Lonhola, and she'd told Mikal that it was his intention to kill him.

"We hadn't really planned to come here—or to travel anywhere in time yet. We weren't really ready. But Haddar—the Amaden—stole one of the time-crafts, and we had to follow him and his companions. The two men I came with were killed when our craft crashed."

"One of them was the man you talked about seeing—with the gash on his face?"

She'd forgotten she'd told him that. "Yes."

"Why did they send you?"

"I'm a historian. I'm a consultant to the project. In all likelihood I would never have been chosen to go if we'd kept to our schedule. It would have been too difficult to send a woman into this time."

"What do you mean?" he asked, and she saw that he was looking less confused and more curious.

"Because women can't move about so freely in this time."

"And how is it different in . . . your time?"

"Men and women are equal in all things, Mikal—and they have been for a long time. Women are doctors and business owners and scientists—just like men are."

He frowned. "What about the army?"

"There is no army in my time, Mikal. The world has been at peace for a very long time. All we have is a security force, like your constabulary—and women serve in that."

He continued to frown, then picked up the stunner again and nodded. "I suppose that if you have weapons like this, then women could fight as well as men."

She smiled. Bit by bit, he was opening himself to her world and its possibilities. Perhaps he would become curious enough that he'd forget about her mission here.

"You said that this man—Haddar—stole a time-craft. Why did he steal it? Were you telling me the truth when you said that he wanted to kill me?"

So there it was: the question. She stared at him and she saw his portrait. She took a deep breath.

"Mikal, there is something I must ask you to think about before I answer your question. Do you want to know your own future? Because if I answer your question, I will have to tell you."

Mikal stared at this woman who was so familiar and so much a stranger. He heard the Elders telling him about a "messenger" from the future and he saw, in his mind's eye, that strange vehicle. He accepted all of this, and yet he didn't—couldn't.

He was reminded of a time in a distant land when he'd experienced an earthquake. He'd known that such things could occur there, but still, in that moment, he could not accept that the very ground on which he stood was not solid.

This felt the same way, but somehow even worse. Now time itself seemed no longer real and understandable. And this woman he loved would never be the same to him.

He could see and hear the differences in her already. She spoke differently: not just her words, but her way of speaking. He'd liked her self-assurance that was so unusual for a woman, but now he felt vaguely intimidated by it. Mikal truly believed that the lot of women needed to be improved, but that was very different from what she spoke of: a world where women did all the things men did.

While they were talking, the brief storm had passed. Now she went outside after putting her question to him. He picked up the thing she called a stunner, the incredible weapon she'd described so casually, as though it were no more than a minor trinket. After a moment he put it down again, barely resisting the urge to fling it into the fireplace.

Anger had been building slowly in him—a dangerous anger because it had no real direction, but was instead born of frustration and of fear. He didn't want to know all this—about her or about her world. But now he couldn't *not* know it. He wanted Shayna back, not this woman from the future who used words she had to explain to him as though he were some particularly dimwitted child.

He let that anger swarm over him for a few minutes,

then pushed it down, deep inside him. He had asked a question and she had countered with another question. He had to deal with that now.

He hadn't forgotten what Bettena had told him—how Shayna had said that he would be a great man one day. In truth, it hadn't really surprised him. Mikal knew his own abilities, and for some time now he'd known that he would one day become commander of the greatest army in history.

Probably she would tell him that—not realizing that Bettena had already told him. But that brought him back to the question she hadn't yet answered. Why then would this man, Haddar—himself an Amaden—want to kill him?

Mikal got up to go outside and find her. He felt queasy inside, but he had to know his future. Whatever it was, he knew that he could not betray his people. Perhaps the man Haddar wasn't Amaden, after all—or perhaps he was simply crazy. How could he know what might happen to men in a time when women were their equals?

He didn't see her at first and thought that maybe she'd vanished somehow. And in that moment of uncertainty, he knew that he still loved her and wanted her, even if he couldn't understand her, and yes, even if she'd cast a spell on him to make him love her.

But then he saw her, sitting beneath a tree at the edge of the slope that led down into the valley. Her head rested on her drawn-up knees, and as he approached slowly, he could see her shoulders heaving and knew she was crying.

Mikal stopped, only now realizing the full implication of what had happened down there in the valley. She'd been searching for the other time-craft so she could return home—and now it was gone. She was trapped here in a world where she didn't belong.

The sympathy he felt for her was tinged with pain. She had intended to leave him. He'd accused her of that the last time he saw her, but he hadn't really believed it. He'd been sure that she loved him too much to leave him, but maybe he'd been wrong. Maybe everything that had happened between them had been part of a plan. She wanted to find this man Haddar and Haddar wanted to kill him, so it made sense that she would stay close to him.

She turned at that moment and saw him, then quickly wiped away the tears and stood up. He waited for her to come back to him and he wondered.

"I want to know the truth," he said when she stopped a short distance away. The truth he wanted was more than the question he'd asked, but he would wait to see what she had to say, and then perhaps he'd have the answer to his other question as well.

"I thought you would," she said softly, her green eyes searching his face. "But I'm not sure you will like it, Mikal."

He felt that uneasiness again, but he tried to ignore it. "Tell me."

Her gaze became distant, even though she was still looking at him. A strange half-smile played over the lips he'd kissed so many times. "Please be patient with me and let me explain it in my own way.

"I fell in love with you years ago—in my own time, that is."

"But—"

She cut him off with a gesture. He felt his anger returning. She was lying. She hadn't even recognized him.

"I didn't recognize you at first because all the portraits of you show a much older man—and because I didn't understand that I'd ended up in an earlier time. You see, we were following Haddar and the others and I'd wrongly assumed that they'd gone to a later time—twenty or thirty years later."

"Portraits of me?" he asked when she lapsed into silence and her gaze became unfocused again.

"Yes, Mikal. There are portraits and statues of you everywhere. And the whole world celebrates your birthday each year." She took a deep breath and didn't seem to notice that he was holding his.

"You will be a great man, Mikal—because you will end the wars and give us the peace we've had now for nearly three hundred years."

Mikal stared at her. What she said wasn't so different from what he'd thought, though he hadn't imagined he would be given that much credit. But she was watching him intently, and he knew that he'd either missed something or that she hadn't yet finished.

"Then why is this man Haddar—an Amaden—trying to kill me?"

"Because your greatness is not the result of battles won, Mikal. You will be great because you *stopped* the wars."

"I don't understand," he said, trying to ignore the growing knot in his gut. "The wars will stop when the Amaden are victorious."

"Yes, that is true—but peace will come only when the Amaden give up their dream of ruling the world. And you will convince them to do that. You will make them understand that true peace can only come when everyone shares the power. It's called democracy."

She went on, but Mikal was barely paying attention. What she was talking about was betrayal. He would defeat his people's enemies and then hand over power to them?

"That can't happen!" he said, interrupting her as she talked about some world council. "The Amaden are meant to rule the world! I'd never betray my own people!"

"That's why Haddar wants to kill you—because he believes as you do. He considers you to be a traitor to your people—but the rest of the world considers you to be a hero."

"Then he has no reason to kill me—because that won't happen!"

"But it will, Mikal."

With her soft but firm voice ringing in his ears, Mikal Har-Amaden turned on his heel and walked back to the cabin.

Chapter Eleven

Shayna watched him stalk away, anger apparent in his every movement. She should not have told him the truth. She'd chosen wrongly. If she'd told him what he obviously wanted to hear—that he would be a great military hero—he would have accepted that and she could have explained Haddar away as being insane—which he was, of course. It wouldn't have been a lie, really—just a failure to tell all the truth. Mikal had more battles to win, and even if he'd never undertaken his great quest, his position in history would still have been assured.

She was angry with herself, but even more than that, she felt the pain of betrayal. He had betrayed every feeling she'd had for Mikal Har-Amaden, the great peacemaker.

But I still love him, she thought. And with that thought, she realized that, finally, she loved the man, and not the mythical giant of history.

She followed him into the cabin, relieved that one thing in her life, at least, was certain.

"What will you do?" he asked the moment she walked through the door. "You were planning to go back—go home, weren't you?"

She didn't want to talk about herself, but it appeared that he didn't want to talk about himself, either. She nodded.

"Yes. I'd intended to go home and bring back some people to help me find Haddar."

"So there are only two of these time-craft?"

"Not exactly. By now, there should be another." She saw his deepening frown and wondered how to make him understand. She was sure that he already resented the knowledge she had that he didn't possess.

"It's complicated, Mikal. Even thinking about it gives me a headache, because I don't really understand time theory, either."

She went on to explain how another craft would be built—had already been built—and then could be sent back to this time even if years had passed in her time. The frown remained on his face as she explained, but finally he nodded.

"Yes, I think I understand. You have to separate the two times—think of them separately. If it took them years to build another time-craft, they could still send it here to arrive at the same time you arrived. But why hasn't that happened?"

Shayna felt a welcome relief even though his question brought back to her her own problem. She could see that he was becoming interested—perhaps even fascinated. Mikal had a very good mind; she already knew that. Everyone who'd written about him in his own time had described him as being brilliant, and his military strategies had reflected that.

"I think it hasn't happened because they're assuming that both Haddar and my own crew went to a future time—to a time when you were already working to bring peace." She noted the scowl on his face, but chose to ignore it.

"That mistake was mine. Because I'm a historian and because I know Haddar, the director of the project asked me where he would have gone, and I chose a time twenty or twenty-five years from now. Then we discovered that by leaving quickly, we could follow a sort of pathway through time that Haddar's craft would have made. And when we arrived here, I assumed it was that time, as I told you before. So I'm sure that they're searching for us in the future."

Mikal nodded his understanding. "It seems to me that this project of yours was ill-conceived. First of all, there should have been better security, so that this Haddar couldn't have stolen the craft. Then they shouldn't have gone forward until they figured out some way to know where the craft was going."

Shayna stared at him, shocked that he had learned so much so quickly—enough that he was now criticizing them. She explained what had happened, which took a very long time because he kept interrupting her to ask questions about the project that she couldn't answer.

"I'm a historian, Mikal, not a scientist," she said in exasperation. "In your world I guess it's possible for one person to understand everything, but it isn't in mine. We all have our specialties."

He was sitting in his chair again, and he drummed his fingers restlessly on the wooden arm. "I don't like that."

"That's because you're a control freak," she flung at him, regretting her words as soon as she'd spoken them.

" 'Control freak?' " he repeated. "What does that mean?"

"It means that you have to be in charge, to know everything there is to know. And that's just not possible in my world."

He was silent for a long time, his fingers still beating out a tattoo on the chair arms. "Maybe you're right," he said at last. "I have been thinking lately that there are so many new inventions that it's difficult to stay abreast of them."

She smiled. "That's why it's important for people to trust each other. I have to trust that those who design and make the aircar I use know what they're doing, so that I won't crash, and—"

"What's an aircar?"

She told him, and she could see his interest growing still more. So she told him about the Wantesa of her time and saw his pride that the capital of the Amaden had not only survived, but was thriving.

But it was careful talk, the conversation of two people who are avoiding the real issues. He wasn't ready to come to terms with the man she'd told him he would become, and she wasn't yet willing to accept that she would never again see the future she was describing to him.

The day faded away to dusk, and then to darkness. There was little food in the cabin, but they managed to fill their stomachs as Mikal continued to deluge her with questions about everything except his own future and the world he would create. He was fascinated by gadgetry, by computers, by the nascent space program—but he showed no interest at all in the structure he'd set up that would allow it all to happen.

At one point during their lengthy discussion, Shayna remembered an essay she'd written when she was twelve. Their teacher had asked them to imagine their fondest wish, and then write about what they would do if it came true. At twelve, she'd already been enthralled by the study of history. Her father was a respected writer of historical treatises, so she'd come to that love early.

Other children had written about becoming space travelers or about underwater exploration or about acquiring some expensive toy—but Shayna had written about traveling back in time to talk to Mikal Har-Amaden.

She'd written a dialogue that was much praised by her teacher, in which they'd talked about his long quest and its results. She'd imagined him as a pleasantly avuncular figure, not the austere man of the portrait. She'd even allowed a few tears to come to his eyes, which had occasioned a comment of "highly imaginative" from her teacher.

But nowhere in that imaginary dialogue had she envisioned him being interested in the unimportant details of daily life in her time, like aircars, spaceplanes, and computers. The great man of her dreams would never have been intrigued by such minor things.

Mikal was disappointing her. It seemed that every time she believed she had set aside that image of him as the man of history, she found that she hadn't, after all.

In the aftermath of the storm, the weather had turned cooler, and Mikal went outside to get firewood, then built a small fire. He resumed his questioning and she continued to explain her world. For the past few hours she had fallen easily, if not always happily, into the familiar role of teacher, with Mikal as a very bright and eager student. Now, however, as night came on and the firelight cast shadows around them, she felt a subtle change coming over them.

She suddenly became aware of her drab male disguise, even though she'd been quite comfortable before. Mikal had long since removed his dashing uniform jacket, leaving him in a formfitting jersey that outlined well-remembered muscles. And when their eyes met, they both looked away quickly—but not quickly enough to prevent a low hum of desire from filling the small silence.

"What will you do?" he asked suddenly after one of these silences. The question had the jarring quality of something he'd been holding back and was now blurting out.

"I don't know," she responded without looking at him. "I must find Haddar, of course. He will not give up, so I think I will have to kill him."

"Leave him to me. We'll find him and take care of that."

"He's my responsibility, Mikal."

His dark eyes lit with an amusement that irritated her. "You may come from a world where women can kill, but you're in my world now, and I can find him far more easily than you can."

He was right, of course, but as long as she could focus on finding Haddar, she could set aside thoughts of her own future. She knew that was what he'd been asking about.

"I don't want to kill him," she said. "I had hoped to persuade him to return. But now that he can't go back . . ."

"Well, I have no such scruples. He intends to kill me, so I will kill him first. But when I asked what you will do, I wasn't referring to Haddar."

"What can I do?" she asked, unable to keep the bitterness from her voice. "I'll have to return to Bettena's—if she'll have me."

Mikal watched her struggling to maintain control. She was doing a good job of it, except for that slight tremor in her voice. He saw her very differently now, but that hadn't lessened his love for her. He admired the bravery she'd shown by making this incredible journey, but bravery was not a quality he'd ever associated with women, and he was having some trouble adjusting his thinking.

But that problem was insignificant by comparison with the picture she'd painted of his future. He wanted to disbelieve her, but all his instincts—which had served him well in the past—told him that she spoke the truth. How could the man he knew he was betray his own people by leading them to a long-sought final victory and then throw it all away by sharing power with their enemies?

He left off those bleak thoughts and turned his attention instead back to the question he'd asked her, and her reply.

"Bett will be happy to have you back. She likes you very much. And I think she will not be too surprised to hear your story."

"I can't tell her the truth," she replied, shaking her head.

"Why not? You've told me."

"That's different. I had no choice. You saw the time-craft. I told you that I'd sworn an oath. It's a protocol that I helped to draw up for time-travel. And the most important part of it is that under no circumstances are we to tell the truth about where we've come from."

"Why is that so important?" he asked, unable to stifle a wish that she hadn't told him his future. He could certainly understand why that shouldn't happen, but as to the rest of it . . .

"The chief reason is that we don't know whether or not the future can be changed," she said with obvious reluctance. "You see, the fear is that if anything we say changes something, it could affect the world of the future: my world."

Now he understood the reluctance in her voice, and his thoughts seized on those words and turned them over carefully. So what she'd told him about himself wouldn't necessarily happen. It was only one of several possible futures. He immediately felt better. He was still in control and could easily guard against becoming what she said he would become.

It wasn't much different, he thought, from listening to a fortune-teller. By hearing what she had to say, one could guard against certain things.

He saw her staring at him intently, with fear in her eyes. "I know what you're thinking, Mikal—but you can't do that. You would destroy everything if you change your own future. That's what Haddar is trying to do, and that's why I'm here: to prevent that."

"How can you know that it would destroy everything, as you put it, if my people rule the world?"

"Because then the world would never truly be at peace," she replied, leaning forward with an intensity that came at him in waves. He'd never felt such a force, and wondered if, consciously or unknowingly, she was using her magic.

"The world would be at peace if we stay strong and are ready to put down any rebellion."

"The absence of war isn't the same as true peace."

Mikal was taken aback by her vehemence, and for a

brief moment he considered her words—but only for a moment.

Her ferocity had died away, and now she had a haunted look. All of Mikal's protective instincts resurfaced. Despite her strength and her great knowledge and all the rest of it, she needed him now, and that put things back to where they should be.

"We'll do as I planned," he told her gently. "You will return to live with Bettena as her cousin who was recently widowed, and after a suitable time we'll get married."

She said nothing, and he felt his anger with her returning. It astounded him that she could affect him this way, make him veer crazily from one feeling to the next.

"I'd go back to my people if I could," she said after a time. "But they believe that the gods sent me here from the future, and they will surely expect them to send me back."

He nodded. "And if they don't believe you're a messenger from the gods, then they might ally themselves with the Maccavi."

"Yes, but it's more than that. I told them something else as well." She drew in a ragged breath. "I also told them about you—that you would come to them one day and ask them to join the World Council, and to renounce their magic."

Mikal stared at her. Now he understood why the Elders had been willing to talk to him, when they'd always refused in the past to talk to Amaden leaders. But surprising as that was, what really shocked him were her final words.

"Are you saying that they agreed to renounce their use of magic?" he asked in disbelief.

"Not now. But they will do so when you come to them years from now to ask them to join the council."

Suddenly Mikal recalled the statement she'd made right after he'd found her about not being able to use her magic. "Is that why you told me you couldn't use your magic?"

She nodded. "The Astasi gave up their magic."

"But you've used it since then."

"I had no choice. Besides, they didn't give it up yet, and I'm here now. Anyway, I was given permission to use it if it became necessary to capture Haddar."

"And they never used it after that?" Mikal asked. Somehow this seemed even less believable than anything she'd told him. How could any people give up such power? And the fact that they would give it up on the order of an Amaden . . . Mikal couldn't believe it.

"No. They signed the pact and gave it up. They continued to use it in small, harmless ways, for healing and to bring the rains or hold them off, but they never again used it against other people."

"But it's obviously still there," he pointed out. "You used it."

"Of course it's still there. It's part of who we are. But that's the price my people paid for peace."

Mikal still couldn't quite believe it. While it was true that Astasi magic was no longer a match for Amaden weaponry, it was still an incredibly powerful force, and one that virtually guaranteed their safety, unless his people were willing to sacrifice many lives—probably many more lives than they'd sacrificed in other wars.

Within the top ranks of the Amaden military, the Astasi, despite their small numbers, were seen as being the most formidable of foes. Not only did they possess the magic fire, but they could easily repel any attempt at an invasion of their valley, thanks to that spell.

"Will they even give up the spell that protects their valley?" he asked.

"They would have, but no one knows how to end it. The Astasi have tried and scientists have tried, but it can't be broken."

Mikal felt better. She might think they'd tried, but he knew better. They'd saved some of their power. He was about to point that out to her and use it to explain why his people couldn't give up all their power, when she spoke again.

"The spell doesn't matter anymore. It hasn't for more than a century. When people come to the valley they fly in. And of course most of us no longer live in the valley."

Of course. He should have thought of that. What incredible weapons these flying machines would make—not just against the Astasi, but against their other enemies as well. With them the Amaden could easily control the world.

"Who invented these flying machines?" he asked, certain it must be his own people.

She frowned. "Many people worked on them for years, but the two men who are usually credited with inventing them are Amaden. One of them is a descendant of yours. Your family will finance many such things."

Of course. That didn't surprise him at all. Har-Amaden money was already being used to finance weapons research. Except for that nonsense about his betraying his people, the future she was talking about wasn't so different from what he might have imagined, if he'd ever thought about such things.

Then he saw that she was once again staring at him intently, and he feared that she might be reading his thoughts. He had no intention of arguing with her again about his future. By the time that future arrived, she would be his wife and the mother of his children, and . . .

His thoughts stopped there. If that was going to happen, she would know it. And it couldn't happen, could it? She had come here from a future time, so how could she also be here and married to him?

Mikal frowned. He'd thought that he had this all figured out, but now he knew he didn't. Except that she'd said that the future could be changed. His thoughts spiraled as he tried to make sense of it.

She got up. "I'm going to check to make sure that the spell I cast before is still in place. I don't think Haddar would come here now, but I can't be sure."

He merely nodded, too distracted by his thoughts to pay attention to her words. But when she didn't return quickly, he set aside his confused mental wanderings and got up to go find her. As he opened the door to the night, Mikal felt a return of that icy fear that she had vanished. Once he had feared that her magic would take her away from him. Now, in addition to that, he worried that her friends from the future would find her and take her.

He didn't see her at first, but then his eyes adjusted to the dark and he saw her standing at the edge of the hill, her back to him as she looked out over the valley. Instead of going to her immediately, he stood there for a moment watching her and wondering if he would ever truly understand all that she was.

But whether or not he ever understood her, he loved her. There wasn't much he was certain about right now, but he knew that. He loved her and he would have her—and he would keep her.

As Mikal stood there quietly watching her, his desire for her—his need to possess her—surged through him more powerfully than ever before. Now there were no more lies between them. Now he understood her differentness that had both attracted and disturbed him. He started toward her and she turned. He saw a slight wariness in the movement, and then in her eyes as he stopped only a foot from her.

"I love you," he said simply.

She smiled—nervously, he thought. "Even now that you know the truth?"

"More than ever—*because* I know the truth."

"But you don't like that truth, Mikal—or at least you don't like the truth about yourself."

"I meant because there are no more lies between us," he replied, not wanting to talk about what she saw as being his future.

Her pale green eyes searched his face carefully. "They will come for me one day, Mikal. Sooner or later, they will figure out where I am."

But they won't take you away from me, he thought, but didn't say. *If I have to kill them to prevent that, I'll do it.*

He reached out to brush away the strands of red hair that the night wind blew across her face, and his fingers lingered to trace a slow line across her cheek and down to the slender curve of her neck. Her skin was cool and she shivered slightly.

"I need you, Shayna. Come to bed with me."

For a moment it seemed that she would refuse. She backed away from him, even though he could see the reflection of his own desire in her eyes.

"Mikal, I don't think you understand how . . . difficult it can be for me sometimes. It's as though you're two men: the man I see here now and the great hero of history whose portraits and statues are everywhere."

"I'm a man—not a statue or a painting."

She continued to stare at him, then moved to him and wrapped her arms around him. "Yes, I know that—and I love you too."

Desire swarmed through him like a thousand angry bees, deafening him to everything but the need to possess her, to eradicate every trace of that other man who wasn't him, couldn't be him. He picked her up and carried her back into the cabin, not stopping until he had reached the bedroom.

Dimly, through a heat-haze of passion, Mikal knew that he wasn't being gentle. He tore her clothes away, eager to get beneath the rough peasant's garb to the soft, sweet flesh beneath. She lay back on the bed, watching as he tore off his own clothes after he'd lit the oil lamp so he could see her. The light flickered over her lush curves and he saw his own hunger reflected in her eyes. He didn't have to be gentle; she understood.

He fell onto the bed and drove himself into her moist, welcoming heat, feeling her body arch beneath him and her fingernails dig into his shoulders as a long, low moan poured from her throat.

He didn't want it to be over quickly, even though every fiber of his being was crying out for release and he could feel her straining against him, wanting what he wanted. But it was too late for restraint. His body ignored his brain as he poured himself into her.

Her cry mingled with his groan of release, but he knew that he'd been selfish, that he hadn't carried her with him. He kissed her—a soft, lingering kiss of apology—then withdrew from her and began to caress her, his hands tracing her curves slowly until his fingers found their goal.

She lay back in his arms, her body still arched and taut with need—a need he satisfied quickly while he watched her writhe and tremble beneath his touch, giving herself over completely to the pleasure his own need had denied to her earlier.

"Now I understand something," he said in the quiet afterward.

"What is that?" she asked as she curved herself about him.

"You said that I seemed to be two men, but I thought that you could seem to be two women."

"What do you mean?" She raised her head to stare at him.

"Women—most women, that is—aren't so, uh, uninhibited in bed. But then, at other times, you seem almost shy. I think I understand that now."

He was feeling a bit inhibited now himself. Men didn't talk to women about such things. And it didn't help at all that she was definitely amused. He wished that he'd never broached the subject. But now that he had, he found that other thoughts were crowding in: things he didn't want to think about.

"I'm sure that's true of most women in your time," she said with a smile curving her lips.

"But it isn't true in your time?" he persisted, seemingly unable to keep his mouth shut even though he didn't want this discussion.

"No. Remember that I told you that men and women are equal—and that includes in bed too."

Mikal frowned. He still couldn't accept this equality business, but he was beginning to see that it had its advantages.

She was sitting up now, one leg tucked through the other in a pose he'd seen dancers use that looked very uncomfortable to him, even though he was enjoying the view and her total lack of embarrassment at her nakedness. She arched one brow and smiled again.

"You said once that you didn't believe women are inferior to men—but you didn't really believe that, did you?"

How had he gotten himself into this discussion? he wondered.

"I do believe it," he insisted, even though he was sure they weren't talking about the same thing.

"Equal, *but,* is more like it," she said, tossing her head. He wished she hadn't been forced to cut off so much of her hair, because he liked it when she did that and created a cloud of wine-red.

"Maybe," he admitted.

"I'm sure you're much more enlightened than most men of your time, but you still have a long way to go, Mikal."

He frowned at her, certain now that he was being compared to someone—a lover or even a husband. Why hadn't it ever occurred to him that she must have someone back home in her own time? He supposed that it was because if she had, surely he wouldn't have allowed her to make this dangerous journey. But from what she was saying, permission didn't enter into it.

"There isn't anyone," she said, leaning forward to kiss him. Her nipples brushed lightly against his chest and he felt himself becoming aroused again.

"Are you reading my mind?" he demanded, even though he was greatly relieved at not being forced to ask the question that had been hammering at him.

"No—at least not by magic."

"You've never been married?" he asked, then amended the question. "Or have women decided that they don't want marriage any longer since they can support themselves?"

"No, I've never been married." She shrugged and the movement drew his attention to her full breasts. He was definitely aroused now, though she seemed to be paying it no attention.

"Most people do still marry, but at a later age. I just never met anyone, and I really love my work."

He already knew that she was a historian, but now she explained that she taught at the university that was located at the fort on High Point. He thought about his college days and the teachers he'd had: all men, of course. How did the youths she taught pay attention to the lectures?

She threw back her head with a sigh, then laughed. It was a sound he realized he hadn't heard very much.

"You can't begin to understand what a relief it is to stop pretending—to be myself again."

Mikal smiled. The "self" she was talking about was going to take some getting used to, but he took pleasure in it nevertheless. He reached for her.

"I want you again."

"Shayna! I'm so glad to see you again!"

Bettena enveloped her in a warm cloud of scent, then motioned them both into her apartment. "I was afraid that you'd gone back to the valley to stay."

When Bettena released her, Mikal bent to kiss her softly. "I have to go to the fort. I'll see you later."

"Take off that dreadful hat," Bettena ordered. "It must belong to Hana—and the dress too. That woman has no taste—and no bosom, either," she added, frowning at the fabric that was stretched tightly across Shayna's chest.

"Yes, they're hers," Shayna confirmed, then added dryly, "We didn't think it would be wise for Mikal to come back to Wantesa with a peasant boy in his carriage."

She removed the offensive hat she'd worn because she didn't have her wig with her. It felt good to be back with Bettena, whose unquestioning acceptance of her had come to mean quite a lot to Shayna.

But the truth was that neither she nor Mikal had wanted to return. It had seemed very important to them both to reaffirm their love after Shayna's revelations. Still, although Mikal had clearly been reluctant to leave their bed, she suspected that a part of him wanted to return to a life he understood—and could control.

"Did you go to the valley?" Bettena asked.

Shayna nodded. "I think you'd better sit down, Bett. I have something to tell you—and it may take a while."

Bettena sat and Shayna explained everything. To her credit, Bettena heard her out without interruption.

"I knew there was something you weren't telling us," Bettena said when Shayna had finished. "But *this?* It's incredible!" Then she frowned. "And how is Mikal taking all this? I thought he looked a bit stunned, to tell you the truth."

"I imagine he is, and I also think he doesn't believe all of it."

"What part of it doesn't he believe? You said that he saw this time-craft."

So she told Bettena about Mikal's future. "He says that it can't happen because he'd never betray his people, which is how he sees it."

Bettena nodded. "He would see it that way, but you said that's years in the future. Mikal will change."

"I'm not so sure. I worry that telling him will make him determined *not* to change."

"But he must. You've seen his future."

"Yes, but I'm not sure that it couldn't change. It's very complicated."

Bettena frowned. "I've seen Mikal when he returns from war, and I've heard him say how he hates it—all the deaths. I think he is already weary of war, but he doesn't know any other way. Maybe what you've told him will help him to change his mind."

Shayna stared at her. A chill slithered along her spine. Bettena could be right. She was silent for a moment, caught again in that incredibly complicated web of past and future. Was it possible that Mikal would change the world because she had told him about a future that her own words had created?

"I have so many questions that I scarcely know where to begin," Bettena said, drawing her out of her shocking thoughts. "But there is something I must tell you first. I worry that it's going to cause problems for both of you, and now that you've explained everything, I think I know where it must have come from.

"There is a rumor going around that Mikal has gotten involved with an Astasi witch. Jan came by just a short time ago to tell me about it."

"Oh no!" Shayna cried, then clenched her fists. "Haddar! It has to be him! I should have guessed he'd do something like this! He knows that his original plan to kill Mikal has little chance of success now, because of me, so he's changed tactics. Instead of killing Mikal he will destroy his reputation—and by doing that, will prevent Mikal from becoming the great peacemaker!"

"Now that I've heard your story, I think you must be right," Bettena agreed. "He's realized that he might well achieve his goal without killing Mikal."

"And the fact that people know the Elders talked to Mikal will only lend credence to Haddar's story," Shayna said sadly.

"I'm afraid so. Everyone knows that they've never been willing to talk to outsiders before."

"I must find Haddar!" Shayna said, thumping the arm of her chair. "And when I do, I'll make certain that he never says anything to anyone—ever again!"

Mikal strode into the office of the commander, his thoughts still half lost in the day and night he'd just spent with Shayna. They exchanged greetings. The older man was Mikal's uncle, his mother's older brother. He was fit and hearty, but Mikal knew that he hoped to retire to his country house soon, and that he'd long ago handpicked Mikal to succeed him.

They exchanged greetings, and the commander gestured Mikal to a chair, then asked his aide to close the door behind him. With his thoughts still on Shayna, Mikal was slow to notice the commander's grave expression—and when he did, he wondered what disaster was bearing down on them now. He didn't want to leave Shayna, but his mind was already turning over the possibilities. Was it trouble in the south again? There was an armistice, but no real peace treaty—not that that mattered much, in any event.

"Mikal," the commander said without preamble, "there's a very unpleasant rumor going about in the city."

"What's that?" Mikal frowned, having expected to hear a report from one of their agents somewhere.

"That you've become involved with an Astasi witch."

Not a trace of emotion showed on Mikal's face, but his thoughts bounced wildly about in his brain. Haddar! It had to be him. Damn the man!

"That's absurd," he said evenly, even managing to laugh. "Maybe it got started because of my meeting with the Elders. Everyone at Lonhola knew that I met with them."

"What I don't understand is why they were willing to meet with you. They've never done that before."

Mikal affected a shrug, hating the fact that he had to lie to this man he both liked and respected. "They didn't say, but I suspect that they wanted to be sure we knew they don't intend to make war on us. They probably guessed that we knew about the visit by the Maccavi agents."

The commander nodded. "Yes, that's what I thought as well. But this rumor is very disturbing. Sandri told me that he saw you recently, dining with your actress friend and another woman—a woman with green eyes."

Mikal nodded. "She's Bettena's cousin, a widow who's just recently arrived in the city. It's true that she has green eyes, but they aren't unheard of among Amaden." Mikal chose his words carefully, not wanting to lie any more than was necessary.

"It seems that she's also the woman who was picked up—wearing the disguise of a prostitute—when the men were searching for those three who tried to break into Lonhola."

"Yes, I'm aware of that. She was trying to find one of them because he had been making a nuisance of himself. It was a foolish thing for her to have done, and I told her that."

"Not only foolish, but rather strange, don't you think?"

"She's a bit . . . different," Mikal said in what was certainly one of the greatest understatements he'd ever made. "Very forthright—not unlike Bettena herself."

"Yes, I know Bettena's reputation. She's determined to stir up trouble among the women. I can't think what you see in her, Mikal."

"What I see is a very intelligent and talented woman whose company I enjoy. And the same goes for her cousin."

"You should get married, Mikal—and to the right kind of woman."

Mikal's anger caught even him by surprise. He leaned forward, his hands planted firmly on the arms of the chair. "The army can lay claim to my talents, Horace, but not to *all* my life. The rumors be damned! I'll see whoever I want!"

His outburst had no effect on the commander, who regarded him thoughtfully. "I keep thinking about what that midwife who attended your birth told your parents. She predicted that you would be a very great man one day—and you're already well on your way to greatness, Mikal. But great men can ill afford to have troubled personal lives."

"My personal life is not 'troubled,' Horace. In fact, I may be married sooner than you think."

The commander brightened briefly, then grew sober again. "Do you mean this widow?"

"Yes. I have every intention of proposing marriage to her as soon as decency permits. She's beautiful and intelligent and she just needs to be, uh, taken in hand a bit."

Chapter Twelve

"Will you have some sherry?" Mikal asked, picking up the sparkling crystal decanter.

Shayna nodded. After another too-large meal, she wasn't at all sure that she could fit in even a small glass of sherry—but it *was* delicious. She watched him pour it and worried about his probable reaction to the news she had to give him about the rumor.

If she knew Mikal—and she thought she did at this point—his reaction was likely to present a problem. He would either dismiss it out of hand, or he would insist that the best way to lay it to rest was for them to marry right now, thereby erasing any "blemish" to her name.

They had just finished a late dinner at his house, after he returned from the fort. Mikal had been unusually quiet during dinner, but she supposed that he had plunged himself into his work. She envied him that and wished that she too had work to keep her mind occupied. As it was, she had little to do but make plans to find Haddar. And beyond that her life was a dark, blank space: an unknown amount of time to be spent waiting and hoping that Teres and the others would find her.

She could not marry Mikal, that much she knew. As yet, she'd done nothing that would change the future from what she knew it to be. She'd persuaded the Astasi to cooperate and she'd told Mikal of his own future—but if in fact that had changed things, her intervention had done nothing more than to cause the future she already knew to come to pass.

Marriage would be different. In the future she knew, Mikal had never married, and it must remain that way.

She took a sip of the sherry. "Mikal, Bettena told me that there's a rumor going about the city that you have become involved with an Astasi witch."

His reaction was scarcely what she'd expected. He merely nodded and even smiled. "I must never again discount Bett's ability to gather information."

"You knew about it?" she asked in astonishment. Bettena had said he was unlikely to hear it this quickly, that the military tended to live insular lives.

His expression remained neutral. "The commander confronted me with it when I went up to the fort."

She studied him, searching for the anger she was sure he was trying to hide. "But what will we do about it? It's dangerous for me even to be here with you."

"The army isn't likely to be spying on my home," he said dryly. "I told him about you—not that you're Astasi, of course. I gave him the story we've come up with. And I told him that I intended to marry you as soon as decency permits."

Shayna wondered how long that was. She was supposed to have been widowed six months ago. The society Mikal lived in had very rigid social rules.

"I think we needn't wait much longer," he went on, answering her unspoken question. "Six months would be sufficient if I'd known you all that time. But since you arrived here only a month ago, we'll have to wait a bit longer."

She didn't ask how much longer because she didn't want to create the impression that she was eager to marry him. That might cause him to shorten the time.

"I don't give a damn what people think," Mikal stated firmly, "But I don't want to cause problems for you."

"What do you mean?"

"Mainly my sister, Estella," Mikal said with a faint grimace. "She lives here in Wantesa and she's a very powerful figure in society. She could make life very difficult for you. In fact I shall have to invite her and that husband of hers to dinner soon, so she can meet you. Otherwise you'll already be off on the wrong foot with her."

"I met her," Shayna told him, then explained the circumstances. "I doubt that she's going to be very friendly toward me in any event, because I'm sure she doesn't like Bett."

Mikal laughed. "She doesn't. Bett has spoken her mind one too many times. And besides that, Essie has regularly trotted out marriage candidates that I've rejected, and she fears that I'll end up marrying some actress."

"All this is very interesting, Mikal, but I don't see how it solves the problem. The fact is that the rumors are true: I am Astasi."

A slight smile still clung to Mikal's lips and Shayna could tell that this was another of those times when she hadn't spoken like a woman of his time. She was learning—or rather relearning—what it meant to be female in this time. A "lady" didn't change the subject or suggest that a man wasn't getting the point.

"I think it likely that Haddar started this rumor," she went on. "Since he hasn't yet succeeded in killing you, he's trying to destroy you in another way."

"You're right, and that means he's still here in the city. Tell me about him—everything you know about him."

She sighed. "More than I want to know. He's a colleague of mine at the university—a historian just like me. To understand him completely, you have to understand a bit more about our world than I've already told you.

"For the most part, there are no tribes anymore. Over

the years and the centuries, people have intermarried and most have long since ceased to live in their tribal lands. I know that ownership of land is very important in this time, but it isn't in my world. People largely derive their wealth from their talents.

"Initially the World Council consisted of representatives from each of the tribes, but over the years, because of intermarriage, that has changed. Now the council is elected by everyone, without regard to tribal origins.

"But it isn't quite as perfect as it sounds—because of two tribes. The Amaden have intermarried less than the other tribes, and my own people haven't intermarried at all. So there are always Amaden and Astasi on the council.

"Most Amaden—in fact all but a handful—are happy with the world as it is. We are at peace and all the intermarriage over the years has guaranteed that tribal warfare could never break out again. The Amaden have always been—and remain—an excessively proud and arrogant people, but not even they want a return to the past."

She paused to gauge his reaction to this truth, but he merely nodded.

"There are a few Amaden—and Haddar is their most outspoken member—who believe that the Amaden were robbed of their destiny, which was, of course, to rule the world."

She hesitated again, wishing now that she'd found a way to explain Haddar without offering this confirmation of Mikal's own beliefs.

"I debated him once on this issue: a public debate at the university. I was chosen by my colleagues to represent our view, even though nearly all of them are senior to me. Haddar resented that. He's accused me more than once of using my magic to further my career."

Shayna paused, recalling that well-attended debate. Haddar had declared Mikal Har-Amaden to be the greatest villain of history, which had aroused the audience to such anger that the debate had very nearly ended right there.

"When the Time Project was announced and I was chosen as its chief historical consultant, Haddar became enraged. He was senior to me and, despite his radical beliefs, he *is* an accomplished historian.

"Anyway, as time went on, his anger didn't lessen and I had begun to worry that he might attempt to sabotage the project. I told the project director this and urged him to set up better security. But it was too late. Haddar had managed to gain the cooperation of an engineer at the project, and they broke in and stole the time-craft.

"Haddar is a driven man. He isn't insane, at least not in the usual sense of the word. And he's also brilliant—and cunning too, which explains how he came up with the idea of spreading the rumor.

"He would have no problem fitting himself into this world. In fact he's almost certainly much better at it than I am, because he must have planned this journey for a long time, and would have researched everything very carefully. I would have done the same thing, if there'd been time. He knew exactly where he was going in time, while we were just following him."

"How will he be surviving here?" Mikal asked. "Surely the money has changed."

"It has, but my guess is that that would pose no problem for him. He's a wealthy man, and he could simply have hired someone to duplicate the money of this time—which is what the project would have done once we settled on a time period for our journey. As it is, Teres, the director of the project, borrowed coins from a museum, which were lost when the craft self-destructed."

"So he came well prepared to live in this time," Mikal said thoughtfully.

"I'm sure he did. He had the luxury of time for planning all this. For a time I worried that he might have brought weapons with him other than stunners, but apparently he didn't, or he would surely have used them by now."

"What sort of weapons?" Mikal asked with considerable interest.

"Explosives of the sort we use for mining or to take down buildings. I've never actually seen them myself, but I know that they're very effective and quite small."

"But he could have brought them?"

"I don't think so. First of all, they're extremely difficult to get, and secondly, as I said, if he had them, he would have used them—on this house, for example."

"And your spell couldn't protect against that?"

"I don't know, but I doubt it."

Mikal got up and began to pace restlessly. "Then you're undoubtedly correct. If he had them, he would have used them. Now tell me about the stunners: their range and direction and so forth."

She did so. "Their range is quite limited because they're meant for personal protection only. But Mikal, it's because of those stunners that I must be the one to find him. If your men find him, he'll use the stunner and, before long, there could be panic among your soldiers over this new weapon."

"I'm aware of that. Fortunately the commander at Lonhola has totally discredited the guards' story by saying that they were merely trying to cover up their dereliction of duty, but we can't risk another report of them."

As he spoke, Shayna heard someone tap at the closed doors to the parlor. Mikal opened one of the ornately carved wooden doors and she could see one of his servants in the hallway. He turned back to her.

"You'll have to excuse me for a few moments," he said formally, then disappeared, closing the door behind him.

If he'd been summoned away at any other time, she would have simply assumed it to be army business, but in light of their discussion, she wondered. It sounded to her as though Mikal had decided to call off the search for Haddar by the soldiers, but she doubted very much that he was giving up the search itself.

When she had discussed her intent to find Haddar with Bettena earlier, and had expressed the concern that the soldiers might find him first, Bettena had thought that unlikely. According to Bettena it was likely that Haddar and his men had remained in the waterfront area of the city, where they would be less conspicuous—and where the presence of soldiers could be guaranteed to send out an alarm.

The waterfront was the source of most of the illegal activity in the city and undoubtedly a base for enemy agents as well. The result was that there was a highly effective, if primitive, communications system that meant that everyone would quickly know about the presence of soldiers in the area.

Shayna had no doubt that Haddar knew this and would take advantage of it. According to Bettena, the fact that soldiers had been there already asking about him would have given him a certain status, and if he were spreading gold around as well, he could virtually be guaranteed that the soldiers wouldn't find him.

She wondered what Mikal had in mind, and if his being called away had anything to do with his plan. Given the fact that she had plans of her own, she decided that she'd better find out.

So she opened the door a crack and peered out into the hallway. No one was there, but she could hear faint male voices coming from the back of the house. Mikal had a small study there, and as she began to creep quietly down the hallway, she could see that the door to the study was closed.

Even with her ear pressed against the heavy door, she couldn't hear most of what was being said. But she heard enough to know that Mikal's visitors were being ordered to find Haddar—and that Mikal was even telling them about the stunners their quarry possessed.

She backtracked quickly to the parlor and closed the door. If he was telling them about the stunners, they must be men he trusted completely—and that suggested they could be family members. She thought that it behooved her to get a look at them when they left, in case she ran into them while she was searching for Haddar herself. She couldn't begin to guess what story Mikal had told them, but it was possible that he would tell them to be on the lookout for her, as well.

No doubt he would be describing her prostitute disguise to them, which was fine with her, since she intended to use the poor peasant boy disguise this time. Perhaps she would ask Bettena to change it a bit just in case they knew about it as well.

It was, she thought, a great stroke of fortune that Mikal had introduced her to Bettena, with all her cosmetic disguises and her access to all sorts of costumes. The only problem she was having with Bettena was that she wanted to disguise herself and accompany Shayna.

A fine mist was falling outside, but Shayna pushed open the glass-paned doors that led to the terrace along the side and part of the rear of the house, then stepped out and closed it behind her. Mikal's visitors must have come by way of the kitchen door, since she hadn't heard them rap with the big brass knocker at the front door. So no doubt they would leave the same way.

In an effort to establish a reason for her to be out here in the misty night, Shayna hurried off the terrace and ran to the shadows near the wall at the edge of the property. She could tell Mikal that she was just checking the spell she had cast to protect him.

She waited, crouched in the shadows behind several big forsythia bushes near the wall. From this spot she had a clear view of the kitchen door. She knew there was a gate at the rear of the property and that they were likely to be using that.

Only a few minutes had passed before light spilled out from the kitchen and two figures emerged. They headed toward her, just as she'd hoped when she chose this spot less than twenty feet from the rear gate, where a lantern sat in a recess in the wall.

"What do you think?" one man asked as they approached the gate, obviously not in a hurry.

"I don't like it," the other man said. "But Mikal's right. If it gets out that these men stole some magic weapon from the Astasi, there's going to be hell to pay. We've got to find them fast."

"Yeah, he's right. We don't need a war with the Astasi,

and it's good to know they don't want that, either."

Their words then became unintelligible as they passed through the gate and vanished into the mews beyond it. So Mikal had told them that the stunners were magic weapons stolen from the Astasi, who wanted them back. It was a risky strategy, because if word got out that the Astasi possessed such weapons, it could easily bring about the war he wanted to avoid.

They must be family, she thought. There was no one else he would trust so completely. Cousins, perhaps. She'd gotten a good look at them both and thought there was a strong resemblance. By now she'd become adept at picking up the differences in accents and speech between the upper and lower classes, and the two men she'd just seen were definitely the former, despite their rough clothes. But they were probably also good at mimicking the speech of the lower classes, or Mikal wouldn't be using them.

She got up and hurried back to the house, hoping that Mikal might have remained in his study for a few minutes. But before she had even reached the edge of the terrace, he had opened the doors.

"I decided to check on the spell," she said, slipping past him into the parlor.

"You might have taken the time to cover yourself."

"I didn't think it was still raining."

Mikal closed the doors and stood looking down at her. "You have many talents, little witch, but lying isn't one of them."

"Stop calling me that, Mikal! It's offensive—and patronizing as well."

"Patronizing?" he echoed. "What do you mean?"

"You sound as though you're talking to a child."

"In my experience it's children who listen at doors and hide in bushes."

Well, he certainly had her there. Her irritation drained away, but she refused to smile. "I just wanted to see who they were."

"Then why didn't you just ask me?"

"Because you wouldn't have told me."

He smiled, then chuckled. "Are you telling me my future again—at closer range, perhaps? I'm surprised that you didn't just transport yourself out there and then back in here. I've always understood that the Astasi can do that."

"They can, but I can't. It takes a lot of practice." And I'm going to practice, she thought. She hadn't wanted to do it because she still felt uncomfortable using her powers.

"It could make traveling between Bett's apartment and my house easier and safer," he pointed out.

"I don't like using my powers, Mikal. When the council gave me permission to use them, they didn't have that in mind. And anyway, you're straying from the subject. Who are those men? I know you hired them to find Haddar and his friends."

"I didn't hire them. They're my cousins, and they've undertaken a few missions to the waterfront before, when I've wanted to see what enemy agents were lurking about in the city."

"And when you wanted them killed."

"Yes. Are you satisfied now?"

"I think there are things about you that I'd rather not know."

"Then you shouldn't be listening at doors. Might I remind you that this isn't your world?"

"When I thought about you, I never imagined you to be hiring assassins," she said, knowing that what he was doing was necessary and that she herself might be forced to kill Haddar and the others.

He put his hands on her shoulders. "Shayna, it's time you gave up your ridiculous dreams about me and accept me as I am."

"That isn't so easy," she said softly, knowing again that he was right.

"I didn't say it was—and I'm glad that you lived in a time when such things aren't necessary."

She moved away from him. "But you're not glad enough to make that come true, aren't you?"

He stared at her in silence for a moment. "I think we

should both agree not to have this discussion again."

She felt like screaming at him or pounding on him until he saw the truth, but instead she merely nodded. For all his behavior and words now, she knew he was a good man, and she would have to trust that he'd find his way to an acceptance of his future. So she nodded her agreement.

He took her hand. "Come to bed with me. At least we don't fight there."

It seemed that all she had to hear was that slight huskiness in his voice, and all her anger and fears just vanished. Never had she imagined that she could feel this way about a man—not even the Mikal Har-Amaden of her old fantasies. The raw force of their mutual desire took her breath away.

On this night Mikal reverted to the tender, considerate lover, holding his own hunger in check as he used his lips and tongue and his big, hard hands to draw from her sensations she still couldn't quite believe.

They seemed to float, bodies entwined, in some secret place, far from either of their worlds. It was here and only here that she could truly love him with a wild abandon: a place where the impossible became—for a little while—real.

"Yes! That's perfect! Perhaps I should put you on the stage." Bettena smiled wickedly. "I know of a play being cast soon that requires an Astasi witch."

Shayna laughed. Bettena was in a gay mood that she found irresistible. And she knew the reason—or rather, reasons—for that mood. Not only was she enjoying instructing Shayna in how to portray a peasant youth come to the city, but she was also looking forward to her own return to the stage—the stage in this case being the waterfront. She had persuaded Shayna to let her accompany her on her search for Haddar.

Shayna had resisted the idea until Bettena pointed out that if Mikal should discover their scheme, Bettena could say that at least she hadn't allowed Shayna to go there alone. Shayna seriously doubted that would make much difference in Mikal's mind, but she didn't want to be the cause of a strain in their relationship.

Besides, she admitted to Bettena that she didn't really want to go alone to that teeming place of dark, narrow streets and drunken men and thieves. She wasn't in any real danger, of course, but using her powers to save herself was in itself dangerous.

Under Bettena's watchful eye, she practiced her walk some more. Bettena was a marvel. Shayna could now understand why she'd been such an accomplished actress. In a blink she had transformed herself from a woman who carried herself with a proud, erect dignity to a farm boy who shuffled along, shoulders slouched and head down as though "he" had no real right to be walking this earth, but must do so.

Shayna had also become more accomplished at lowering her voice—which Bettena did effortlessly—and mimicking the accent and speech patterns of a country boy. She was sure that she could now withstand all but the closest scrutiny, and Bettena said that no one was likely to give her that close scrutiny, if only because most of them couldn't withstand it themselves.

"Now let's see how well you do if you're challenged in any way," Bettena suggested. "I'll pretend to be a constable—not that you're likely to encounter any of them. They avoid the area as much as possible."

Bettena stepped up to Shayna with a fierce look. "You there, boy! What's your business here?"

"Why, nothin' sir. I wuz just wantin' t' see the city—and mebbe find some work." Shayna adopted an expression of wide-eyed innocence and slouched even more.

"Very good, but watch the eyes. You shouldn't look straight at anyone—especially anyone challenging you. Besides, it only draws attention to your eyes. The cap helps to hide them, but looking down works even better."

She drew Shayna over to the big mirror in a corner of her bedroom, where they stood side by side, staring at their reflections. Shayna laughed. They were a pair, all right. Bettena had acquired two wigs of lank brown hair, which she'd then proceeded to hack away at until she was satisfied that they looked as awful as possible.

Then, with skillfully applied makeup, she'd managed a subtle transformation of their features—and for good measure, had thrown in a wicked-looking scar that ran from just beneath Shayna's right eye to her jaw.

Their clothing was much the same as Shayna had worn when she went to the valley: coarsely woven, drab, and loose-fitting, with cracked and scuffed boots and billed caps pulled low over the ugly wigs.

"Remember, no smiling or laughing. Onstage we can blacken teeth, but that won't stand up under close scrutiny. Your teeth, especially, are entirely too perfect."

Shayna smiled—this time without showing her teeth. "If I didn't know it was us, I'd never believe it myself."

"I think we're ready for our debut. I'll have Mogun drive us to the edge of the district, then pick us up again later. We have a lot of walking to do, and these boots are already uncomfortable."

Shayna hugged Bettena impulsively. "I don't know what I'd do without you, Bett."

Bettena returned the hug warmly. "Don't thank me. My life was in danger of becoming downright dull until you arrived on the scene."

Shayna laughed. "Your life will never be dull, Bett."

She had meant it as a joke, but even as she spoke, she realized that she knew it to be true—and Bettena seemed to realize that. Shayna could see the unspoken question in her eyes, and she nodded slowly.

"Yes. I know your future."

For the first time in Shayna's acquaintance with this remarkable woman, she saw Bettena flustered. "I didn't think you would know anything about me. I'm not Mikal."

"But you will be famous, Bett. Your plays are still performed even in my time. I saw one of them only a few months ago. I'm not an expert on theater history, but I do know that of all the playwrights you've mentioned, you're the only one whose name is still known to the general public."

Bettena's eyes filled with tears. She dabbed at them carefully to avoid destroying her makeup. "Is that how you knew about the dollhouse?"

Shayna had forgotten about that. She rolled her eyes. "Yes. That's one of the mistakes I made."

"Well, it was a good mistake. I've changed the play—but of course you know that." She shook her head. "This is all very confusing."

"It is for me as well, but it's a great relief to be able to be honest with you and Mikal, at least."

Bettena stared at her solemnly. "You won't marry him, will you?"

"I can't, Bett. So far I've done nothing that would change his future—but that would."

Bettena nodded sadly. "Then you will go home."

"Why do you say that?"

"Because if you stay here, Mikal would talk you into it sooner or later. I've been observing him for years now, and if there's one thing I know, it's that Mikal gets what he wants. And there is nothing he wants more than you."

Now tears were threatening Shayna's makeup as well, and Bettena quickly handed her a handkerchief. "No crying when we're in disguise. We'll just have to save that for later."

"I really do love him, Bett."

"I know you do. Impossible love is a constant theme in literature and on the stage, you know. But I don't think anyone could ever have imagined *this*."

Then she shook off her somber mood and took Shayna's arm. "Let's be on our way. There's nothing like a bit of adventure to take our minds off our problems."

Less than an hour later, the two women were walking along one of the narrow, winding streets that led to the waterfront. When there was no one within earshot, Shayna described this area in her time.

"It will all be rebuilt two centuries from now, after a

terrible fire that destroyed hundreds of houses. Now it's filled with wonderful little stone houses and is home to many artists and writers. In fact, rebuilding this area used up the last of the golden stone. Everything built after that is built from a synthetic stone that still looks very real."

"What an improvement!" Bettena exclaimed as they passed by the squalid little wood-frame houses that seemed to stand only by leaning against their neighbors. "But where do the poor live?"

"No one is truly poor. The government helps those who cannot help themselves."

They both stared at several malnourished children who played in the gutter nearby. "How wonderful!" Bettena murmured.

"It is Mikal who will create the lasting peace that will make it possible," Shayna said, as though by saying it she could guarantee that he would do it.

"You need to make him understand that," Bettena said. "Have you considered the possibility that if you hadn't come here, Mikal might not have sought peace?"

"Yes, I've thought about it. But he's a good man, and I think he will come to that decision on his own."

"But we'll never know, will we?"

Bettena's comment echoed in Shayna's mind as they left the ugly houses behind and emerged on the wider street that bordered the harbor. There were many more people here, and both women began to covertly study the crowds, no longer conversing as they searched for Haddar and his men.

An hour later they had traveled the entire waterfront street with no sign of them. They were jostled a few times by drunken men and propositioned once by a thin, ragged prostitute—but otherwise, they encountered no problems. Finally they made their way to an empty pier and sat down.

"Well, I guess our disguises are a success." Bettena smiled, referring to the encounter with the prostitute. "I recognized her. She's been to the settlement house a few times. She'll be dead within a year—but not before she spreads her disease around some more."

"What disease?" Shayna asked.

"Syphilis. It's become quite a problem. But I suppose that it doesn't even exist in your time."

"No, it doesn't—but I've read about it."

Bettena sighed. "How wonderful your world must be. Tell me what the harbor looks like in your time."

"It's quite beautiful. There's a lovely park and all the boats there are pleasure boats. Nothing is shipped by sea anymore because it can be moved much faster by air. I have friends who have a beautiful sailboat and I've sailed here many times."

A vivid image of those times came to her, surprising her with its clarity. Would she ever sail with her friends again? And if she did, would she enjoy it as much? How could she, when a part of her would always remain here with Mikal?

"Mikal has a boat, you know," Bettena said, breaking into her thoughts. "It's just down there, past the bend. He loves to sail, though he doesn't get much opportunity."

Tears sprang to Shayna's eyes, and Bettena stared at her. "What is it?"

Shayna shook her head and turned away, hoping that Bettena would think it was only the mention of Mikal's name that had affected her. But she was, of course, thinking about his death.

It felt so strange. Mikal would live many more years—and be gone centuries before her own time. There was no reason for her to feel this way. But thoughts of his death seemed to open that awful chasm between them: the darkness of the centuries that really separated them.

They continued to stroll along the waterfront, watching the ships being unloaded or readied for sailing again. They bought meat pasties from a street vendor, and even visited a few taverns that were, even in daytime, filled with foul-smelling, drunken men. Bettena had told her that the taverns all watered down their brews so that, if she could stand the taste, she at least didn't need to worry about getting drunk so easily.

Shayna cast off her bleak mood and concentrated instead on studying these people. Bettena's earlier remark about her returning home had made her realize that she had a unique opportunity to add to the knowledge of this period. She was determined that when she got back to Bettena's apartment, she would begin to set it all down.

When they were leaving one of the taverns, Shayna very nearly ran into a man she recognized only after they had passed each other. It was one of Mikal's cousins! She turned back involuntarily, then hurried away when she saw him pause at the entrance to the tavern to stare at her.

"What's wrong?" Bettena whispered.

"That man I nearly ran into—he's Mikal's cousin." She'd forgotten to tell Bettena about them and did so now. "I think he might have recognized me."

"Did you meet him?"

"Oh. No, I didn't." Shayna relaxed.

"I may have met him, though I can't recall. No worry, though. He's probably just keeping a sharp eye out for Haddar."

Shayna hoped that was the case—and also hoped that he wouldn't find him.

They were ready to give up and return to meet the carriage when Bettena suddenly laid a hand on Shayna's arm. Shayna had been studying the laborers who were just ending their long day's work at the docks.

"Over there, near that pile of crates," Bettena whispered, gesturing discreetly.

"Yes!" Shayna whispered. "That's Haddar's student. If we can follow him . . ."

The two women set off in the direction the young man was taking. Shayna hoped that he might lead them to Haddar's lodgings. But their timing was wrong. The waterfront was now filled with men hurrying away from the docks to the taverns and their homes. They did their best but, in the end, they lost him.

"Well, at least we know they're here." Shayna sighed

as they both collapsed onto the seat in the carriage.

"Perhaps we should come back at night," Bettena suggested. "This man Haddar might be lying low during the day."

Shayna agreed. "But how can I manage that? Mikal expects to see me every night."

"You could arrange to feel indisposed."

Shayna smiled at that old ploy. "Fine. We'll do it tomorrow night. Unfortunately I have to dine with Mikal's sister tonight."

"Oh? 'Unfortunately' is putting it mildly. And the fact that she knows there's a connection to me won't help."

"Mikal is determined to force her to befriend me."

"Of course. If you were really going to marry him, it would be important."

Shayna lapsed into silence. It helped to have Bettena understand her situation, but that didn't lessen the pain of knowing that she was living a lie where Mikal was concerned. *Still* living a lie, she amended sadly. She'd just exchanged one lie for another.

Shayna was certain that she'd never spent a more uncomfortable evening than the one she was enduring now. She simply could not imagine how a family that had produced Mikal could also have produced Estella.

The worst of it, as far as Shayna was concerned, was the excessive politeness. She'd already known that this was an era that made much of appearances—and to all appearances, Estella was charming to her. But her conversation consisted entirely—or so it seemed to Shayna—of carefully veiled insults and hidden barbs.

When she began to probe—delicately, of course—Shayna's background, Shayna wondered if she might have heard the rumor. She glanced at Mikal and he shook his head, a careful gesture intended only for her. When Shayna had arrived, Estella and her husband were already present, and she assumed Mikal was letting her know that the rumor had not come up in their conversation.

Fortunately Shayna had a carefully plotted background. Bettena had simply borrowed one from a young actress of her acquaintance who had since left Wantesa.

It was only because of Mikal that she managed to get through the evening. In his eyes she saw apology and love in equal measure, and a few times he intervened to prevent Estella from becoming even worse.

Estella's one redeeming feature, as far as Shayna was concerned, was her very apparent love for her brother. But of course that only served to make her more determined that he shouldn't marry someone unsuitable.

After dinner, as was the absurd custom in this time, the men withdrew for cigars and brandy, leaving Shayna alone with Estella. For one brief moment Shayna, who by now had a very genuine headache, was tempted to cast a spell on this abominable woman. It shocked her that she would even think of doing such a thing, and it worried her greatly that she'd become so accustomed to her powers that she might find it difficult to bury them again.

"Well, my dear Miss Hartaman, you certainly seem to have entranced my brother in a very short time," Estella said, no longer hiding her disapproval now that the men were gone. "Hartaman" was a surname borrowed from the same actress whose background she'd stolen.

Shayna thought that her choice of words was interesting, but probably only coincidental. "He's been very kind," she replied noncommittally.

"Oh, Mikal is that. He was always kind—even to the peasants and the house servants. It's his nature. But I sense more than kindness here." She stared hard at Shayna. "What remarkable eyes you have, Miss Hartaman. Astasi eyes."

"Yes. Or so I've been told. I've never seen an Astasi, of course." Shayna met her gaze easily.

"Your accent is interesting too. I've never heard one quite like it."

Shayna feigned embarrassment. "I've been trying to correct what I suppose must be a country accent to people here. Perhaps what you hear is that effort."

"I'm sure Bettena must be helping you. She has many talents."

"Yes, she does." Once again, Shayna's gaze met hers unflinchingly.

"Mikal has shown a propensity toward . . . arrangements with unsuitable women. But given his position, he would never marry one."

"I'm sure you're right," Shayna said, then couldn't resist adding, "But it's possible that his idea of a suitable woman could be somewhat different from yours."

When she saw Estella's reaction to that, she pushed it a bit further. For the first time this evening she was beginning to enjoy herself, headache or no.

"It seems to me that Mikal's position is such that he could choose whomever he wanted. In fact, he's said as much himself."

Estella was by now very nearly choking on her anger. "Are you saying that you've actually discussed the subject of marriage?"

Shayna affected a careless shrug. "In theory only. I haven't known him that long, and I'm in no hurry to marry again. I'm not even certain that I'll stay in Wantesa."

Estella's anger turned quickly to disbelief, but before she could pursue that, the men returned—rather more quickly than Shayna supposed was the custom.

Soon after that, Estella and her husband left—but not before offering to see Shayna home in their carriage. Mikal slid an arm around her waist in a gesture that was obviously shocking to his sister.

"She'll be staying for a time," he told her. "We have some things to discuss."

As soon as the door had closed behind them, Mikal drew her into his arms. "I'm sorry she was so unpleasant. But when she knows that she can't prevent me from marrying you, she'll change."

Shayna wrapped her arms around him. "I don't want to talk about her."

"Oh?" He arched his brow with amusement. "And

what subject would you care to discuss?"

She smiled. "As I recall, you're the one who said we had something to discuss."

He chuckled and glanced meaningfully toward the staircase. "What I had in mind is a *very* informal discussion."

Chapter Thirteen

"Mikal will have both our heads if he finds out about this," Bettena said, frowning into the mirror.

"He won't find out," Shayna said confidently. "If his cousin had recognized either of us, I'd know it by now."

She smiled into the mirror as her thoughts spiraled back to last night. Little shivers of remembered pleasure ran through her: tiny echoes of their lovemaking. Mikal never failed to surprise and delight her. Sometimes he was fiercely possessive, and other times—like last night—he was wonderfully tender and even playful.

"I know that smile." Bettena chuckled as she put the cap onto Shayna's head. "I used to smile like that from time to time myself."

Her slightly wistful tone caught Shayna's wandering attention. "Why haven't you married, Bett?"

"Because men are best appreciated at a distance. Even the best of them tend to think they own you once they've exchanged marriage vows. There." Having put the cap onto Shayna's head and then fussed a bit with the cropped wig, Bettena stood back to admire her handiwork. "Even Mikal wouldn't recognize you now."

Shayna thought she was probably right, even though it didn't matter. They weren't about to run into Mikal drinking the night away at some waterfront tavern. When he'd stopped by earlier, Bettena had told him that Shayna was feeling ill and was resting. According to Bettena, the cause was an overindulgence in sweets at the tearoom this afternoon. Bettena, it seemed, couldn't help embroidering on a story, cleverly using Shayna's past remarks about the quantity of food eaten by people of this time.

Shayna, who'd been listening at her bedroom door, heard Bettena sigh. "It must have been those cream cakes. I warned her they were very rich, but she'd never had them before." Shayna had in fact had only two of them. They were delicious, and as far as she knew, didn't exist any longer in her diet-conscious world.

Mikal had accepted the excuse easily and told Bettena to give her his love. He'd spend the evening catching up on his reading.

So now here they were, once more disguised as poor farm boys, about to set off for the waterfront again in the hope that night would bring out Haddar and his companions.

This time, since it was dark, Bettena instructed her driver to drop them closer to the waterfront. He pulled into the shadows across from the bawdy house Shayna had seen that day with Jan, and the two women got out. Across the way, an elegant carriage pulled up in front of the house and two men got out. Shayna drew in her breath sharply, then released it with a sigh of relief. For one brief instant she'd been sure that one of the men was Mikal. But then he half turned in her direction and she saw she was mistaken.

Bettena followed her gaze as the two of them stepped into the street. "Mikal came here from time to time in the past, but he wouldn't do that now."

Shayna knew that, but it still felt good to have Bettena confirm it. "It bothers me that he came here at all."

"He's a man," Bettena said with a shrug. "Better than

most, of course, but still a man."

They made their way slowly along the crowded streets. It seemed to Shayna that there were even more people here now than there had been in the daytime—and most of them were drunk. Skinny, garishly made-up prostitutes plied their trade. Furtive deals seemed to be taking place in shadowy alleyways. Here and there bodies sprawled in foul-smelling gutters. Within the space of two blocks they saw three fights taking place, with onlookers cheering them on and laying bets.

It was difficult for Shayna to keep her attention focused on finding Haddar, and she realized that in the semidarkness and the crowds, she might well pass within a few feet of him and not see him. But at least no one was paying the two of them any attention, except for the hungry prostitutes who approached them from time to time.

There were at least a dozen taverns along the street that faced the harbor. After they had walked its entire length, Bettena said it was time to begin searching them, and so they made their way into the first one they came to.

The foul odors of unwashed bodies and strong brews and tobacco assaulted Shayna's nose and eyes, and the din nearly deafened her. She glanced at Bettena, who seemed to be taking it all in stride. Bettena had told her that she'd come down here before in disguise, with friends. She'd wanted to "savor the experience," as she'd put it. Shayna wondered how she could come back again.

Although the tavern wasn't large, it took them nearly a half hour to establish that their quarry wasn't there and then make their escape. When they were back out on the street, Shayna gulped in the salt-scented air and waited for her ears to stop ringing. Then she turned to Bettena.

"I just can't see Haddar going into a place like that. I think we're wasting our time."

Bettena frowned in thought. "As I recall, some are better than others. Perhaps we should be trying a few of the ones on the side streets."

Shayna groaned aloud. She hadn't realized there were even more of them. But Bettena was already turning a corner. "There are two up this way that aren't half bad."

Bettena was right—but Haddar wasn't there, either. Nor was he in any of the next five they checked. Although she'd taken no more than a sip of the brews they bought at each establishment, Shayna was beginning to feel slightly drunk. Bettena, on the other hand, was fine and, furthermore, seemed to be enjoying herself immensely. She even got into conversations at a few places, astonishing Shayna with her performance.

Her feet aching from the cheap, ill-fitting boots, and her eyes burning from the smoke, Shayna declared that she was ready to give up what had obviously been a bad idea to begin with. But Bettena was staring down another side street.

"There's another one down here, a quiet place. It caters to local merchants more than to sailors."

"This is the last one," Shayna declared. "I think I'm being punished for the lie we told Mikal."

Bettena had started down the narrow, dark street, then turned to Shayna and frowned, looking behind her to the busy street they'd just left.

"What is it?" Shayna asked as she too turned.

Bettena shook her head. "Nothing. I just thought for a moment that I saw someone who looked like Mikal. But he's gone now."

The two women made their way to the tavern. Shayna paused in the doorway. "Quiet" was not the way she would have described this place, although the noise level was somewhat lower than the other places they'd visited. A moment later, as she followed Bettena inside, she had to admit that it didn't smell quite so strongly of unwashed bodies, either. But the other smells were just as strong and the crowd was every bit as thick.

She stood inconspicuously in a corner while Bettena went up to the bar and then returned with two tankards. Here, as elsewhere, it was difficult to see faces clearly amidst the swirls of smoke and the dim lighting. But she scanned the ever-shifting crowd. Then Bettena tugged at her sleeve.

"Over there—in the opposite corner at that table. Is that him?"

Shayna followed Bettena's gaze, but was unable to see the table she'd indicated through the crowd that was constantly milling about. She thought about trying to get closer, but if it *was* Haddar she couldn't confront him here. It wasn't likely that he would recognize her, but she didn't want to risk it.

"I'm sure it was him," Bettena said, leaning over to speak into Shayna's ear. Bettena had, of course, seen Haddar the day he'd spoken to Shayna on the street.

More customers came into the tavern and joined their friends, further blocking Shayna's view. At least, she thought, he won't be able to leave without my seeing him. The spot they'd chosen was within clear view of the tavern's entrance.

Finally, after the two women had stood there in frustration for many minutes, Bettena turned and poured the remainder of her beer into the corner, then announced with a wink that she needed another mug. As she made her way slowly through the crowd to the bar, Shayna continued to try, without success, to see the table in the corner.

Only now, when it appeared likely that she had found Haddar, did Shayna begin to face up to what she would have to do. Could she actually kill this man who, however terrible his crime, was a colleague of hers?

She thought about Mikal's remark that perhaps women in her time could kill, and she shuddered inwardly. Killing in self-defense was certainly morally acceptable, but she had lived her life up to now in a time when even that wasn't necessary, thanks to the invention of stunners.

And yet she knew that even if Haddar promised to give up his scheme of killing Mikal, she wouldn't be able to trust him. As long as he was alive in this time, he remained a threat to Mikal—and to her as well, since he seemed bent on exposing her as an Astasi.

She knew that she should have left this to Mikal's cousins and began to question her determination to handle it herself. When there was a risk that the soldiers would find him and learn the truth, she'd had good reason to hunt him down herself. But now Mikal had men he trusted to go after Haddar.

She realized that her determination sprang from something far deeper than the risk of exposure. She'd been sent here to find Haddar, and, after having broken the protocol, she was trying to redeem herself by carrying out the mission that connected her to her own world.

Bettena had disappeared into the crowd, but now Shayna saw her making her way back, her body slouched and her eyes downcast—every inch the farm boy out of his element. Only when she reached Shayna and had her back to the crowd did she look up with a gleam in her eyes.

"I was right!" she announced triumphantly. "But the men he's with don't fit the descriptions you gave me of the other two."

Shayna wondered what had happened to them. She'd been so focused on Haddar that she'd nearly forgotten about his friends. Would she be forced to kill them as well? The student was particularly troubling. He was young and impressionable—but did he deserve to die for his foolishness? She could probably justify killing the engineer from the project for his treachery, without which Haddar couldn't have accomplished this, but the boy . . . ?

Bettena sipped at her ale. "It looked to me as though he could be here for some time. Why don't we find someplace to wait for him outside?"

Shayna nodded eagerly. Nothing would please her more right now than to get away from the smells and the noise and the oppressive heat of too many bodies packed into too small a space. Perhaps then she could think more clearly.

They left the tavern and surveyed the surrounding

area. Most of the neighborhood consisted of small shops that were now shuttered, and what appeared to be storage facilities. She gestured across the narrow street.

"We could wait over there in that alleyway between those two shops. It's dark enough to hide us." Thankfully they were both wearing dark clothing.

So they hurried across the street and into the narrow space between two buildings. There were no street lamps here as there were in the better parts of the city, and the darkness quickly swallowed them up. Shayna sank to the ground and Bettena slid down beside her.

"What do you intend to do when he comes out?" she asked.

"I'll have to follow him—and kill him," Shayna said in a bleak tone.

Rather to Shayna's surprise, Bettena didn't look shocked. Instead she seemed merely curious. "Can you do that?"

"Of course. I can use the fire."

"That isn't what I meant. Have you ever killed anyone?"

Shayna was the one who was shocked. "No, of course not."

"It isn't as easy as it may seem—not even if your own life is in jeopardy."

Shayna turned to her in surprise. "Are you saying that *you've* killed someone?"

Bettena nodded, then produced a small but deadly looking knife with a carved mother-of-pearl handle. "With this. It was a long time ago, when I was just beginning my career. Two men followed me home from the theater one night and attacked me. I'd just bought the knife a few days earlier because there'd been attacks on other actresses."

"You killed both of them?" Shayna asked in astonishment.

"No, only the one. The other one ran away. But even though I knew that they intended to rape me and probably kill me, it still wasn't an easy thing to do." She shuddered. "I had nightmares for months. I still have them sometimes."

She glanced at Shayna. "Maybe it would be easier to kill with magic."

"I don't think so."

"You could leave this for Mikal's cousins to deal with," Bettena suggested.

Shayna shook her head. "What if they don't find him before he kills Mikal? We still can't be sure he won't try."

"There is that," Bettena agreed.

"I have to do it," Shayna said, as much to convince herself as to persuade Bettena. "I was sent here to prevent Mikal's being killed."

"Do you really believe that your friends will find you?" Bettena asked after a long silence.

"Yes, I think they will . . . eventually. Sooner or later they'll figure out that Haddar came to an earlier time."

"But how soon will that happen? You told me that even if it took them years to build another time-craft, they could still come back to this time."

"I don't know how long it could take," Shayna admitted. "It depends on how much time they spend in other time periods. As far as we know, that's *real* time."

" 'Real' time?"

"Yes. If they travel to a period, say, twenty years from now, and then spend a month there, that time is real. Or so we think. There are some disagreements about it.

"You see, what was planned was for a crew to go back only a few years and stay for only a few minutes. That way, if something happened and they couldn't return—or if we're wrong about its being real time when they were there—it wouldn't have been such a problem. But Haddar's theft of the time-craft changed all that."

Bettena was silent for a time. "Mikal will never let you go, Shayna."

The certainty in her voice sent a chill through Shayna. "He'll have to let me go, Bett."

"Don't be so sure of that. I think he'll do whatever he

has to do to keep you. I've seen that in his eyes when he looks at you."

Shayna turned to her, but before she could speak Bettena grabbed her arm. "There he is!"

Shayna looked back toward the tavern and saw Haddar emerge with two other men. They stood in front of the tavern talking for a few seconds. Then the two men walked off in one direction and Haddar strode off in the other.

Shayna's heart was pounding as they emerged from their hiding place and began to follow him, weaving through the still-crowded streets. Several times she saw Haddar turn and scan the street behind him, then walk on. There was no doubt in her mind now that he knew someone was after him, though she suspected that he would be looking for soldiers.

Then, abruptly, she saw several soldiers up ahead, coming in their direction. Haddar apparently saw them at the same time because he turned quickly onto a very narrow street. Shayna and Bettena followed him and discovered that it was really only an alley. It was also very dark, surrounded on both sides by the backs of shops and other buildings.

"Wait here," Shayna said, taking Bettena's arm. "I don't want to put you at risk. He has a stunner, and perhaps other weapons too."

"I'm coming with you," Bettena insisted.

They made their way slowly down the dark alley, and as their eyes became accustomed to the dim light, Shayna could see the end of the alley and a narrow gap between one of the buildings and a high stone wall. Haddar was nowhere in sight, and she assumed he must have slipped through that gap.

As they neared the dark opening, Shayna summoned the fire and heard Bettena's sharply indrawn breath as her hands began to glow. She wished she hadn't brought Bettena with her. Bettena knew about her powers, of course, but as with Mikal, knowing it and actually seeing it were very different matters.

Shayna peered into the dark space. It wasn't a dead

end, as she'd expected. Instead another alleyway branched off from it. Shayna felt a strong sense of danger but chose to ignore it, more determined than ever to deal with Haddar herself.

She moved cautiously into the dark space, her eyes straining to see into the corners. Bettena was just a short distance behind her. Then suddenly Bettena made a sharp sound that was abruptly cut off. Shayna whirled around—just in time to see Bettena make a desperate attempt to defend herself from Haddar, who had one arm around her throat. In his other hand he held a stunner, aimed at Shayna!

As Bettena struggled to stab him with her knife, his arm merely tightened against her throat, and the knife flew from her hand to clatter off into a corner behind some crates—undoubtedly the same crates Haddar had used for concealment.

"I wouldn't have known it was you if it hadn't been for the fire," he said, his voice cold and deadly.

Shayna silently cursed herself for her mistake. If she hadn't called the fire, their disguises might have held.

"Let her go!" she ordered.

"You can't use your magic now," he scoffed. "If you do, your friend here will die too."

"And you can't kill me with that," Shayna reminded him, referring to the stunner he continued to aim at her.

"No, but I have a knife as well. All I need to do is to use the stunner—and then kill you both."

"It won't work, Haddar. Mikal knows everything. He'll find you and kill you."

As she spoke, Shayna's mind was spinning. She didn't dare use the magic fire because of Bettena, but she *could* cast a spell on Haddar. It would probably affect Bettena as well, but it would do her no harm.

The problem, as she soon discovered in the few seconds that she had to consider it, was that she couldn't find that quiet place within her that allowed her to cast spells. Someone more experienced could surely have managed it, but she couldn't. Paralyzed with fear for both herself and Bettena, Shayna watched as Haddar's thumb slid toward the activator for the stunner.

Then he paused and his head began to turn. A half second later, Shayna saw a tall, dark figure emerge from the alleyway behind Haddar.

Bettena used the moment to her advantage and pushed away from Haddar, causing him to lose his grip on the stunner as well. It fell away into the darkness—only to be replaced with a long, deadly knife as he confronted their rescuer.

Shayna missed the moment when she might have used her fire against Haddar—before he rushed at the other man, his knife already swinging in a deadly arc.

"Traitor!" Haddar screamed, just before an explosion that momentarily deafened Shayna, then left her ears ringing as she stared at the tableau before her.

Haddar lay unmoving on the ground, the deadly knife still clutched in his hand. The other man bent down and wrenched it away, then felt for a pulse and grunted with satisfaction. The gun that had caused the explosion was still in his other hand, and there was an acrid odor in the air.

The stranger's face was still in shadows, but Shayna allowed a tiny hope to rise within her. The stranger was dressed like the man they'd seen earlier—the one they'd briefly thought was Mikal. But before she could ask the question, it was answered. He set the gun down on a nearby crate and closed the small space between them.

"Are you both all right?" Mikal asked, his gaze encompassing them both. Bettena had sunk down onto a crate nearby.

Shayna nodded. "Is he dead?"

"Yes. I'd hoped to take him alive, so I could find out where his friends are, but . . ." He shrugged.

In the brief silence that followed, Shayna could hear echoes of Haddar's accusation. She knew that Mikal had had no choice but to kill Haddar, but she also suspected that Haddar's fate was sealed the moment he had spoken. Mikal Har-Amaden would not stand for being called a traitor. In his world it was reason enough to kill.

"How did you find us?" Bettena asked as she slid between the crates and came out with her knife.

"There's no time for explanations now," Mikal stated. "We have to get out of here. Someone will report that gunshot, and I don't want to have to answer any questions."

They ran back through the alley to the street. Shayna saw some men running toward them. Mikal grabbed both their arms and propelled them rapidly in the other direction, not slowing down until they were surrounded by a mostly drunken crowd.

"Do you have a carriage nearby?" he asked Bettena.

"It's at the other end of the street," Bettena replied, gasping for breath after their run.

"Mine is closer then," he said, and began to push his way through the crowd, leaving them to follow in his wake. When they reached the next corner, he told them where his carriage was and said they should follow him—but at a distance.

"They'll be looking for a man and two boys," he explained before turning away from them and then crossing the street.

Shayna and Bettena continued down the side of the street they were on, keeping Mikal in view. "Are you really all right?" she asked Bettena worriedly.

Bettena nodded. "I know I am . . . now. But I thought I was dead for a few moments back there."

"How did he get here?" Shayna asked, still watching Mikal as he walked along the far side of the street.

"He must have followed us."

"But how did he guess what we were going to do?" Shayna persisted.

"I'd wager my diamond brooch that Mogun told him we were coming down here," Bettena said, referring to her driver.

Across the street and about half a block ahead, they saw Mikal get into his carriage. They both hurried after him, and as soon as they were inside, Mikal rapped on the roof to signal the driver to get moving. Then he settled back in his seat and glared at the two of them as they sat across from him, looking for all the world like two scruffy boys very much out of place in the elegant carriage.

"Dammit, Shayna!" he exploded. "Why did you risk your life like this—and Bettena's too?"

"She tried to stop me from coming with her," Bettena put in, but Mikal's stormy gaze remained on Shayna.

"I was sent here to stop him," she stated. "It was my mission." She thought that he'd understand, if only she weren't a woman.

Suddenly there was a commotion outside the carriage: the sound of horses and men's voices. Mikal tore off the seaman's cap he was wearing and thrust his head through the opening in the curtains.

"What is it?" he demanded in a curt tone that she was sure must be sending shivers through whoever was out there.

"Your pardon, sir," was the reply in a chastened tone. "There was a shooting nearby. Sorry to have troubled you, sir."

Mikal settled back onto his seat. The horses clattered away and the carriage began to move again. After a few moments he opened the small panel in the front of the carriage and spoke to the driver.

"Find Miss Halward's carriage. It's at the other end of the street—if it's still there."

He closed the door and turned to Bettena. "Mogun probably had enough sense to get out when he saw the constables."

Shayna and Bettena said nothing, exchanging glances that signaled their agreement to remain silent for now in the face of his wrath. The carriage turned onto a side street, then turned again and soon came back to the main street. Mikal opened the panel again, and the unseen driver's voice floated down to them.

"It's there, all right, sir. But there's a constable there as well."

"Pull up beside him," Mikal ordered. "I can't get out dressed like this."

The driver did as ordered and Mikal once again thrust

his head through the curtains. "What's going on here, Constable?"

"There's been a shooting, sir, and we're questioning everyone in the area."

"I can vouch for this man and for the owner of the carriage."

"Yes, sir. Thank you, sir, and good night to you."

As soon as he'd gone, Mikal told Bettena's driver to follow them back to her house and they set off again.

Shayna cast a sidelong glance at Bettena, still worried about the danger she'd brought to her friend. She reached over and seized Bettena's hand. "I'm truly sorry, Bettena. I shouldn't have allowed you to become involved in this."

"Neither of you should have allowed the other," Mikal said curtly.

"Oh, stop it, Mikal!" Bettena said, proving that she wasn't as cowed as Shayna had feared. "All we did was to provide you with the opportunity to play the role you like best: protector."

Mikal's dark eyes swept over them both. "And if I hadn't played that role, you'd both be dead. The least you could do is thank me."

"Thank you, Mikal," they both chorused, then abruptly broke into simultaneous laughter—though it was laughter with a hysterical edge.

When the laughter died away in the face of Mikal's stony silence, Shayna shivered. "I was wrong to have trusted my powers. When I needed them most, they failed me."

Bettena protested that she couldn't very well have used her powers with her in the way.

"That isn't what I meant. I tried to cast a spell and I couldn't do it. I was too frightened. I can't imagine how my people were able to do that in battle."

"Well, I can assure you that they did," Mikal said. "What about the other two? Do you know where they are?"

Shayna shook her head. "We followed Haddar from a tavern and he was alone there."

An image of Haddar's body, sprawled in a pool of his own blood, haunted her. She'd disliked the man and she knew that Mikal had had no choice but to kill him, but still she could not reconcile herself to his death.

She also knew that Mikal—and most likely Bettena as well—would never understand her horror at his death. They lived in a time when death was an acceptable punishment and violence was common.

She forced herself to think about Haddar's allies. "They were followers of Haddar, that's all, especially the young student. I think that when they learn what has happened to him, they will try to go home."

"You mean return to the time-craft?" Mikal asked.

She nodded. "I don't know what they'll do when they discover it's gone. I doubt they could know that yet."

"Then I'll send someone out there to wait for them."

"Don't kill them, Mikal! What they did is wrong, but they don't deserve to die."

"They would have helped Haddar kill me," he pointed out coldly.

"But they won't try to kill you now that he's gone."

"I fail to understand your reasoning, Shayna, but I'll have my men capture them—and then I'll decide what to do with them."

"They'll be punished when Teres and the others find us," she insisted. "They'll face justice when we're back home."

Mikal said nothing, but the look he gave her made Shayna recall Bettena's statement that Mikal would never allow her to leave. A chill went through her. What would he do when they came for her? She'd never seriously considered that before.

Their carriage pulled up in front of Bettena's house. Mikal got out, then handed Bettena out. Shayna started to follow, her thoughts still on the question she'd asked herself.

"Wait here. I'll just see Bett to her door."

He was gone before she could voice any objections. Bettena turned back briefly, but Mikal took her arm and propelled her toward her front door. Shayna sank back into the carriage seat. She was irritated at his high-handed attitude, but she realized that he'd earned the right to be angry now. He'd saved their lives.

Mikal returned quickly, but remained silent for the time it took them to reach his nearby home. Shayna's thoughts shifted again to Haddar's companions. She had to prevent Mikal from killing them. He'd had no choice but to kill Haddar, and she knew she must accept that. But there was no reason to kill the other two, and she must convince him of that.

The problem was that she didn't know what could be done with them until the new time-craft arrived—and even raising that issue again would be difficult.

She raised her eyes and found Mikal staring at her intently, almost as though he were reading her thoughts. She looked away quickly. It seemed as though every time one problem was solved, another rose to take its place. She no longer needed to deceive Mikal, and now she didn't have to worry about Haddar—but instead she had the other two to consider, not to mention Mikal's reaction to the rescue mission.

The truth was that she had no idea when they would come. It all depended on their guesses as to the time period Haddar had chosen. She was a historian, and yet she had mistakenly assumed he'd gone to a much later period: the great period of Mikal's life, at least from their perspective. She wasn't at all certain that, even if she'd had more time to consider it, she would have chosen this time, because she wouldn't have thought as an assassin would. Once Mikal achieved his greatness he would become much less accessible to a killer.

There was also the question of how much time they would be forced to spend in whatever period they chose. It wasn't as easy as popping in and out again. They would have to search and do so unobtrusively.

Did she have mere days—or weeks, or months, or even years? She just didn't know, though years seemed highly unlikely.

They reached Mikal's house and as they entered the

study she turned her thoughts back to the present. His silence was unnerving, and she wondered if he intended it to be. She recalled that Maltus, the historian, had written that Mikal had a tendency to remain silent at times, using only his very formidable presence to bend others to his will. It was a clever tactic, as she now saw, and one that served him quite well.

"I'm afraid that I don't quite see why you wanted me to come with you," she said, "when it appears that all you intend to do is to brood."

"You think I'm brooding?" he asked, arching one dark brow as he poured himself some brandy.

"It appears that way to me," she replied, shaking her head to refuse his offer of a brandy for her as well. She was only now beginning to be rid of the effects of the foul brew she'd drunk earlier.

He sank into a chair, his long legs stretched out. His rough seaman's garb contrasted jarringly with the elegant furnishings. She remained standing, thinking with a fleeting amusement that his manners had vanished along with his fine clothes.

"I want you to promise me that you won't kill those two men."

He sipped the brandy and stared at her. "Conspiracy to commit murder is a crime punishable by death. If I were to haul them into court—which of course I can't do—that sentence would be pronounced."

"I don't doubt that. These are barbaric times. But they don't come from this time, and they should be dealt with in their own time."

"Barbaric, are we?" he asked, his face betraying nothing.

She regretted having said that, but since she had, she wasn't about to retract it. "Killing, whether in wars or through the courts, is barbaric."

For a moment she thought she saw a flash of anger in his eyes. But then his gaze slid away from hers and he seemed to be contemplating his brandy. In the corner of the room, a huge old clock ticked noisily.

"At times like this I realize the great distance between

us," he said softly, once again raising his gaze to her. "In three centuries people have forgotten about war and have become soft."

" 'Soft' is not the way I would describe it," she replied, both surprised and relieved at the change in his tone. "And we still have violence, though it's much more the exception than now."

"What do you do with murderers—and would-be murderers?"

She explained their system: the remote island penal colony. "Many think it is also cruel, and there is discussion about changing it. Drugs have been developed that can alter the brain and rid it of aggressive tendencies."

Mikal threw her a look of distaste. "If you can't understand our ways, I can't understand yours, either. It seems to me that a quick death would be preferable to life in such a colony or to altering the brain."

Then, before she could reply to that, he waved a hand. "All right. They'll only be killed if my men have no choice. Then, if I'm satisfied that they're harmless, the family can find some work for them until they can be sent back."

Shayna held her breath, waiting for him to move on to that subject. But he remained silent and she finally thanked him, though his silence on the subject of the rescue craft was nearly as troubling as any questions he might have asked about it.

Later, as Mikal slept beside her, Shayna decided that this man was still capable of surprising her. She'd expected a fierce possessiveness to his lovemaking this night, that wild, nearly uncontrollable passion that left them both breathless and slightly stunned.

Instead he'd been tender and solicitous, moving with a deliberate slowness and great thoroughness, allowing each separate moment to be savored and cherished until they were both swept away to that time out of time where nothing mattered but that pounding, driving need that melded them together with its heat.

Now, as she lay there waiting for sleep to take her as well, Shayna heard the words he hadn't spoken as clearly as she'd heard his husky-voiced words of love. "I will keep you." He might as well have spoken them aloud.

She was swept away by her memories of this man: memories of the time before she'd met him, his daunting power, and his monumental certainty that what he wanted would come to pass. Mikal Har-Amaden would one day force the entire world to accept his dream, and the man who lay quietly beside her now must surely be just as certain that he could keep her with him.

She raised herself up carefully so as not to disturb him, and stared at him in the moonlight that poured in through the partially open drapes. Its harsh, silver light created shadows and planes, almost mimicking the face she had known before she met him. She felt again the wonder of it all: that she had actually come to know this man—and to be loved by him.

She lay back down again, and her thoughts turned to Teres and the others on the project, who would even now be searching for her through time, riding their craft through the black void, then returning to reconsider.

Perhaps they wouldn't find her, after all. Or perhaps many years would pass before they did. Her thoughts became more and more confused as she began to slip down into sleep. Perhaps by the time they reached this period, she would have moved into a future they had already searched: a future she had changed merely by her presence in it.

Or perhaps they would one day return to the future of her time—but find it changed irrevocably, with every trace of her existence obliterated because she had remained here.

But when thoughts turned into dreams, they were dark, terrible dreams where she was lost in time, tossed about among different worlds, never belonging to any of them.

Chapter Fourteen

Four days passed before Haddar's accomplices surfaced. Through a wondrous network of contacts that amazed Shayna, Bettena learned that Haddar's body lay unclaimed in a mortuary, destined for a pauper's grave. It was widely believed that he'd been shot by the soldiers who were known to have been seeking him and his missing companions for unknown reasons.

Horrified to think that Haddar would end what had been, after all, a long and illustrious career in such ignominy, she persuaded Mikal to provide for a decent burial for him, with the arrangements made through a discreet friend of Bettena's, a man known for his ability to undertake delicate missions for a price, with no questions asked.

So, instead of being unceremoniously tossed into a pit in a weedy patch of land at the edge of the city's cemetery, he was laid to rest in his own plot beneath a tree, with a small gravestone that bore only his name. In attendance at the ceremony were Shayna and Bettena, clad in black and heavily veiled, as well as Bettena's friend, who had posed as his distant cousin.

A rosebush was planted on the grave because Haddar's only hobby had been growing roses. Shayna was glad that he no longer posed a threat either to Mikal or to her, but her tears were nonetheless genuine. She knew that he wasn't, as Mikal and Bettena thought, an evil man. Instead he'd been the victim of Amaden arrogance and pride, and it was perhaps fitting, therefore, that he was being buried in a time when those qualities had been at their zenith.

It was the next afternoon, on a sultry day that marked the beginning of summer in Wantesa, that Shayna received the news about Haddar's accomplices. She had begun her project of recording her impressions of life in this time, laboriously writing them out as she wished for her computer—and for the climate-controlled comfort of her own world as well.

The message arrived from Mikal, delivered to her by one of his aides. Even before she broke the seal engraved with his crest, she knew that the two men must have been found, and she hoped that they were alive.

Only the young student had survived. In the struggle to capture them, the engineer had been killed as he aimed his stunner at Mikal's cousins. The student was being held at Mikal's cabin, and Mikal's message said that they would go there the next day.

Shayna was sorry about the engineer's death, but glad that the student had survived. Of the three, she believed he was the least culpable, having certainly been drawn into the scheme by the force of Haddar's powerful personality.

She was also pleased that Mikal planned to take her with him to speak to the student. She'd been expecting an argument over that. Now she felt confident that the young man's life would be spared.

By the next day, however, Shayna was less certain. Mikal's anger was very apparent. By now she knew that one of his cousins had been struck by a stunner and was still in bed, racked with pain, the result of having been struck at very close range. The fact that he would survive intact and that the stunner in question had been wielded by the engineer and not by the student had made little impression on Mikal.

In a desperate attempt to save the student's life, Shayna suggested that they take him to an Astasi truth-teller who could easily ascertain if he posed any further threat.

"What's a truth-teller?" Mikal asked, turning to her with a frown as they rode across the valley from the keep to his cabin.

"It's a special talent that a few Astasi possess," she explained, having forgotten that people of his time knew less about the Astasi than in her own time.

"They see auras around people, and the color of those auras change if they lie. So they have only to watch as questions are asked, and they know if the answer is truthful."

Mikal was silent for a moment, and Shayna suddenly realized that they couldn't do it because she couldn't return to the valley, and she doubted that the Astasi could be persuaded by Mikal to do it. She expected him to say just that, but his silence apparently had another reason.

"When I went to speak to them, there was an old woman who stood apart from them and stared hard at me the entire time I was talking to them. I was disturbed by her behavior at the time, but I'd nearly forgotten it. Was she a truth-teller?"

"Probably. I wasn't there long enough to know, but from what you said, it sounds as though that's what she was."

He lapsed into a brief silence again, then said that they couldn't go to the valley for the reason she'd already given herself.

"He's very young, Mikal, only eighteen or nineteen."

"That's scarcely a child," Mikal scoffed.

"You don't understand. Children grow up more slowly in my time—his time. They don't really assume adult responsibilities until after they've completed their education." She'd been writing about that, having already known it but not truly understood it before. In this place, a boy of twelve seemed as mature as her students did.

Mikal said nothing as they rode up the hillside. His cousin came out of the cabin as they dismounted. Mikal introduced them, then asked about the student, who was apparently in the cabin.

"He hasn't said much. He told me his name and he claims to be nineteen, but I think he's lying about that. He seems to be much younger."

Shayna shot Mikal a glance, hoping that his cousin's observation would bolster her own argument.

"Does he know we're coming?" Mikal asked, glowering at the door.

"No. I merely told him that someone was coming to talk to him, and that he'd do well to answer any questions honestly."

Then he asked how his brother was, since he'd been forced to remain here and hadn't had any news of him today.

"He's better," Mikal assured him. "But he's still in pain."

"But he'll recover, won't he?" the man asked, glancing uncertainly from Mikal to Shayna.

"He'll be fine," Shayna said. "No one has ever died or been permanently injured by a stunner."

She already knew that both cousins had been told the whole story, and even if she hadn't known that, she would have guessed from the man's nervousness as he looked at her. During their stop at the keep, Mikal had also told his brother everything, but had requested that the truth be kept from his mother and his sister-in-law. Derik had initially been horrified, but had recovered quickly and become as fascinated as Mikal himself had been. In fact Mikal had been forced to put an end to his questions so they could get away and come up here to the cabin.

They walked into the cabin. The student, whose name she learned was Hattis, was sitting in Mikal's chair and sprang to his feet the moment they entered.

His reaction was interesting. He was surprised to see her and definitely recognized her even with her dark wig—but it was Mikal who drew his full attention. She'd assumed that he'd already seen Mikal at some point, but now she decided that she was wrong. Mikal was wearing his uniform, and even though this was a much younger Mikal than the man familiar to him from history, his expression told her that he knew immediately who stood before him.

Although he certainly had reason to fear this man he and his dead companions had intended to kill, Hattis's expression was one of awe, not fear. And he confirmed that with his words.

"You're really him!" he blurted.

Shayna glanced at Mikal and saw that he was surprised at the question. But he recovered quickly. "If you mean by that, am I the man you intended to kill, the answer is yes, I am," Mikal stated in a hard, cold voice.

The young man's face grew pale, then flushed crimson. "I . . . I wasn't going to kill you. That was Haddar. I thought I could talk him out of it."

"But you came with him, knowing that was what he intended," Mikal pointed out in the same tone.

"Yes, but I was sure I could talk him out of it—or stop him. And I did stop him. He wanted to build a bomb and use it on your house. He was gathering all this stuff to make an old-fashioned bomb, and that night, the night he was killed, I got rid of it all.

"Then I was going to go home. I knew I'd be in trouble, but I thought if I told them that I'd stopped Haddar . . ."

He ran out of words all at once as tears welled up in his eyes. Mikal turned to Shayna, a look of disgust on his face. "I think I'm beginning to believe you. He does sound like a child—one who's given no thought to the consequences of his actions."

"He is a child, Mikal," Shayna said. "However much he might look like a grown man to you." She turned to Hattis.

"You can't go home now, Hattis. I accidentally destroyed your time-craft when I was trying to go home myself. And my own was destroyed when we arrived. The men with me died in the accident."

Hattis stared at her in horror. "You mean we're trapped here?"

"I'm afraid so—for now, at least. They will come for us, I'm sure. But I don't know when."

As she spoke to him, she was aware of Mikal's gaze on her, and now he interrupted as she was about to attempt to soothe Hattis, who once more had tears in his eyes.

"If it was your intention to stop Haddar, why didn't you do it before he left your world?" he demanded.

A good question, Shayna thought, though she suspected she already knew the answer. And Hattis confirmed those suspicions in a low voice, his face once more flushed with embarrassment.

"I wanted to come here—to see what it was like."

Mikal was silent, his wide mouth curved with contempt as he stared at the young man. Shayna wanted to help Hattis, to try to make Mikal understand the temptations of such an adventure, particularly to a youth like Hattis. But she said nothing, fearful that any plea on her part might have the effect of hardening Mikal, who clearly saw before him not a child, but a man.

"Very well," Mikal said after what seemed an eternity. "So the question now becomes: what do we do with you?"

"I won't cause any trouble," Hattis assured him. "I'll do anything you want."

Mikal turned to his cousin. "Can you find work for him that will keep him out of trouble?"

"Well, I could probably use him at the stables, if he can keep his mouth shut, that is. We can't have him telling anyone else who he really is. It's bad enough that he's not Amaden."

"But I am!" the boy blurted out. "I mean I'm half Amaden on my mother's side. She always said that we were descended from you," he said hesitantly, glancing shyly at Mikal. "Or from your brother, actually, Derik."

Mikal looked down at him from his impressive height. "I hope your mother was wrong. Considering your behavior, I wouldn't want my brother to be burdened with the knowledge that one of his descendants tried to kill me."

"But I didn't! I was sure I could talk Haddar out of it!" the young man protested, his face once again flushed. Then, seeing the need to improve his chances of coming out of this alive, he said that he knew all about horses and was good with them.

"My uncle—my mother's brother—raises Amadens. I've worked at his farm in the summers."

"Amadens?" Mikal queried with a frown.

"That's what we call the breed your family originated," Shayna put in. But she decided not to add that Hattis must be telling the truth about his being a descendant of Derik's. She knew that the Har-Amaden family still bred Amadens on a farm not far from here. It was possible that Hattis would be going to that very farm.

Mikal turned back to Hattis and spoke sternly. "Very well. You may go with Hari and work at the stables. But I hope that if you are able to return to your own time, you will do better with the rest of your life than you seem to have done thus far."

"Y-yes, sir. I promise I will."

"Do you think he spoke the truth when he claimed to have been descended from Derik?" Mikal asked as they watched the two ride away.

"Yes, I think so," Shayna replied after a hesitation. She'd spoken briefly to Hattis before his departure, mostly to encourage the young man to be patient until they were rescued. He'd told her his uncle's name. Hattis was still dazed from his encounter with Mikal, and she had the impression that he'd been so overwhelmed at meeting him that he hadn't really understood just how dangerous his own situation had been.

"It seems to me," Mikal said, "that for all the inventions you have, you've lost something as well—at least if that young man is any indication. Who is teaching the children values and a sense of responsibility?"

Shayna smiled. "Actually, there's been much debate about that lately. I never said that our world was perfect, Mikal, but it's still far better than this one. There's no war and no real poverty, and there is true equality."

As the carriage made the return trip to Wantesa, Mikal remained quiet, lost in his thoughts. He kept hearing Shayna's words to the boy about how they would "come for them." She'd told him this before, of course, but he'd paid her scant attention.

He looked across at her, their gazes locking for a moment before she turned to stare out the window. Unconsciously he clenched his fists. He would not let her go. He couldn't believe that she could *want* to go, but he was afraid to put that question to her, lest he be proved wrong.

He knew that she'd told Bettena that she couldn't marry him because he must remain free to follow his destiny—but the destiny she had in mind wasn't going to happen. He would never betray his people. If she stayed she would see that and would come to realize that it hadn't been necessary for her to leave, after all.

Mikal knew it wouldn't be easy for her. She would have to spend the rest of her life living a lie: pretending to be Amaden instead of Astasi. But he would do his best to make her happy, and he thought she *would* be happy.

Still, there were nagging little doubts in his mind. Could he really force her to stay here if she wanted to leave? What rights did his love for her give him?

The days and then weeks passed. High summer settled over Wantesa, with only the ocean breeze at night to drive out the heat. Mikal divided his time between the fort at High Point and the council and Lonhola. War with the eastern tribes began to seem inevitable.

Shayna poured her energies into her writing and began to spend time in the city's settlement houses with Bettena, who had been volunteering there for some time. Those dreary places with their sad, defeated people depressed her even more than the ever-present heat, but she did her best to help turn around lives that were mired in poverty and hopelessness.

Mikal said nothing to her about it, but she knew that another war was looming. Her memory of the exact date it would commence was uncertain, since she wasn't a military historian, but she knew that by next spring the Amaden would again be at war, and that, in the midst of it, Mikal's uncle, the commander, would be forced to resign because of ill health, leaving Mikal in charge of the mighty Amaden army, and unquestionably the most powerful man in his world.

Maltus, the historian, had written that it was after this war that Mikal began his quest for a permanent peace, but Shayna saw no indication that he would have such a quest in mind, and she worried that by telling him about it she had doomed it—and with it, the world she knew.

At one of those times when she allowed herself to think about the confusing subject of time theory, she wondered if the world she knew even existed. If it didn't, then in all likelihood the Time Project didn't exist either, and there would be no rescue. And even if it did exist, would she be returned to a world that was any better than this one?

She became depressed, weighted down by the inequities of this time and by her fears for her own future. Mikal saw this, of course, though he made no reference to its cause. Instead he listened quietly to her complaints about the injustices of his world, and even visited the settlement house where she volunteered.

The visit was unannounced. Neither Shayna nor Bettena had known he was coming until he stepped through the door into the usual chaos of hungry children and desperate mothers.

He came alone and he didn't stay long, but Shayna

could see the dismay in his eyes, and she wondered if she might have given him a subtle push toward his destiny. But he didn't mention the visit when she saw him that evening.

Then, on a day when the oppressive heat had reached its peak, Mikal suggested a day's outing on his boat. Bettena had been hoping for such an invitation, but Shayna hadn't mentioned it to Mikal because the boat brought painful memories of how he would one day meet his death.

Nevertheless, she went along with Mikal and Bettena and Mikal's banker friend, a widower who had been paying cautious court to Bettena. The son of Mikal's housekeeper was taken along to help sail.

Bettena was in high spirits because her new play was in rehearsal and doing quite well. Since she was one of those rare people who could effortlessly draw everyone along with her mood, Shayna found herself casting off her depression as they sailed out of the harbor.

As she watched Mikal and the boy maneuver the handsome boat, she saw that Mikal too was in high spirits. It was clear that he relished the thought of a day at sea. It amused her to see this man who was so often stern and serious behaving like his young helper.

They cleared the busy harbor and began to sail along the rugged coastline. She was standing at the rail and watching a flock of white birds—doves, she thought, rather than seagulls—as they rode the invisible currents where land met sea. Then Mikal suddenly appeared at her side and handed her a glass of lemonade.

She took it and forced herself to smile at him. She'd been half lost in a daydream where she and Mikal were sailing this coast in her own time. He startled her by asking if people still sailed in her world. It was almost as though he'd reached across the barriers of time to join her daydream.

"I've sailed this coast many times," she told him. "And it's much the same, once you get away from Wantesa. No building is permitted along the cliffs, to preserve the beauty." She pointed to the distant flock of white birds floating along the cliff face.

"Are they gulls or doves?" she asked.

He glanced at them. "Neither. They're eidens."

"Eidens," she repeated as a deep sadness came over her. She'd heard the name, had probably even seen pictures of them somewhere. But they'd long since vanished by her own time, victims of a world that had existed between this time and her own, a time when too few people had understood the fragility of that world.

Mikal slipped an arm around her waist and drew her closer. "I'd like to stay out here forever with you."

A tidal wave of pain engulfed her now. He *would* stay out here forever—though not with her. His body had never been recovered.

"What is it, my love?" he asked in that gentle tone he seemed to reserve for her alone.

She shook her head, not trusting herself to speak.

"Shayna, I won't let you go. I can't let you go. I would be losing a part of myself."

She leaned against him as the boat rocked in the gentle swells. In the distance the eidens continued to drift along the cliffs, blissfully unaware that their time was soon coming to an end. She wished that she could share that innocence.

Mikal's great strength and determination almost made her believe it could happen—or that she would let it happen. But the cost was far too great. Her very world was at stake.

When Shayna's gaze first swept along the busy street, she almost missed him. She and Bettena were making the rounds of the shops, planning their wardrobes for the party Mikal was giving to celebrate Bettena's birthday and the opening of her new play. Mikal also wanted to use the occasion to announce their impending marriage. He'd admitted that war now seemed inevitable, and he wanted them to be married before he went off to battle.

The end of the summer's heat had brought many people out to the busy street, and when she first saw the man she thought only that he looked familiar. If he hadn't come to a sudden stop in the middle of the sidewalk, staring at her as others were forced to detour around him, Shayna would have paid him no further attention.

But suddenly a wave of dizziness swept over her as she realized why he seemed so familiar. He was one of the Time Project engineers! She couldn't recall his name, but there was no doubt in her mind that it was he.

"Shayna?"

Reluctantly she tore her gaze away from the man as Bettena spoke to her.

"Is something wrong?" Bettena asked with a frown.

"No. Would you excuse me for a moment?"

Without waiting for Bettena's reply, Shayna turned back—but the man had vanished. She stood there, paralyzed by fear. Had she imagined him? Or was he real, but he'd failed to recognize her?

"Shayna, what's wrong? Are you ill?" Bettena took her arm. "Come. Let's have some tea."

Bettena started to pull her toward the nearby tearoom, but Shayna resisted as she scanned the crowds desperately. They were at a busy corner, and he could have gone in any direction. For one brief moment she thought she'd spotted him, and began to pull free of Bettena. But then she realized it wasn't him as the man in question turned to speak to a woman who held his arm.

She allowed Bettena to lead her into the tearoom as her mind skittered about, trying to make sense of what she'd seen. Surely he hadn't been a hallucination! There had been times recently when she'd searched the faces in crowds, hoping to spot someone from the project—but this hadn't been one of those times. Her thoughts had been on Mikal's party and how she could persuade him to delay their marriage.

Besides, she'd somehow expected that whoever came, it would be people she knew well—probably including

Teres himself. And she barely knew this engineer. But he was Amaden and that would have made him a likely candidate for the journey.

She thought about that surprised look on his face. He'd obviously recognized her, even in her disguise. But why had he vanished, instead of waiting for her to approach him?

They had found her! She clung to that belief as her mind spun. Perhaps he hadn't approached her because of Bettena. Unlike her own mission, this one would have been carefully planned, and they would be very cautious.

What should she do now? She realized that although she'd thought of this day constantly, she'd given no thought at all to the details. Should she simply wait for them to find her again and make contact? It seemed she had no other choice.

"Was it that man?" Bettena asked her after they'd been seated and had ordered. "Do you know him? He was certainly staring at you."

Shayna shook her head quickly. "No, I have no idea who he is. It was just very . . . upsetting."

"I shouldn't wonder, after all that business with Haddar. Could he have brought someone else with him that you weren't aware of?"

"No. There were only the three of them."

"Well, he must have been just an admirer then," Bettena said, smiling. "Though I must say that he was very well dressed to have had such poor manners."

Shayna murmured agreement, then quickly changed the subject. She was certain that Bettena would soon forget about the incident because she was so busy with her new play about to open.

That evening Shayna wrote to Hattis, telling him the news and asking if he could get away to come to Wantesa. She told him to be careful and to do nothing that would cast suspicion upon himself. If he couldn't find an excuse to get to Wantesa, they would come for him there.

The next morning she hesitated before posting the letter. What if she was wrong? It wouldn't be fair to Hattis to let his hopes rise. But if she was right, it was important for him to be here. She had no idea where the time-craft—or time-crafts, since they must have brought more than one—would be, and the longer they were forced to remain here, the greater the danger would be.

In the end she posted the letter, hoping that by the time Hattis arrived she would have made contact with the crew. Then she set out—alone this time—to the area where she'd seen the engineer. Bettena was at rehearsal and Mikal was still at Lonhola, where he'd gone two days earlier. He would be returning this evening.

When she reached the spot where she'd seen the engineer, she found the streets just as crowded. She'd decided that she should come at the same time of day, even though that meant it would be more difficult to spot him in the throngs of shoppers and strollers.

She moved along slowly, pausing to peer into every shop window, then turning to scan the crowds. With each passing moment she became less and less certain that she'd actually seen the man. Then, as she stood before the window of a shop that sold clocks, a low, familiar voice spoke her name.

"Teres!" Tears were already stinging her eyes as she turned to stare at the well-remembered face of her friend.

"Are you alone?" he asked, his gaze darting about.

"Yes."

"Is there someplace we can go to talk?"

She gave him Bettena's address. "I'm staying with a friend, but she won't be home until this evening."

"Then go back there now and I'll follow you."

Shayna hurried back to Bettena's carriage, but could not resist turning several times to assure herself that Teres was really there. When she reached Bettena's she stood impatiently at the window that overlooked the street, waiting for him to appear. She was so eager to talk to him, to reassure herself that her world was the same.

He arrived twenty minutes later and she barely managed to close the door behind him before wrapping her arms around him. He returned her hug enthusiastically.

"Maron wasn't completely sure that it was really you," he said, holding her at arm's length and smiling at the wig.

"I thought I was hallucinating," she admitted. "How long have you been here?"

"Five days—on this trip, that is. We were searching in the future at first. Then our panel of historians suggested the possibility that Haddar might have gone to an earlier time. Our last journey was to just a few months from now." He grinned ruefully. "I think by now I know everything there is to know about Wantesa over the years."

Shayna had been studying him intently. She saw subtle changes. There seemed to be a bit more gray in his hair, and the lines in his face were deeper.

"How much time has passed since I left?"

"Not quite four years. It took us that long to build a larger craft and then to work out the problems. I had to weigh the passage of time for you against the advantages of making improvements—and I chose the latter."

"I understand," she told him. She'd lost four years of her life: four years during which all sorts of things would have happened to people she cared about. But if she'd been in Teres's position, she would have made the same choice.

"Where are the others?" Teres asked. "You're the only one we've seen."

"I'm the only one left—except for Hattis, the student who came with Haddar."

She gave him a quick synopsis of everything that had happened, but left out Mikal's name, saying only that she'd met a man who had helped her and who had then killed Haddar when he tried to kill *her*. Finally she drew in a deep breath. But before she could explain about

Mikal, Teres asked if the man who was helping her knew the truth.

"Yes. He knows everything. I had no choice but to tell him the truth. When he found me after the accident, he told me his name was Kaz. As I told you, I had temporary amnesia, but I kept thinking that he somehow looked familiar. And when I recovered my memory, I thought I was in a time twenty or so years from now." She paused and drew in another breath.

"Then I found out that Kaz wasn't his real name. It was only a pet name the family had for him when he was a child."

"So who is he? Is this his place?"

"No. This belongs to Bettena Halward."

"The playwright?" Teres was astonished and began to look around.

"Yes. She's a good friend of the man I knew as Kaz." She hesitated. "Kaz's real name is Mikal Har-Amaden."

Teres's mouth dropped open and his eyes nearly bulged out from their sockets. Then he laughed, albeit nervously. "You're joking, aren't you?"

"No, Teres, I'm not joking. I didn't recognize him right away because all the portraits of him show a much older man. In fact, when I finally realized who he might be, *I* didn't believe it—until I read his journal."

"Are you saying that he knows *everything?*" Teres asked, still wearing a stunned expression.

"Yes. As I said, I had no choice but to tell him the truth. He saw Haddar's time-craft just before it self-destructed."

Teres got up and began to pace around the room. "Tell me about him. What's he like? I can't believe this!"

Mikal's image sprang into her mind and she felt a deep coldness inside. She had to see him again, to make him understand. But a part of her wanted to leave now.

"Maybe I'll be able to talk about him someday, Teres, but not now," she said quietly.

Teres stopped pacing and turned to her sharply. "What do you mean?"

The tears she'd been struggling to hold back now

streamed down her cheeks. "I love him, Teres—and he loves me. He wants me to stay here—and marry him."

"But—but that's impossible!" Teres blurted out.

"I know that," she said, wiping the tears away. "If everything is the same at home, then I haven't done any damage yet—but that could change everything."

Teres nodded, dropping into a chair across from her. "If it were anyone else, maybe it wouldn't matter so much, but . . ." His voice trailed off.

Shayna nodded sadly. "But I can't just run off without seeing him again and trying to make him understand. Besides, there's Hattis to deal with." She told him where Hattis was and that she'd sent him a message, then asked where the time-craft was.

"About forty miles north of here, in the woods near the cliffs," Teres said distractedly, then reached out to take her hand.

"Shayna, I'm sorry about this. But I guess it justifies the decision that was made."

"What decision?"

"The council—on my recommendation—has discontinued the project. When we return it will be terminated."

She nodded. "It's the right decision. I was going to recommend it myself. Even though I've tried very hard not to change anything, I think I have."

She explained about Bettena's play and about the Astasi. And then she told him her fears about Mikal. "He swears that he would never betray his people by defeating their enemies and then sharing power with them. I shouldn't have told him his future."

Teres was silent for a long time. "Is it possible," he wondered, "that by coming here and meeting him, you've *created* the future we know?"

"I've asked myself that question," she admitted.

Teres stared thoughtfully into space. "We know so little about time theory now. That's why the project is being discontinued. Years from now we might find the answer, though. We're not stopping the research."

"I hope you don't find that answer in my lifetime,"

Shayna said softly. "I'm not sure I want to know."

"But it wouldn't change who he is," Teres protested. "Even if you planted the seed, he's the one who will nourish it. I wish I could meet him."

His wistful statement reminded her of the look on Hattis's face when he met Mikal—and reminded her as well of the awe she'd once felt. But it also reminded her of Bettena's statement that he would never let her go—and of Mikal's own words.

"Teres, I'm worried that he might not let me go."

"What do you mean?"

"I know that you're thinking of him as I once did, as the giant of history. But he's also just a man—a very determined man. And he wants me to stay here."

She could tell that Teres was having difficulty grasping the notion that Mikal Har-Amaden could actually cause a problem for them, so she hurried on.

"Tell me where you're staying, but don't come back here or approach me in any way. When Hattis arrives I'll be in touch with you. It'll probably be a few days. And if he can't get away to come to Wantesa, then I'll have to go get him."

Teres gave her the name of the inn where they were staying, then stood up. She followed him to the door and he kissed her cheek. "I'm sorry about all this," he said, then slipped out the door and started down the steps to the first floor.

Shayna closed the door behind him and let her tears begin to flow again. They were tears of joy—and tears of pain.

Mikal told his driver to wait and then, for the sake of the aide who was traveling with him, forced himself to walk and not run into Bettena's house. He hoped Shayna would be there, and not at the theater with Bettena. Three days away from her and he was feeling like a lusty schoolboy.

As he opened the front door, a man stepped off the stairs and started toward him, then stopped and stared at him before hurrying past and out the door. Mikal turned, frowning. He knew most of Bettena's friends, but he'd never seen this man before, and something about the way he had stared at Mikal bothered him. The man hurried off down the sidewalk, but not before casting a quick glance over his shoulder in Mikal's direction.

Mikal took the stairs two at a time, forsaking dignity now that he was out of view of his driver and aide. The stranger was thrust from his mind to make way for thoughts of Shayna's soft, warm flesh pressed against his. He knocked at Bettena's door, then was startled when it opened so quickly.

Shayna seemed just as startled, and it flashed through Mikal's mind that she must have been expecting the stranger to return. Furthermore, even though she rather belatedly smiled at him, her beautiful green eyes were rimmed in red and her long lashes were wet with tears.

Mikal drew her into his arms and felt a brief resistance that quickly melted away—though not before an emotion he barely recognized swept through him: jealousy.

"Who was that?" he asked, loosening his hold on her as he stared down at her. "Why are you crying?"

She kept her face averted. "Just a friend of Bett's. I thought he'd returned for some reason."

"Why are you crying?" Mikal asked again, trying to ignore the instincts that were telling him she was lying.

"It had nothing to do with him," she replied, moving out of his arms, but still avoiding his gaze. "I wasn't expecting you until tonight."

Mikal said nothing. She hadn't answered his question and his jealousy grew, even though he couldn't believe she would seek pleasure in another man's arms.

"You don't understand what it's like for me, Mikal," she went on after a moment. "Sometimes I feel so . . . trapped. I don't belong here, and I hate the way I must pretend to be something I'm not."

Mikal's jealousy faded away. Her soft words had the unmistakable ring of truth. "I do understand," he told her. "But I have tried—and I will try—to make you happy, dearest. I intend to spend the rest of my life doing just that."

She smiled at him, then ran to him and wrapped her arms tightly around him. "I love you, Mikal. I'll never love anyone else."

Mikal picked her up and carried her back to her bedroom, but her final words echoed through his brain, mingling with an image of that stranger.

She was as hungry for him as he was for her, and they barely managed to remove their clothing before their combined passion exploded into a frenzy of lovemaking. Sometimes, when the need inside him was as great as it was now, Mikal worried that he would hurt her. But this time her own hunger matched his—perhaps even surpassed it. She welcomed him into her with a shudder and a deep moan, her fingers clutching at him as though he might vanish before her eyes.

When it was over and she lay quietly beside him with a satisfied smile curving her kiss-swollen lips, Mikal heard her words again: "I'll never love anyone else." He thought about her tears and about the stranger—and then he knew.

"Yes, that's him. You've captured him perfectly."

Mikal picked up the sketch and stared at it for a moment, then paid the artist and dismissed him with another expression of gratitude and a warning that he was to tell no one about this. The artist was a friend of Bettena's, but Mikal had made use of him before and he thought the man could be trusted, thanks to a very generous payment.

When the artist had gone, Mikal added some comments about the man's age, height, and build to the bottom of the sketch, then folded it carefully and put it into his pocket. He'd already sent word to his cousins that he had need of them, but they wouldn't arrive in Wantesa until tomorrow. And he'd included a warning that someone should keep a close eye on the youth, Hattis.

If he was right, the boy was likely to be coming to Wantesa himself.

He stared out the window of his office at the fort. The city lay below him in all its splendor, framed by the restless sea. It was a view he never failed to enjoy, but it gave him no pleasure now. He clenched his fists helplessly.

The man he'd seen was most likely not alone, so Mikal could only hope that when his cousins found him, they would find his companions as well.

A dark voice had been whispering to him that he should kill them, arrange for some sort of "accident" that Shayna would believe, and then find and destroy the time-craft as well. The voice was seductive, whispering to a warrior who'd planned many a battle.

But Mikal knew he couldn't do it. Not only were these men wholly innocent, here on a mission of mercy, but it would mean living his life with Shayna as a lie.

He would talk to them instead, try to convince them that she should be allowed to remain here—because he needed her.

Chapter Fifteen

Hattis arrived the following evening, just as Shayna was preparing to join Mikal at his house. Fortunately Bettena was at the theater. The opening of her play—and her party—were only a few days away. She herself had spent the better part of the day at the theater with Bettena, watching the rehearsals. She had performed in amateur historical productions herself in college, and had enjoyed seeing the preparations for this play, which was—or would be—one of Bettena's finest.

Bettena's housekeeper was off for the day and had gone to visit relatives, so Shayna herself opened the door to find Hattis there, his dark eyes lit with anticipation. For a brief moment she felt angry with him. How could he be so eager to leave this place when she was filled with grief? But she pushed that thought aside and ushered him in.

He looked around hopefully. "Are they here now?"

"No. How did you manage to get here?"

"I just went for a ride to exercise one of the stallions—then kept on going."

"Hattis!" she said in exasperation. "I told you to make some excuse to get here, so they wouldn't be looking for you."

"I couldn't think of any," the young man said stubbornly. "And anyway, what does it matter? We'll be gone before they can find me."

"It matters because we're not leaving for a few days."

"Why not?" He frowned.

Shayna didn't want to try to explain herself to this annoying young man, but she supposed she owed him that—and, in any event, she'd already sent a note to Teres explaining why she wanted to wait.

"A friend of mine has a play opening in two days, and it's also her birthday. There will be a party for her. Her name's Bettena Halward. I assume you recognize her name. This is her home, and she's been very kind to me. I want to attend the party before I leave."

"Does she know?" Hattis asked curiously.

"She knows who I am and where I come from—but she doesn't know that I'll be leaving."

"What about him?"

"Mikal also knows everything, but he doesn't know that I'm leaving, either."

Hattis ran his hand through his dark hair. "I can't believe I really met him!" he said in a voice that was still tinged with awe.

"He saved your life, Hattis. That's what you'd better remember."

Hattis nodded, then peered closely at her. "You're in love with him, aren't you?"

"Yes. You can't stay here. I'll give you the address where Teres and the others are staying. They'll take care of you until we leave."

She gave him the address and some gold coins, since he had nothing. Then, as he was leaving, he turned to her. "Does he love you too?"

"Yes, he does."

Hattis shook his head in wonder. "I guess that's why he never married."

Shayna didn't reply as she watched him run down the

stairs. His words triggered a resurgence of that ever-present pain inside her. Since Teres's arrival, she'd been drifting through the hours as though a part of her had already left this place. It surprised her that Mikal hadn't commented on her behavior. Bettena certainly would have, if she hadn't been so preoccupied with her opening.

Later that night, as she lay in Mikal's arms, she thought about the lonely future to which they were both doomed by their impossible love. Separated by three centuries, both of them were condemned to live forever in their memories of this brief time.

In the quiet aftermath of their lovemaking, she let her mind touch the possibility that she could stay here with him. If she didn't marry him, but instead remained his mistress . . .

No, she told herself firmly. Married or not, her presence in Mikal's life could change his future. Only by leaving could she free him to pursue his destiny. And she thought that she was seeing the change in him that preceded that great quest.

His surprising visit to the settlement house was only one indication of that. He had begun to ask her questions about the period of time just ahead for him, though he'd carefully avoided asking for any specific details about his own role.

Curved against him, Shayna fell asleep and dreamed of an impossible place where they could be together, adrift in time itself.

"We've found them—and the boy Hattis is with them."

Mikal nodded. He'd known that Hattis had left the farm, and his joining the others only confirmed what he'd already guessed.

"There are three of them, plus Hattis," his cousin went on. "They're staying at Seacliff."

Mikal knew the place. It was a handsome inn at the northern edge of the city, built, as its name suggested, on a cliff overlooking the sea. Beyond its grounds was wilderness.

"Their craft is probably not far from there," Mikal said.

"No doubt, but it would be impossible to find it without sending out a large squadron of men."

"I can't do that. I don't want to be seen at the inn, either." He frowned in thought. "There's a small cove just north of the inn by a few miles. Do you think you can capture them and bring them there?"

"It shouldn't be a problem. We'll take them at night. They've been going out for most of the day, just roaming around the city."

Mikal nodded. "Just remember that they'll have stunners, but I doubt they'll have any other weapons, and I don't think they'll be expecting an attack."

"We're not likely to forget those damned stunners. But I don't understand why they're still here."

"I do," Mikal said. "They'll be planning to leave the day after tomorrow. I'll sail into the cove about an hour after dawn. Be sure you have them there by that time."

Mikal slipped quietly out of bed and dressed hurriedly in the pale dawn light. Then he stood there for a moment, staring at Shayna as she slept. Her red hair was beginning to grow out again and it spilled across the pillow. A faint smile curved her lips, and Mikal wondered if she was dreaming about being back in her own world. He left quickly, before the thought that he might never again see her in his bed could seize his mind.

An hour later, as the sun was glittering at the crest of the hills to the east, Mikal maneuvered his boat out of the harbor. He'd told Shayna that he had a very busy day and would be leaving at dawn. She would be busy as well. Tonight was the opening of Bettena's play, followed by the party, and he'd asked her to supervise the party preparations. It wasn't really necessary, because he had a highly competent household staff, but he wanted to think about her there in his home.

The boat was difficult for one man to sail, but Mikal

had managed it before. He enjoyed the challenge—and on this day, it was necessary for him to sail alone.

The sun had risen on a clear, cool morning by the time the small cove came into sight. As Mikal trimmed the sails and began to bring the boat into it, a group of men emerged from the thick forest and made their way down to the sandy shore. He picked up his spyglass, then grunted with satisfaction. They were all there, including that young fool, Hattis. One of them was the man he'd seen at Bett's, and he wondered if this could be the man Teres that Shayna had mentioned.

When he drew near the shore, one of his cousins waded out to help him, and after dropping the anchor Mikal leaped into the water and waded with him to shore.

"No problems?" Mikal asked.

"None at all. Like you said, they weren't expecting anything, and we've got all their stunners." He slanted Mikal a glance.

"Teres—that's their leader, the one you saw—guessed right away that we'd been sent by you."

Mikal wasn't surprised. He'd already guessed that Shayna must have told him everything. Maybe she'd even begged him to let her stay. He clung to that hope as he walked out of the water and approached them.

Their reaction to his appearance did surprise him. He'd expected to see fear, but what he got instead was openmouthed amazement—even though they'd apparently known he would be coming. It was the same reaction he'd seen with Hattis, and he now heard in his mind Shayna's clear, certain voice: "You will be a great man, Mikal."

His gaze swept slowly over them all, including Hattis, who smiled uncertainly at him. The other two were of indeterminate lineage, but the man Teres was clearly Amaden. In light of what Shayna had said about women being equal to men, he wondered at this all-male crew. But then he recalled her saying that under normal circumstances, they would not have sent a woman to his world because of the limitations placed on them: limitations, he reminded himself, that she would be forced to endure for the rest of her life if she remained here.

He addressed himself to the man Teres, asking without preamble the question whose answer he dreaded. "Has Shayna asked to remain here?"

The question clearly caught Teres by surprise, but he had no difficulty meeting Mikal's eyes as he shook his head. "No. She understands that she cannot stay. Has she explained this to you?"

"She is unaware that I know you have arrived," Mikal told him. "If she wanted to stay, would she be permitted to do so?"

Teres's brows drew together. "I couldn't force her to return, though I'd try to persuade her to do so."

"Why?"

"I know that she has told you of your future. Perhaps if you were not who you are, it wouldn't matter. But as it is . . ."

Mikal sensed uncertainty in the man's voice, so he pressed on. "How can you be so certain that her staying here would change the future?"

Teres gazed at him steadily. "I can't be sure; no one can. We're only beginning to study time theory. But when the consequences could prove to be so great . . ."

His voice trailed off again, and Mikal was left with the impression that while this man was undoubtedly very self-assured, his present situation had left him badly off balance.

"This entire project will be discontinued as soon as we return," Teres said after a pause, then added, seemingly at considerable personal cost, "It was a mistake."

"Do you understand that you intend to take from me the woman I love just so I can create a world you want?" Mikal asked coldly.

"Yes, I understand that."

"You ask too much!"

Mikal turned to his cousins. "Get them aboard the boat. I am expected at council and must return now."

They came aboard willingly, rather to Mikal's surprise. As they boarded he searched the face of each man, but found no hint of fear. They set sail quickly, with Mikal leaving the actual sailing to his cousins. He stood at the rail, staring down at the restless sea, thinking how very easy it would be to throw them all overboard. The currents here were strange, and if their bodies were ever discovered, it would probably be many miles from this place.

There was still the matter of the time-craft, of course, but he could send his cousins and perhaps a few other carefully chosen men into the forest to find it. Then they would have to do nothing more than Shayna had done—and it would be gone without a trace.

The temptation was great. One simple order and his problem would vanish forever. Shayna would never suspect that he'd played a part in their disappearance because she didn't know he was aware of their presence. Given time and his love, she would come to accept her life here.

"You asked me if I understood what you are giving up," Teres said, breaking into Mikal's thoughts as he joined him at the rail. "Have you considered what Shayna is giving up? She loves you as much as you love her."

Mikal turned to him, acknowledging his presence, but saying nothing. Still, he saw no fear of imminent death in this man's face. Then he realized the reason for that. They didn't fear for their lives because they believed him to be incapable of such a deed.

"You should also consider what it would be like for her to remain here," Teres went on. "She is a highly accomplished woman from a world that values men and women equally. Put yourself in her place, Mikal Har-Amaden. If the situation were reversed and she was asking you to live out your life in a world where women totally dominated men, would you be willing to do that?"

Mikal stared at him as though he'd gone mad. Then he turned away. "Such a world could not exist," he said dismissively, but the question haunted him.

What are the limits of love? he asked himself. How many demands can be made in its name?

He was still asking himself that question when the city and then the harbor came into view. His cousin Hari approached him.

"So you intend to let them live."

Mikal nodded. "For now, at any rate. Keep them on the boat until I contact you. I'll see that provisions are sent out."

Mikal had not exactly lied to Shayna: he did have a busy day. There was a meeting with the tribal council, a general staff meeting, meetings with several foreign agents who'd just returned from the east, and a demonstration of an improved rifle that had long been in development.

Normally he thrived under such pressures, but on this day, he was just barely able to keep his mind focused on the task at hand. Somehow he managed to field questions, give advice, gain the necessary information from the spies, and fulfill all the other demands on him. But during all this, a part of him was . . . absent.

Some years ago, when he was a new young officer, Mikal had been wounded on the battlefield. The pain was excruciating, but somehow he'd managed to lead his men to victory before having his wound tended to. He could still remember the strange way he'd coped that day—almost by separating himself into two people: one that lived with the pain and another who still performed the necessary functions. Now he felt that way again.

The dark side of his nature was still whispering to him to kill Teres and the others. But the other half of him continued to pose that nagging question. Did he really have the right to commit murder in the name of love?

If he killed them and destroyed their time-craft, it wasn't likely that any more would come. Teres had said that the project was being discontinued, and their failure to return would surely convince any skeptics that further time-travel would be wrong.

He would have Shayna, but he would also have to live with his guilt—and with the knowledge that he'd condemned her to a life for which she was not suited.

He silently cursed Teres for having posed that question about whether *he* could live under such circumstances if the situation were reversed. His response had been quick and dismissive, but the question haunted him nonetheless, and served to point out how little he truly understood her. She was more alien to him than the Astasi had ever been—and yet he loved her.

Late in the afternoon, still undecided about how to proceed, Mikal returned to his house to find it a beehive of activity. Shayna was in the large dining room, arranging vases of flowers. Her back was to him and he stood there for several moments, watching her.

No one seeing this beautiful woman in her simple but elegant gown would ever have suspected that she didn't belong to this place and time. Her entire attention seemed to be focused on perfecting the flower arrangements. She'd chosen reds and pinks: Bettena's favorite shades. He was about to announce himself when he had a sudden urge to talk to Bettena—the one person to whom he could confide his feelings and his fears.

So he left the house quietly and went to the theater, only to discover that Bettena had gone home just a short time ago. Back on the street, he hesitated. Bettena was a good friend, but Mikal had never been in the habit of confiding his most personal feelings to her—or to anyone else, for that matter. Except for Shayna, that is, and even then, only in the aftermath of lovemaking when his guard was down.

He opened his mouth to tell his driver to take him home, but what came out instead was an order to drive to Bettena's house. Upon his arrival he hesitated again, but only briefly this time. The urge to pour out his pain was nearly overwhelming now.

The housekeeper answered the door and informed him that Shayna wasn't there. He asked for Bettena and she went to fetch her while Mikal paced around the pink and cream living room, feeling like a fool, but unable to do anything about it.

"Mikal! What brings you here? Isn't Shayna at your house?"

Mikal turned to her, thinking, not for the first time, that Bettena was the sister he'd never had. He and Estella had never been close, and from the time he'd first met Bettena, nine years ago, he'd felt comfortable with her.

He knew that many people assumed he and Bettena were lovers, but he'd never had those feelings toward her, despite the fact that she was a handsome woman. It occurred to him now that perhaps what had drawn him to her was an unconscious sense that if he had been born a woman, he would have been much like Bettena. That he was thinking such thoughts now could only be the result of Teres's damnable question.

"Yes," he responded rather belatedly. "She's busy with preparations for the party. But I must talk to you."

Bettena searched his face in silence for a moment, then sank onto a chair. "They've come for her, haven't they?" she asked in a soft voice.

Mikal stared at her. "How did you know?"

"I didn't, really. I've been so busy these past few days that it wasn't until a few hours ago that I realized how . . . different she's been. And then I remembered the man she saw."

"You mean Teres?"

"I don't know who he was." Bettena described the encounter on the street. "I should have guessed right away, but I didn't because I was preoccupied."

"There are three of them," Mikal told her. "I've taken them captive—including the boy, Hattis. They're being held on my boat."

"Oh, Mikal, what are you going to do? Shayna doesn't know about this, does she?"

"No, they plan to leave tomorrow. She persuaded them to stay until after the party, I think. I don't know if she intends to tell me—or just to disappear."

"She wouldn't do that," Bettena said, then frowned.

"Or maybe she will. I told her that you would never let her go, and she may fear that you'll try to stop them."

Mikal told her about his conversation with Teres, and Bettena nodded slowly. "He is right, Mikal. This world is not for her. She has survived in it thus far only because she's had no choice."

"But she loves me, Bett. As much as I love her."

"I know that, dear, but even if she stays she won't marry you. She is convinced that by doing so she would change your destiny—and the future. And you said that Teres confirmed that."

"He didn't confirm it. He doesn't know the truth any more than she does."

"But it is a risk she cannot take," Bettena pointed out. "Mikal, put yourself into her place in another way. If you were forced to consider such a risk, what would you do?"

"Dammit, Bett, stop throwing impossible questions at me!"

"If I didn't, you would be asking them yourself sooner or later, Mikal. What you don't seem to understand is that Shayna has just as strong a sense of duty as you do. You wouldn't be questioning that sense of duty if she were a man."

"If she were a man, we wouldn't be having this conversation, because I wouldn't love her."

"Then perhaps you need to think of her as a man trapped inside a woman's body. It isn't so far from the truth, in some ways—and I also think that's one of the reasons you love her. The qualities you love best about her are qualities generally associated with men—in our world, that is."

"You're saying that I should let her go."

"Yes, Mikal, that is exactly what I'm saying. But let her go because you love her, not in spite of that love."

Shayna stared at herself in Bettena's mirror. Her glossy black wig had been restyled into a high mass of soft curls, with a thin gold chain strung with tiny diamonds threaded through it. The simple gown she'd chosen was a creamy yellow, in the low-cut fashion that had just made its appearance.

She lifted her hand and stared at the ring Mikal had just given her. It was a large fire opal that Bettena had told her was exceedingly rare. Mikal said that he'd chosen it because the ever-shifting colors reminded him of her. Diamond engagement rings had only just become fashionable in this time, and when he'd produced the tiny box she'd feared that he was going to raise again the issue of their marriage.

Now, as she stared at the opal, twisting it to catch the fiery display, she wondered why he had chosen this instead. She'd seen him only briefly, because he'd returned just as she was about to leave his house to return to Bettena's. Something about him had troubled her, but she couldn't figure out what it was.

What was she going to do? She was to meet Teres and the others tomorrow morning at the inn where they were staying. By this time tomorrow she would be home: three hundred years away from Mikal.

She didn't want to run away, but she couldn't face that final good-bye, either. She'd already tried writing him a letter, but she'd torn up each draft. And she continued to fear that he would try to stop her.

"How lovely you look," Bettena said, coming into the room to stand beside her.

Shayna turned to thank her, and for just a moment she thought she saw a sadness in Bettena's dark eyes. But Bettena smiled and hugged her, then said they should be off to the theater.

Shayna had been surprised to learn that Bettena would join Mikal and her in their box, rather than arriving early at the theater and staying backstage. But Bettena had said that she had done all she could do, and she wanted to be in the box where she could watch the reactions of the audience.

The theater was completely filled. From the box, Shayna looked down on the well-dressed crowd and wondered if they would appreciate this play as much as people of her time did. How very daring it would seem to them—too daring, she suspected, at least for the men. But it would speak to the women, which was Bettena's intention. Bettena had admitted frankly that if it weren't for Mikal's patronage, she could never have drawn such a crowd.

Shayna had been surprised to discover that Mikal's friendship with Bettena was well known to his contemporaries. Not one word about it had been mentioned in Maltus's biography of Mikal—no doubt because he considered it to be both shameful and irrelevant. Theater historians and those who studied the long quest for women's rights would be thrilled with her report.

She slanted a glance at Mikal, who was chatting with Bettena as they waited for the curtain to rise. Merely looking at him was painful now, but she could not take her eyes off him. Every word, every moment was magnified as she faced their final hours together.

She still didn't know what to do. She'd left a letter for Bettena on the pillow in the guest room that she'd used, but she hadn't yet found any words for Mikal. How could she?

The performance was flawless: the best production Shayna had ever seen. She found herself eager to tell her friend about the differences. A tug-of-war was going on inside her. Part of her was eager to be going home, while the rest of her clung to Mikal and this time.

At intermission, when everyone streamed out into the ornate lobby, Mikal introduced her around. She met his uncle, the commander of the Amaden army, and felt the strangeness of knowing that even though he appeared to be in good health, he would be forced to give up his command to Mikal in mere months.

Mikal also introduced her to several members of the tribal council: the Amaden nobility. One couple had with them their teenage son, and when the boy was introduced to her, she just barely managed to control her shock. This boy, who appeared to be pale and rather sickly, and who gazed at Mikal in open adoration and hero-worship, was Maltus, who would grow up to write the history of Mikal's exploits. She came very close to telling him to write the whole truth about Mikal, and to tell him that he too would achieve a lasting fame.

Shayna tried to eavesdrop on the many conversations going on around her. It was much as she'd expected. The men seemed to be avoiding the play completely to talk business. But among the women she heard the beginnings of a movement that would gain adherents rapidly in the years to come.

The play ended to applause: polite clapping from most of the men, with rather more enthusiasm from most of the women present. Bettena pronounced herself well pleased and Shayna nodded, speaking to her across Mikal.

"It is a beginning, Bettena. You've planted many seeds here tonight. Within a few years, women will be marching in the streets to demand the right to vote and to own property."

Mikal frowned at her, but said nothing.

They left the theater for Mikal's house, where Bettena would soon be joining them, after she visited with the cast and stage crew. Adrift in a sea of uncertainty and misery, Shayna failed to notice that Mikal too was very quiet.

She had decided that she would tell him of her departure after the party. She wanted desperately to spend one last night in his arms, but she feared that if she did, leaving would be impossible. To her mind, it was better for them both for their memories of lovemaking to be untainted by their mutual knowledge that they would be parting forever.

Guests began to arrive soon after they reached Mikal's house, and before long the place was filled to capacity with a lively crowd. Bettena's friends were mostly from the theater world, with a liberal sprinkling of artists and composers and musicians. But included among them were members of the newly emerging Amaden middle class: owners of businesses and even some skilled craftsmen.

Champagne and wine from Mikal's family vineyards flowed freely, and happy voices and laughter nearly drowned out the efforts by a quartet of musicians ensconced in one corner of the larger parlor. Bettena's arrival was heralded by applause and the traditional birthday greetings.

Moving from group to group, Shayna was a part of all this—and yet apart from it. At moments it seemed impossible to her that she would be back in her own home by the next night, picking up the pieces of her interrupted life. But at other moments it seemed that a part of her had already made that long journey into the future.

Mikal was busy with his duties as host, but every time Shayna's gaze turned in his direction, she found his eyes on her. He had eschewed his uniform in favor of formal evening clothes, and Shayna was glad that her last memory of him would not include the trappings of war, even though she would be returning to a world where all his portraits and statues showed him in uniform.

The guests began to depart shortly after midnight—including Bettena, who was clearly in a state of happy exhaustion. Even though she'd left the letter for her, Shayna still followed Bettena to the door, wanting desperately to say more than just "good night" to this woman who'd become such a good friend.

Bettena took both her hands as tears sprang to her dark eyes. "I just can't walk away without saying goodbye," she told Shayna.

Shayna was shocked. "Did you go home and find my letter?"

Bettena shook her head. "Mikal told me this afternoon."

Shayna just barely managed to resist the urge to turn around. She could hear Mikal behind her, saying good night to some other guests. "How did he know?"

"Let him explain that." Bettena drew her into her arms and kissed her cheek. "I was never blessed with a sister, but if I'd had one, I would have wanted her to be just like you."

Shayna felt Bettena's tears on her cheek, and felt her own eyes fill with them as well. "I'll never forget you and all your kindnesses, Bett. And I know that you'll be a good friend to Mikal in the years ahead. He'll need you."

Bettena nodded, brushing away her tears. "He may yet try to stop you, but I think he is beginning to understand."

Then, after another quick hug and kiss, Bettena hurried through the door and into the night. Shayna watched until she got into her carriage. The few remaining guests followed her, and then the only sounds were those of the departing carriages. Shayna could feel Mikal's presence behind her, but she didn't turn. Bettena's final words of caution were still ringing in her mind.

"Let's go out into the garden," Mikal said, wrapping a long arm around her waist.

She merely nodded, still avoiding his gaze, and they walked through the house, where his staff was busy cleaning up. The night was clear and cool, and a crescent moon shone brightly without upstaging the millions of stars. The lush scents of summer were gone from the garden, and the cool night hinted of frost to come. Shayna, who loved the fall best of all seasons, knew that she would never again feel that glorious season's approach without sadness.

"You know," she said quietly.

"Yes."

She didn't care how he'd found out, and she also didn't know if it made this any easier. She forced herself to lift her head and look at him.

"Do you understand, Mikal?"

"Yes, I understand."

Shayna could hear in his voice the terrible cost of those words. This was a man who had never been denied anything, and who would, in the end, gain everything he wanted—except for her.

"Teres and the others are on my boat, at the harbor. The time-craft is not far from a cove where I can put you all ashore."

Shayna was temporarily shocked out of her anguish. "But why are they there? How did . . . ?"

"I had them captured and then brought there. At the time, I thought I might kill them and then destroy the time-craft."

He spoke these words in a low, neutral tone, his eyes holding hers all the while. He could not beg her to understand, but he seemed to come very close to that. She reached up to touch his cheek.

"I understand, Mikal—more than you can know. More than you yourself can know, I know the greatness that is in you—and the goodness as well."

Mikal drew her into his arms and simply held her, saying nothing. She expected him to suggest they go upstairs, but instead, after a few minutes, he released her.

"I want to make love to you again," he said in a voice thick with emotion. "But if I do, I may not be able to let you go."

They returned to the house, where Mikal summoned his driver. A short time later they were riding through silent streets down to the harbor. They sat across from each other, not touching, already preparing themselves for the final separation.

Teres and the others were waiting for them when they boarded the boat. She gave him a tremulous smile that was met by the warmth of his understanding. Mikal's cousins cast off and they moved slowly out of the harbor.

Shayna stood at the stern rail, staring for the last time at Wantesa. Her gaze went to the dark hills above the city—to the place where her home was—and to the fort, where a light blazed in a tower. Through her mind ran all the adventures she'd known in this place. How would it feel to see it again, with all the differences of three hundred years?

Mikal came up behind her and wrapped an arm

around her waist, drawing her back against his long, hard length.

"Teres tells me that historians have searched for my journals, but that they never found them."

She nodded, even though her mind could just barely focus on his words.

"My family must have destroyed them to prevent anyone from finding out about you. You are in them already."

She turned in his arms, searching his face in the semidarkness. "I hadn't thought about that."

"Teres says that if I were to leave them somewhere to be found, it wouldn't change the future, since everyone will know of your journey here."

"Yes, that's true."

"There are old dungeons in the keep that haven't been used in a century. When I was a child, we sometimes played down there. In the farthest cell there is a large, loose stone. Perhaps at some point, a prisoner had pried it loose in an attempt to escape. Beyond it is a short tunnel that Derik and I dug years ago. I will take each journal there as I finish it, and I have told Teres that they are yours to do with as you wish."

He paused for a moment and stared out at the dark sea. Shayna could see the wetness on his cheeks. "You already know my future, but I know this. There will never be another woman for me, my love—and my journals will tell you that."

The moon had set by the time they reached the cove, where a narrow strip of sand was just barely visible beneath the starlight. The sailboat dropped anchor in shallow water. Shayna and Mikal had spent the journey standing at the rail, arms around each other, neither of them able to speak.

Teres approached them as the others began to disembark. He put out his hand and Mikal released Shayna long enough to grasp it.

"I know that Shayna has already told you that you have a long, difficult life ahead of you, Mikal. But I also know that nothing you will ever face will be as difficult as this moment. And on behalf of the millions of people who will benefit from your sacrifice, I thank you."

Mikal said nothing, and Teres walked away. He drew Shayna into his arms again, holding her gently even though she knew that every fiber of his being must be crying out to hold her tightly and never let her go. She knew it because she shared his anguish.

At last he bent to kiss her. Their lips trembled together in a sweet, tearstained touch. And when it ended, they stared into each other's eyes and knew there were no more words to be said. Mikal remained where he was, and Shayna walked to Teres, who waited to assist her off the boat.

An hour later the sky began to lighten. Shayna was still standing on the sand, staring out to sea where Mikal's boat had vanished into the darkness. A deep, cold numbness had settled into her. Her mind was blessedly empty.

"There is enough light now for us to find the timecraft," Teres said when she belatedly acknowledged his presence. "It should be only a few miles."

Shayna nodded as he took her arm and led her off to join the others.

Chapter Sixteen

Shayna would never really know how she arrived at this moment. The mind has its own peculiar rhythms, and somehow, on this quiet winter evening, with the threat of snow hanging over Wantesa, that strange rhythm had brought her here to the deserted campus. The students were gone on break—most of them to warmer climes, along with many of the faculty.

She got out of her aircar and began to walk across the windswept campus. A few flakes had begun to fall, presaging the storm that was predicted for tomorrow. The night sky was leaden, but the campus was lit by silvery globes on tall poles.

The parking for aircars was in a lower lot surrounded by tall evergreens, so she couldn't see the fort until she had walked partway up the hillside. She stopped and stared at it. Spotlights placed out of sight beneath the tower illuminated it, making it rise ghostlike in the night. Somewhat indifferent to its presence in the past, Shayna had come to cherish it, as she cherished all the other buildings that remained from the old Wantesa.

She walked on, crossing the wide quadrangle, where flower beds had been dug up in preparation for spring planting, still several months away. Then she stopped again in front of the history building and got out her keys. Her office was in this building, but in the three months since her return she had never once entered through the handsome lobby.

The big carved wooden door was a relic of times past, but no one in the department was willing to mar its beauty with a handprint screener. She fitted the key into the lock and pushed open the door.

The lobby was darker even than the night outside, but she felt along the wall until her hand found the light-pad. Immediately the lobby was filled with a warm, mellow light. She drew in an audible breath and turned to face the portrait.

It was huge—life-size in fact—and lit by its own softly glowing brass fixture. She walked slowly across the marble expanse, her soft boots barely making a sound. Then she stopped about ten feet from the painting.

At first he seemed a stranger to her, though she had known this portrait all her life. It wasn't the original, but it was an excellent copy. She could have requested a private visit to the original, which hung in the council headquarters not far away, but she came here instead because she wished to draw no attention to herself. There had been all too much of that the past three months.

She studied the austere figure in military uniform and felt faintly disappointed. This was not Mikal—at least not the Mikal she had known. And yet, as she stood there, studying his face, she could see something of him. Or perhaps her mind was simply rearranging that unsmiling face, transforming it into the Mikal who had smiled at her, his eyes lit with love.

It hadn't been easy for her to avoid seeing his likeness these past three months, but somehow she'd managed it. And now she thought that perhaps that avoidance hadn't been necessary. Perhaps she would always be able to separate them: the man she loved and the giant of history.

Her hand had probably been resting on her stomach for some time before she became aware that she had placed it there. She smiled, although it was a sad, slightly nervous smile.

Barely a month ago, following several bouts of sickness in the morning, Shayna had gone to see her physician, certain that it couldn't be what her instincts were telling her. But the test had confirmed her instincts: she was carrying Mikal's child.

At first she'd cried bitter tears. She'd even considered terminating the pregnancy because she couldn't bear the thought of living with a constant reminder of him. But that had only been a brief thought, arising from shock. Now she thought of the child she would bear as a gift from Mikal—far more precious than the ring she wore constantly.

Still, she was filled with fears for their son. Soon she would have to decide if she wanted his paternity to be known. Although the media had speculated endlessly about her relationship with Mikal, neither she nor the few others who knew had ever confirmed those speculations. She had met him, as had the others, but the details remained their joint secret.

In the end, she thought, she would be forced to admit that he was Mikal's son. It would be obvious to everyone that he'd been conceived very close to the time of her return, and if he should resemble Mikal, no lie would be accepted.

She stood there for a long time, staring at the portrait, but thinking of the man she'd known—and of their child. His life would be no easier than his father's life had been. She could only hope that he would inherit his father's great strength and patience. He would need that to cope with the burden of being the son of Mikal Har-Amaden.

Finally she turned away from the portrait and crossed to the door, then gave it one last glance before she turned out the lights and left. Now there was one more thing she must do.

"I haven't been down here for years," Davo Har-Amaden said as they descended the winding stone steps, where the dust lay thick on everything and cobwebs trailed along the stone walls. "But I too played down here a few times when I was a child."

He turned to smile at her, his face glowing in the beam of the big flashlight. "My own children were never interested in the dungeons. In fact I'm not certain they even know of their existence. But I think I remember that loose stone."

They reached the bottom and began to make their way through a large, empty room where pieces of rusting metal clung to the walls. Davo shone the light on them.

"People were tortured here once," he said in a solemn whisper. "As a child I found that rather intriguing. Now I find it appalling, of course. But that was long before Mikal's time."

They began to walk down the corridor, where small cells lined one wall. Under any other circumstances Shayna would have been thinking about the men who'd been kept here, and had probably died here as well. But the only thing on her mind now was the stone and the tunnel Mikal had described—and the journals.

She had as yet told no one but Davo, the current family patriarch and a descendant of Mikal's brother, Derik. Davo had contacted her soon after her return, at the time when she was near to collapse under the weight of media scrutiny. He had said that he hoped one day to talk to her about Mikal, but he was calling only to offer the sanctuary of the family's home to her. She'd spent two weeks at the old keep, but the portrait of Mikal had been removed at her request before her arrival. She was everlastingly grateful to Davo for understanding that request, and at the end of the two weeks she'd told him everything.

Everything, that is, except for the fact that she was

carrying Mikal's son. She hadn't known it then. She intended to tell him after they found the journals.

No one yet knew of the existence of the journals—except possibly for Teres, who'd mentioned them to Mikal and who might suspect that he'd told her where to find them. But Teres remained a steadfast and undemanding friend who, if he knew, had decided to wait for her to raise the issue.

Davo paused in the open doorway to the last cell. The iron door had long since rusted and fallen from its hinges. "There!" he said in a hoarse whisper of excitement. "That must be it. See how the mortar is gone?"

"Will we be able to pull it out?" she asked, her stomach churning with excitement.

"We can try. If not I'll go back up and get a tool."

The stone wasn't large, only about two feet square. And the mortar must have been thick, because the space it had occupied was large enough for Davo to get his fingers between the stones. It gave way almost immediately, and he set it on the floor. Shayna, who now held the light, aimed it at the darkness behind the stone.

Wedged in against the earthen walls was a large trunk, its brass fittings tarnished almost beyond recognition and its leather straps rotted away. They stared at it, and then at each other.

"Until this moment I'm not sure I believed it would be here," Davo said in a wondering tone. "Let's see if I can get it out."

It took far longer to coax the trunk out of the tunnel than it had taken to remove the stone, but Davo finally lowered it to the floor, then stepped away from it.

Before Shayna could bring herself to open it, he squatted down in front of it and shone the beam directly on it, then began to rub away the dust. The lettering that emerged was faint, engraved into badly tarnished brass. MIKAL HAR-AMADEN.

Shayna's fingers trembled as she touched the rusted hasp. There was no padlock. She struggled with it for a moment as her vision became blurred by tears—and then it was open and she raised the lid.

The trunk was nearly filled with leather-bound journals bearing the Har-Amaden family crest. Somewhere in there, probably near the bottom, was the journal that had confirmed his identity for her. Cautiously she lifted out one of the volumes on top and opened it as Davo leaned toward her with the light.

Shayna could not stifle the cry that welled up in her as she saw the first page. Mikal had written his name and the beginning and ending dates. She had unwittingly selected his last journal. The date he'd filled it was only three days before his death.

"I . . . I can't read it now," she said, putting it back into the trunk and turning away.

Davo laid a hand gently on her shoulder. "I can have the trunk brought up to your room, and you can read them whenever you're ready. They belong to you, Shayna, though I'm afraid that you'll soon have to decide what to do with them."

"I've already decided," she told him. "After we've both read them—and the rest of your family as well—I'll allow them to be copied for publication. But I would like the originals to remain here."

"That's very kind of you," Davo said sincerely. "I will see to it that they are preserved. We're fortunate that they're in such good condition."

"There is something else I have to tell you, Davo. I wanted you and your family to know before anyone else. I'm carrying Mikal's son."

Davo stared at her in openmouthed amazement. He was a tall, dignified, gray-haired man who had probably never in his life been seen with such an expression.

"I'll never marry. I couldn't. So I hope that you and your family will accept my child. My father is dead, so it would be wonderful if he could think of you as his grandfather."

Davo's dark eyes grew wet with tears as he opened his arms to her. "Shayna, my dear," he said as he held her gently, "nothing would please me more. Not only will he have a grandfather, but he'll have more aunts and uncles and cousins than he may want."

Then he released her and smiled. "Grandfather to the son of my ancestor. It's a strange world."

She smiled too. "And I'm afraid it will be a difficult world for him once the news is out. That's why I want him to have the security of a family."

"Will you consider giving him the Har-Amaden name as well?" Davo asked rather shyly.

Shayna hadn't thought about that, but she nodded. "Since the world will think of him as the son of Mikal Har-Amaden, it seems only fitting that he should bear that name."

Then she smiled again. "But I think I will call him Kaz. That was Mikal's pet name when he was a child, and it was the way he first introduced himself to me."

Shayna closed the final volume of Mikal's journals, the one she had first opened down in the dungeon three days ago. Davo had arranged them in chronological order for her after the trunk had been carried upstairs.

She walked over to the window of her sitting room and stared out at the snow-covered landscape. Earlier in the day she had ridden alone on one of Davo's Amadens to the spot where Mikal's cabin had once stood. The hilltop was empty now; the cabin had been destroyed many years ago, crushed by a huge hemlock that had been struck by lightning. Davo had told her that it had happened sometime in the last century.

Shayna had sat there for a long time, remembering: memories that were for her only months old, of a love that had actually happened three centuries ago.

All the far-flung Har-Amaden clan was gathered at the keep, having arrived within a day of receiving the news from Davo about the discovery of the journals. As Shayna finished each one, she passed it on to Davo, who read it and then in turn gave it to the others. The huge keep was filled with Har-Amadens reading alone and in groups and talking in hushed tones.

This morning a team of experts in the copying and preservation of ancient manuscripts had arrived, sworn to secrecy by Davo until he and Shayna were ready to make the dual announcement of the journals' existence and of the impending birth of Mikal's son.

Shayna was touched by the excitement of these people over the discovery of the journals and by their warm acceptance of both her and of Mikal's son. In today's world the Har-Amadens were the closest thing to a true nobility.

Instead of feeling sad that she'd finally completed her reading of Mikal's life, Shayna felt a deep, warm happiness that she hadn't felt since her return. For three days it had felt as though Mikal himself were there with her, pouring out his thoughts and hopes and fears.

No one, not even Shayna herself, had expected the journals to be so personal. The only one she'd seen had been nothing more than a dry recitation of battles planned and then executed. But that had begun to change even before her departure from his life, and her belief that he'd already begun to change his thinking was confirmed.

Following her departure, the journals were clearly being written for her, even though he didn't forget his obligation to history. He wrote about their love and about his pain at her loss with far more eloquence than he'd ever spoken to her, but he also wrote long passages that gave more detail about the Period of Unification than had previously been known.

It was difficult for Shayna to read the journals as a historian, but she managed enough professionalism to know that her colleagues would be intrigued by his recounting of his long quest, during which he'd experienced far more doubts than had been believed until now.

Two entries stood out, and both had reduced her to tears and an inability to continue reading for a time. The first was his anguish over Bettena's death, five years before his own fateful sailing voyage. Bettena had been mentioned a few times, but when he wrote of her death, he stated that he'd lost his only link with Shayna, and now had no one to whom he could pour out his heart.

The other entry that had brought her to tears was the

last entry in his final journal, and it left Shayna wondering if he knew his own death was imminent. The newly elected Tribal Council—later to be renamed the World Council—had just ended its first two-month-long session. He was weary, he wrote, then went on to say that his life's work was complete and he could finally rest. His final sentence was now smudged by her tears: "I have given my beloved Shayna the world she first showed me."

As she thought about that entry now, Shayna smiled through fresh tears. Historians would spend an eternity arguing over whether Mikal would have created this world without her. She believed that he would have. Perhaps she had given him the knowledge that it was possible—but the actual doing was his.

"Each time I see him, he is more Mikal's son," Teres marveled. "Though of course he has your eyes."

Shayna smiled as Kaz tried to destroy the new toy Teres had brought him. At three, he already had an unquenchable thirst to know how everything worked, and an astonishing patience as well. He would sit quietly for hours taking apart his toys and reassembling them.

"I saw the birthday interview on the vid," Teres said. "You were very forbearing."

"At least they've held to our agreement," Shayna said with a smile. "I agreed to give an interview on the anniversary of Mikal's birth, as long as they left us alone the rest of the time. And so far most of them have done that."

She shuddered, thinking of the way she'd been hounded after her announcement, and then again after Kaz's birth. But Davo Har-Amaden had stepped in on both occasions and carried her off to the keep. Then he'd built her a home on fifty secluded acres in the hills north of Wantesa, where she lived now and where Teres had come to pay a visit after a long period spent at the new Space Center. When the Time Project had closed down, he'd been invited to join the staff there. Unmanned space probes had begun ten years ago, and

Teres was now the director of the first project designed to carry a human crew into the solar system.

"The news hasn't been released yet, but I thought you might be interested to know that Hattis has been selected for the astronaut training program."

"Oh, Teres, that's wonderful news. He was here only a month ago, and he was so worried that he wouldn't make it." She smiled. "When Mikal met him, just after Haddar's death, he told Hattis that he hoped he would do better with the rest of his life than he'd done thus far. And so he has."

Teres studied her carefully. "You've made peace with yourself, haven't you? You can speak his name without pain."

She nodded. "Kaz has helped. I feel close to Mikal just by seeing him."

She saw that Kaz was yawning and got up. "Time for bed, Kaz. You can finish destroying your new toy tomorrow."

He protested halfheartedly, then allowed her to take his hand. She told Teres that Kaz's nanny was off for the night and that they could have their dessert in the garden after she put him to bed.

Then she led Kaz off to his bright, airy bedroom, where his tiredness became evident, because he didn't even demand a bedtime story. Seconds after giving her a sloppy kiss, he closed his eyes. Shayna smoothed back his dark curls, then paused for a moment to stare at the small, framed portrait on the table beside his bed. Shortly after his birth, she'd had a miniature made of Mikal's portrait. It wasn't the Mikal she wanted him to know, but one day she would tell him about the other one.

She went back downstairs to the kitchen, where she picked up a bowl of luscious peaches. She put them onto a tray with a bottle of Davo's best wine and two glasses, then carried it all out to the terrace, where Teres was already seated, looking strangely pensive.

"What is it, Teres? Have you been working too hard?"

He shook his head as he accepted a glass of wine. "No, it isn't that."

"Then what is it?"

"I'm wondering if I made a mistake."

"Teres, it isn't like you to talk this way. What mistake?"

He stared at her in silence for so long that she began to feel uncomfortable. What could possibly be troubling him, and why was he reluctant to talk about it?

"I must tell you, since I've carried it this far—but I think I may have been wrong." He paused briefly, then went on.

"Ever since we returned, I've been haunted by the memory of what it cost you and Mikal to give us this future. And each time I saw you, I felt that pain all over again.

"One evening, after I'd seen Kaz for the first time, I started to think." He smiled slightly. "I confess that I was a bit drunk at the time.

"Anyway, I thought about how you had to give up Mikal so that he would be able to fulfill his destiny—which of course he did, just before his death. Then I thought about his death. He was only fifty-seven, and as far as we know, still in good health. And of course his body was never found.

"I knew that night what I wanted to do, but it took me nearly a year to put action to my thoughts. I suppose I was afraid of being rejected. Then I went to the minister of science. She went to the council, and it has taken them nearly another year to give me an answer—but they gave it yesterday."

By the time he stopped talking, Shayna was holding her breath and trying very hard not to think what she was thinking. But then Teres confirmed it.

"The Time Project was closed down, but nothing was destroyed. And now the council has given me permission to make one more journey. But they understand that the decision to make that journey is yours. I told them that I didn't want to tell you about it until I had their approval."

Shayna's mind spun. She was silent for so long that Teres frowned questioningly at her. "Do you understand what I'm talking about?"

She managed to nod. "I can go back and get Mikal—and bring him here."

Teres nodded eagerly. "Everyone agreed that it could have no effect on the future if we catch him at the end of his life. His work was done, and since his body was never recovered, nothing in his time will be changed."

She nodded, unable to speak, and Teres went on. "But I'm thinking now that I should have talked to you first. You've made peace with yourself and bringing him here could . . . destroy that."

Shayna wasn't even aware that she'd started to cry until she felt the wetness on her cheeks. She swiped distractedly at the tears.

"Oh, Teres, what a wonderful friend you've been. Of course I want him here. Making peace with myself isn't the same as being happy."

"But there is something you should consider. Only four years have passed for you, and you're still young. But Mikal has lived nearly twenty-five more years, and he won't be young anymore."

She stared at him, realizing that she'd been thinking about the Mikal she'd known. But the man she would meet now was the man from the portrait. A strange uncertainty came over her.

"Of course," Teres said, "with the medical science we have now, he can undoubtedly live many more years, but—"

"I would want him here even if he had only a year to live," she stated with a certainty that hadn't quite settled into her yet.

"Do you think he will want that?"

"Yes, I think he will." She thought about the love that had been there right to the final journal entry, and let go of her own doubts.

"He may guess why we've come, you know," Teres said. "A lot of people who read the journal thought he knew his death was imminent.

"The council was divided on the issue for a while, but in the end, they saw it as being a gift we could offer him in return for all he gave us."

"When can we leave?"

"In about a month, I think. We will need to reassemble the old team, but they'll come quickly. Then we must run some tests. I'll begin calling them tonight." He stood up.

Shayna stood too and wrapped her arms around him. "Thank you, Teres—for me and for Kaz."

Teres had been optimistic. One month turned into two, then edged toward three. The Time Project crew had commitments they couldn't drop quickly, however much they wanted to do so. Then it was decided that some of the equipment was outdated and needed to be replaced. Four years was a long time in a world where technology advanced seemingly by the minute. And the new equipment meant more testing.

During this time Shayna rode the crest of a wave of happiness, only to fall into black despair. She would watch Kaz and think how wonderful it would be for him to have his father with him. Davo and his family had been wonderful to Kaz, but the day could surely not be far off when he would begin to question the absence of his father.

But then she would worry about whether or not Mikal could adjust to this world. Despite the fact that history spoke of him as a peacemaker and a diplomat, Mikal remained a warrior. That realization had come to her when she read his journals—and had been noticed by others as well. His great lifelong quest had been plotted and executed like a battle plan, albeit one fought with words and persuasion, rather than with guns.

The world had turned Mikal Har-Amaden into something very like a legend. What would happen when they discovered that he was only a man, after all, with very human frailties? And how would this affect Mikal, who had achieved near-mythic status in his own time as well?

And, finally, she wondered how he would react to the news that he was a father. He'd never spoken of children, and she'd had no opportunity to see him interacting with them. The closest she'd come to that was his confrontation with Hattis, who of course wasn't really a child, though Mikal had regarded him as such. Men of his time were stern, authoritarian figures, and he'd demonstrated that very clearly with Hattis.

So there were times when she would awaken in the night and smile, thinking that soon Mikal would be lying there next to her. And there were other times when she wished that Teres had never conceived his plan, and had instead left her to her memories.

Then, finally, on a cool morning that presaged autumn, Teres called her to say that the date had at last been set. One week from today, the time-craft would make its final journey.

Shayna had been at loose ends for months. She'd written a few treatises and had begun to work on a book project long postponed about the daily lives of people in Wantesa three centuries ago. Normally she would have been busy now preparing to teach in the fall, but following Teres's stunning announcement, she had requested a leave of absence and would be giving only the odd lecture.

Teres's call had the effect of making it all real. The time for equivocating was past. They would be spending three days in the old Wantesa, so, ten days from now, Mikal would be here.

Suddenly she was forced to consider details that had failed to capture her attention. Mikal would want a study, a place of his own. He would need clothing. He might well find the food she was accustomed to eating inadequate. He would need someone more knowledgeable than she was to acquaint him with all the technology of her time.

She dealt with all this in her usual efficient manner. A sunny, unused room in her overly large house was fitted out with antique reproductions in an effort to recreate his study in the house in old Wantesa. She ordered a small selection of clothing, keeping it to the minimum since she could only guess at the sizes. She told her cook and housekeeper to study old cookbooks she'd unearthed and learn to prepare the heavy, meat-rich meals he would want.

She met with Davo and revealed the plan to him. As yet, no public announcement had been made regarding this final time-journey, and Shayna hadn't wanted to tell Davo until it was set.

He was ecstatic, as she had known he would be. As he spoke excitedly, Shayna realized that the Mikal who would be arriving here was close to Davo's age. While that seemed to bode well for a close relationship between the two men, it also forced Shayna to face for the first time the question Teres had raised when he told her of his plan. Mikal would be the same age as her father, if he were still alive.

Davo quickly suggested one of his grandsons as a tutor for Mikal. Shayna had gotten to know the young man quite well, because he was a student at the university and had taken one of her courses. Karon called her that evening, after his grandfather had contacted him. He was excited and a bit awed by the task assigned to him. When Shayna suggested that he might wish to consider moving into her house for a time, he accepted the invitation immediately. A house that had once seemed far too large was now shrinking by the moment.

"Karon," she said, in an effort to get his feet back on the ground, "you must remember that Mikal comes from a very different time. And you must also understand that he is a man, not a mythical giant."

Karon laughed. "But he's a Har-Amaden—and I know what that means."

It was true, she supposed. Over the past four years she'd gotten to know that legendary family quite well. They were unfailingly kind and generous, but they were also proud and arrogant and very sure of their place in the grand scheme of things. Perhaps Mikal would fit in better than she'd thought.

On the day before their departure, following a

lengthy meeting that had taken her back to the Institute for the first time since her return, Shayna went to the old Wantesa cemetery. The newest graves in the place were nearly two hundred years old, and the city now surrounded it on all sides. It was a lovely, peaceful spot on a hillside, with great oaks and hemlocks shading the ancient graves.

She left her aircar in the small lot at the entrance and walked along the old gravel paths, past the graves of many who had been contemporaries of Mikal's. If she'd had the time, she could no doubt find tombstones with familiar names on them: friends of Mikal's or of Bettena's whom she'd met.

It gave her an eerie feeling to be here, and she almost regretted coming. This was, in its own way, a journey through time. And it was also a reminder that what they were about to do was unnatural.

She found Bettena's grave and stood there quietly, remembering her friend: a vibrant woman in the prime of her life, who had actually been dead for more than two centuries. How she wished that she could bring her here as well, to have with her the one person besides Mikal capable of understanding her thoughts and feelings.

She turned and stared down through the trees at the city, which glowed in the late-summer sun. White marble tombstones of all shapes and sizes filled the space in between. But Shayna was thinking about another cemetery: the old military cemetery at Lonhola. A huge monument to Mikal had been erected there, though of course the grave itself was empty. In front of it was an eternal flame and two large urns that were always filled with fresh flowers.

She shuddered, even though the day was quite warm. What would Mikal think when he saw it? What would it be like to see your own grave? Was it really fair for them to disturb time?

She turned back to Bettena's grave, and for just a moment she thought she could smell the rose scent her friend had always worn. And she could feel Bett's approval as well, her certainty that she and Mikal belonged together, even if that did mean stealing him from time itself.

Chapter Seventeen

Teres opened the door to the time-craft, and Shayna paused for one moment before climbing in. Beyond the thick plex window, she could see most of the project staff gathered to watch, together with the minister of science, a very tall, coffee-skinned woman whom Teres said was the person most responsible for gaining approval for his plan.

When they returned in three days, the room beyond the window would be filled to capacity. The entire council planned to be there, and Davo would be present to represent Mikal's family. No public announcement had yet been made, but the media was already abuzz with rumors that another time-journey was being planned. Shayna had received numerous calls, but had denied any knowledge of such a thing.

The council had initially wanted to televise Mikal's arrival, but Shayna and Davo had persuaded them that he would need time to adjust before facing the glare of publicity. It would be difficult enough for him to be confronted with the entire twenty-member council, though Teres had remarked wryly after reading Mikal's account of the first council meeting that he should be well prepared to meet the current group.

She climbed into the time-craft, followed quickly by Teres and Hattis. The choice of Hattis as the final member of their crew had surprised Shayna, until Teres reminded her that Hattis knew old Wantesa as well as she did, and furthermore had experience with the craft itself, from his ill-fated journey with Haddar. And Hattis himself had pointed out that he was, after all, distantly related to Mikal.

Shayna strapped herself in as Teres began his preflight check with the project's chief engineer in the control room. She was beyond nervousness at this point and edging ever closer to numbness.

To keep her mind off Mikal, she thought about Kaz. This was the first time she'd been away from him for more than a day, and she'd tried to explain to him that she wouldn't be there to put him to bed. He was very fond of his nanny and of their housekeeper as well, so she thought he'd be all right.

Kaz didn't yet know that his father would be returning with her. She hadn't told him because she didn't quite believe herself that it would happen. But she wondered if he had sensed something in that part of him that was Astasi. Several times in the past week, she'd seen him staring at Mikal's portrait—something he'd never done before. He knew, of course, that Mikal was his father, but he'd never asked any questions about him.

She left off her thoughts about Kaz as Teres completed his checklist, then said to her and Hattis, "We're off!" A moment later the craft began to vibrate slightly and the many displays lit up and began to change rapidly.

Shayna forced herself to relax even as her mind replayed that disastrous journey that had ended in the deaths of her companions. It was that first journey she thought about now, because she'd been too lost in a haze of pain at the time of her return trip.

Still unable to believe that this was actually happening, Shayna started nervously as a triple chime sounded. But Teres announced calmly that they had arrived, and a few moments later she was climbing shakily out of the craft.

Teres had chosen as their landing place a point in the woods not far from the spot where his rescue team had arrived. This time the coordinates he'd selected would put them closer to the cove.

Their plan was a simple one. They had arrived three days before Mikal's death, allowing them plenty of time to get into Wantesa and either hire—or if necessary, steal—a boat. When Mikal sailed out of the harbor, they would be behind him. Then, with Mikal aboard, they would sail into the cove and make their way back to the time-craft, while Mikal's boat sailed on into the storm.

Teres and Hattis unloaded their old-fashioned luggage. Unlike on her previous trip, they had come fully prepared this time. The inn where Teres and the others had stayed was about an hour's walk, and their arrival was timed to get them there under cover of darkness, so that no one would question the fact that three city-dressed people had come walking out of the forest with luggage.

Shayna pulled her wool-lined cape more closely around her. It was early spring here, and the air had a damp chill. They set off through the woods at a brisk pace, not wanting to be caught out there after dark.

They reached the inn just at dusk and stopped within the shelter of the woods. No one was out on the wide terrace at the rear. They began to circle the place, staying in the woods and waiting for full dark. During his brief stay here, Teres had discovered that many people came out from Wantesa for dinner, creating a veritable traffic jam of carriages. It was his hope that they could arrive at the inn during such a commotion, with no one noticing that they hadn't arrived by carriage. Shayna had worried that there might not be rooms available, but Teres considered that to be unlikely on a weekday night in the early spring.

They were in luck. No sooner did they reach a point in the woods where they could see the front entrance to the inn than three carriages clattered up the drive and disgorged three groups of laughing, chattering people.

"Let's go!" Teres said, and they stepped out into the drive just as a fourth carriage rounded the bend. Shayna saw a woman look out at them with a startled expression, but no one else gave them a second look, including the harried staff of the inn as they made their way into the high-ceilinged lobby.

She waited nervously with Hattis as Teres strode up to the desk, cutting a fine figure in his obviously expensive attire. She was supposed to be his sister, while Hattis pretended to be his son.

As she waited, Shayna scanned the crowd of people coming into the inn. It was unlikely that she would see anyone she knew—and even less likely that she would recognize them if she did—but since they would have no trouble recognizing her, she was eager to reach the privacy of a room.

Through the door now came a high-spirited group that included the woman who'd seen them leave the woods. Shayna's gaze swept over them, then stopped. Among them was a tall man with salt-and-pepper hair whose face was vaguely familiar to her. He didn't turn her way, so she studied him as the group headed toward the large dining room. And then, just as they disappeared, she realized who he was: Bettena's friend Jan, who'd accompanied her on her search for Haddar in the waterfront district.

Seeing him had a strange and powerful effect on Shayna. She knew intellectually that nearly twenty-five years had passed here, but only now did she feel that passage. Jan had been a few years younger than her, and now he looked nearly old enough to be her father.

She was still lost in thought about this when Teres returned and informed them that he'd procured a two-bedroom suite, with an adjacent third room. She followed the two men up the staircase, her thoughts still on Jan. Four years for her and twenty-four years for him. It felt wrong—unnatural.

Teres and Hattis were eager to go to the dining room, but Shayna explained that she could not risk being seen by Jan. It was even possible that some of his companions were friends of Bettena's whom she'd met at Mikal's party.

So they went off, leaving her to devour the small supply of fruits and grainbars they'd brought with them. When she had satisfied her hunger, she began to think about the next few days.

Perhaps it would be safer for her to remain secluded here, while Teres and Hattis found a boat. They were far less likely to be recognized: Teres because he'd been here only briefly and Hattis because he'd been transformed from a rough workingman into a young gentleman.

But she longed to see the old Wantesa once more. For all its many disadvantages, the old city had a charm that the splendid city of her time lacked.

When Teres and Hattis returned, she told them of her concerns and her wish to see the city again. The highly practical Teres had an immediate solution. They would need to hire a carriage in any event, and she could use it to roam about the city. She would have preferred to walk, but she accepted his suggestion as being the best possible solution.

The two men talked animatedly about their plan, while Shayna remained mostly silent, thinking about Mikal. It was unlikely that he was in Wantesa at this moment, or if he was, he would most likely be leaving in the morning. His final journal entry had been made on this very day: three days before his death. And he must then have taken the journal to the keep before setting out on his boat.

Shayna shivered involuntarily at that thought. It hadn't occurred to her before that his final entry was made on the very day she returned. Teres saw her shudder and asked if she was cold.

She shook her head, then told them both about the coincidence.

"I wonder if it is just coincidence," Teres said thoughtfully. "Everyone who has read the journals has felt that Mikal knew his death was imminent. And there was that final reference to you."

"Well," said Hattis with an insouciant grin, "we'll just have to ask him."

Hattis had been in high spirits ever since their arrival, and Shayna, who understood what it meant to him to be part of this mission to "rescue" Mikal, as he'd put it, managed to smile at him. He was, as she'd once tried to explain to Mikal, still little more than a child.

When she turned away from him, she caught Teres watching her with a troubled expression, and later, after Hattis had left the small sitting room to go to his own room, Teres voiced his concern.

"You're worried about Mikal, aren't you—about whether he can fit into our world?"

She nodded, surprised that Teres had guessed the cause of her concern. "He's so . . . different, Teres. I don't think I realized just how different he is until after I returned."

"He's a warrior." Teres nodded. "No one thinks of him that way, of course, because all the histories have concentrated on his role as a peacemaker. I did too—until he captured us."

Shayna stared at him in surprise. She'd known how Teres and the others had come to be aboard Mikal's boat, but in her pain at losing Mikal, she'd forgotten about it. And in all the time since, they'd never spoken of it.

"He wanted to kill us," Teres said, his gaze far away, reliving that episode. "I knew it, but I couldn't believe it. It was only later that I came to understand it—to understand him. I think he came very close to tossing us overboard."

Shayna knew that was true; Mikal himself had admitted it. But like everything else about those final days, the truth had gotten lost in a haze of pain.

"But he didn't do it," she said quietly. "And he did bring lasting peace."

Later, as she lay in bed, Jan's much-aged face swam in her mind's eye as her conversation with Teres replayed itself. And as she hovered on the edge of sleep, the question she'd suppressed until now haunted her.

Had they made a mistake in coming here to "rescue" Mikal? Was it fair to him to offer him a new life in a world he could neither understand nor accept—a world, furthermore, where he could not hope to live out the final years of his life in peace and quiet?

Was it fair to Kaz to bring him a father so different from other men, a man from a world where fatherhood had a very different meaning?

And finally, what about her? Teres had been right when he'd said that she'd made peace with herself. The months she'd spent with Mikal had receded into the soft, gentle haze of memory, and she was content with her life.

Perhaps, she thought, it has been the same for Mikal. Perhaps he too was content, cherishing his own memories of their time together.

And Teres had reminded her of something else as well: Mikal's intent to kill him and the others in order to keep her. Mikal had never told her why he'd changed his mind—but she knew why. He had decided that the rights conferred by love were not without limits.

And now, years later, she was facing that same question herself.

Mikal laid down his pen and rubbed his eyes. Writing by lamplight was difficult for him these days, but he'd been determined to finish his account of the first Tribal Council, so he could take this journal to the keep before returning to Wantesa.

He got up and put another log on the fire. The cabin was growing cool. Then he went outside to check on his horse before turning in. As he was walking slowly back to the cabin, his mind still on the future of the council, he heard thunder rumbling off in the distance, and when he turned in that direction, he saw lightning flash across the valley.

Twenty-four years, he thought—nearly a quarter of a century since another storm had brought her into his life. Sometimes he could feel the weight of all that time, but at other times it seemed to have been only yesterday that he'd fallen in love with an Astasi witch.

She'd been on his mind almost constantly for the past two days, ever since he'd visited the Astasi. They had signed the pact and had renounced their magic—as Shayna had said they would—but they'd been unwilling to send a representative to the council. Instead the Elders had told him that they trusted him to represent their interests, and he'd done that, then had gone to report on the council to them. He now thought—hoped—that they would join the council.

There was one thing he hadn't told them, though he intended to make it a reality on his return to Wantesa tomorrow. He was going to change his will to leave his entire fortune to the Astasi, to help them join the world. During his many recent meetings with them, he'd discovered that many younger Astasi were curious about the world beyond their isolated valley, and now that there was lasting peace, they would want to see that world for themselves. It pleased him to think that his money would aid them in taking those first steps that would one day, several centuries from now, result in Shayna's being completely accepted in her world.

He went back into the cabin and undressed for bed, his thoughts still on Shayna. She was right, after all, and he decided that he would have to put that into his journal. If she had stayed, he would have given up long ago on his quest for a lasting peace. There would have been no reason for him to concern himself with the future if she'd been in his present. As his wife, she would have been safe within the circle of Amaden power.

He hadn't been completely honest in those journals, even though he'd often vented his frustrations at the slowness of the endless rounds of talks. Knowing that she would be reading them one day, he'd deliberately left out any mention of the times when he'd been tempted to end the talks and bring in the army to reassert Amaden supremacy.

But always, in those dark moments, she had come to him in her quiet intensity, her voice and her luminous green eyes begging him to go on.

Later, as the storm came closer, Mikal stirred in his sleep and reached out. He smiled in his dreams, feeling her warmth there beside him. And when he awoke in the morning, he was half convinced that she'd been there.

Shayna knew what she was going to do the moment the carriage turned into Mikal's neighborhood. For several hours now she'd ridden around the city, noting all that was familiar and all that had changed, leaving this place to the last.

She crawled across to the opposite seat and opened the small door just behind the driver. "Please stop here," she ordered. Then, after he had pulled over, she got out and told him to wait, that she wouldn't be long.

They had stopped near the intersection with Mikal's street, and as soon as she was far enough away that the driver couldn't see her, she stopped next to a huge old elm and studied the street. There was no one in sight. She closed her eyes, summoned her powers, and visualized a secluded spot in Mikal's garden.

Then she was there. She put out a hand to steady herself against the stone wall. She'd been practicing for weeks now, ever since they'd developed their plan. At first she'd felt terribly dizzy even after 'porting only a short distance, but by now she could manage far more than the distance that would be required at sea.

The garden was exactly as it had been twenty-four years ago. She might have walked out here with Mikal only last night. She remained hidden behind the shrubbery next to the wall as she studied the house. She was sure that Mikal couldn't be there now, but it was likely that the staff would be.

She saw that the terrace doors were open to the spring breeze and smiled. Unlike many people of his time, who seemed content to live in stuffy houses, Mikal had always insisted that the big house be properly aired.

She watched for a time, then, seeing no one about, 'ported into Mikal's study, knowing that he'd always kept the maids out of there and cleaned it himself.

Tears sprang to her eyes as she caught the lingering odor of cigars. When she'd been here she hadn't liked that smell, but now she breathed it in as though it were the finest of perfumes. Her memory of this room had indeed been very good, she saw. The study she'd created for him was almost identical, though she was still searching for many of the books he had in his library here.

Her gaze lingered on the brass humidor containing his cigars. She lifted the lid and saw that it was nearly full, so she took three cigars and slipped them into her bag. He'd never smoked more than one a day, as far as she knew, so this would give her time to find some for him. She'd forgotten all about them until now.

Several sheets of heavy paper lay on his desk, covered with his bold handwriting. She picked them up and studied them—then gasped. They were his notes for changes he intended to make in his will. She'd known, of course, that he'd left his fortune to the Astasi, but seeing it in his own writing brought a fresh burst of tears to her eyes.

She was wondering about the significance of his making that change now when she heard footsteps and voices beyond the closed door. She didn't think anyone would come in here, but she knew that she'd taken enough risks, so she quickly 'ported back out to the garden, then left by the rear gate.

A short time later she was back in the carriage, where she directed the driver to return to the waterfront to pick up Teres and Hattis.

They had good news. After nearly giving up their quest to find a boat to rent—without a crew—they'd managed to find one that was for sale. Fortunately they'd brought plenty of money with them.

"It's berthed some distance away from Mikal's boat," Teres told her, "but that shouldn't be a problem. We'll be able to see him when he sets sail."

"I still wish there were some other way," Shayna said. "I think what we're doing is risky."

"Not really. According to the records, he didn't encounter the storm until he'd sailed another hour or so up the coast from where we'll be intercepting him."

"But what if the records are wrong?" she persisted, envisioning them all being caught in the sudden squall.

"I had someone going over those records for months. According to him, that area where Mikal's boat went down was known for rough seas and sudden squalls. It still is, as a matter of fact. I've been there myself."

"If that's the case, and it was known even then, why did he sail there?" she asked.

"For the same reason I go there sometimes: the challenge. Of course, it's much safer now, with better boats and life-floats and good communications.

"We have to do it this way, Shayna. He can't just disappear without a reason that people here will accept."

She nodded, but she was barely listening. Seeing his house again had brought back to her all the happiness she'd known there, all the nights of lovemaking. Could they find that happiness again? Or had those brief moments been snatched from time—and then lost forever?

His solicitor was waiting when Mikal returned to his house. He ushered the man into his study. He picked up his notes and handed them to him, then watched as the solicitor put on his spectacles. He was probably going to be forced to wear them himself soon.

As Mikal sat there waiting for the solicitor to finish reading the notes, a strange feeling came over him. He couldn't quite identify it at first, but then Shayna came abruptly into his mind and he remembered. It was the same feeling he'd had when she'd returned to him that evening after casting the protective spell on his house. It had been stronger then, but he was certain it was the same feeling, a sort of vibration in the air.

The solicitor broke into his thoughts to ask a question, and Mikal soon dismissed the feeling. He was tired after the long ride back to the city; that was all it was. And now that the first council was concluded, he'd allowed his thoughts to dwell on her far too much.

"That's him!" Hattis called out, pointing excitedly to the boat that was making its way out of the harbor.

"Right!" Teres said. "Let's get under way."

Shayna stood at the rail, watching the handsome boat as Mikal maneuvered it expertly out into the open water. After all this time and all this planning, the moment would soon be upon them. Mikal was only two hours away from his death—and his new life.

During the largely sleepless night that had just passed, she had suddenly begun to fear that he might choose death. That she could even imagine that proved to her how little she trusted their love. Over and over in her mind, she'd imagined their meeting and their conversation, but none of it felt right to her.

With the passage of only four years for her, her memories of him and of their love were still very clear. But could his memories be that clear after twenty-four years? He hadn't forgotten her, of course; his journals proved that. But had his memories been transformed over the years, until the woman he loved no longer resembled the woman she was?

She knew she hadn't been herself then. She'd been frightened and vulnerable and totally dependent on him. Now that situation was about to be reversed. He would be vulnerable and dependent on her. Did he love her enough to risk that—or would he choose to go to his death? She was filled with cold terror because she could not answer that question.

They sailed out of the harbor beneath a cloudless pale blue sky. There were a few other small boats dotting the outer harbor, and a large steamship also making its ponderous way out to sea. Teres called out to her that it must be one of the first of its kind. She nodded, but she barely paid any attention to it. Her eyes remained fixed on Mikal's boat.

"You're letting him get too far ahead," she told Teres a short time later, as they reached open water.

"Don't worry about it. I've made this trip a dozen times the past year, in a boat not very different from this one. We can catch up. He's alone, so he can't maneuver as fast as we can." He glanced at her long dress. "Why don't you go below and change, in case I need your help. He might as well get used to the fashions of our time."

She went down to the tiny cabin, where they'd left their luggage. After taking off the dress and the annoying petticoats and the uncomfortable corset, she pulled on a pair of second-skin shorts and a knit shirt, then slipped her feet into her boating shoes.

Teres was right—perhaps more right than he knew. Perhaps it would be easier for Mikal to meet her again as the woman he'd known, but she wasn't that woman.

When she came back up onto deck, she saw that they were already closing the gap between their boat and Mikal's, and now there were no other boats in sight. She would prefer for them to get even closer, but she knew that, if necessary, she could 'port from this distance.

For the next hour they sailed along the coast, narrowing and then widening the gap. At one point, when the space between them had narrowed to less than a quarter-mile, Hattis picked up his binoculars and trained them on Mikal's boat. They had brought along glasses that were far more powerful than Mikal's spyglass would be.

Hattis lowered the glasses with an eager grin. "He looks just like his portrait." He offered them to Shayna.

She shook her head. She didn't want to see him yet. She needed more time to prepare herself to meet this stranger—more time than they had at this point.

Teres took the glasses. "You're right. The portrait is

a good likeness. When was it done, Shayna?"

"About two or three years ago," she replied automatically, thinking about that time she'd gone to the history building to see the copy, and how she'd told herself then that it wasn't the Mikal she knew.

Then the breeze became trickier and they were all busy keeping the boat on course. Teres remarked that Mikal was a good sailor and must be accustomed to sailing alone. Then, not long after that, he pointed toward the distant coast.

"The cove is just beyond that spot where the cliffs bulge out. It's time to get closer."

It took all three of them to maneuver the boat closer to Mikal. Hattis said that he might be growing suspicious, and Teres turned to Shayna.

"He's soon going to be able to get a good look at us through his spyglass. I doubt if he'll recognize either of us, but if you don't want him to see you yet, you'd better go below. We can handle it now."

She escaped gratefully. All the conversations she'd had with him in her mind were replaying themselves now, and none of them sounded any more real. With each passing moment it seemed that Mikal was becoming more and more a stranger.

She didn't realize that she'd drifted off into a sort of trance until she heard Teres calling her. Fearing that something had gone wrong, she ran up the steps—and saw the cove about a mile away.

This was where she had said good-bye to Mikal—where the happiest part of her life had ended. Was it possible to pick up those pieces again, as though they'd been drifting all these years on the tide, waiting for her—for them?

She walked toward the bow and saw Mikal's boat, less than a quarter-mile ahead of them, headed north. She closed her eyes and summoned her magic.

For a few seconds she could not see him clearly. Then the dizziness passed, and the figure at the helm came into sharp relief against the pale blue sky. She had landed as planned in the stern. The boat rocked gently in the swells. The sails strained against the strong breeze.

In the portrait Mikal's hair had been a soft gray, but in the sunlight it gleamed like silver as it was ruffled by the wind. He seemed bigger, but she knew that was because he'd lost the trim waist and hips of youth. Nevertheless, as he stood there at the helm, he was the perfect picture of a healthy man in his prime.

But he was also a stranger. She had tried to prepare herself for this. She'd spent hours staring at the miniature of his portrait that she'd gotten for Kaz, telling herself that this was still the Mikal she knew, regardless of the passage of years. And none of that had done any good.

Keeping one hand on the wheel, he reached for a spyglass and trained it on their boat. Teres was closing in on him. They were now near the center of the cove's entrance. From this distance Mikal could probably see them fairly well, but since both Teres and Hattis were wearing seamen's clothes like Mikal, with the addition of caps, she knew it wasn't likely that he'd recognized them.

She wanted to stand there unnoticed, to let herself accept the reality of him, but as he set aside the spyglass he must have caught sight of her in his peripheral vision. He turned abruptly, his body twisted as he kept one hand on the wheel.

Mikal Har-Amaden, the giant of history, stared at her, the expression on his face remarkably like the one in the portrait: harsh and slightly frowning. Then he turned away—toward the other boat. She knew he must think he was hallucinating, and she knew that she must announce her presence.

He turned back, still wearing the same expression. She spoke his name, but it was carried off by the wind. She tried again, forcing it out from a tightly constricted throat.

"Mikal."

She saw his lips move, but she couldn't hear what he said. The boat was rocking more now, and she put a hand on the rail as she moved toward him on unsteady legs. Time seemed to stretch out to an eternity as she made her way to him. Beyond him she could see Teres bringing the other boat closer still.

She stopped some six or seven feet from him. Tears were blurring her vision. "Mikal," she said again, as though his name was the only word she knew.

He was frozen in place, one hand still on the wheel. She closed the remaining space between them and looked up into a pair of dark eyes where she could see only shock and confusion—no love at all. Nothing about his changed appearance hurt so badly as that. The eyes of the man she'd known had always been lit by the fires of love.

"Mikal, I'm really here," she said in a husky voice. "I'm not a ghost."

Then, when he didn't respond, she reached out tentatively and touched his cheek, withdrawing her hand quickly when he flinched.

"Teres and Hattis are in the other boat. Do you remember them?"

He nodded, then spoke a single word: "Why?"

Shayna blinked away her tears, and with them her dream of a glorious, passionate reunion. She tried to understand the shock he must be feeling. She'd had time to prepare for this, but he hadn't.

"We've come to make you an offer," she said, wincing at her choice of words. "We'd like to take you back with us."

For the first time he dragged his eyes away from her and raised his head to study the sky. She thought about their suspicions that he'd known his death was imminent.

"An offer," he echoed, turning back to her. Then he nodded.

"You'll come?" she asked, uncertain what that nod meant.

"Yes."

She gestured to the forest beyond the cove. "The time-craft is up there—not far. Teres will bring the boat closer so that we can board it."

She expected him to say that he would sail his own boat into the cove, but he merely nodded again, then turned his attention to the other boat. He said nothing at all as he held the boat steady in the water while Teres maneuvered to within a few feet, then tossed two lines across the empty space. Shayna secured them and turned back to him.

He knows, she thought. *He knows what his choices are. Otherwise he would be asking why we're doing this instead of sailing into the cove.* But at a deeper level, she knew something too. The life she'd dreamed of would not happen. Mikal loved the memory of her—but not her.

She closed her eyes and 'ported into the other boat. It was a short leap, and there was no dizziness, so she saw Mikal climb up onto the rail, then make the leap with surprising agility. The deck heaved beneath his weight, and Teres reached out a hand to steady him while Hattis cast off the lines that had bound the boats together.

Shayna made no move toward him as Teres and Hattis reintroduced themselves. Even the irrepressible Hattis was solemn and wary in the face of Mikal's silence.

Teres and Hattis brought the boat around and headed into the cove. Mikal stood at the rail, watching his boat as it rode the waves, moving north on a strong breeze. She walked over to stand beside him, wondering if he understood the decision he'd made—and if he might already be regretting it.

"You were in my study," he said without turning to her.

"Yes," she replied, startled. "How did you know?"

"I felt . . . something. It was the same thing I felt that time after you'd cast the spell on my house."

He was still staring at his boat, and she realized now that he didn't want to ask the question. She recalled thinking that he would be as vulnerable as she'd been when they met. The difference was that she understood that, while he hadn't. But she remembered his kindness and gentleness, even though he'd believed her to be an enemy. She drew in a breath, and he half turned toward her.

"Everyone assumed that you encountered a sudden squall. Pieces of your boat washed ashore, but your . . . body was never found."

He merely nodded again, and said nothing for a moment. Behind them, Teres and Hattis were trimming the sails to ride the currents onto the sand.

"So that's why you could come now."

"Yes, Mikal. Your work was finished."

He stared at her, his dark gaze running slowly over her face and then down over her body. It was a frighteningly neutral inspection. She thought he seemed less confused now—but no less wary.

"How . . . how much time has passed for you?"

"Only four years. It took—"

"Then you can't understand, can you? You're all playing with time as though it were merely a toy."

She recoiled from his harshness. "Mikal, you don't understand either."

At that moment the boat struck bottom, jolting them both. He staggered backward, grabbing for the rail, while she was flung against it. Somehow the sudden movement shook loose all the volatile emotions she'd bottled up.

"Would you rather that we'd left you to die, Mikal? Is that what you want?"

She knew that he understood she was asking if he preferred death to a new and uncertain life with her, and for a long, agonizing moment she was sure he would say yes. But instead he shook his head, then followed Teres and Hattis to shore.

Shayna stayed on the boat for a few moments, clenching her fists helplessly. This man had written only days ago that he'd worked all his life to give her world to her. Was she no more than a symbol to him, an ideal he'd kept in his mind all these years?

Then, abruptly, she saw the terrible irony. Mikal had been an ideal to her when she met him, and now she had perhaps become that to him.

"I do understand, Mikal," she said softly to herself as she followed the men to shore.

Hattis and Teres had started up the hill into the woods, but Mikal remained on the strip of sand, waiting for her.

"I want you to listen to me, Mikal," she said, stopping a few feet from him. And then she told him how it was Teres who had conceived the plan and then finally obtained permission from the council before telling her about it.

"I could have stopped it. The decision was mine to make," she said. "But I thought . . . I found your journals and read all of them and . . . and I wanted us to have another chance."

By the time she'd finished, she was in tears again and she started to wipe them away. But then his fingers touched her face tentatively, and he rubbed his thumb across her cheeks.

"I'm not the man you once loved, Shayna. I'm fifty-seven years old."

She seized his hand when he started to drop it. "I know that. It doesn't matter, Mikal. I still love you."

He drew her into his arms, his chin resting on top of her head. She breathed in the scent of him and felt his strength, and her hopes began to rekindle.

"I don't think I can ever be that man again," he said softly.

She drew back in the circle of his arms and stared up at him. "You're wrong, Mikal. I was in love then with the man I knew you would become—and now you are that man."

For the first time, he smiled at her. "Ah, Shayna. Did I spend my life becoming what you wanted me to become? There were so many times when I thought about that."

"Does it matter?" she asked.

"No. It's done now." He hooked a finger beneath her chin, but then gave her only a chaste kiss on her forehead.

"Come on, little witch. Take me to my new future."

Hope blossomed within her, bright and warm. Mikal held her hand as they started up the hill toward the time-craft. She thought about how long it had been since she'd felt that hard, callused hand curve around hers and about how many times she'd smiled at the memory of his calling her his "little witch."

She cast him a sidelong glance and saw that rugged profile and the thick silver hair, and the memory of the other Mikal faded into the dark recesses of her mind—still cherished, but now a part of the past.

That other Mikal had protected her when she was vulnerable—and now she would protect him from a world he couldn't understand.

Chapter Eighteen

"Welcome back!"

Mikal started nervously as the voice came over the comm from the control room. Shayna reached over to touch his hand.

"We're here. There are people waiting to meet you, Mikal: the entire council and Davo Har-Amaden, who's a descendant of Derik's. I'll get us away as quickly as possible."

But he seemed not to have heard her. He had already unlocked the seat straps and was leaning forward to watch Teres as he shut down the systems.

Mikal was the last to emerge from the craft as eager faces crowded into the window to watch them. He stared back at them, and something in his expression told Shayna that he was only now beginning to realize his position—and perhaps to understand how she'd felt when she'd first realized who he was.

The door slid open into the decontamination chamber and she explained it to him as they stood there in the bright light. Then the outer door opened and Teres stepped back to allow Mikal to leave first.

He stood quietly as the introductions were made, then frowned slightly when he extended his hand and the council president was hesitant to take it. Probably he thought that the gesture was inappropriate, when the real reason for the president's hesitation was humility. He was, quite simply, awestruck.

Someone was recording the meeting on video, and Mikal frowned again when the woman repositioned herself and aimed the camera at him. Shayna leaned close to him and tried to explain what it was, but once again she wasn't certain that he'd heard her, because Davo had now come forward.

"Mikal, this is Davo Har-Amaden," she said, even though she realized that the introduction was unnecessary. It was obvious as the two men shook hands that Mikal knew immediately who he was.

"On behalf of the family, I welcome you, Mikal," Davo said as the camera continued to whir. "Everyone looks forward to meeting you."

Mikal nodded. Then his gaze swept over the entire assemblage. "Thank you," he said into the sudden silence. "Thank you for giving me back . . . my life." And as he uttered the final two words, his gaze returned to Shayna.

"Your aircar is parked just outside on the lawn," Teres told her quietly, materializing out of the crowd. "I'm afraid that the word got out. There's a huge crowd outside."

Shayna took Mikal's hand and they walked down the long hallway, where the Institute staff who hadn't been able to get into the control room lined the walls. She tried to hurry him, but Mikal seemed content to walk slowly, his head swiveling constantly to peer into the offices.

They emerged from the building into a chilly day, where the late-afternoon sun had tinted the undersides of fluffy clouds. The crowd was enormous, and she could see still more people at windows of adjacent buildings and even on the roofs. Mikal stopped, then raised his hand in greeting. Abruptly the silence was shattered by thunderous applause and thousands of voices calling his name. She turned to him to see how he was taking all this and saw that his gaze was fixed on something off to the left. The tower of the old fort rose above the trees at the far edge of the quadrangle.

She squinted at the flag that was fluttering over the tower. It wasn't the university's emblem. She couldn't make it out clearly, but then she realized what it must be. Some enterprising student had run up the old flag of the Amaden, which bore Mikal's family's crest. She laughed and, when he turned to her questioningly, she explained. Mikal smiled, and then with one final wave, he strode across the lawn toward her aircar, which was surrounded by uniformed security people.

They climbed into the aircar, and this time he needed no assistance in fastening the safety straps. "Are you all right?" she asked, thinking that he was certainly taking it all in stride so far.

He touched her face gently, his fingers grazing her jaw. "Yes, love, I'm fine."

Shayna turned away and busied herself with the controls, unwilling for some reason to let him see how his casual use of that endearment had affected her. Then Kaz's face swam into her mind and she wondered how he would take that news. Uncertainty began to gnaw at her again.

"Would you like to see the city before we go home?"

He nodded. "Where is home? You don't live in the city?"

"Not anymore. I have a house in the woods north of the city." And you have a son waiting there, she added silently, struggling against the tight knot that had formed in her stomach.

They flew over the city. She pointed out buildings from his time, though he seemed just as interested in the aircar, which she was operating manually at the moment. Then she keyed in the coordinates of her house, and the aircar banked in a wide arc out over the harbor and headed north.

Mikal was turned away, his face pressed against the window as he stared at the land below them. She realized too late that she should have told him about Kaz before this. He had probably already awakened from his nap and would run out to greet her if he saw the aircar. She cut the speed back to minimum.

"Mikal, there is something I must tell you that I should have told you before."

Her tone of voice drew his head around sharply, and she saw that wariness return to his eyes. She drew in a deep breath.

"There's no easy way to tell you this. We have a son. I named him Kaz."

She held her breath as she searched his face. What she saw was a shock as great as she'd seen when she appeared on his boat.

"Did you know you were with child when you left?" he asked in a harsh tone.

"No. I didn't know until I'd been home for more than a month." And as she spoke, she wondered for the first time what she would have done if she had known it before she left.

He abruptly turned away from her, and she felt that lump inside her turn to ice. "Mikal, I'm sorry," she said in a choked voice. "But I wanted him. At first I didn't, because I didn't think I could stand to be reminded of you. But then I thought of him as a gift from you."

He turned back to her and his eyes were filled with tears. "I wanted you to have my child. I kept hoping it would happen, and then you would have been forced to stay—or I would have felt justified in forcing you to stay."

He reached out and took her hand. "When you said that you had something to tell me, I thought you were going to say that you'd . . . found someone else."

"Oh, Mikal, how could I ever love anyone else?"

"We had only a few months together—and not much time to ourselves. And always, you seemed beyond my reach, no matter how much I loved you."

For the first time Shayna felt the presence of the

Mikal she'd known and loved. His voice was low and almost halting, as it had always been when he spoke of his feelings. Then and now, she believed that no one else saw this side of him—except, perhaps, for Bettena.

"We have each other now, Mikal, and I'm not beyond your reach."

His dark eyes searched her face and she knew he didn't quite believe that. But he will in time, she thought, after he becomes comfortable here.

He said nothing more as they flew north, over the forest that was dotted with isolated homes like hers. This was an area of country homes for the wealthy of Wantesa—a place she could never have afforded herself. She told him that Davo had paid for her home here, so that she could bring up Kaz in a comfortable environment safe from prying eyes.

Mikal's only response to this was a nod, and she grew ever more apprehensive about his meeting with his son. He'd said that he'd wanted to have children with her, but he'd asked nothing at all about Kaz.

"Davo and his family have been wonderful to Kaz—and to me," she went on. "Davo's been like a grandfather to him."

Still Mikal said nothing, and as she heard the echo of her final words, Shayna saw—too late—her mistake. He'd met Davo, and it probably had not escaped his notice that Davo was only a few years older than Mikal himself.

"There it is," she told him as she spotted the clearing ahead. "It's much bigger than I need, but it's a lovely home."

She cast a sidelong glance at him as he studied the big stone house with its handsome tiled roof and gardens and big swimming pool. She was thinking about the guest room she'd had prepared for him. It had been a last-minute thought, born out of her increasing nervousness about this meeting. And now it seemed that her fears had been justified.

She switched off the autopilot and brought the aircar down to a gentle landing, with Mikal watching her actions intently. After switching off the power, she turned to him with a smile.

"They're very simple to operate. You'll learn quickly. Either I can teach you or Karon can. Karon is Davo's grandson, and he'll be staying here for a while to help you learn everything you need to know. I asked Davo for help because I thought you would have many questions I can't answer."

Then she realized that Mikal wasn't paying any attention, but was instead staring out the window. She followed his gaze and saw Kaz running toward the aircar, followed by his nanny. His sturdy little legs were pumping furiously as he ran across the grass. Until this moment, Shayna hadn't realized just how much she'd missed him, and she got out quickly. Kaz flung himself into her arms.

"Mama, mama, Demmi messed on the floor. Bitty said you'd be angry, but you're not, are you?"

Shayna kissed him and tried to look stern. "I thought we'd agreed that Demmi couldn't come into the house until he's trained." Demmi was his puppy, a golden retriever given to him by Davo.

"But I missed you, so I brought him in the house."

Shayna couldn't quite suppress a smile. He was only three, but he was already learning just how to manipulate the adults in his world.

Then Kaz twisted about in her arms and became very still as Mikal got out of the aircar. Father and son stared at each other in silence, their expressions mirror images.

"Kaz," she said in a choked voice, "this is your father. He's come a very long way to be with us."

Kaz clung to her, but he was studying Mikal very intently—a scrutiny that was being returned measure for measure by Mikal. Then he squirmed and she set him back onto his feet. He looked up at the silent Mikal.

"Do you want to see my puppy? His name is Demmi, and he's a good dog."

"Yes, I'd like that," Mikal said, then acknowledged Bitty with a nod when Shayna introduced them.

Kaz grabbed his hand, which seemed to startle Mikal for a moment, but then he started across the lawn with Kaz, matching his long strides to his son's. Shayna watched them through a haze of tears.

"He looks just like his portrait," Bitty said in a wondering tone.

Shayna nodded, blinking back her tears. "Bitty, we will all have to be patient with him. He's come here from a very different world."

"But he's happy, isn't he—about Kaz, I mean?"

"I think so, but it may take him a while to become a father to Kaz. Men of his time were authority figures, not fathers."

Kaz and Mikal had disappeared around the side of the house, headed toward the large screened porch where the puppy was being confined until he could be trusted inside. Shayna couldn't tell if Mikal had said much, but it was clear that Kaz, at least, wasn't tongue-tied. Shayna thought wryly that he might well be the only person in this world who wasn't struck dumb in Mikal's presence.

She went through the house, listening to Bitty's report on Kaz's activities during her absence, then pausing for a brief chat with the housekeeper, who wore the same expression Bitty did, after having glimpsed Mikal.

Then she went to the porch. Mikal was seated in a chair, with Kaz and the puppy at his feet. Kaz was still chattering away, while Mikal wore a bemused expression. It was, she thought, a sign of the problem she faced. Any other father would be down on the floor with his son. She walked in and settled down beside Kaz.

"I have a pony too," Kaz said to him. "And we have horses. Can you ride a horse?"

Mikal was startled at the question, but then he laughed. "Yes, I can ride a horse. I've spent a lot of years riding horses."

"Granpa takes me for rides on his horse sometimes when we're at the keep. But I can ride my pony by myself."

"Do you like the keep?" Mikal asked.

Kaz nodded eagerly. "It's so big and it's really old. Have you ever been there?"

"Yes, I was born there," Mikal said.

Kaz studied him in silence for a moment. "But you were never there when we went there."

"No." Mikal looked at her helplessly.

"Kaz," she said, "your father was far away when you were born, and he's just now come back."

"You mean in space?" Kaz waved an arm toward the sky. "Hattis is going on a spaceship someday—and so am I."

"Hattis has been accepted into astronaut training," Shayna explained. "Teres is working on the space project too. The first manned launch is only a few years away."

"I want to ride my pony now," Kaz said, having apparently lost interest in asking Mikal questions. He got up, then looked at Mikal with a wary hope. "Do you want to come riding with me?"

"Kaz," Shayna said quickly, "go get Bitty and you can ride with her in the ring. We'll join you later. Your father needs to change into riding clothes."

Kaz bounded off, calling for Bitty. Shayna watched Mikal's gaze following him. Then, when he turned to her, she smiled.

"I guess he can be a bit overwhelming at times."

"He's . . . different," Mikal said cautiously.

"Yes," she agreed. "All children are different in this time, Mikal." And so are fathers, she added silently.

Then, to her surprise, Mikal chuckled. The sound echoed down the long corridors of her memory and sent a thrill of warmth through her.

"So he's going to be a . . . what did you call it?"

"An astronaut. Him and every other child."

Mikal smiled. "When I was growing up, all boys wanted to be soldiers. Maybe it isn't so very different."

"Granpa lets me ride with him," Kaz stated, tilting his head back to peer up at Mikal.

A brief puzzled look passed over Mikal's face. "Do you want to ride with *me?*"

Kaz nodded solemnly and Mikal lifted him into the saddle, then swung up onto the magnificent Amaden stallion that Davo had sent over for him. They set off on the path that wound through the woods.

Shayna had been surprised when Kaz indicated that he wanted to ride with Mikal. He'd only recently been permitted to ride his pony into the woods, using a special saddle that held him securely. He wasn't particularly shy, but she was surprised that he seemed to be warming up to Mikal so quickly, given the fact that Mikal had done little to encourage that.

As Kaz chattered away, Shayna thought about Mikal's reaction when she'd shown him to his room to change. Or rather, she thought about his lack of a reaction. Their situation seemed so fragile, filled with the carefulness of two strangers thrown together under intimate circumstances.

She reminded herself, for perhaps the hundredth time, that twenty-four years had passed for him—nearly half his lifetime—and that, furthermore, he'd been thrown into a situation he could not hope to control, then confronted with fatherhood to boot.

"Are you going to stay here?" Kaz asked suddenly, his words capturing her attention only because they came after a brief pause.

"Yes," Mikal told him. "I'll be here." Then his dark eyes met hers, and she saw—or thought she saw—less certainty in them than in his words.

What could she do to change this untenable situation? Was it only a matter of time? She'd come to hate that very word. It occurred to her that she'd been spending far too much time worrying about herself and Mikal and too little thinking about the effect of all this on Kaz. She was about to try to explain to Kaz why Mikal had been unable to be with him before this, when, to her very great surprise, Mikal began to talk about it himself.

"I couldn't be here before, son," he said carefully. "It's very complicated. When you're older I'll explain it all to you. But I won't be going away again."

"Bitty says that you're very famous," Kaz said. "She said that you're the most famous man in the whole world. Are you more famous than Estrella?"

Mikal looked at her helplessly and she explained. "Estrella is the host of a children's show he watches every day on the vid." He'd already seen the comm room with its huge vid screen.

"Yes, Kaz, your father is more famous than Estrella. You'll be seeing him on the vid soon too."

Kaz twisted around to stare at Mikal with big eyes. "Wow!" he cried, now just as awed as the others had been.

Mikal laughed, then urged his stallion into a gallop as they reached a straightaway on the trail. Kaz's childish laughter joined his, and Shayna began to believe it would all come out well, after all.

She bent to kiss Kaz, then tucked the covers around him. His eyes closed, then opened again as he stared behind her expectantly. Mikal's arm wrapped around her shoulder as he leaned forward somewhat awkwardly and kissed his son's cheek.

"Will you still be here when I wake up?" Kaz asked in a tiny, fearful voice.

"Yes, son, I'll be here—tomorrow and all the mornings after that too. We have a lot of catching up to do."

Mikal turned to her as Kaz's eyes closed. Her breath caught in her throat when she saw the love gleaming in his eyes.

As soon as they'd left Kaz's room, Mikal drew her into his arms. "Did you really intend for me to sleep in there?" he asked softly, nodding toward the room she'd prepared for him.

She smiled. "I . . . I didn't know what to think."

He hooked a finger beneath her chin and drew her face up to meet his. "Do you still want me, Shayna? I'm not the young man you loved."

"You've forgotten something, Mikal. Long before I met that young man, I'd already fallen in love with the man who's here now."